D1569469

WITHDRAWN

2

Fates Awoken *(Fates Aflame, Book 2)*
© 2018 by P. Anastasia

Cover illustration by Fernanda Suarez
Bonus story illustration by Cristiana Leone

No part of this publication may be reproduced in whole or in part, or stored in a
retrieval system, or transmitted by any means, electronic, mechanical, photocopying
recording or otherwise, without written permission of the author.

This book is a work of fiction. Names, characters, places, and incidents are either the
product of the author's imagination or are used fictitiously, and any resemblances to
actual persons, living or dead, business establishments, events, or locales is entirely
coincidental.

ISBN 978-0-9974485-6-6
Library of Congress Control Number: 2018900013

Other books by P. Anastasia:

Fates Aflame
ISBN 978-0-9974485-3-5

Dark Diary (Paperback / Special Edition Hardcover)
978-0-9862567-8-3 / 978-0-9974485-1-1

The Fluorescence Series:

Book 1: Fire Starter
ISBN 978-0-9862567-0-7

Book 2: Contagious
ISBN 978-0-9862567-2-1

Book 3: Fallout
ISBN 978-0-9862567-4-5

Book 4: Lost Souls
ISBN 978-0-9862567-6-9

The Complete Tetralogy
ISBN 978-0-9862567-7-6

Trust and prevail

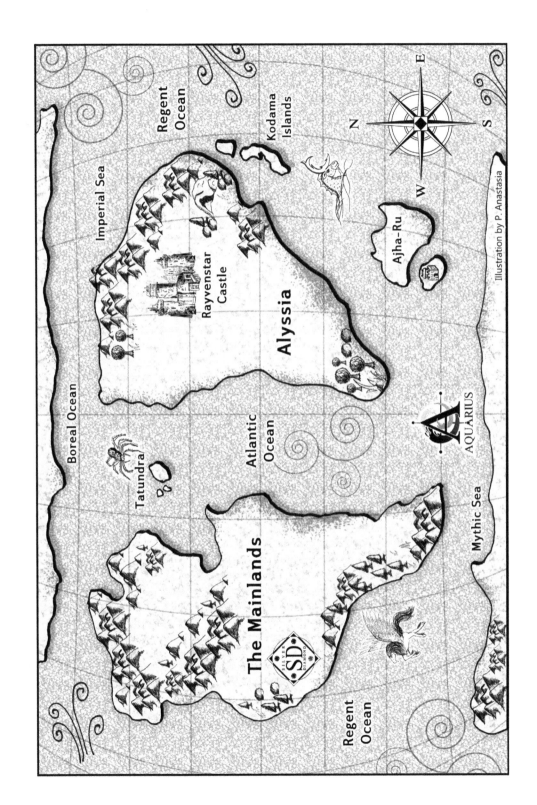

Boreal Ocean

Imperial Sea

Regent Ocean

Kodama Islands

Tatundra

Atlantic Ocean

Alyssia

Rayvenstar Castle

Ajha-Ru

The Mainlands

Mythic Sea

Regent Ocean

AQUARIUS

N E S W

Illustration by P. Anastasia

Archive Record# SD-A2179.9.18
CLASSIFIED | TEXT OMITTED

They're dead. All of them.

Dead.

My entire team wiped out by that... *thing*.

The beast had broken free in the night and snatched up my colleagues one by one, until I alone remained.

I survived because I'm a coward.

Instead of sending out a warning alert, I barricaded myself in the central laboratory and watched security camera feed of the creature seizing the lives of the other scientists.

I remained where I was, hiding quietly, knowing my next exhalation could be my last and contemplating how irresponsible we were to toy with Mother Nature. ██████ ███████████████ ████████████ ██████ ██████████████ As team lead, their blood was on my hands. After our associate team overseas uncovered an ancient scale fragment from an archeological dig, I suggested we try to resurrect the bloodmane—that we manipulate the beast to be used in biological warfare. They are strong, and their scales harder than titanium.

But we underestimated the beast's intelligence.

The bloodmane had no weakness that I had been able to discover, and that naiveté left my entire team vulnerable. █ █████████████ ████████████ ███ ███████████████████ ███████████████████████████ ████████████

Something scratched on the doors; I held my breath as I glanced over at the monitor displaying real-time footage from the hall. A creature stood hunched over with the tip of its muzzle pressed to the bottom of the door. It raked long, onyx talons through ceramic tiles, tearing them as if they'd been made of cardboard. The beast sniffed the air in search of my scent, its bushy, lion-like mane swaying as it moved, dyed scarlet with the blood of those who had died before me. ██████████████████████

My heart raced, and my mind began to wander, poisoning my thoughts with fear. No. I could not—*would not*—allow instinct to control me. I'd come this far and survived. I had to live. I had to warn others of the dangers of genetic engineering. Bloodmanes had gone extinct for a reason. A reason we discovered far too late in the experiment.

Nothing can stop them. Mother Nature must have decided to fix her mistake by plunging the species into extinction centuries ago. And there we were, going against all laws of the universe to resurrect the death-machine.

The beast wound up and bounded forward, busting the laboratory doors open and landing inside with a powerful thump that shook my bones as I watched from my secret perch on the second floor rafters overhead. My knuckles turned white as I squeezed the safety railing to stop myself from shaking as the thing skulked through the lab, pausing to investigate aisles and periodically sliding shelving units to the side with deft hands while peering behind them for signs of life.

Bloodmanes have opposable thumbs. Articulate hands and a powerful bite are massive advantages in the

evolutionary food chain. ███████████ ████████████
██████████████████████████████████████ With the strongest
bite force on Earth, its jaws could crush a man's skull with
over 5,300 psi (pounds per square inch) of brute strength.

This was one of the many haunting facts I could not
push from my mind as I watched the monster trawl the
laboratory, its tail sweeping from side to side as its snout
wrinkled and searched the air, its narrowed, yellow eyes
darting in various directions. A row of large, armor-like
scales trailed from the bridge of its nose to its crown, ending at the hairline of its mane, and then continuing in a large
row from between its shoulder blades to the tip of its tail,
with additional segmented chains stretching down the
outer sides of each arm and leg. A long, hook-shaped piece
of cartilage sloped down over its muzzle like a beak or ros-
trum, just passing the lower jaw, like a war helmet fashioned
to instantly impale anything the beast clamped down upon.

████████████████████████████████████
███████████ ████████████████████████████
█ ████████████████████████████████████
███████████████████████ As the creature continued
through the aisles, pushing chairs to the side and angrily
smashing cabinets, I slowly followed the guardrail toward
the emergency bunker entryway, squeezing tightly to stabilize myself as I stepped, though sweaty hands made it
difficult and slippery.

If I could reach the containment bunker, I could hide
there and call for help. The doors were made of reinforced

tungsten. Nothing, well, *hopefully* nothing could breach them.

I inched toward the stairwell, slick, clammy, sweat-covered fingers sliding along the guardrail while my breath quaked. Then my fingers slid over a short, rough piece of metal and a line of flesh split open in my hand.

My lips separated, and I used all my might to hold in the yelp of agony seizing in my vocal cords. I gazed down at the culprit: a welded seam in the bars had become exposed, re-vealing jagged edges of old solder that had cut into my palm. The subtle noise snatched the attention of the beast. It veered its head and stood up on its hind legs—instantly becoming five feet taller—as it voraciously searched its sur-roundings for me. Iridescent scales on its muzzle reflected the overhead fluorescent lights, glimmering with intense shades of yellow and green.

I hunched down as it hobbled toward the guardrailing and stretched its face up to graze the second floor rafters with its upper lip. I remained where I was, holding my breath, swallowing the lump in my throat while enduring the pounding of my frightened heart.

It would hear me. It would sense my fear and smell me soon enough. ████████████████████████ ████████████████████████

Just another step closer, perhaps. I forced my heavy, tingling legs to move nearer to the door at the end of the metal bridgework. I picked up speed as the bunker entry came into view. A lighthouse in the storm, a piercing red beacon flashed in the shadows, just above the door.

The keypad came into focus and I reached out a trembling hand, clumsily pressing a code into the number pad. My fingers smashed the keys in as far as they would go. Five. Seven. Two. Six. Three—

A yellow light blinked and I gasped; code rejected.

I took a deep breath.

Then I tried again, glancing behind me, though I could no longer see the monster from where I stood. I pressed in the code a second time and it was accepted, then I slid my ID card through a security panel. The door beeped and a loud clanking sound filled the room as metal gears engaged to unlock the door. The creature snarled. I pulled on the door, but the hydraulic pistons made it open slowly.

So slowly. Precious time slipped through my fingers.

The giant beast lunged and climbed up onto the steel rafters, scrambling to get all four paws onto the walkway.

The door had opened just enough for me to squeeze by. I sucked in my gut, shimmied through, and pulled as hard as I could to close the door, while the creature's fangs came at me at breakneck speed.

The door closed, the pistons hissed, and the bloodmane crashed into the metal, sending a tremor through the floor that vibrated into my bones. I flipped a few switches on the other side of the room and they caused a large steel bar to lower across the panel. Noisy gears and locks secured everything in place.

I backed away from the door, gasping for breath and holding my chest as my heart banged against my ribs. A riveting howl stung my ears, resonating simultaneously with a deep, thunderous roar. The sound was unnatural—two tones in one. The way the bloodmane's breath split around the curve of its vestigial beak penetrated metal and stone, producing a sharp, ear-piercing wail.

The beast slammed itself into the door again, making the room quake, but the tungsten remained steadfast. It would hold until help came.

If help came...

All Jacksiun could provide me with was a brief journal entry by an Old-World scientist documenting the experimentation and utter failure of an attempt to resurrect and utilize a genetically-modified bloodmane for biological warfare. After the event, the lab had been decimated with chemicals and fire, destroying every last trace of evidence, except the journal, which had been leaked over a hundred years ago.

The Mainlands had a history of unethical genetic engineering and animal mutation experimentation, but the vile nature of the experiments had been kept secret for many years.

Jacksiun's kingdom was under attack, and vague information would not be enough for me to assess the situation properly. Anything less than a well thought-out strategy could be life threatening.

"How can you expect me to fight a creature I know next to nothing about?" I asked, clapping the old government conspiracies book closed and dropping it onto the desk with a thud. When I had originally agreed to help, I had assumed he had more information for me to work with. "Jacksiun, how can you put me in this position?" I stood from my seat. "You know I would do anything for you, but bloodmanes are strong. Perhaps stronger than anything I've faced before." I clenched my teeth and avoided eye contact.

"Compose yourself, my dear." Firagia stirred inside me, his calmness soothing my anxieties. It helped. A little.

"Valhara." Jacksiun reached across the table to place his hand atop my frigid, trembling fingers. "You are so cold." His eyes grew wide. "I'm sorry, Valhara. I would never put you in harm's way, but my people are dying and I didn't know who else to go to for help. Please consider it. Please come back to Alyssia with me and speak to my father. You don't have to make a decision until after you've spoken to him. Could you at least do that for me?"

"What good will that do? You and I both know we'd never go to war without fully evaluating the situation in advance."

"You're an Elemental Guardian, Valhara." Jacksiun released me and then came around to my side of the table so he could press a hand onto my shoulder. "You were chosen for this—whatever your fate may be—and you may be far more powerful than you're giving yourself credit for."

Jacksiun had yet to experience even a flicker of my abilities, so I decided to enlighten him.

Firagia. His name swirled in my thoughts. *"Come to me,"* I spoke to him in my mind.

A flash of amber and scarlet shot from my necklace, arcing around me, and then the dragon appeared nearby, which made Jacksiun gasp and take a step back.

"Your Highness," Firagia said softly, bowing.

"Th-that's a dragon!" Jacksiun stammered. "How?"

"He is my Spirit Guardian—part of the package of becoming an Elemental Guardian. May I introduce you to Firagia." I turned. "Firagia, you already know my dear, childhood friend turned crown prince, Jacksiun." I was unable to hide a trace of malice in my voice as I recited the newly discovered royal status of the man I *thought* I knew like the back of my hand.

"It is my pleasure to serve you, dear prince," Firagia said with a toothy smile. "Alyssia was my birthplace, and I hold the land in the highest regard. I will lend all my efforts to your plight, should my Guardian deem it necessary."

"Th-thank you, F-Firagia," Jacksiun said, shaking. He had the rare ability of hiding his discomfort—most of the time.

"Can you tell me anything more about bloodmanes, Firagia?" I sat in a chair and gestured for Jacksiun to do the same. Firagia came around to the other side of the small, round table and cupped his hands together.

"I do not know much more than you," the dragon began, "but they are incredibly dangerous and robust. All actions towards them must be carried out with the utmost precision and forethought."

"As you have heard, Jacksiun would like us to go with him to Alyssia and evaluate the situation further before deciding what to do. What are your thoughts on this?"

"It would do no harm for us to see where we stand," the dragon replied. "I will protect you, and you surely will not go alone."

"They've killed many of the king's soldiers," Jacksiun added. "We cannot let this continue. While Celestial Galaxy and Silver Diamond have offered their assistance, I would not ask them to sacrifice warriors in a fight we do not yet know how to win. We have both studied war tactics, Valhara, but this isn't a war we can negotiate terms over. We aren't fighting men and women; people are being hunted and murdered by *creatures* with strength beyond anything we have in our arsenal. How can we protect ourselves?"

The laboratory in which the original bloodmane experiments were held had supposedly been destroyed with chemicals and fire. Maybe fire was the key.

Fire demolishes many things, including organic matter.

Jacksiun may have come to me for help because he was thinking the same.

Firagia smiled at me, as if he agreed with my theory.

"I'll go with you," I said. "We'll speak to your father and see what we can do."

"Thank you, Valhara," Jacksiun replied, a look of relief softening his distressed expression. "Thank you. The king will be honored to have you." He looked toward the door. "Will Commander Draven join us?"

"I'm not sure. He has responsibilities here."

"I understand."

"If I may interject, Valhara," Firagia spoke.

I nodded for him to go ahead.

"Although he had some trouble with Emerald and the ice dragon, Commander Draven is a worthy ally with much experience in diplomatic issues. He is a good leader and will be able to provide us with defense strategies we may not take into consideration on our own. The Pegasus Sword is a great asset and it may be of help on this new venture."

"If he's here, he'll be safe," I responded sternly. "I won't have to worry about his well-being."

"But he will have to worry about yours," he said, tipping his head.

True.

I sighed, defeated.

My body hadn't completely healed from the last battle, which had taken place just over a week ago, but I had to keep moving. I would need to assemble a team to go with us to Alyssia, and that would take time we didn't have. Perhaps Mattheia could assist me in expediting that, too.

I excused myself to make a call.

"Admiral," Mattheia addressed me with a nod and his usual, charming smile as he entered the meeting room. He *thoroughly* enjoyed using my new title. Not that I minded his enthusiasm.

"Thank you for coming," I replied. "We'd like to depart soon, but I want to organize a small crew to go with us, and I would appreciate suggestions for those personnel."

"I'll come," he said without missing a beat.

I hadn't asked him yet.

"Y-you will? But I thought you had responsibilities here, and that Captain Lansfora needs you around."

"He does, but per the request of the president of the Mainlands, I've been granted diplomatic release to oversee this mission."

So I didn't even have to ask?

"Valhara, your best friend is Crown Prince Jacksiun of Alyssia, and while our governments may be run by different entities, Rayvenstar Castle has long been our strongest ally. We've been at peace for years thanks to their ordinances. We can't ignore the contributions they've made to the well-being of our own economy. And... my eyes have also been opened to the fact that the Alyssian throne has ties with Celestial Galaxy we were previously unaware of. I am not at liberty to disclose all the details at this time, unfortunately, but King Vincent's influence is much greater than we have been led to believe."

"That would explain why our regulations have become out of sync—why Celestial Galaxy and Silver Diamond haven't been able to agree on many academy standards."

"Yes. That's all I can say at this time." He straightened up. "Is there anyone you would like to bring, specifically?"

Ironically, I chose the girl who couldn't stop fangirling over my best friend because I truly felt Private Amanda Quill's skill set would be beneficial to us. She was young but smart. I'd leave the remaining choices up to the commander. He had more expertise and knowledge of qualified candidates.

"Private Quill," I said. "I would like to recruit her into the Citrine Exploration Division, as well as on this mission, if she agrees."

"If you appoint her, she has no choice," Mattheia replied with an air of poise.

I propped a hand on my hip and cocked an eyebrow.

"Because I'm the type of person who would do that to someone against their will?"

"Ah." Mattheia shrugged. "Sorry. The whole admiral thing has me excited. You do have the power to recruit nearly any student, and even some staff members, to your team."

"So if I wanted Chef Amelia to make pizza for us while we're there, she *has* to oblige?" I smirked.

"I said 'nearly' anyone. But yes, in theory..." He furrowed his brow and then laughed. "We need to get going. I'll assemble a list of suggested personnel to recruit. We have to hurry. Those bloodmanes aren't going to wait for us to make up our minds before they decide to attack again."

"I know," I said. "Jacksiun—the prince," I corrected myself, "is worried, too." I looked over at a nearby intercom box and turned. "I'll reach out to the private and—"

A swirl of dizziness shook me and I lost my balance. I wobbled and threw out my hands to stop myself from falling against a table.

"Whoa!" Mattheia lunged after me and braced me, just as a prickly sensation throbbed up my legs and I bit down in pain. His arms came up around me and supported my weight until I could lower myself into a chair within arm's reach.

"Are you alright?" He cupped my face and gazed into my eyes. "Maybe you should rest and let me take care of this until we're ready to leave. You're still recovering."

"I'll be fine," I said, lifting a tingling arm out toward him. He knelt in front of me and I clasped onto his shoulder. "I just need to take things slow, that's all." Heat flushed my face and my entire body felt heavier.

The commotion caught the attention of the others, and Jacksiun and Firagia hurried over to me.

"Valhara!?" Jacksiun reached toward me. "I didn't mean to push you so hard. Please rest, if you need to. Recover, and then we'll pursue this."

"She will be fine," Firagia said confidently. "I feel her strength growing, but she requires a little more time before she will be at her best."

"Yes. I'll be fine." The dizzy spell had passed; I reached out toward Mattheia. He stood and offered me his hands. I took them, and he pulled me to my feet. "I'd like to depart in the next 48 hours."

"Are you certain that is enough time for you?" Jacksiun asked.

"Yes." I lifted an open hand and spread out my fingers. A small spiral of gold and lilac fire bloomed from my palm. Jacksiun gasped. "I'll be okay," I added, then closed my fingers around the light to snuff it out.

"You'll get used to it," Mattheia said, smirking at Jacksiun.

"If I could say 'yes' a hundred times, I would," Amanda replied, her eyes bright with excitement as she shook my hand vigorously, almost squeezing too tightly. "I would be honored to be part of your department Lieu—*Admiral* Hawksford."

I hadn't thought she'd give me much trouble if I had requested her on my team, but I also hadn't told her Jacksiun was involved, either. She had a lot more news coming;

hopefully her adorable, overly-enthusiastic heart could handle it.

"Good. I appreciate your willingness to participate. Things might get a little hairy and…" I paused, not realizing the phrase was quite literal this time, with reference to the bloodmanes. "Well, it will be challenging and dangerous, but I could use a good markswoman like you."

"Thank you, Admiral," she said, beaming. "If something needs to be shot, I'll do my best to hit the mark!" She laughed excitedly.

"I'll let you know, Private." I handed her a new keycard to identify her as a member of my crew. She took it from me with both hands and examined it closely. "This is beautiful. Can't wait to swipe it for the first time." She tucked it into her front pocket and straightened. "So, when do I get briefed?"

"Now, if you'd like."

"Yes!" She cleared her throat. "I mean, yes, Admiral. Please. Now would be the perfect time."

I escorted her to the meeting room and prepared to introduce her, yet again, to my friend.

The doors slid open and she followed me inside. Firagia had made himself scarce, for now, and only Jacksiun remained in the private room, sitting quietly at the end of the table with a cup of steaming hot tea and a laptop in front of him.

I heard a breath catch in Amanda's throat as we passed the threshold.

The words "Your Highness" were on the tip of my tongue, though he'd already asked me not to use them here, so I stifled the urge and cleared my throat loudly instead.

He looked up from the computer.

"Private?" He jolted up from his chair and brushed at the wrinkles in his sleeves. "It is... nice to see you again." His voice was unusually tense.

"I've decided to enlist Private Quill on our expedition," I announced. "I know she will be a valuable asset."

"Nice to see you again, too, Lieutenant." She tangled her fingers together and glanced over at me. "He's not wearing his glasses today?"

"Have you... explained things to her?" Jacksiun asked, approaching us.

"Not yet. I wasn't sure if you wanted to tell her yourself."

His jaw tightened as he hesitated.

Amanda gave me a very inquisitive look.

"Private Quill, may I introduce to you Prince Jacksiun Rayvenstar of Alyssia."

Her sharp breath echoed across the room and she covered her mouth, embarrassed.

"It's okay," I said, glancing sympathetically at her. "I had a similar reaction, myself, when he first told me."

"I am *so* sorry, Lieutenant!" She shook her head. "Sir. Um... Your Highness." She whined beneath her breath. "I apologize for my behavior. I just—"

"Relax, Private," Jacksiun said with a cordial smile. He reached out to her and cupped a hand against her forearm. "Please do not think of me as any man other than the one you knew before today. There's no need for formalities. At least, not while I am still on the Mainlands."

She exhaled and a little smile of relief curled her lips. "Thank you," she uttered. Then she glanced at me with widened eyes. "Your best friend is a prince!"

I let out a laugh. "Yes. I've been made aware."

H aving rested up for almost two days, I felt much better now, and I was confident I could make the trip without another dizzy spell striking me down. Firagia said I was strong enough to go, and he knew me better than I knew myself.

Traveling to Alyssia aboard the Goliath was not Captain Lansfora's preferred choice for me, my crew, and the prince, but Captain Ventresca of Celestial Galaxy insisted we utilize it since it was already on academy grounds after having transported Jacksiun to Silver Diamond.

Some firm convincing on my behalf and Mattheia's persuaded Captain Lansfora to give in, but only under the condition that his second commanding officer—Mattheia— escort us with his private jet. The Tetra Haizon may not have been as large or durable as the Goliath, but it was fast and equipped with powerful artillery. We weren't too concerned about being attacked along the way, but splitting up the most prestigious members of our team made sense, strategically.

Mattheia had chosen the remainder of my crew, and I trusted his judgment. Amanda, still smitten by Jacksiun's new title, remained surprisingly calm, though I could tell she had been holding back a lot of thoughts and feelings over the last day and a half. She'd never been so quiet.

Once the others had boarded the ship and had taken their eyes off us, I kissed Mattheia goodbye and wished him luck on the flight. He wished me the same, and a hint of worry sparkled in his azure eyes.

"I'll be fine," I said, sweeping my fingers across his cheek. "Jacksiun got me here in one piece; he'll get me there in one, too."

"I know," he replied. "I trust him."

"Thank you."

Mattheia's trust in Jacksiun meant a lot to me, because I knew it was difficult for him to put my life in another man's hands. If it weren't for the two of them having worked together, though, I'd be dead already. He knew that.

He climbed up into the cockpit of the Tetra Haizon and I watched the vivid yellow canopy close. I boarded the Goliath and we departed from Silver Diamond Academy.

The brief, half-hour flight came to a close, and we approached Alyssia. We were given permission to land on a designated tarmac behind the castle, from where we would be escorted to the main gates by the king's royal guard.

As we disembarked, we were separated from each other, and a sliver of fear weaved through me. Jacksiun was whisked off to the front of the group by the king's Royal Allegiance—special guards distinguishable by the elaborate silver details marking their dark grey-blue uniforms, and a single, colorful medal of gold, silver, and some type of gemstone positioned above their hearts.

As we exited the ramp, two guards came to my sides and escorted me to the front of my team, forcing the others to the back—a motion I did not appreciate at all. After exiting the Tetra Haizon, Mattheia was then guided over to our group and directed to file in behind me.

"Why are we being separated like this?" I spoke quietly to the guards at my sides. "And should I be concerned with the threat of a bloodmane attack any time soon?"

"King's orders," one replied, without turning to acknowledge me. "Do not fret about the beasts attacking; they have only ever struck at nightfall."

"Oh." *King's orders?*

There wasn't much else I could say until I spoke with the king, but I felt relieved knowing we weren't going to get assailed in the middle of the day while walking toward the castle gates. We'd been asked to land our ships a considerable distance from the entryway, and while the walk wasn't necessarily daunting, it was inconvenient.

As we rounded the side of the massive stone building, I had a lot of time to take in the spectacle that was Rayvenstar Castle. It was much, much larger than I had ever imagined it to be, and the ancient-style turrets and spires were adorned with gold finials and shimmering Victorian metalwork spirals.

I narrowed my eyes as we approached the massive black metal gates surrounding the castle entrance. I'd seen those exact same design elements before on...

The Goliath!

On the ship's bridge, along the corners and trim of the ceiling and tables, I'd seen identical golden spirals. I had thought they represented Celestial Galaxy—seeing how many interlocking pieces were also green—but I knew now that the similarities were too close to be coincidental.

The guards stripped us of our weapons, documented our personal information on a digital tablet, and then presented each of us with a diplomatic visitor badge. For having been friends with the crown prince, I thought we'd be treated less like outsiders.

After all formalities had been performed, we were ushered through the front gates and guided under a towering archway leading into the castle. I'd lost my precious sword, the Azure Phoenix, once again, but trusted it would be safe within Jacksiun's kingdom.

My crew and I were led down several hallways, past various security checkpoints. By now, Jacksiun was so far ahead of us, I'd lost track of him.

Finally, we were brought to a round room with wall-to-wall vibrant blue carpet. At the far end were tall double doors painted bright gold, which featured the same swirling patterns I'd seen throughout the castle. Two guards in silver and blue uniforms stood at each side, at the ready, with gleaming silver tridents. In this century, I assumed the spears were more decorative than functional, but anything was possible.

A woman in an all-white, satiny pant suit approached me and bowed slightly. "The king will see you now," she said flatly. "Follow me, Admiral."

The golden doors eased open and she ushered me through. They were then shut tightly, forcing Mattheia, Amanda, and the remainder of my team to stay behind. I wanted to object to our being separated, but it appeared King Vincent's guards had very specific instructions to allow me alone into the throne room.

Sunlight shone through crystal clear windows inset along the walls on both sides of the walkway. At the far end, a small flight of carpeted steps led up to a pair of intricately-carved wooden thrones, upon which the king and queen were seated. An overhead skylight allowed more natural light into the throne room, lighting up the hall with warm tones of afternoon sun.

The woman in white walked up ahead of me, and while I tried not to stare at Jacksiun's parents, I quickly surveyed the royal pair.

The king wore all black, an embroidered tunic with metallic accents, and a navy-blue cape trimmed with golden-brown fur. Atop his head rested a striking silver circlet crown, encrusted with shimmering red gemstones. The majestic colors and glimmering accents shifted with each subtle movement, catching the sun. Like his son and wife, King Vincent had jet-black hair. Unlike his son, he had a chiseled, square jaw line and trimmed mustache and goatee.

The queen's attire matched in grandeur. She sat quietly beside her husband with her hands intertwined in her lap and a serene expression on her face.

The woman in white bowed before the king and queen, then raised an arm out toward me. "I present to you Voyage Admiral—"

A door off to the side of the platform opened and a pair of guards entered the room with Jacksiun in tow.

The king veered his head toward them. "It has been too long!" He bolted up from his throne and rushed to the side, swinging open his arms. "Come, Son. Let me see how you have grown!"

The woman in white glanced at me, embarrassment flushing her face, and then ducked away and backed off the steps to stand beside me.

Jacksiun straightened his shoulders and stood tall as he made his way across the platform toward his father, our eyes meeting momentarily as he passed in front of me.

"Hurry up!" the king raised his voice. "I have waited eight years to see you; quit dawdling!"

Jacksiun's pace hastened. His father grabbed him by his forearms and shook him excitedly, his eyes gleaming with pride. "Look at you! You are taller than I am!" he said, looking him up and down. "But you could use more sun," he said, scowling. "You are as pale as a lady."

Jacksiun's complexion was incredibly fair, attributed mostly to the fact that we worked and lived in space. I glanced over at the queen, who appeared to have the same gentle curve to her eyes as Officer Angela Meadows, and a skin tone identical to her son's. If I had to make an educated guess, I'd presume she had ancestors from Kodama. I couldn't see her very well from where I stood, but Jacksiun had definitely inherited much of her delicate, refined facial features. His father's face was square and masculine, while Jacksiun's was more rounded and soft, granting him a gentler appearance, more reflective of his personality.

"Do not just stand there, speak up!" The king rattled him again, but Jacksiun seemed to be holding his tongue.

"It..." Jacksiun started, nearly inaudibly. "It is nice to be home."

"What was that?" The king scowled and looked back at the queen. "Are my ears deceiving me? Did you hear it, too? Never mind it." He turned Jacksiun around forcefully and then pointed at me. "Introduce me to your companion—the legendary Elemental Guardian."

"Father," Jacksiun spoke up, looking at me nervously. "May I introduce to you Voyage Admiral Valhara Hawks—"

"Barbaric!" The king interrupted him again.

"P-pardon me, Father?" Jacksiun shifted toward him.

"Why the ridiculous accent, my boy? Were you not born in Alyssia!? I demand you speak properly in your mother country!"

"I am sorry, Father," Jacksiun said, hanging his head low. There was a tremble in his voice.

It hadn't occurred to me that he'd been speaking with a Mainlands accent the entire time.

"I... will do my best," Jacksiun added, his voice now spiced with Alyssian flair. "It has been many years, but I will try."

"Good! Now, where were we?" The king looked down at me. "Come here, at once, young lady."

I did as I was told and approached the platform, slowing as I reached the first step, as I was unsure of how far I was allowed to go. The burly king tromped down the stairs and reached a large, open hand out for mine. I slowly lifted my fingers and placed them in his.

"It is a pleasure to meet you, my dear," he said, tipping his head slightly. He clasped my hand and brought it toward his lips to lightly kiss my knuckles. I barely felt anything at all, but still flinched because the gesture was new and unexpected.

"A pleasure... to... meet you, too, Your Highness." I couldn't stop myself from stammering. I glanced over at Jacksiun, who was looking back at me with an encouraging grin, and then my eyes met the king's once more.

I, too, spoke with the "barbaric" accent he'd shunned moments ago, but he didn't say anything to me, at least.

I also wasn't Alyssian.

"The crown prince tells me you have the power to control fire. Well, we can use your strength against those wretched beasts running amok. They have slaughtered two battalions thus far in their attempts to breach the castle walls. Tell me, Guardian, how might we put a stop to this madness? I simply cannot lose any more soldiers or put the prince in harm's way."

The king's dark brown eyes gazed at me imploringly. "Do not be shy. We must hear what you have to say. That is why I ordered you to come here."

I narrowed my eyes. "*Ordered*?" The word slipped out of my mouth before I could censor myself.

"Yes. Of course. I demanded your immediate presence.

That is why you are here, is it not?"

I furrowed my brow and turned to look at Jacksiun, who was now staring guiltily off to the side.

"No one commanded me to come here," I said, holding my ground in front of the rough-edged, intimidating king. He smelled of deep woods, suede, and ash, and the overbearing scent made me uncomfortable, now that he had gotten so close to me.

"No one ordered you to come?" The king turned toward his son and huffed angrily. "Hmm." Then he returned his attention to me. "We have much to discuss, Guardian." He flicked his hand toward the guards at the base of the steps. "See the others to their private quarters while I speak with the Guardian, alone."

"Your Highness," I pried in. "What about the commander and—"

"I will call upon them when they are needed," the king snapped.

Anger sparked in me, fueled by His Majesty's crassness, and—while I sensed fire inching to the surface of my fingertips—I did my best to contain my feelings, snuffing out the flame before it could manifest and threaten the king.

I didn't need to start a war.

They'd made multiple attempts to separate me from my team since our arrival and I couldn't understand why, nor were they in a hurry to offer an explanation.

"Take the prince to his room. Get him out of that uniform and into something befitting of the Alyssian crown prince."

In the blink of an eye, Jacksiun disappeared from the throne room and two stately older men—decorated soldiers with uniforms of distinctly high rankings—came in through the side entryway.

"Your Highness," they chimed in unison, bowing deeply.

"Guardian," the king started, "this is General Cain and Colonel Hammonds." He pointed to the men. The taller man with white hair, narrow shoulders, and a stern look on his clean-shaven face was the general; the colonel was a shorter, stouter man with a trimmed, peppered beard and glasses. At first glance, his expression seemed more inviting and friendlier in nature than the general's.

"Admiral Hawksford," I introduced myself, tipping my head to the two men. "Nice to meet you."

"We must discuss, at once, this infestation and how to deal with it," General Cain grumbled. "There is no more time for idle chatter. Come with me, Admiral. Good day, Your Highness." He bowed to the king and then turned on his heel and began marching off. Following a quick bow, the colonel did the same. I panicked, unsure of how to properly dismiss myself from the room. I glanced over at the king, who stared back at me with a cocked eyebrow and flicked his hand in a gesture of dismissal. I looked briefly at the queen—whom I'd been unable to speak with—and she smiled calmly at me. It was obvious from whom Jacksiun had acquired his levelheadedness.

Not far from the platform was another door set off to the side of the room—a very plain door in comparison to the many distinguished ones. We entered and I looked around the large, poorly lit room.

The room had no windows or natural light, but with the flip of a switch, the walls became illuminated by vivid white overhead lamps. A series of soft buzzing sounds clicked on and dozens of brightly lit, electronic maps and holographic dioramas of different provinces and continents came to life, each 3D illustration set atop its own marble pedestal and placed along the perimeter of the room. Standing between flickering blue and green holograms were tall wooden shelves filled end to end with old leather-bound books.

Colonel Hammonds pulled out a chair near the head of a massive black table and gestured for me to sit. "Admiral," he said with a kind smile.

I sat and he helped push my chair in closer to the table.

Together, they dragged out a larger, more stately-looking chair and placed it at the head of the table for the king, who had popped into the room from behind us. He took his seat and placed his large hands atop the table.

I really didn't know how to act around royalty, and I hadn't realized I'd be working one-on-one with the king.

Was I allowed to speak without being spoken to first? How much did they know about me, and what did they think I could do? Would I be thrown into the dungeon if I said something unsavory or unfavorable in front of the king?

Did they have a dungeon?

Why hadn't Jacksiun explained these things to me before I had been shuttled off into some war room?

I clasped my hands together in my lap and sat there quietly, awaiting instruction.

General Cain brought a long, metal oval to the table and laid it out in front of us. He used a remote to switch something on, and then a three-dimensional terrain map came to life upon the plate in shades of electric blue. A 3D image of Rayvenstar Castle appeared at one corner of the map and, with the click of a button, the image shifted to a nearby building and then sunk below the surface, revealing an array of underground tunnels.

"Here are the locations of the electrical caverns," General Cain stated. "This intricate network of tunnels surrounding the castle houses the majority of our emergency resources and power stations." The map rotated again, and the angle of the shot sunk down to a clearing beneath a pile of rubble at the edge of the castle grounds. "Here is the location of the bloodmane lair. We have theorized that one of the generators installed near the old ruins must have generated enough heat to disrupt and awaken the pride from a state of hibernation. They have since destroyed that generator and dug an exit tunnel nearby. At night, they use this underground network to emerge and hunt and attack soldiers."

I leaned forward in my seat to get a closer look at the projection. The map vanished and a detailed, animated diagram of a bloodmane appeared. The creature had a shape similar to a lion, but more muscular, and had a large, hooked bill covering its upper jaw like a helmet. A line of armored scales ran from the bridge of its nose all the way to the end of its tail. Thick tufts of fur sprouted from each ankle. The bloodmane reminded me vaguely of something I'd seen in an old mythology book—a thing called a manticore—only the manticore was a myth and the bloodmane, well...

A projection of a little human popped up beside the beast, illustrating the substantial size difference. The man's shoulders lined up at about the same height as the creature's head. Until I'd seen them compared side-by-side, I hadn't realized how incredibly large bloodmanes were.

The animation proceeded to show the monster attack, swiping at the man with its enormous paws and then impaling him in the back with the long, scythe-like beak, clamping down onto the man as if he were a twig.

"We have yet to acquire a living or dead subject to study," the general said. "But we will continue to make attempts to capture one. You have experience fighting beasts. A dragon, for example. So we believe these much smaller nuisances should not be a challenge for you."

"With all due respect, Sir, my department at Silver Diamond wasn't formed to handle these types of things," I clarified. "The Citrine Exploration Division specializes in artifact research and the acquisition of unique weaponry. We don't plot battle strategies or fight... *monsters*. And, surely, my solitary experience with a single dragon does not automatically qualify me for such an undertaking."

"But you were trained to follow commands," the king interrupted. "Were you not?"

"Yes, Your Highness, but—"

"Then you will do as I have commanded and aid us in this fight. You have fought a dragon *and* a mahora spider, according to the prince. Why should these creatures be any more difficult?"

I stifled an anxious laugh of disbelief. "Your Highness, I almost *died* in both battles. Just because I fought those battles doesn't mean I'm experienced in fighting bloodmanes, or that I have any chance of defeating something I know so little about. Actually, my superior, Commander Draven would—"

"Enough!" The king stood and slammed a fist onto the table, sending a tremor across the wood which made the bloodmane animation ripple. "You *will* discuss what you know with my general and colonel, or I will have you locked away for treason."

"Treason!?" I scoffed. "I'm *not* from Alyssia! You have no jurisdiction over me."

"You *are* from Celestial Galaxy," he added gruffly.

"Not anymore. I've been transferred—"

"Celestial Galaxy has been under our control since the prince began his term there." The king's brow furrowed.

What!?

"*Any* transfers can be reversed or denied by me within 90 days of initiation. It is well within my power to choose who may come or go. If you should choose to defect so quickly and refuse your duty to your country, I will overturn your reassignment to Silver Diamond, reclaim your citizenship, and ban you from leaving the country."

"Your Highness!" I clenched a fist and heated, tingling sensations coiled down my arm.

"Admiral." Colonel Hammonds pressed a hand to my forearm. "Please, do not worry."

I looked him in the eye; there was a glimmer of assurance on his face, as if he were trying to say things would be okay if only I would calm down.

The fire extinguished from my hands, right before the king could take notice, and I took in a deep, shuddering breath, collecting myself.

"I will do my best to assist you," I said quietly, under duress.

"That is better," the king replied with a nod of triumph. "Thank you, Guardian. I knew you could be reasoned with. Now, I must spend time with my son before he decides to scamper off in rebellion again."

Again?

The king left the room without any fanfare.

"Here." General Cain handed me a small tablet computer. "There are documents on here which will bring you up to speed. Read over them as quickly as possible and relay your thoughts to us, please. It was a pleasure meeting you, Admiral Hawksford." He tipped his head. "Good day."

I was left in the room with Colonel Hammonds.

"I must apologize for the king's behavior, my dear," the colonel said, keeping his voice down in case the general was still within earshot. "His Royal Highness can get quite wound up about matters concerning his people, and sometimes the feelings of others slip his mind."

"I understand, but I've never been treated this way before. I've worked very hard to get where I am today, and I would appreciate being recognized for *who* I am, not *what*."

"Give him time. He will grow to respect you," the colonel added with a friendly smile. "You must be tired from the hectic afternoon. I recall you mentioning that your department studies ancient artifacts. Is that so?"

"Yes."

"While you are growing acquainted with the castle, may I show you to the library? I believe there are several items there that may be of interest to you. The king has quite an arsenal of ancient weapons and trinkets."

"Thank you, Colonel. I'd appreciate that very much." Perhaps the detour would take my mind off the king's rudeness.

I'd heard about the Rayvenstar Library, but never thought I'd ever have an opportunity to peruse it. It housed some of the oldest, rarest books in the world.

Colonel Hammonds directed me out of the war room via a different door than we had entered by (the castle was beginning to seem like a maze of hidden corridors) and took me back into the main hall. We walked together down the lengthy passageway with cathedral ceilings, lush cobalt carpet stretched as far as I could see, and grey walls trimmed with complex metalwork accents.

We approached an archway with guards posted at each side. With the colonel as my guide, I was allowed entry. The library easily dwarfed Silver Diamond's and ascended at least half a dozen floors, each massive wall of shelves cascading with books.

In a glass case illuminated by soft white light rested a long, stately silver sword. The blade had strange markings etched across it, and the hilt and guard were encrusted with gemstone insets. Its crossbars had been inlaid with strips of shimmering blue.

I'd seen the sword before—in a vision of the past.

Excalibur...

I moved closer to the case and stared at the prominent blue gemstone set in the guard between the crossbars. Subtle white light sparkled within it and I gasped, pulling back from the case.

"I see that has caught your eye," said the colonel, coming up beside me. "It is a magnificent piece; one of our prized acquisitions from the Great War."

"How did Rayvenstar Castle acquire it?" I asked, pretending not to know what the sword was. "Do you know anything about it?"

"It was taken from the last king of the Pendragon reign when King Westin Rayvenstar overthrew Camelot."

"It must hold incredible power," I muttered, entranced by the masterful blending of colored metals forming the fine broadsword.

The colonel grinned. "Silver Diamond was right to appoint you head of such an eclectic department. You have an otherworldly sense of wonder about you. This sword has been in our custody for centuries, but we know very little about it."

The glitter I had witnessed inside the gemstone piqued my interest and I knew I'd have to return to the weapon later to examine it more closely.

I turned toward the colonel. "King Arthur was one of the first Elemental Guardians," I said matter-of-factly.

He stared at me with widened eyes.

"G" ood evening, Admiral," said a guard, bowing toward me. He had short, dark blonde hair combed back and parted two-thirds to one side. Though young, his under-eye shadows gave him a rigid, weathered edge. "I am Officer Alistair Cassian of the Royal Guard, and I will be your personal liaison and escort during your stay here at Rayvenstar Castle."

His cobalt, nearly black uniform had crisp pleats in the slacks. White piping cord trimmed his high collar and cuffs and ran in a stripe down the outer side of each leg. A thick band of braided, metallic silver cording diagonally crossed his chest from left shoulder to right hip, and two small silver star emblems had been affixed to it over his heart.

Although he had a pleasant air about him, I was far from enthusiastic about having to be followed by Officer Cassian during my stay.

"If you would come with me, please," he instructed, turning to face the long stretch of hallway before us. "I will take you to see Prince Jacksiun."

Rayvenstar guards had a distinct way of carrying themselves—chest pushed out, shoulders back, chin slightly raised, and eyes ahead and vigilant. They kept their arms very straight, bending minimally and mechanically with each step. I'd watched some of the guards earlier and admired their perfect form. They walked stiffly, but with great poise and presence, their strides perfectly in sync with each other, not unlike the military precision I'd become accustomed to over the years, but somehow more polished.

A compact pistol resided in a holster at one hip and a bright saber in a scabbard on the other. I didn't recognize the type of gun, but it was similar to my own and likely used kinetic rounds as well. The sword appeared to be made of steel, and the crossbars shimmered with gold highlights.

"Watch your step, please," Officer Cassian alerted me, pausing to point out an upcoming staircase.

"Thank you." I followed, and we ascended to the second floor hall.

At the end of the hallway, we were greeted by a woman in a pristine white uniform. Her shoulders had bands of silver cording draped over them, and a golden star badge gleamed above her heart. Nothing else colored her minimalistic, but elegant, pant suit.

"Admiral Hawksford," she began with a brief curtsey— she put her arms out to the sides, rested her weight on her left leg, and then briefly bent her knees as her right foot came behind her left to tap against the floor. Then she straightened back up.

I never thought I'd be bowed to, and so frequently.

"The crown prince will see you now." The woman flourished her hand and stepped away from the ornate archway. Officer Cassian silently migrated to the other side of the hall to wait.

I made a conscious decision to perfect my posture—since I was being watched—before walking into the room. Muffled voices sounded up ahead, and then a few unarmed personnel in less decorated uniforms came scuttling past me, taking their places at attention beside the entryway.

"Admiral?"

A warm, familiar voice called to me, and I looked across the room at a stately figure seated on a glossy, carved wooden throne. Armed guards stood on both sides.

"Please do not feel out of place," Jacksiun said as I approached.

No longer in a green Celestial Galaxy uniform, the prince donned deep blue slacks and a long dress jacket with a high collar—closer in design and cut to Mattheia's than my own. A silver and black belt wrapped around his waist and bright metallic platinum roping draped both shoulders and trimmed his epaulets. Crisp white gloves covered his hands. Upon his head rested a delicate, woven silver circlet, embellished with red gemstones—like the king's. With a brand new uniform, no glasses, and a stiffer appearance overall, he looked like a different man.

"You will bow in front of the crown prince!" barked one of the nearby guards.

I panicked, and in an attempt to immediately do as I

was told, I stumbled and hit my knee hard on the ground. A grunt of pain welled in my throat, but I fought to keep it in.

Jacksiun bolted up from his seat and rushed to my side. He reached for my hands and assisted me to my feet.

The offending guard gasped in disbelief.

"Are you alright, Valhara?" Jacksiun whispered, a tinge of regret and sadness in his voice.

"I'm fine. Thank you." I stood and swept off my slacks, grinning appreciatively.

Jacksiun veered toward the guard and narrowed his eyes fiercely.

"You will not speak to Admiral Hawksford that way!" he said, sneering; his accent was much more Alyssian now. "You will treat the Elemental Guardian with respect, for she came here—by her own free will—to assist our kingdom in a battle we have failed to win on our own."

"I-I apologize, Your Highness," the man said, his voice trembling as he bowed very low. "Please forgive me, Admiral Hawksford," he said, making brief eye contact with me before lowering his head again.

I tipped my head in acknowledgement.

Jacksiun dismissed the guards, and then he brought me over to a plush velvet chair off to the side of the room and asked me to sit. Not in a royal sort of way, but in a friendly manner that reminded me how close we were, even if stature put a wedge between us.

"I am sorry for the mess I have gotten you into," he said. "I did not mean to bring you in to such a callous environment, and I sincerely hope you do not see my kingdom in a poor light because of it."

"Never." I smiled. "This is your home, Jacksiun." I cleared my throat and twisted my lips to the side. *"Prince Jacksiun,"* I corrected myself.

He gazed at me with sympathy, as if he didn't like the way I now had to address him.

"Thank you for standing up for me," I said quietly. "I don't know if your father would have done the same. I admit, he's different from how I'd imagined he'd be. I'm not sure how to describe it. Less patient?"

Jacksiun nodded. "I am very sorry. You deserve more respect than they have given you thus far. I was certain my father would come to his senses upon your arrival and revere your presence, but... he has slipped into his old ways, yet again. As he always does." He shook his head and sighed; his jaw tightened and he clasped his hands in his lap.

"Your new uniform is striking," I whispered, trying to steer the subject away from the uncomfortable one. "That blue goes well with your eyes."

"Thank you." He attempted to smile toward me, and then looked back down at his hands and sighed.

We sat there quietly for several awkward moments.

I waited for him to speak, but he didn't.

"Your father mentioned something about you *rebelling*," I said, breaking the silence. "May I ask what he meant by that?" I'd never known Jacksiun to revolt against anything other than a grade less than one-hundred on a one-hundred-point exam.

He nodded, but pressed his lips thin before responding. "I was sent to a school on the Mainlands to learn to fit in and socialize, but he hadn't expected me to join Celestial Galaxy and leave Earth without permission. It made him furious, because he had no way of assuring my safety while up in space. I am his only heir." He said the last few words with a hint of disdain.

"Is that why he now owns part of the academy?"

He raised an eyebrow. "Did he tell you that?"

"In a way."

"Hmm." He straightened and unclasped his hands. "*Owns* is not quite the word for it. *Sponsors*, perhaps."

"Oh? He called me one of his citizens. I was born on the Mainlands. How can he say something like that?"

"He notified the president of the Mainlands about my recruitment and offered to donate a substantial sum of money to alleviate much of the government debt, in exchange for a hand in governing the academy. In doing so, he claimed diplomatic control of the station."

"Why didn't I know about this before? How can we be told the academy is run by the president, when it's not!?"

Jacksiun looked me firmly in the eye. "Do you know what kind of backlash would have occurred if the people of the Mainlands discovered one of their largest military stations had been assimilated into the only other super-power government in the world? It would have caused chaos and, no doubt, a war."

"I see." I looked away. My fingers rested at my sides and my nails brushed against the velvety seat cushion. "Where are the others?" I hadn't seen Mattheia since he and the rest of my team had been separated while I was speaking to the king.

"I believe they are being kept—*put up*—in rooms in another wing of the castle."

"Why would they be housed in another wing? I need to discuss things with them. Commander Draven needs to be part of this and so does—"

"Private Quill," he solemnly finished my sentence.

"Yes." I tilted my head. "And the rest of my team." There was an odd look on his face, as if something troubled him. "Are you *concerned* about her?"

"Amanda?" His brow twitched. "I mean, the private?"

"Yes."

"Well, not *concerned*, per se, but..."

"You can tell me," I said, brushing my shoulder against his.

"It is more a problem of prejudice."

"Prejudice?"

"I understand things were different with you and Commander Draven when you were getting acquainted, but my father will not allow me to speak to whomever I choose."

"But you are the crown prince." My brow crinkled.

"Yes, but upon my return, I have become a prisoner in my own home. Once you and your crew return to Silver Diamond, I may never be able to speak to your friend again. I was hoping to get to know her better. She seems... nice."

His words pulled at my heartstrings, and I smiled. "You're sweet," I said. "I'm sure she'd like to get to know you better, as well." In fact, I *knew* she would.

"Really?" His eyes grew wider, and a hopeful grin curled his lips. "Do you think so?"

"Yes."

He smiled and a faint flush of pink colored his face; I'd never seen him blush before.

"I'll find a way for you two to talk while we're here."

"Thank you. I am sorry to burden you with such trivial problems when much more pertinent matters are on the horizon."

"Friendship is no trivial thing," I replied. "But I do have a small favor to ask of you while I am here."

"Anything."

"I visited the library; Colonel Hammonds took me there to show me around."

"Did he?" He gazed thoughtfully at me. "What do you think of it?"

"It's incredible; so many pieces of history in one place. I could stay there all day."

"It is quite humbling," he added. "So, what is it you wished to ask of me?"

"Are you familiar with the broadsword with the blue metal accents? The one in the glass case just past the main entrance?"

"Yes. It has been in our collection for as long as I can remember."

"It's Excalibur."

"What!?" He raised his voice and shifted closer to me, then composed himself and asked again. "What did you say?" His narrowed eyes glinted with disbelief.

"Excalibur, King Arthur's sword."

"How do you know that? My father commissioned at least a dozen experts in ancient arms to examine it over the years and not one has suggested such a thing."

"He never commissioned me." I smirked.

"What makes you think it's Excalibur?"

Knowing that what I was about to say would sound crazy to anyone *other* than my best friend, I decided to say it exactly as it came to my mind. "I saw it in a dream," I replied. "It's a very long story I can tell you later. In summary, the sorceress who tried to kill me was King Arthur's half sister. He wielded the sword in battle when he fought her to the death many years ago. It was taken from him and buried. Since you have it, I'm assuming someone uncovered it."

"Rayvenstar acquired it after the Great War. It was the same year all remaining traces of Camelot were wiped from Alyssia and Rayvenstar Castle erected in its place. It was the last surviving relic from the Pendragon Era. Have you told anyone this news?"

"Not yet. I was with Colonel Hammonds at the time and I was hoping you could grant me permission to study the sword further. I believe there is some kind of magic inside it, considering it was once held by another Elemental Guardian."

"I wish I could grant you such permission, but it is not up to me. I will ask my father on your behalf."

"Thank you. I would appreciate that."

"Perhaps Excalibur could be of some use to us." Jacksiun composed himself and cleared his throat. "I know my father can come across as rather abrasive at times, but please know he is doing the best he can for this country, and that he *does* care about his people. As do I."

"I understand."

"I do not want any harm to come to you or your team. I

know I said you could decide what you wanted to do once you arrived, but it seems my father is not allowing you freedom of choice. Please, Valhara, if this becomes too much of a burden for you, tell me and I will do anything in my power to keep you and the others safe." He glanced down at my hand—the one with the engagement ring. "You and Mattheia have a long life ahead, and I would like to see your wedding day as much as you. I surely did not bring you here on a suicide mission."

"And I didn't come all this way to run away from a challenge." I thought to reach out and press my fingers to his shoulder, as I had done in the past, but the strict environment had me fearing the consequences of touching Prince Jacksiun Rayvenstar in such a way. Instead, I lifted my head, smiled confidently, and said, "I came to fight beside my best friend."

Jacksiun and I had a good heart-to-heart.

He told me he had missed his mother terribly, and while he had returned home with the intention of seeing her before going to Aquarius, the bloodmane threat kept him from departing, except to come to me for aid. With monstrous danger now circling the castle walls, Jacksiun's father had prohibited him from transferring to the sea academy, demanding he stay in Alyssia until his coronation—however many decades away that might be. He and his father rarely saw eye-to-eye, and this made Jacksiun miserable in his home.

I was beginning to understand how he felt—like a prisoner in the guise of a guest.

"I would like to speak with Commander Draven," I said to Officer Cassian, after leaving the prince's quarters. "We need to discuss plans." The sun had begun to set, and light filtering in through stained glass windows in the cathedral ceiling had warmed to an auburn hue.

"I apologize, Admiral," he replied, peering up at the skylight. "But you are not permitted to wander the castle halls at dusk."

"Excuse me?" I squinted in disbelief. "Dusk? Why is it too late to speak with a member of my team inside the castle?"

"It will have to wait until sunup. *Tomorrow*," he replied firmly.

"Tomorrow? There are viable work hours left tonight, and I thought this matter was urgent?"

"It is, Admiral." His jaw tightened and he glanced off to the side as if my interrogation made him uncomfortable. "We do not conduct business matters after dark, per the king's order."

"This is..." I bit my lower lip to hold my tongue and then inhaled deeply, holding the breath a moment before exhaling.

"I apologize if it is out of the ordinary for you," he added. "I am following commands. If you have further questions about the ordinance, you may speak to the chamberlain or make an appointment with His Majesty."

"I understand."

Officer Cassian and I were subject to orders from our superiors. You join the military with the expectation that you will be part of a group, and you don't make waves. I wouldn't cause him any more grief over this.

"Where will I be staying?" I asked.

"The king has granted you lodging in the Regent Suite in the north wing."

"And my crew?"

"They are in the south wing."

I couldn't hold back a disgruntled huff.

"I assure you their lodgings are as adequate as your own," he added.

It was my first day at Silver Diamond all over again. Now, King Vincent was putting me up in a special room, most likely to keep an eye on me.

Regardless of how I felt, it was neither the time nor place to let my discomfort be known. I'd speak to the king in the morning—if possible—and see if we had other options. I wasn't about to spend the entire stay separated from my team.

As we came upon the Regent Suite, Officer Cassian stopped and turned to me. "Here is your room," he said. "Your things have been placed inside. Should you require anything, you may request it of me or any other guards in this hall."

I'd passed several along the way.

"Thank you." I turned toward the strange door, which was devoid of any handle, knob, or keycard reader, and cocked my head. The outline was flush against the wall with only a faint indent tracing the perimeter. "How do I enter?" I felt childish asking, but I really couldn't tell.

"Clearly state your rank and name," Officer Cassian instructed.

"Lieu—" I cleared my throat and smiled awkwardly at the officer before trying again. "*Admiral* Valhara Hawksford."

The door slid up with a soft whoosh, disappearing into the ceiling.

"The door will recognize your voice," he continued. "We made an imprint of your vocal inflections upon your arrival. Those were used to program the door."

What? A twinge of anger made my fingers squeeze into a fist. I felt violated, but didn't have the power or patience to challenge yet another castle policy.

"Officer, could you deliver a message to Commander Draven on my behalf?"

"I would be happy to do that for you." He grinned. "However, there are tablets in your rooms through which you may communicate, and they are already logged on to the castle's network. Please keep in mind that all electronic transmissions are monitored and recorded for security purposes."

"Monitored? *All* of them?"

"Yes, Admiral. It is within our jurisdiction to do so for the safety and security of our king. Do not worry. It is only a precautionary measure."

"Thank you for letting me know."

"I will be resigning for the night and another officer will take my place outside your room. If you should require anything, please do not hesitate to let him or her know." He bowed his head. "Have a good night, Admiral."

"Good night, Officer."

I entered the room and the door slid closed behind me. A huge bay window with lattice shutters gleamed at the far end of the spacious suite, the final hints of sunlight peeking in. I approached it and unclasped the latch so I could swing open the shutters. A cool evening breeze gushed into the room, and I filled my lungs with Alyssian air. Rayvenstar Castle resided in the mountains, which meant the temperature would always be cooler than in other parts of the region. I had also been told that it snowed very early in the year. I'd never seen snow on the Mainlands, and in space, well...

I surveyed the suite. Off to one side of the bedroom was a large shower and bathroom, and on the other side, a separate sitting or reading room with a stone fireplace surrounded by shelves of leather-bound books. End tables beside my bed had been decorated with small marble statues of mounted knights and the woodwork engraved with the royal Rayvenstar crest. A menagerie of colorful tapestries woven from shimmering threads hung on the walls.

The place was reminiscent of someone's lush home, not a temporary lodging, and I hoped the rest of my team had been as well accommodated.

My bags had been laid out on the bed and a small tablet computer set up on the desk across from there. An app had been loaded to the main screen that resembled a messaging program, and all the names of my crew members had been pre-loaded. Though I hadn't planned on saying anything that might be interpreted as suspicious by the kingdom's transmission moderators, I didn't feel comfortable knowing *everything* I said to my team would be monitored and recorded. We were there to assist the king. He needed to trust us, especially since I was the crown prince's friend, and, possibly, the only person on Earth with the ability to save the kingdom.

I walked over to the desk, tapped Mattheia's title on the open application, and typed a brief message.

"I hope you are well. I'll try to fill you in on what happened tomorrow. Have a good night."

I watched the screen for several moments.

A blinking dot appeared, indicating he was typing a response.

"I'm okay, but not happy with the current situation," he replied. "We can discuss it tomorrow. Have a good night, Admiral."

I might have typed something else were we not being monitored, but I didn't feel like disclosing our relationship to the castle staff.

"Goodnight, Mattheia," I muttered and turned off the screen.

I withdrew the needle from my thigh and capped it. The injection was supposed to help me focus by tricking my body into thinking I was back on my usual sleep schedule, but the effects of yesterday's injection had been marginal.

Someone knocked on my door at what had felt like three in the morning. I'd been awake for almost an hour, begrudgingly, and had been attempting to get my bearings in between chatting with my crew. The time difference interfered with my circadian rhythm. The effect was likely worse on Mattheia and the rest of my crew because they had been running on RST (Regent Standard Time) for most of their life while Rayvenstar Castle ran on NST (Noble Summer Time). Why it was called "summer" I'll never know. They were about 10 hours ahead of Silver Diamond, and four hours ahead of Celestial Galaxy. Kinasetsu's island was 14 hours, give or take, ahead of Silver Diamond, which made it four hours ahead of NST. In short, I felt terribly jetlagged.

The injections they'd given us right before we'd left did help adjust the melatonin and hormones in our bodies, but time zone shots can only help so much.

Someone knocked on my door again.

"Just a moment," I said, raising my voice so whoever was there would hear me. I glanced at the tablet computer on the desk across from the bed. A string of messages had been sent since I'd last looked. Mattheia. Amanda. Lieutenant Claire (a specialist in animal biology). We were using a group chat to discuss plans for the day.

I approached my door and looked around. I'd forgotten there were no handles or knobs of any kind.

"Abracadabra?" I shrugged. "Open says me?"

It slid open and I laughed. *Whatever works.* They were voice activated both ways, apparently.

"Good morning," Mattheia said with a smile that was more subdued than usual—probably because he was flanked by an escort.

I smiled back, caught off-guard because I hadn't expected to see him at my door first thing.

He cocked an eyebrow. "You seem surprised. Did you not get my last few messages?"

"Oh." I chuckled sheepishly. "I didn't check it for a little while. I'm sorry. I'm still very tired."

"No worries."

I peeked over Mattheia's shoulder at Cassian, the officer who had been assigned to escort me around the castle.

His shift had been taken over by someone else last night, but now he was back.

"I hear breakfast is being served in the south dining hall," Mattheia said. "Care to join me?"

I thought it quite odd how everything moved so slowly in the kingdom. They were under attack—giant, bloodthirsty creatures had been taking the lives of their military for over a week.

I couldn't fight on an empty stomach, but the lack of urgency here felt very out of place.

"Yes. I would enjoy a nice breakfast," I replied, stepping past the threshold of my room. The door closed behind me.

Our escorts moved to our outside shoulders so we could talk as we walked to the dining hall. Being watched so closely made me uncomfortable, and as I glanced into Mattheia's eyes every now and then, I could see he was disconcerted too.

Rayvenstar Castle did not operate the way Silver Diamond or Celestial Galaxy did, but we would have to adhere to their different (albeit, unusual) ways.

"May I present to you Royal Chamberlain Sir Isaac Grennings," Officer Cassian announced with a bow toward the unfamiliar face.

Sir Isaac Grennings, a tall, broad-shouldered man with silver hair, a square jaw, and vivid green eyes, greeted us at the dining hall entrance.

"I see you have met my nephew," he said, gesturing toward Officer Cassian. "I do hope he has made you feel welcomed here."

I nodded. "He has."

"It is a pleasure to meet you, Admiral Hawksford and Commander Draven," the chamberlain continued. "If I may be of any service to you whilst you are here, please do not hesitate to ask."

From my knowledge, Chamberlain Grennings was next in line for the throne should something happen to both King Vincent and Prince Jacksiun. With so much authority at hand, there were a lot of things I wanted to ask him. Such as why we couldn't take a step in any direction without someone on our heels, why the palace had ridiculous rules about evening curfews, and why my team was separated so quickly yesterday.

But I said nothing; I knew better than to challenge authority in this new place.

We had not been in Rayvenstar Castle long enough to ask prying questions. A time would come for those. *Hopefully.*

The chamberlain left us and we entered the dining hall. An elaborate table had been set with seats for at least a hundred people. The ivory table runner spanned the length of the table, and places had been set for many more people than were on my team. Elegant wine flutes and crystal glasses had been buffed to prismatic shine. Silverware shimmered on the left side of each setting, and delicate, embroidered napkins had been folded into neat little triangles standing at attention near each plate.

The cathedral ceiling in the room made me feel so small, and the oversized tapestries hanging along the walls reminded me we were in the presence of royalty.

"Admiral," a perky voice called from nearby. I turned toward Amanda, who had already been seated. She appeared to be halfway through eating a fluffy biscuit with butter and jam spread on top. A cup of tea in an elegant blue, silver-accented teacup sat steaming near her right hand.

A castle server seated Mattheia and me beside each other and then pushed my seat in.

"You have to try these," Amanda said with an ecstatic grin. "These biscuits are amazing." She shoved the remaining bite into her mouth and nodded vigorously.

I turned to Mattheia, who observed a server pouring bright golden red liquid into the teacup at his setting. The server filled my cup next.

I'd not had tea in the past, though Jacksiun had recommended a few types to me. Now was as good of a time as any to try the beverage of choice for royals.

He'd also told me to add a small amount of milk and sugar, but I did not know how much to add or when to add them, so I watched steam drift out of the elegant porcelain cup for several moments, waiting to see what Mattheia would do.

He did nothing, and as he lifted his cup to take a sip, a server came between us and said, "If I may, Commander Draven, I suggest you add a hint of sugar and milk before you indulge. You may find it slightly more palatable and it is generally how we enjoy tea."

So there was a *right* way to do it.

Mattheia set down his cup and gestured toward it. "If you wouldn't mind. I'm not sure how much to add."

"If you could," I interrupted. "Mine, as well. I'm sorry

to be a bother."

"Not at all, Admiral." The server smiled genuinely at me. He seemed very happy to do his job and was more than thrilled to show us foreigners how to enjoy tea properly.

Jacksiun had, at one time, attempted to explain to me about the different types of tea, but considering Celestial Galaxy only offered one blend, everything had slipped my mind.

The server added a cube of sugar to each of our cups and then tipped a dainty milk carafe over each until the mixture turned pale brown.

"Thank you," we both said to the server, who then cheerfully reached between us to remove a metal dome lid from a tray of biscuits on the table.

"We will bring out the rest of your meal shortly," he added and then left the dining room.

Mattheia was first to take a sip of the tea. His mouth wrinkled slightly after he swallowed, but he tried very hard to hide the look of discomfort from fully manifesting on his face.

"Not your thing?" I asked.

"Maybe it's an acquired taste," he said with a subtle shrug.

I sipped mine next. It had a malty aroma which carried over to the taste, but the sugar and hint of milk softened it to a mellow, creamy sweetness. It wasn't bad. It wasn't something I was used to drinking, but it certainly wasn't bad. I could see why Jacksiun enjoyed it.

"It's not terrible," I said to Mattheia. "It's different."

"Yes, it is."

"I like it!" Amanda beamed, taking a dainty, but enthusiastic sip from her cup.

I chuckled beneath my breath. Of course.

Mattheia cracked open a fresh, piping-hot biscuit and slathered strawberry jam on each side with a silver buttering knife. At the same time, another server came out with a tray of eggs and breakfast meats.

I wasn't accustomed to being pampered this way, but it was nice.

"So, what are we doing today?" Mattheia asked, stabbing a piece of ham on his plate and then forking it into his mouth.

"I think we should take a look at the ruins where it all began—the temple the king was having excavated. It would probably be a good place to start gathering information on these creatures. Lieutenant Claire may be of some help there. I've been told bloodmanes only come out at night, so we should be safe to investigate during daylight hours."

Mattheia nodded and let out a grunt of agreement; he was chewing.

"I'll ask for permission to leave the castle as soon as we finish here." I was in no hurry to escape the quiet, delicious array of things the castle chef had prepared for us.

A bsolutely not!" General Cain growled. "What good is it for you to drag your team all the way out there to observe a pile of stone?"

Lieutenant Claire stepped up. "Sir, we must gather information about the bloodmanes in order to fight them. We're blind right now and we have nothing to go on. We don't know when they will strike again, and we must be prepared for when they do."

General Cain narrowed his eyes. "I do not see how you will find anything helpful there. Is there not something in the library or in the international database network you can use to conduct your research?"

"No," I cut in. "She's right, Sir. I would like to see the site where the bloodmanes emerged. Any tissue sample, scale flake, or tuft of fur could provide us with more insight than we have now."

"Hmm." He crossed his arms.

Another soldier leaned closer and whispered something into his ear, which he acknowledged with a nod.

"Very well," the general said. "If it satisfies your curiosity, then go. We will provide you with a map at the castle gates and I will send a team along to assist you."

"We don't need your soldiers," Mattheia said firmly. "This team is more than capable, Sir."

I could tell by his wrinkled lips and judgmental glare that General Cain was not happy with the commander's audacious rebuttal, but I was proud of Mattheia for standing up for us. This was his team, too, and as second-in-command at Silver Diamond—a rank on par with the colonel of the Rayvenstar army—he deserved to be heard.

"Fine," the general grumbled and turned away from us. "Report your findings back to me."

The ruins were about a three-quarter-mile trek northwest from Rayvenstar Castle, and the cool, early morning temperatures made for a comfortable walk. The time zone injection had finally kicked in and I felt more alert.

Broken stone, dirt, rocks, and shattered wood were all that remained of the temple. It was in ruins alright, but I wondered what condition it had been in *before* excavation had begun. A brief survey of the surrounding area revealed no claw marks or tracks. If the creatures had actually been birthed from this place, there should have been signs of their emergence.

I ducked down beneath a crumbling archway of shattered stone and wood pillars and peeked inside. It was dark, dusty, and probably unstable; we had to tread carefully.

"Admiral, wait." Mattheia reached for my forearm as I took a step forward. "How do you know it's safe? What if what's left of the place collapses when we enter?"

"You're right." I shook my head and backed away from the entryway. "I'm not sure what I was thinking going in headfirst. Let me summon Firagia and see what he suggests." I looked over Mattheia's shoulder at the rest of my crew. "Please brace yourselves." I raised my voice to be sure they heard.

"Whatever you see, stay calm," Mattheia added.

Amanda's brow twitched. Lieutenant Claire clasped her supplies close to her chest and recoiled several feet.

"Many of you have probably heard about Admiral Hawksford's powers," Mattheia said. "She can summon fire to her hands and bend it to her will."

"I have other abilities, too," I added. "I'd like to introduce you all to my friend. Please do not be frightened of him. He is here to help us."

I willed Firagia to join us, and in the blink of an eye, a burst of red light shot from my necklace. My crew gasped and Amanda stared in awe.

Firagia manifested a few feet away from me, first on all fours, and then he stood up on his hind legs because it was more comfortable.

"Greetings," he said in a cheery voice. Then his smile went straight and he looked at me. "Are they alright?" He looked over my team members; their expressions were mixed with fear, inquiry, and anticipation.

A wide smile stretched across Amanda's face. "It's a dragon!" she squeaked, breaking the silence as she rushed over. "Nice to meet you," she said, tipping her head. "Where are you from? Oh, your scales are so beautiful." She looked him up and down quickly. "How old are you? Oh!" She smacked her palm to her forehead and grinned sheepishly, backing away a step. "Wait. I'm so sorry. I apologize. I'll be quiet now, Admiral."

"My name is Firagia," he said to her and then looked at the others. "There is no need for you to be afraid of me. I am Admiral Hawksford's Spirit Guardian—an enchanted being bound to her. Our fates are intertwined because of her ability to wield fire."

"Please do not tell the king about him," I said. "I don't believe he needs to know about my friend just yet. I hope you all can understand why."

Lieutenant Claire bobbed her head and then the others snapped out of their frozen-like states and approached us.

"You may speak to him later," I said. "Right now," I turned to Firagia, "I need you to tell me if you believe it is safe for us to enter the ruins. Your slender body and slick scales should allow you to maneuver through the entryway much more easily than any of us. Do you think you can do that without getting injured?"

"Yes," he said with a bow of his head. "But I must be very careful, as I am now attached to my skin." He smirked.

Firagia resided in my necklace, but he had a physical form that could get injured, so he had to take care of himself. Dragons heal more quickly than humans, so small scrapes and scratches wouldn't last long.

He approached the entryway and ducked his head down to squeeze inside. His long, iridescent tail slowly disappeared from view, and I waited for him to share his sight with me.

Dust fell into my eyes and I shuddered; Firagia shook off the discomfort as he inched over broken boulders and crushed, sharp-edged rocks scattered across the ground.

"Careful," I spoke to him in my mind. Mattheia's hand pressed onto my shoulder reassuringly, a signal that he realized I was now seeing through the dragon's eyes.

Firagia pulled his long neck down to avoid a low hanging slab of stone, and then shimmied his way through a narrow corridor just wide enough for a single person (or small dragon) to squeeze through.

At the end of the lengthy, claustrophobic stretch of rock and debris was a larger entryway barricaded with slats of wood nailed diagonally across the door.

"I cannot get through, Valhara," Firagia spoke to me. *"It is completely blocked off."* He took a step closer to the barricade and peered at a row of symbols etched in the wood. *"There are old Alyssian runes carved here. 'Condemned. Do not enter.'"* A royal seal had been left near those marks. Next, he investigated the nails and boards. *"These are new. The nails are clean, not rusted, and the wood is hard and fresh. This was done recently."*

"How did the surrounding walls get destroyed while the inner doors remained intact?" I said out loud so everyone could hear me.

"It would appear as though the doors had been nailed

shut in an attempt to keep the beasts inside."

"Or to keep us out," I suggested.

"*That is possible. The outside walls were clearly destroyed with purpose. Most likely with explosives.*"

"Can we get inside?" I asked.

Firagia pressed the side of his face against the crack between the doors and peeked through. There was a huge room on the other side, with small specks of light shining where sun leaked through cracks in the ceiling stone.

"*We could burn the doors open,*" he said.

"Yes."

I released Firagia's vision long enough to turn to my team and say, "There are doors, not far beyond this crumbled entryway, which are blockaded off. I can probably break through them with my fire so we can get inside to look around. Does anyone here object to my clearing an opening for us to enter?"

"I don't object," Lieutenant Claire spoke up. "But I would advise your friend to be very careful. The structural integrity of the building could be compromised once the framework around the threshold is destroyed."

"Good point, Lieutenant." I focused on Firagia again.

"*I will return to you before we move forward,*" Firagia said.

A few moments later, he emerged and several members of my team gasped again as if they were seeing him for the first time.

Amanda's face lit up and she gravitated closer to hear what he had to say.

"I'm going to burn the wood away and hope the stone

archway remains," I announced.

Mattheia's brow furrowed. "Why? Shouldn't we—"

"Together, we can move some rubble to make a pathway to the main entrance, but the doors at the end are sealed shut. If I destroy them, we can get inside."

"What if the bloodmanes attack?" Officer Franklin, another team member Mattheia had appointed, asked sternly.

"Look around you," I said. "Do you see *any* sign whatsoever that a bloodmane has been anywhere near here? There are no prints. No claw marks on the stone or in the dirt. If they escaped from the ground, they didn't do it from here. But if King Vincent wants us to get to the bottom of this, then I need to know what's beyond that door. We must get inside."

Officer Franklin lowered his head in shame and nodded. "Yes, Admiral. I understand, and I apologize for questioning your judgment."

"Everyone stand back, please," I said, holding out my arms.

Mattheia backed away and everyone followed his lead.

I focused on the massive pile and tried to visualize how far beyond the stones the door stood. With Firagia's help, I could locate the approximate placement. I lifted both hands and concentrated, willing vagrant energy in the air to come to me, drawing in what power wafted through Alyssia.

Soft white-gold light emanated from my fingertips and then vivid sparks of fire licked up off my skin. I pressed my hands forward and forced the fire at the ruins, igniting the area with an immense wave of light. Fire consumed the stone as if it were kindling, causing rocks to fall upon each other as the wood beneath collapsed to ash.

Smaller stones near my feet trembled, and the ground shook with a deep, thunderous growl. A stream of golden light skittered toward my boots and the dirt ignited to a molten orange. *What's happening*!? I knew something was wrong, but it was too late to snuff out the light swallowing up the pile of stone.

"Get back!" I shouted while turning to run. An explosion sent splintered wood and debris toward the sky, and a force pushed me to the ground; my knees hit the earth hard, and my torso slammed into the dirt.

A humming noise hung in the air.

No. It was in my head.

A dull buzzing sound coiled through my brain. Sand rubbed against my face, scratching the skin.

I came onto my elbows and blinked, trying to focus through the cloud of dust surrounding us. People coughed. Mattheia, who wasn't far from me, stood and brushed dirt from his pants.

"Is everyone alright?" I asked, raising my voice as I staggered to my knees.

"I believe so," Lieutenant Claire replied. The dust settled and the rest of my team crowded around.

Firagia came to my side and looked me over with concern.

"What was that?" I asked, rubbing the back of my neck.

"I am unsure," he replied. "I believe there may be more energy here than you have trained with in the past. All the vagrant energy must have come together much too quickly, amplifying your power and causing that terrible blast."

That had never happened before, and Kinasetsu had not warned me about such a risk. I needed to be more careful. The land surrounding Rayvenstar Castle was saturated with magic.

"On the plus side of things," Mattheia started, lifting a hand to point, "the entryway is clear." He coughed.

The surrounding rubble had been blown away and only a massive stone archway, scorched black, remained.

"So it is. Firagia, let's go first." I turned to my crew. "Please wait while I check to see if it's safe. I'm also not sure if the area is big enough to accommodate us all."

"No," Mattheia said, grabbing me by the forearm just as I turned away. Our eyes met. "I'll go with you."

"Okay," I agreed. "But you need to be careful, too."

"Of course."

The three of us ventured through the charred entrance and down a rocky corridor, which eventually opened up into a round room with a high ceiling and ornate metalwork stretching up toward a fractured stone skylight overhead. Beams of light sprinkled through cracks in the perimeter, and a larger stream of white flecked with dust shone through the massive opening in the center of the ceiling.

"Stop!" I swung out an arm to block Mattheia.

Firagia leapt into the air, flew past him, and then swooped down in front of me, hovering over a large chasm where the floor of the room had completely collapsed. I peeked over the ledge but couldn't see far into the hole.

"I will take a look," Firagia said, drifting down into the darkness until his radiant firelight began to subtly color the nearby walls.

"How far is the drop?" I asked the dragon, who was flitting around the perimeter of the room like a hummingbird, his fiery glow bouncing off metallic panels on the walls.

"Twenty feet or so," he replied. "Much too far for you to drop down safely. You could break something, or worse..."

The flooring had collapsed from the center out, and there weren't piles of stone large enough for me to climb down anywhere near the edge of the pit.

"Is there some other way for us to get down there?" I shouted into the chasm.

"I could catch you," Firagia said.

"What?"

"If you jump, I can catch you."

I wasn't one for jumping blindly into dark holes, but I did trust my dragon.

"Are you sure you want to do that, Valhara?" Mattheia asked. "If we return to the castle, we can gather supplies and rappel down safely, with the rest of the team."

"I don't know if we have time to go back," I replied. "Firagia, is there another way?"

Firagia rose from the hole and drifted in the air before us.

"You're worried about jumping," he said softly. "I understand your concern." He flew behind me and Mattheia stepped back. "I have an idea, but it means the commander must wait here. May I try it?"

"I think I should investigate while I'm here, don't you?" I glanced at Mattheia imploringly and he appeared to hesitantly agree. "Yes. Let us try your plan."

Firagia faded into light; a gentle pressure in my chest was the dragon returning to my necklace and assimilating with me.

"Perhaps we can share powers," his voice resonated in my head.

A warm sensation pushed through me and my back felt hot. A burst of wind knocked me forward, thrusting me into the hole. I let out a shriek of fear as the ground came into view, but then I stopped falling and my body hung in the air, as if suspended by an invisible harness. I craned my neck back to look over my shoulder at the raging wings of flame dancing behind me.

My feet came down and my head up as my body orientation righted. The ground beneath me reflected the bright glow of colorful fire, the light fading as my boots touched down.

Firagia emerged from my amulet and his fire illuminated our surroundings. It was a circular room, with large metal nameplates perched above various cutouts.

"Come look," Firagia said, pointing at a nearby plate covered in cobwebs and dirt.

I couldn't make out anything on the plaque until Firagia took in a deep breath and blew away a puff of dust.

A scrollwork design framed the entire plate, and swirls of metallic shimmer danced across lines of raised text. Letters had been obscured by ridges from deep claw marks, but I could still decipher most words.

"King Westin Rayvenstar," it read, and below it, "Brave. Virtuous. Loyal. Fight and we fight. Fall and we fall. A king to lead all men."

"And this next one," Firagia added, brushing his hand across a second metal name plate that was a few feet away.

I neared it and leaned closer. "King Edward Rayvenstar,

son of Westin. Blood of a king in his veins. Mark of a king on his flesh."

"Why are these here?" I asked. "Why would all the kings' names be posted in a cave underground?"

Firagia paused and lowered his head. "I'm afraid they are not merely the names of past kings. These markers are burial plaques put here to designate the final resting places of Rayvenstar kings passed. This is a mausoleum. Or at least it *was*." He frowned and traced the deep scratch marks defacing Westin's tomb marker. "Those terrible beasts have marred this sacred place."

"I see that." I turned around; almost every tomb had been vandalized. Stones had been crushed and torn from the walls. Grave markers clawed—some completely illegible. "Why would they do this? Why would they desecrate the old kings?"

"Valhara, look!" Firagia glanced down at the ground and then staggered back. "Blood!"

My eyes followed his line of sight down to the desolate floor. Deep trenches of fractured stone had been darkened with rusty bloodstains. I leaned down, willing an orb of bright light to my fingertips so I could better see the evidence. Tufts of hair had been scattered around. Light reflected off a curl of something wedged into the dirt; I reached for it, uncovering a glossy, black claw fragment at least three inches long.

"Did they drag someone down here?" My stomach churned at the thought. Those monsters had killed someone or something, carried them all the way down here to this sacred place, and then brutally fed, leaving blood all across the stone. I clenched my teeth and growled beneath my breath.

The Rayvenstar kings who died for their country deserved more respect than this. King Vincent had been forced to seal off their tombs in order to protect his people from the raging nightmares that had taken up residence here.

"Is everything okay?" Mattheia called from the upper floor.

"I'm fine!" I shouted back. "Can you get something from Lieutenant Claire that I can use to gather samples?"

"Sure. I'll let her know. Give me a few moments to get back to her."

The room went quiet while Firagia and I listened intently for movement, just in case the beasts decided to return prematurely to their feeding ground. We didn't want to be caught off-guard.

"Here." Mattheia shone a flashlight down toward me, and Firagia's flames brightened to compensate for the low visibility. "Catch!"

I reached out my hands and Mattheia tossed down a small plastic box. I flipped open the lid to reveal several plastic jars with screw-on lids.

"I noticed fur scattered near one of the grave markers," Firagia said. "Would you like me to gather a sample?"

"Yes." I handed him one of the jars. He wandered off and it became very dark once again. "Commander! Shine your flashlight down here, please."

A blue-white beam of light brought the ruddy bloodstains near my feet back into focus. I knelt, used a wedge of plastic from the kit to shovel some of the red dirt into the jar, and then screwed the lid back on. "Thanks!"

"Are you coming back up?" he asked.

"Yes. Firagia, will you help me again?" I turned toward the green and red glimmering nearby. He perked up and hurried over to my side.

"You will have to take this," he said, handing me the sample jar containing the fur. "Stand back from the ledge, Commander!" Firagia raised his voice so Mattheia could hear. "Are you ready, Valhara?"

"Yes."

The first time he'd merged his wings with my body, the sensation was strange and new. Now, I knew what to expect and took a deep breath in anticipation of the pressure build-up.

His firelight faded and my necklace grew hot again as he returned to it. A burst of yellow-orange fire sparked from my back, and wings formed behind me, pushing through my skin with subtle force.

"*Brace yourself,*" he said in my mind.

I tried, but still gasped with surprise as I was thrust up off the ground toward the ledge overhead, where Mattheia stood. My feet came down and I tumbled forward, scrambling to retain the box of samples.

Mattheia grasped me by my shoulders before I could hit the rocks and instantly the wings faded.

"*My apologies for the harsh landing,*" Firagia said. "*It is something we can work to improve.*"

"I agree," I muttered, clutching Mattheia's arm as I caught my balance and straightened up.

"Agree with what?" he asked.

"Oh, sorry. I was talking to Firagia."

"So... I take it that's new?" Mattheia asked. "The wings."

"Yes. Firagia suggested it. We'll need more practice with the ability, but I think it will be a useful one."

"It looked amazing. You were sort of, kind of, *flying*..."

"Yes."

"But... I thought you didn't like to—"

"Don't even," I interrupted. "*That* was far from *flying*."

"Yes, I know." He smirked. "I'm sorry I keep poking fun at you for that. I really am lucky to be part of your life."

I feared flying, *and* I was engaged to a pilot.

Two things he'd not soon let me forget.

H ave you found anything?" I asked Lieutenant Claire.

We'd returned to the castle, been stripped of our weapons (yet again), and set up a makeshift laboratory in the on-site medical facility. The lieutenant had been working for a few hours, analyzing the samples we'd collected in the ruins.

"Yes and no." She withdrew from a computer screen and turned toward me. "This is the fur sample you brought in. Do you see this pattern?" She pointed at a 3D projection emitted from a metal disc nearby her workstation. It displayed segmented lines of various shades of color in stacked patterns. I recognized it as DNA but could tell nothing more.

"This isn't the pattern of any animal species in the international biological database," she added.

All medical records from the Mainlands' experiment

years ago had been destroyed, so we couldn't compare our findings to those.

"We don't have bloodmanes on file, right?"

"No. Which is why I am going to make an educated guess that this *is* bloodmane DNA." She swiveled around in her chair and pointed at her second monitor. "Take a look at this. This is the DNA from the blood sample found in the dirt. It's human."

Just as I had suspected.

"So the creatures are bringing people down there to... eat?" I asked.

"Possibly, but there were no bones, you say?"

"Nothing that I saw." I began to wonder if they devoured prey whole, like owls.

"There are no other skin or tissue particles in the dirt you brought back, either," the lieutenant continued. "I don't know exactly what this means, but it does indicate the creatures were, or still are, inhabiting that area. I'd tread carefully from now on if you decide to venture back out there."

"Should I report this to the king now, or do you want more time to analyze the samples?"

"The royal chamberlain has already asked me to send copies of all reports to him, as well as to General Cain. I'll do that as soon as I'm finished."

"I see. Thank you for your work so far, Lieutenant. I'm going to relay the information to him personally and see how he thinks we should proceed."

"No matter what, I suggest you proceed with caution," she warned.

"Always," I replied flatly.

"What were you doing *inside* the ruins?" Chamberlain Grennings spoke through gritted teeth. "That area is off-limits and was clearly marked as such. We granted you permission to investigate, but never said you could *enter* the ruins. You put yourself and your team in great danger."

I chewed my lip while waiting for him to come to a full stop.

He narrowed his eyes. "How did you even get inside? We had boarded everything off and—" He looked as if he had said too much and stopped himself.

"I am the Elemental Guardian," I said firmly. "It wasn't that difficult for me. Besides, you *did* give me permission to access the grounds and did not forewarn me of any limitations."

"But we did not give you permission to pass the barricade."

"No one told me there *was* a barricade." I kept my gaze firmly locked onto his, holding my ground.

"Hmm." He grumbled and then shook his head and shrugged. "Well, what did you find?"

"Tissue samples we believe to be bloodmane, and a sample we know to be human. The lieutenant running the tests was unable to determine the bloodmane one because there are no records of such DNA in the international database, but we have a good hunch that it is. And then we found human bloodstains on the dirt inside."

"The monsters are using it as a feeding ground, no doubt." Chamberlain Grennings scowled. "Anything else?"

"Do you have any idea why they would take up residence inside the temple of the old kings?"

"Hush." His voice became low and gruff. "Do not speak of such things here. The citizens are not yet aware of the unfortunate... incident, and we wish to keep it that way."

"You're hiding the truth from your people? Why? Don't they deserve to know what has happened?"

"We have informed them that a sinkhole opened up beneath the excavation area and that we are working to stabilize the site."

"And no one has come to pay homage to the kings ever since?"

"The location of the tomb has not been made public, and the area is off-limits to civilians."

"If your people don't even know what the ruins truly are, then they can't know about the monsters, either. Th-that's..." I glared at him and he shifted his eyes to look away. A plume of anger billowed in me. "Your people deserve to know the truth! They need to be prepared. They need to be able to defend themselves. This is an incredibly dangerous outbreak. By keeping quiet about it, you're endangering the public. Does King Vincent know you're doing this? Does he—"

"Quiet, Admiral!" Chamberlain Grennings loomed over me, his brows knitting together as an angry sneer bent his lips. "Do not forget whose country you are in. Tread lightly and follow orders, or you *and* your team will be punished for poking around in places you do not belong."

"Is that a threat?" I rolled my shoulders back.

"You are dismissed." The chamberlain swerved on a

heel and turned his back to me. "Escort her away," he said with a flick of his hand toward his guards.

I was taken by the forearms—quite forcefully—and shuttled back into the main hall where I was released and the doors behind me closed to keep me from reentering the chamberlain's office.

If Captain Lansfora and Captain Ventresca knew how I was being treated, they'd have an awful lot to say. I was beginning to prefer the constitutional republic of the Mainlands over the parliamentary democracy and constitutional monarch of Alyssia. Some Alyssian officials are elected, but many gain positions through power and hierarchy. As long as I stayed in this country, I was at the mercy of these people.

If everyone kept secrets and I couldn't talk to others about what I had seen, how could I help the king? Again, more roadblocks. More unnecessary stalling. We had to get to the bottom of this attack soon, before the monsters struck again.

Come to think of it, I'd seen no evidence since my arrival that the bloodmanes were an active hazard. I took Jacksiun's, and his father's, word for it, but the creatures hadn't so much as stepped foot near the castle since we'd touched down. In part, I wanted to go exploring the perimeter on my own, but I knew that wouldn't be an option. It was as if they wanted me to swoop in, clear out all the pests with some magical smoke bomb, and then swoop out, returning to the Mainlands as if nothing had ever happened.

My personal guard (or watchman) and palace escort, Officer Cassian, came up to me and tipped his head with respect. "Admiral," he said with a friendly smile. "I am at your disposal. Let me know where you wish to go."

"To speak with Commander Draven," I declared. "He told me he'd be in the library."

He acknowledged my request and we began walking.

As we traveled down the long, elegant hallways of the north wing—where most castle dignitaries resided—toward the east wing, Officer Cassian remained as silent as a ghost.

"You're welcome to speak freely when you're with me," I said, smiling slightly as his face turned toward mine. "You don't have to treat me like royalty, even if they told you to."

"Thank you, Admiral, but it is not my business to pry in your affairs."

"You wouldn't be prying," I replied. His eyes met mine and then darted away. It was a strange, almost shy movement that surprised me. Did I intimidate him?

We turned a corner and walked down another hall before he said anything more.

"Did you... really defeat a dragon?" he whispered.

I glanced over at him. "Yes—an ice-dragon larger than an elephant."

Cassian gasped and then swiftly composed himself. "That is incredible. You must be a powerful warrior. I have heard you are skilled with a sword."

"Yes. I've been studying since I was very young and the department I work at now—the one at Silver Diamond—specializes in rare artifact and weapon attainment and research."

"Really?" Cassian raised his brow in awe.

After a few more moments of silence, he asked, "How

does it feel?"

"How does *what* feel?"

"The fire," he said, speaking from the corner of his mouth while looking off to the side, as if he didn't want any other castle personnel to witness our conversation. "What does it feel like to draw upon it and wield it in battle?"

I had to think on that briefly, because the sensation was not easily describable.

"It's similar to evaporation," I started. "Imagine if you poured water onto your arm, and then the room became so warm that the water began to evaporate. That's what it feels like sometimes. Other times, it's almost a subtle pressure building up under my skin, as if something is pushing to get out of me."

"Hmm." His brow furrowed. "Does it hurt? Or *burn*?"

"No." I shook my head and lifted a hand out in front of me, cupping my fingers and pulling my arm in closer to my chest so as to not draw too much attention. A ball of flame sparked to life within my fingers.

Cassian stumbled.

"Ah!" I reached for him, but he caught his balance and dismissed my help with a flattened hand.

"I am fine." He stopped walking and turned to me with widened eyes. "I-I will admit, I did not believe it, at first, but... y-you just made fire in the palm of your hand."

The stretch of the hall we had arrived in was quiet and lengthy, and the only other people in sight were far ahead of us at the next archway.

"Actually, I don't create it; I manipulate the energy that's already in the air and all around us."

He cocked his head.

I put my hand up in front of him and willed another small coil of flame to life.

"Touch it," I said.

He lifted his hand but hesitated.

"It will not... burn me?"

"No. I assure you, it won't."

I uncurled my fingers and he slowly lifted his toward the reddish swirl of sparkling light.

He quickly passed his hand through the flame and pulled back.

"No heat," he said, astonished. Then he made a second pass and let his fingers drift through the changing colors. "I..." He shook his head and took in a deep breath. "I-I cannot find the words."

"Not many people can." I squeezed my hand closed and lowered it to my side.

W hat weren't they telling me?

Why would they drag me all the way to Alyssia under the pretense that their kingdom was under siege, only to block my every move to acquire information that might assist me in battle?

The creatures hadn't attacked since we'd arrived, which left me with no way to judge their strength or numbers. We found a possible lair, but I wasn't about to hang around waiting for them to return to confirm it.

"Should I contact Captain Lansfora and request he speak to the president about how we're being treated here?" Mattheia spoke quietly as he slid a book from a library shelf and then gently tucked it back into place in an attempt to appear busy. We weren't really looking for anything in particular, but if the king would not allow us to speak freely anywhere else in the castle, we'd do it while pretending to research his cause.

"No," I replied in a low voice. "I can't tell you everything, but we don't have as much power here as we think we do. And if I don't do as the king asks, there's even a chance I could get my transfer revoked and then be sent back to Celestial Galaxy."

"Excuse me!?" Mattheia's eyes widened and he dropped the book he'd been holding. "What do you mean!?"

"Shh." I pressed a hand to his shoulder. "I can't explain everything here, but it turns out King Vincent is a..." I twisted my lips to the side trying to decide which word to use, "sponsor of C.G., and that means—"

"He can deny your transfer request if it hasn't been 90 days," Mattheia completed my sentence, bending down to retrieve the book.

"Exactly." I nodded and frowned.

"I knew King Vincent had a hand in some of the governing of the academy, but I didn't realize he could do that. That's not right."

"No. It's not, but I don't make the rules, and telling Captain Lansfora might worsen the situation. We need to keep our heads down and play nice, for now."

He growled beneath his breath. "Play nice," he hissed, sliding out another book, looking at the cover image briefly, and then shoving it—less than gracefully—back into its place on the shelf. "They took our weapons away *again*."

"I know." Being without the Azure Phoenix frustrated me beyond words.

"Valhara..." He turned to look me in the eye. "*Admiral*, we are delegates from Silver Diamond, and we should be treated as such. Respected, at the very least, for our ranks and our expertise. But, instead, they segregate us on different sides of the castle, as if we're lab animals in some experiment, and you want me to *play nice* with them?" He stared at me, awaiting a response.

I stood there in silence, thinking of an answer but unable to find one.

Then Mattheia heaved a sigh and his irate expression changed to a neutral one.

"Technically... I'm secondary on this mission," he said. "Because you were the one summoned here, and it was your choice to come. I don't want to step on your toes or tell you what to do." He swallowed hard and looked down. "I'm sorry for my outburst. It was unprofessional."

"What do *you* think we should do?" I asked. "I respect your ideas and your choices, and you know a lot more about these types of things than I do. What should I do, Commander?"

His gaze met mine and he sighed. "Okay. But only since you asked. I feel like we don't have time to waste playing games and solving riddles for their amusement. Prince Jacksiun asked for your help and you came here to help *him*. Maybe you should discuss your next steps with him instead. Maybe he'll have suggestions about how to deal with his father's peculiar way of asking for help."

I nodded. "You're right. Thank you for your advice."

"You're welcome. I want us to get out of this in one piece, but I also am becoming skeptical that there's any threat at all. Perhaps they only wanted you here to show off your powers." His eyes darted to the side and his voice lowered even more. "I was planning on keeping this thought to myself, but what if they really called you here to manipulate you into using your powers for a different purpose? Something we've yet to discover? What if—"

"I won't be pushed around," I said sternly. "I won't let them push me or my team around anymore."

"I knew I liked you for some reason," Mattheia said with a proud grin.

"I'm going to see if I can speak to the prince about getting back our weapons permanently and also see if he has any suggestions."

"Good. Let me know what you find out." He shrugged and rolled his eyes. "That is, if they'll even let you tell me. Who knows anymore?"

"You should take a very close look at that blue and white sword near the entrance." I pointed over his shoulder. "Don't tell anyone, but that is Excalibur. I looked at it yesterday and saw something strange inside the crystal on the hilt. I haven't had time to investigate it further."

Mattheia turned to look back toward the glass and wood display case on the other side of the library and his brow furrowed as he turned back toward me. "You're serious? *Excalibur?* King Arthur's Excalibur?"

I nodded.

It took more energy than it should have to get permission to speak to Prince Jacksiun a second time, but Officer Cassian was determined and worked diligently to arrange such a meeting. I never thought I'd be making appointments to speak to my best friend!

I entered the long, ornately decorated room accented with metal wall hangings and tapestries primarily in silver and royal blue. At the far end, at a desk made of glossy redwood, sat Jacksiun, pen in hand, head down, analyzing a document printed on off-white paper. A brightly lit tablet had been propped beside his right hand, and he appeared to be making comparisons between two texts.

"Admiral Hawksford," a woman in a fine white pantsuit announced. She bowed before the prince and lifted her hand out to the side in a long, sweeping motion.

It made me feel important, but it also made me realize how very unequal Jacksiun and I had become.

The prince's head rose and a look of relief came across his face.

"Dismissed." He gestured toward the woman who had introduced me and she turned on a heel and exited the room.

He pushed the document to the side and turned the tablet so the screen rested against the desk and was no longer a distraction.

"How have you been?" he asked, standing from his chair. His eyes avoided mine as if he knew the answer wouldn't be a comfortable one.

"I'm holding up," I said, approaching his desk. "May I sit?"

"Of course," he replied, gesturing to a chair beside me.

I took my seat. The cushion was plush and comfortable and I sunk into the chair just enough. I ran my fingers across the high-gloss varnish of the arm rest and they slid over the satiny-smooth wooden curves.

"How are you being treated?" he asked, retrieving a matching chair from nearby and setting it down across from mine so we could sit eye to eye, as equals. It made me feel valued—for the first time since I'd arrived—and I appreciated the courtesy.

"I sincerely wish we weren't required to be escorted around the kingdom 24 hours a day. We are, in a way, dignitaries, and we shouldn't need to be constantly observed."

"I am sorry about that, but I had no say in the matter," he said, shrugging and slumping over in his chair—an unprincely thing to do, I thought. "I had asked my father to treat you and your team with respect, and to trust you, but he continues to do as he wishes. Who is your officer, by the way?"

"Officer Alistair Cassian."

"Cassian?" He repeated the name in a soft, nostalgic sort of way. Then he nodded and smiled warmly, as if he had recalled a pleasant memory. "I remember him very well."

"You do? So you know him?"

"Yes. Alistair Cassian—Chamberlain Grennings' nephew—was a childhood friend of mine. He and I were very close until I left for the Mainlands. Before you, there was Cassian." A smirk curled his lips. "I am glad you came along. My life may have taken a very different path had you not walked into it."

"I'm glad we met, too. So much has happened and I'm here now, alive, because of you."

"And your fiancé, of course. Cassian's personality reminds me a lot of Commander Draven, actually. At least, the Cassian I once knew. He is grown now and likely changed."

"He's very polite, but also a little reserved, probably

because being a king's officer demands it of him. I can see how you might think he and Mattheia have similar attributes."

I clasped my hands together in my lap and sighed. I didn't want to bring up the unpleasant news, but... it was the real reason I had come to see Jacksiun. He needed to know what was happening in his kingdom.

"I'm afraid I have some bad news," I began, shifting in my seat.

"About Cassian?"

"No. Sorry. I didn't mean to confuse you."

"Ah. What then?" He leaned closer.

"The temple your father had been excavating..."

"For the new generator? Where the bloodmanes erupted from? What of it? Did you find anything?"

"Were you aware of the temple's original purpose?"

"No. It has been there for a very long time and I do not believe it has been in use for many years. It was abandoned, to my knowledge."

"It wasn't abandoned."

He perked up. "Oh?"

"That temple is the tomb of Rayvenstar kings passed. It was a mausoleum for the old kings."

"The old kings?" Jacksiun narrowed his eyes. "You mean... my father destroyed the entrance to the Tomb of the Old Kings? I did not realize it was so close to the castle. I had been told of the great mausoleum of Rayvenstars passed when I was a child, but I had always assumed its location had been kept secret to deter thieves."

"Yes, and when I questioned Chamberlain Grennings about it, he became very irate. I managed to enter the crumbling temple; Firagia helped me inside. But then I quickly learned that…" I dropped my head down. "Most of the tombs had been destroyed by the beasts."

"No!" Jacksiun clutched his chair's armrests tightly.

"We found samples. What we believe is bloodmane fur and… human blood."

He gasped, then swallowed hard and furrowed his brow sharply. "Those monsters will pay for desecrating the sacred ground of my ancestors. Please do not allow them to go un-punished for this." He looked at me. "I will fight to protect my kingdom and I will do anything I can to put an end to this disaster, even if my father insists upon keeping me penned up here doing trivial things and paperwork."

"If we're going to fight," I started, "we're going to need our weapons back. I need the Azure Phoenix and Mattheia and the others should have their weapons, too."

"I may not have the authority to change the laws my fa-ther has enacted, but I do have the authority, as crown prince, to pardon visitors from some castle sanctions. I will see to it that you and the others get your weapons back as soon as possible. You are not a threat to our kingdom; in fact, you are precisely the opposite. I will also request pri-vate access to the sword in the library so that you and I may better investigate its origins and the possible power it may have locked inside. I know it has been daunting thus far, but I will make certain these things are seen to at once."

"I know you will, and I know your power here is limited. Although Colonel Hammonds seemed open to suggestion, General Cain was more abrasive and demanding than nec-essary. I'm doing my best to learn as much as possible, but it feels like all my attempts are being blocked. Even the king wouldn't listen to me. I'm starting to feel like I'm wasting my time here too."

"Too? What else has occurred?"

"I was speaking with Commander Draven earlier and he's feeling very isolated and uncomfortable with this situation as well."

"I see. Well, for him to feel that way, it must be very troubling, indeed. He is very collected and I respect his feelings."

Jacksiun paused to think.

"I will go now to get your weapons returned to you and your team. Why not try to find some way to get your mind off this matter for the remainder of the day? You have been more than patient thus far, but I ask for you to please extend that patience a little longer."

"I will."

"Thank you." He smiled appreciatively. "We have many great training areas where you can exercise and practice whatever you wish. Cassian was a great fighter when he was young, and to make the league of castle officers, still is, no doubt. He may be able to teach you and Commander Draven new skills. I know that is a silly and unhelpful suggestion at this time, but it is all I can really offer now."

He shifted in his seat and heaved a sigh. "In the meantime, I will speak to my father and see if I can instill any sense into him. He is stubborn, as you have learned, and I apologize for his behavior. I assure you my mother is much more reasonable, but she is not the one making these decisions."

"I understand. I'm sorry I had to come to you with these

problems, but I didn't know what else to do. I'm sure you know your father better than anyone."

"Sometimes I wonder if I know him at all..." He lowered his head and a frown tugged his lips.

"I'm sorry," I whispered, refraining from reaching out to comfort him. "I know you're doing the best you can. If anyone I know can handle this type of atmosphere with grace and poise, it's you."

"That means a lot to me, Lieu—" He cleared his throat and stifled a chuckle of embarrassment. "I mean, Admiral. I apologize, I just—"

"A lot has changed in very little time, my friend," I assured him, smiling.

The crown prince tells me you're sharp with a sword," I said to Officer Cassian as we walked through the hall. We had been told my crew was now gathering in one of the meeting halls in the south wing.

"Did he?" Cassian replied, raising an eyebrow while trying to hide a budding smile. "It has been many years since we have practiced. The prince was quite good with a blade, as well. His father placed a sword in his hand the moment his fingers had the strength to grasp one."

"Can you teach?" I asked.

"Teach what? To whom?" He cocked his head.

"Could you teach someone to fence? I'd like to get Commander Draven more acquainted with a blade. None of my other team members have sword experience."

He pondered, and an intrigued grin drew across his

face. It seemed that my very suggestion had flattered him.

"I could try," he said with a nod of agreement. "When would you like to start?"

"Today, if he's available, and if your superior allows for it."

"I will see what I can do," he replied.

"I appreciate that."

We passed a few other officers as we walked and another question brewed in my mind. "Officer Cassian?"

He glanced over at me. "Yes?"

"I heard you are the chamberlain's nephew. Is that why you became a member of the royal officers?"

"Yes, I am Chamberlain Grenning's nephew, but it was my mother's idea to train to try out for the castle guard. The queen and my mother have been close for many years. Perhaps that is how the prince and I met. I was very young at the time, so I do not remember the exact circumstances, yet I am proud to serve in his military."

His mother and the queen were close? Perhaps she could provide me the information others were withholding. For now, I had to find a way to burn some time as I waited for Jacksiun to look into getting our weapons back, among other things.

"We are just about to the South Assembly Hall." He flicked his hand forward. "It is just down there and to the right."

An ornate banner arcing across the top of the grand entryway in the distance confirmed his statement.

"Would you like me to wait in the hall with the other officers?" Cassian asked, referring to a handful of other royal escorts who had gathered outside the room.

"No. Please come with me so we can speak to the commander about training," I answered.

Inside were several round conference tables, and it was obvious the hall had been created to host large, formal events; my tiny crew of less than a dozen people looked insignificant amidst the backdrop of hundreds of pieces of furniture.

Amanda was the first to notice me enter. She dismissed herself from the group and hurried over to see me.

"Good afternoon, Admiral Hawksford," she said with a salute, and then turned toward Officer Cassian. "Good afternoon, Sir." She tipped her head.

"Good afternoon." He bowed more deeply toward her than she had toward him.

I peered past Amanda at Mattheia, who was looking back at me now.

"Commander!" I raised my voice, though he was already making his way toward us.

"Hello, again," Mattheia greeted Cassian. "I don't believe we've been properly introduced. High Commander Mattheia Draven. Nice to meet you." He offered out his hand.

"Officer Alistair Cassian," the officer replied, cordially shaking the commander's hand.

Cassian cleared his throat. "The admiral tells me you are interested in the art of swordplay."

"Uh." Mattheia appeared caught off-guard by the question, but quickly gathered himself to respond. "Yes. Well, I had a very nice rapier, but it's currently in lock-down by castle security."

"We have swords we can lend you for practice," Cassian

replied cheerily. "Admiral Hawksford suggested we work together to teach you while you are here."

Mattheia's brow furrowed and he glanced at me. "She did?" He gazed at me with one eyebrow cocked.

"I'm sorry," I said, chuckling slightly. "I didn't fully explain myself. Prince Jacksiun is going to see if he can get us back our weapons, and he needs to discuss a few other things with the king, as well. Meanwhile, he asked that we find something to busy ourselves with while he works to handle those matters. We don't have any new information in this case yet, so I think it would be okay to take some time out for training. You can't simply own the great Pegasus Sword and not know how to use it, Commander." I smirked.

He still looked confused, but a few moments later he surrendered and shrugged. "Alright then. It would serve me well to stay in good shape while we're here anyway." He turned to Cassian. "Where is your training area?"

"Just outside the eastern gate. It is very nice this time of year."

"We could use some fresh air," Mattheia said. "And the rest of our crew? Are they welcome to join in?"

"If they wish," Cassian replied. "They are all welcome to join. I will be able to find additional sparring partners if their accompanying officers do not wish to help."

"I'll ask the others and see who would like to come. Thank you, Officer." I dismissed myself from the conversation and went to speak with the remaining members of my crew.

Only Private Quill desired to come along. Lieutenant Claire and the others chose to sit the offer out, and I was okay with that, seeing how none of the other members had special interests in ancient weaponry. Most of the personnel we had brought along were not necessarily going to become permanent members of the Citrine Exploration Division upon their return, so it wasn't important for them to be educated in swordsmanship. Swords were rarely used in combat nowadays, and had been reserved mainly as decorative elements of stature and heritage in places like Rayvenstar Castle. I chose to pursue this dying art because it fascinated me, and because I often feel a connection with artifacts of the past.

Officer Cassian approached us with two swords—a lightweight, blunt broadsword and a fencing foil (a dull, thin, flexible rapier made for practice).

The foil had a grip that resembled a tree branch, but was made to fit into the hand like a gun, hence the name—pistol grip. But the Pegasus Sword had an older style, simplified, tapered grip. It was a style seen less frequently today than in the ancient and very early Old-World eras.

"Do you have a traditional-grip foil?" I asked.

Officer Cassian seemed surprised by my inquiry and smiled. "Yes, but why would you suggest that over the ergonomic pistol grip?"

"Commander Draven owns a traditional-grip rapier, so it would benefit him to begin learning with that style."

"You have a valid point, Admiral," Cassian replied with a nod of agreement. He returned to the nearby rack of weapons and exchanged his previous selections for two traditional-grip foils. "Private Quill?" he asked, glancing over at her. "Would you like to participate?"

"I'd like to watch, for now," she replied.

"Very well." Cassian handed one of the foils to Mattheia. "And you, Admiral?" He turned to me.

"I'll observe, as well. You seem to have this under control. Please teach him as you wish and I will chime in if I feel the need."

"That will work nicely," Cassian replied with a small bow of his head to me. Then he returned his focus to Mattheia. "Here. Hold the foil like this." He wrapped his fingers around the handle as if he were grasping a small remote control. His fingers curled around the grip, and his thumb pointed straight. "Your grasp must be gentle but firm. You see?" He rotated his wrist, twisting the blade.

"Like this?" Mattheia asked, mimicking the placement of his fingers around the grip and pressing his thumb up to the thumb pad beneath the bell guard—the rounded metal piece between the crossbar and grip which protected his fingers from an offending blade.

Cassian leaned over. "Yes," he replied. "How does it feel in your hand? Is it comfortable? It should not strain your hand muscles if you hold it properly."

"It feels good." Mattheia gave a quick nod.

"Good." The officer stepped back. "In all bouts of practice, there are several things that must be done. First, we salute each other. Obviously, you typically would not deal with this in real battle, but in all practice bouts and competitions, we must show our respect and willingness to try our best to beat our opponents and to fight fair. This is done like this." He pressed his heels together in a V-shape, lifted his arm and blade straight out in front of him, bent his arm at a 90-degree angle until the sword was parallel to his body, and then extended the arm and sword again, straight out in front, before lowering the point to the ground. "This is how you salute an opponent. Now you try."

Mattheia flexed his fingers and adjusted his grasp on the grip of his foil, then he looked down at his feet to make sure they were in the same placement as Officer Cassian's had been. Then he lifted his blade straight out in front, pulled his arm back into the 90-degree angle, parallel with his face, and then lowered the point down.

"How was that?" he asked.

"Excellent, Commander." He approached him from the side and lifted Mattheia's arm with his hand. "Only do try to keep your stance rigid and straight here. Put power and purpose in each movement so they are firm and swift." He adjusted the arm into the bend and then lowered it back toward the ground. "Like this."

"Okay. I'll do my best to keep that in mind."

"That's the spirit. A good swordsman learns quickly. Now I shall demonstrate the other important stances and footwork you need to know before we can begin using the blades." He paused and pointed to the equipment room behind them. "Normally we would wear protective head masks and plastrons—chest guards—but since we will only be covering the basics today, I feel they are unnecessary for this session."

"Realistically," Mattheia cut in, "when you're on the battlefield, no one gives you time to grab protective gear anyway."

Cassian cocked an eyebrow; I couldn't tell if he was

annoyed or amused by Mattheia's comment, until he smirked and nodded. "That is very true," he replied. "A warrior cannot hide from the scars of battle, but he *can* prevent those of a rough practice round."

"Good point. Please continue."

Cassian planted his feet in an L-position, heels together and back straight. "Footwork is universal in most styles and vital to your success. First, face your opponent." He turned to Mattheia, saluted, and began slowly transitioning into the next stance. "Put your right foot in front of you, toes facing the opponent. Put your left leg back, toes facing out and knees slightly bent into a squat. Make your feet about shoulder-width apart. Keep your upper body completely straight." He paused and gestured with his free hand. "Imagine a straight line being drawn from the top of your head to the base of your tailbone. Your free hand is tucked behind your back slightly, which assists in keeping as little of your body as possible in the way of your opponent's blade. Your foil should be tipped upward and your arm out in front of you with your elbow bent. This is the basic en garde stance."

Mattheia moved his feet into the same position and then lifted his foil out in front of him.

"Correct," Cassian praised him. "Now to advance, you step with your front foot first and follow quickly with your back." He did this move swiftly, stepping forward several times in a straight line. Then he waited for Mattheia to copy his actions. "To retreat, move your back foot back and follow with the front. You should practice this to get the general movements down and learn to keep your distance. It is very important, in fencing, that you keep your distance."

Mattheia nodded.

"Am I covering everything satisfactorily, thus far, Admiral?" Cassian glanced over at me for affirmation. I gave him a smile and a thumbs-up.

"This is some of the most important footwork you will ever learn in fencing," Officer Cassian continued. "And it can determine whether you make or miss your mark. We should practice the advance and retreat several times before we progress to the next move—the lunge. However, I recommend you stretch your hamstrings first so you do not damage them." He glanced down at Mattheia's black slacks and twisted his lips to the side with concern. "If you would like, we do have appropriate clothing you may borrow that will assist you with your movements as you practice. It is very difficult to lunge and stretch in dress wear."

Mattheia shrugged. "What I have is fine, for now. I won't be able to change my clothes on the fly in the field, so I might as well grow accustomed to what I have. The fabrics used in our uniforms are more versatile than they may appear." He put his right foot out in front and then squatted to stretch his right leg. "They are made of a special weave and proprietary fiber blend that does allow for good movement. I believe I'll be fine."

"Understood." Cassian moved back into position. "Let us practice the advance and retreat several times, until you are comfortable with the movements."

I watched for a while as they stretched and then practiced stepping forward and backward repeatedly. Mattheia tried very hard to get the flow right, and I knew that, in time, he would.

Cassian was a good instructor, from what I could tell, and he was patient enough to gently correct him when he made an error. After several rounds of practicing the movements, Mattheia pointed his blade toward the grass and waited for the next instruction.

"Now the en garde position is also known as the lunge position," Officer Cassian said. "Its purpose is to close as much distance as possible between yourself and your opponent. Your back foot should be perpendicular to the front foot and your leg should be stretched out as much as possible with your front leg and knee at a 90-degree angle. The movements should flow much like this." He moved forward quickly. "Advance." And again. "Advance." He squatted and jabbed the air with his blade. "Lunge. Pull back." He stepped back quickly and agilely. "Retreat. Retreat." Then he moved forward again. "Advance. Lunge. Close as much distance as possible and get low to the ground." He paused, put his heels together again, and looked over at Mattheia. "These are the basic moves. Would you like to try those?"

Mattheia nodded and assumed the en garde stance to begin.

I watched Officer Cassian instruct Mattheia, correcting his foot placements as he switched between stances. Cassian's confidence and expertise with a blade were obvious in his precise, controlled movements, and in the way he taught Mattheia carefully. I quickly realized why he had been chosen as a member of the king's officers.

I sat beside Amanda, who remained fixated on them as they practiced. She mouthed things to herself, as if she were memorizing their movements and analyzing the order of each one. I wanted to train Mattheia myself, eventually, but if he had the opportunity to learn while we were in the land of great swordsmen, then I'd prefer he take the crash course while we were here. At least one of us might benefit from the trip.

"Admiral!" Amanda poked me in the shoulder. "The prince!"

Officer Cassian froze in place and Mattheia halted, too. I veered around to see Prince Jacksiun approaching us.

"Crown Prince Jacksiun," a guard announced as he neared us, bowing with a flourish of his hand.

I took a cue from the others and bowed. It felt strange to do so toward my best friend, but it was necessary. I couldn't be seen as careless and disrespectful toward the crown prince of Alyssia.

"I see you have taken my advice and found a productive way to pass time," Jacksiun said, his attention shifting to Officer Cassian and Mattheia. They had already set their foils off to the side. "Ah! Cassian, my old friend." He walked over and stretched out an arm. They shook hands heartily and then the prince reached an arm up to wrap around Cassian's shoulders to embrace him briskly. "You and I were only children back then." They separated and Jacksiun pressed a hand onto Cassian's shoulder. "How is your mother?"

"She is well, Your Highness. We missed you while you were away on your... *adventures*." Cassian raised an eyebrow. "You will tell me all about them, will you not?"

"Of course! As soon as matters here calm down. My father is keeping me on a very short tether as of late, and I am struggling to find a moment to get away from all the documents he has requested I review. That, and... the other incident."

Cassian lowered his head. "Yes. It is unfortunate, but I have confidence in Admiral Hawksford." He looked over at me and grinned. "You have a powerful ally, Your Highness."

"I know." Jacksiun tipped his head at me and then at Mattheia. "I am fortunate to have several." He looked past Cassian at Mattheia, his eyes scanning down to the foils resting nearby. "How is he treating you, Commander? I do hope my friend is not being too hard on you with his teachings."

"Not at all," Mattheia replied with a confident shake of his head. "Officer Cassian is a fine instructor. The faculty at Silver Diamond could use someone like him. But, I understand his skills have already been put to good use here as a member of the royal officers."

"Yes. He can teach you many things. I learned some of my first fighting techniques from him when we were barely old enough to hold a foil. Pay close attention and you might be able to best Valhara someday in a bout."

I narrowed my eyes skeptically. "Really?"

Jacksiun shrugged. "No. But he could use a little motivation, right?"

We all laughed.

"Speaking of which, that is why I am here." Jacksiun turned.

A guard came out from behind him with a shimmering platinum blade balanced carefully atop gloved hands—the Pegasus Sword.

"Give it to Commander Draven, please," Jacksiun commanded.

The guard took no time in rushing over to where Mattheia stood, lowering his head, and offering the sword out to him.

Mattheia wiped his hands off on the sides of his slacks and then reached out and took the rapier.

"And the other," Jacksiun added.

Another guard approached me with the Azure Phoenix resting on his arms. He lifted it toward me. "Your blade, Admiral."

It was good to see the shining brass color of my prized, jagged-edged sword. It appeared to be in even better condition than I'd left it. The metal had been polished to a brilliant shine and the gemstones sparkled with fire and color. They must have cleaned it.

I wrapped my hand around the grip and lifted the blade, pointing it away from Jacksiun's guard.

"Thank you," I said. The guard backed away and returned to stand just behind the prince. I raised my head toward Jacksiun and smiled gratefully. "Thank you for returning these to us. Were you able to learn anything else?"

"Unfortunately not," he answered glumly. "But I will continue trying to get through to... *someone.*"

From the corner of my eye, I saw a dark shape hurrying toward us. The commotion got everyone's attention and we turned to face the oncoming soldier. He came to a stop and bent down to rest his hands on the knees of his bright blue and silver-trimmed slacks to catch his breath.

"The general... he..." he huffed. "General Cain demands your presence, Admiral," he finally got out through labored breaths. "It is imperative that you hurry."

"What is it?" I asked.

"I am not at liberty to speak of it, but you must come quickly."

Jacksiun crossed his arms. "I will come, too," he said firmly.

"No." The man stood and bowed his head shamefully. "My apologies, Your Highness, but I was instructed to bring only the admiral. The general specifically requested you not be bothered with this."

I looked back at Jacksiun and wrinkled my lips to the side. What on earth could be so important as to require *my* immediate attention, but not Jacksiun's? I shook off my frustrations and heaved a sigh.

"Okay," I replied. "Give me one moment."

The messenger nodded.

"I have to go, for now," I said, looking at Amanda and the others. "But you can stay and practice, if you'd like."

"Are you sure, Admiral?" Cassian asked, a look of concern twisting his face. "I will be happy to escort you back."

"I'll be fine. Thank you." I lifted the Azure Phoenix toward him with both hands. "Could you see to it that my blade is returned to my room, please? I can't carry it around the castle without my scabbard."

"Yes, Admiral." Cassian gently lifted the sword from my hands, handling it with the utmost respect.

"Commander Draven, good luck with your training." I turned to head back to the castle.

Afternoon, Admiral." General Cain greeted me in the main hall outside the throne room.

"What have you learned?" I asked, eagerly awaiting the answer and hoping it was something I could use to finally move forward in this ordeal.

"We have not ascertained much information just yet, but we are working to do so. We have something very important to show you." He turned on his heel and began walking. "Come." He marched off ahead of me, in the direction of the war room where we had spoken the day of my arrival.

We entered the room and he directed me to the very back.

"Admiral." He looked over his broad shoulder at me. "You must swear to keep everything you see beyond this point in strict confidence."

Confidence? I refused to hide pertinent information from the crown prince or Commander Draven.

"Do I have your word?" He turned and glared at me judgmentally, as if he had expected me to say something other than "yes."

I looked him sternly in the eye. "You have my word, General."

I lied, but what other choice did I have? I would not keep vital information from my team. If it came to it, I'd deal with the consequences.

"Step back, please," General Cain said. He approached the conference table in the center of the room and lowered his hand down, reaching for something on the underside of the tabletop. A motor activated and began churning below the floorboards, causing the furniture to move and smoothly sink down into the floor. Then it slid off to the side and out of sight, revealing a spiraling flight of steps plummeting straight down into what appeared to be endless darkness. We stood there for a moment and then a strip of white lights turned on, tracing the shape of each step so we could see our way down.

"Follow me." General Cain took the first step. His boot made a sharp clink as it came down, indicating the steps were metal.

I followed behind him slowly, clinging onto a very thin guardrail spiraling along the stairway as it corkscrewed downward. The air grew cold and damp as we descended, and I had no way of gauging how far down we'd traveled or how much farther we had to go.

Finally, the bottom step came into view, along with a

boxy, metal room trimmed in blue and white lights which had been wedged into the base of the rocky cavern like an upside-down tree house.

Strange noises bounced off the walls—unusual hisses and growls unlike anything I'd ever heard before—followed by high-pitched wheezing. I rubbed my arms as cold air made my hair prickle on end, and the disturbing acoustics made my heart race; I couldn't tell where anything was coming from in the strange cavern.

General Cain opened the door of the mysterious room and gestured for me to enter ahead of him. Inside, several technicians manned a wall of computers displaying moving graphs and strange patterns scrolling across the screens. A large glass window spanned one full side of the building, overlooking more blackness.

"General." One of the technicians saluted. The other three followed his lead.

"This is Admiral Hawksford, the Elemental Guardian," the general announced. "I want you to show her the—"

"Are you sure, General?" The man's voice shook with fear. "It is a recent capture and is in a foul mood. We should give it time to quiet down first."

"You have your orders." The general sneered at the technician.

"Y-yes, Sir." The man typed in a set of codes on the device on his desk and then swiped his hand across a black panel. A spotlight turned on outside the window, casting a white-hot glow onto an industrial-sized chain dangling in the darkness.

The floor rumbled as a series of motors kicked on in the

cavern, hoisting the chain up until a large metal crate with thick bars lifted into view.

A cage?

My stomach began to twist into knots as my imagination surged with visions of what might be contained therein.

I watched intently as the crate rose and then the spotlight shone down toward the front of the box, casting lines of light and shadow through the front bars.

"Wh-what is that?" I asked, staggering toward the window as a lump formed in my throat and a second wave of unearthly noises resonated around us. The otherworldly sounds vibrated through the walls and into my bones.

The technician touched a button on the keypad in front of him and the white spotlight changed into a sickening yellow color, which then morphed into a bright cyan, alternating between hues several times before turning back to white.

I moved another step closer to the window, squinting to focus on the box suspended several feet away.

A shimmer of deep, iridescent green flickered into view, followed by a thick, muscular, lion-like muzzle. Then a large, round head with rounded ears appeared, layered tufts of dark red and brown fur circling its head. Its eyes glimmered with facets of amber and it wrinkled its lips angrily as it pushed its massive body up against the bars of the cage. Its light brown coat reflected ripples of golden light. As it turned, the scales trailing down its back to the end of its bushy tail glittered.

I knew exactly what it was, but the first thought that came to mind was not one of fear, but of awe. What a magnificent and beautiful beast!

"How did you capture a bloodmane?" I asked, my face only an inch from the glass as I watched the agitated creature pace.

It disappeared back into the shadows near the far corner of the cage and two large dots of yellow eyeshine stared brightly back at us.

General Cain came up beside me and rested his hands on his belt. "For days, we have been setting up snares in the underground networks, but all attempts to make a catch had been futile. This particular bloodmane appears to be the smallest of the pack, and that may be why we were able to capture it. Our traps have been unable to hold any of the larger pack members. This wretched thing took one of our soldiers with it, though, as it thrashed about trying to escape. We moved in, quickly, and coerced it into a cage before it could harm anyone else. The suspended enclosure prevents it from escaping."

"It's... so big," I said, looking at the bloodmane's massive paws.

I'd witnessed Emerald transform into one, and I'd closely examined the hologram on the war room desk, but the real-life creature dwarfed both. This was a *small* one?

"Can I take a closer look?" I asked, eyeing a metal walkway just outside the room that surrounded the hanging cage.

"Why?" the general asked with a scoff. "What would provoke you to want to get any closer to that thing!?"

"Just because you captured it doesn't mean you've learned anything yet. Have you done blood work? Discovered what those armor scales are made of?"

"Well, no, but we have not been able to get close enough. Gas sedatives have not worked on the beast, and its skin is too thick to pierce with standard sharps."

"Then let me go look at it. I want to see how it responds to me."

"I will not allow you to put yourself into harm's way." The general shook his head adamantly. "You have no idea what you are doing."

"I fought a dragon," I said, glaring at him. General Cain was bigger and more muscular than me, but I was the Elemental Guardian, and I could hold my own ground. "King Vincent asked for my help. I have my ways of doing things, and you have yours. If you and your soldiers insist upon walling me off from any knowledge I might use to evaluate the situation I've been flung into, then I'll back out of this fight and leave you to deal with it on your own. From what I already know, you haven't been very successful thus far." I crossed my arms. "Isn't that why you brought me down here to see this thing? Or did you just want to gloat?"

The general's lips pressed thin and he narrowed his eyes at me. Then he scrunched his mouth to the side. "Fine," he growled beneath his breath. "You have five minutes to make an assessment, Admiral, and then I want you back in here."

"Thank you." I lowered my arms to my sides.

A technician opened a nearby door and allowed me to exit onto a narrow, metal grate bridge running the circumference of the cage. The beast had tucked itself away into the far corner, so I moved slowly, taking small, quiet steps toward the other side.

Was it hiding from us? Or... from me? That would mean that it was capable of fear and thus...

"I won't hurt you," I whispered, unsure if it could understand me. "Please come into the light again."

A deep, visceral growl made the metal vibrate beneath my boots.

"It's okay. Please, calm down. King Vincent brought me here because of you, but I don't want to fight if I don't have to."

I lifted a hand and ignited a plume of subtle orange light.

The beast shot out of the darkness and slammed into the bars closest to me, filling the cave with a hollow metal echo that loomed in the air for several seconds. I stumbled back from fright. The bloodmane fell from the impact and roared in pain, hissing and baring its fangs in my direction.

A drop of red splashed onto the floor, highlighted by the gleaming white spotlight, and I noticed a fresh wound across the creature's forehead. They did bleed; I'd learned that much.

I extinguished the flames in my hand and took a step back, wobbling as the treads of my boot snagged on a gap in the grating.

The true severity of the situation rattled my nerves. The visual evoked by the leaked documentation left by the Old-World scientist was no match for the colossal thing glaring at me through thick metal bars. Nothing could have prepared me for the otherworldly eyeshine flickering in the shadows of the isolation cage or the iridescent scales that played with the light and my ability to focus.

The bloodmane shoved its muzzle against the bars and strained to squeeze leathery, furry paws and sharp black claws through narrow gaps, in an attempt to reach me. A terrifying, frustrated growl seethed from the monster as it snapped its jaw down repeatedly and bashed its head against the cage. Over and over again. The loud clanging made my ears hurt.

It backed away and rushed the bars again, thrusting its body against the side. It picked itself up from the floor and shook its head, sending a splash of blood toward me, which I narrowly avoided with a swift sidestep.

"Are you alright, Admiral?" the lab assistant spoke to me from an intercom.

"Yes. I'm fine," I replied, my eyes still locked on the unbelievably strong beast.

I ignited a line of fire at my fingertips and lifted out a hand toward the cage, testing the beast this time. The bloodmane hissed and let out a deafening roar in my direction, winding up to charge at the bars again.

I'd assumed it was fearful, at first, but I was terribly wrong.

How could I strike fear in a creature that appeared to have none?

A wave of dread gave me goose bumps and made my pulse thump faster. Would it come at me, even as deadly fire burned in my hand?

"Are you certain you do not need assistance?" the technician asked via intercom.

"No. I've still got a few minutes."

They were so impatient!

"Yes. Apologies, Admiral." The intercom went silent.

"I don't want to harm you," I said, cautiously avoiding eye contact with the bloodmane. "I am friends with Prince

Jacksiun. He asked me to help him—"

It lunged again, bashing its head against the bars and then hobbling in a circle as if it had become dizzy from the blow.

"Please, stop!"

Intense clanging reverberated through the cavern, making the bridge quake beneath my feet. I grasped onto the safety railing as I tried to steady myself and quickly inch my way back toward the viewing room. "I'm coming back!" My voice trembled. The cage began to swing on the chain, drawing closer to me as the creature bound from side to side.

"Trai...tor..." A sound resembling a word came from the beast and I veered around.

"What?" I froze. "What did you say?" I was absolutely sure I'd heard it speak.

It opened its jaws wide and howled. With its vivid yellow eyes locked onto me, it lowered its head and separated its jaws. "You serve... a false... king." The words were clumsy and rough, but they confirmed that the creature *could* speak.

The cage continued to rock back and forth over the pit like a pendulum and I hurried back inside the observation room before it could plow me straight off the bridge. I bent over near the window to catch my breath. From the corner of my eye, I saw the cage swinging dangerously close to the viewing window.

The bloodmane let out a cringe-inducing yowl of pain— a vile, sharp scream with throaty undertones.

My face came up and I gazed though the thick pane of

glass, watching with widened eyes as visible bolts of electrical energy were released into the enclosure, lighting up the cage from the inside out.

"Stop!" I screamed. The creature convulsed violently as arcs of lightning seized its muscles, and the suspended enclosure shook in place. Sparks of white-hot light bounced between the bars and then ceased, leaving the bloodmane on its side inside the cage, motionless and silent.

"Admiral, are you okay?" General Cain asked.

I huffed. "Of course, I'm okay! You didn't need to do that. It may have calmed down." I pushed past him and ran back out onto the bridge.

It spoke. Didn't it? I thought to myself. *The beast spoke...*

"*I heard it, too,*" Firagia said in my mind, confirming my suspicions.

I raised my hand and formed a small ball of fire which I then willed to drift between the bars. The golden light hovered over the creature's body and I watched quietly, hoping for some sign of life.

Not a breath.

Not a flinch.

I couldn't escape the truth as I stared at the stiffened lump of fur and scales.

Blood pooled at its feet and the iridescence of its body armor turned translucent grey. The entire mound of flesh and bone crumbled to a pile of ash, leaving only faded scales peeking out from the dust.

"You... you *killed it*!?"

"At least we now know it *can* be killed. It was a liability, Admiral," the general spoke over the intercom. "Now we can harvest samples without endangering the technicians. We will finally see what this monster is made of."

Blood and bone, I thought to myself, clenching my fists tightly.

And... something more.

An officer, who was not Cassian, escorted me from the observation cavern back to my suite.

I sat down in a corner of the room near a bookshelf and pulled my knees up to my chest, feeling very small and insignificant after seeing such an ancient and majestic creature slaughtered before my eyes. I rested my hands at my sides and buried my fingers into the thick carpet, squeezing my eyes shut and dropping my head back against the wall with a heavy sigh.

The bloodmane couldn't even reach me, but because it had rattled the cage aggressively, they chose to murder it on the spot. It may have calmed down after a few moments, but they didn't give it a chance.

The creature's brutal, unjust demise wasn't the only seed of worry taking root. I'd heard the creature speak, even though those in the observation room seemed not to notice.

Firagia confirmed he'd heard it, too.

The beast had called me a "traitor," claiming I served a "false king." King Vincent had been king for over two decades, and his lineage stemmed from centuries of other Rayvenstar kings.

What had it meant by that? I was no traitor, unless it had somehow been referring to my transfer from Celestial Galaxy to—

No. That wasn't it. It couldn't be something so absurd.

Now that I knew the creatures could speak, perhaps that meant they were open to negotiation, unless further attempts to do so ended the same—with an attack.

Maybe I had frightened it with my fire. Maybe I had been the one to provoke it.

Still...

Firagia?

Warm red light emanated from my amulet and my Spirit appeared before me from a ray of cascading golden light.

"I am sorry you had to see that horrific event," Firagia said, bending down and curving his long, slender neck to look me in the eye. His warm dragon fingers clasped my shoulder. "Your heart aches very much because of the cruelty you have witnessed. Is there anything I can do to help?"

"I'll fight for my life," I said, gazing up at him. "I'll do anything to protect the people I love, but the fact of the matter was that I was not in immediate danger. They shouldn't have acted so brashly. That bloodmane didn't need to die because of me. I frightened it with my powers and they—"

"It was not your fault, Valhara." Firagia sat beside me and curled his tail around his feet. "They had very clear intentions of destroying that creature whether you had come to witness it or not. That enclosure had been made for such an execution, and I believe it was premeditated."

"Why did it get so angry when it saw my fire?"

"I am afraid I do not know, Valhara. Those are all things we will have to find out if we are to make any progress in this so-called 'war' against the bloodmanes. We have not seen or heard from the beasts since we've arrived, aside from the single, rather timely capture by the king's soldiers."

"You're right, and I'm beginning to wonder if this is some kind of façade to hide a greater threat. A distraction, maybe. I don't know." I lifted my hands and crossed my arms, resting them on my knees so I could lean my head upon them.

"I will always do my best to comfort you," Firagia whispered, softly tracing the side of my face with his dainty fingernail. "But I know there is another whose presence tames your anxious soul in ways mine cannot."

Mattheia?

"Go to him. Tell him what you have seen."

"But... the general said—"

"You know you can trust the commander," Firagia interrupted, smirking. "You have already exchanged rings and loyalties."

"You're right." I pushed up from the floor and Firagia quickly stood to offer me his hands in assistance.

"Thank you." I smiled.

He bowed his head. "Would you like me to wait here for you? Or would you prefer I stay inside the necklace?"

"Either is fine." The room was plenty large enough for a

dragon. Or even five.

I hated leaving him cooped up in my amulet, but it was an unfortunate requirement in the castle, since he could no longer instantly manifest wherever I summoned him, now that he was attached to his body.

"Although I am certain you will be safe with him," Firagia started confidently, "I would rather return to the amulet in case you should require me again. I do not believe roaming Rayvenstar Castle would be the best way to introduce myself to its soldiers."

"I understand."

The dragon faded into a cloud of soft red light and then vanished into my sunstone.

As I exited my room, Officer Cassian stopped me just past the threshold. There was a very stern and perplexed look on his face.

"Is everything alright, Admiral?" he asked. "You left the training field for quite some time, and I was told that another officer walked you back."

"I'm fine. I am not permitted to discuss the events that took place while I was away, but—"

"There is no need to explain confidentiality to me, Admiral. I understand. Unfortunately, though, I must ask where you think you are going at this hour?" He glanced up at the ceiling—at the fading sunlight backlighting the stained glass windows from the encroaching dusk.

The days felt short in Alyssia, and the stringent rules about walking the castle at night made them feel even shorter.

"I-I need to speak with Commander Draven, please."

"I apologize, but I cannot allow you to go right now."

I narrowed my eyes at him. "I thought we were guests here, but you insist upon putting us under house arrest each evening. Why?"

Cassian's face twisted with discomfort and uncertainty, making it clear he did not expect confrontation. "Well, the king has ordered us to see to it that you are cared for and protected at all times."

"Are you telling me we're not safe here?"

"I-I do not believe that is what the king meant, Admiral." Cassian stammered a bit.

"I am the Elemental Guardian of fire. The king specifically asked me to come assist him in a war he, alone, cannot seem to win. And yet, he believes I cannot walk through the castle without a chaperone to 'protect me,' or walk the castle halls in the very early hours of dusk?"

"My orders are from the king, Admiral. I apologize, but I must do as I am told."

I searched his face for an inkling of sympathy and I was sure I could see a glimmer of it in the way his gaze shifted from mine as he spoke.

"Officer Cassian?"

"Yes?"

"Does this mean anything to you?" I lifted my left hand and showed him my silver ring—the ring Mattheia had given me.

"You are *married*?" His brow crinkled and one of his eyebrows twitched. "We were not aware. Is your husband here?"

We weren't *legally* married yet, but if a little stretching of the truth was what it took...

"Commander Draven," I said flatly, looking the officer straight in the eye.

"Oh!" Cassian's eyes widened. "I am very sorry they have chosen to separate you, then. I am certain you were placed in different wings only because this information had not been disclosed to us beforehand. There is nothing we can do right this moment, but I can inform the king and—"

"No." I cut him off. "We..." I drummed up my best look of concern and glanced away. "We didn't want to tell anyone because it could put us in danger. We prefer not to disclose that information if and when we participate in a mission together." I raised my hand to briefly touch his forearm. "Please don't tell anyone."

Cassian took a deep breath and pressed his lips thin, furrowing his brow as he appeared to lose himself in thought.

I didn't want to abuse his trust, but I had to try something.

The officer looked over at me with an air of defeat sweeping across his face. "I will retain your secret, Admiral, but please understand that it is not within my right to amend the rules we have in place here." He looked back up at the ceiling windows and sighed. "Perhaps it is still early enough in the evening. I will escort you to the commander's room and then take my leave from there, as my shift ends shortly. Should you require anything or an escort back to your suite, you will have to request it from one of the guards in the south wing."

"Thank you." I smiled gratefully at him.

"How did training with the commander go?" I asked quietly as we walked down the hall.

"It went very well. Commander Draven is a quick learner. You have a very skilled husband, Admiral," he said in a hushed tone. "He is driven and dedicated, and that is something we all strive to be."

"Yes. He is. Thank you for your help, Officer. I appreciate your willingness to work with someone with no previous sword training, and I'm glad your supervisor allowed time for it."

"It is no problem at all. He was a pleasure to work with and any concern of yours is a concern of mine, while you are in my care."

"You are very kind, Officer," I said, grinning. This time, he looked away, as if my words had made him uncomfortable. When he glanced up ahead again, I saw a subtle hint of color flush his face.

At first, I had thought he was intimidated by me, but now I could tell his actions were those incited by admiration. He was earnest and good-natured, and I felt a little guilty about exploiting his kindness.

"The commander's room is here on the left," he said, pausing and stretching out an arm to gesture toward the door. "If I may." He lifted a fist to knock.

He waited several moments until Mattheia came to the door.

"I'm sorry," Mattheia said with a look of embarrassment. "I couldn't get the door to open right away. I apologize for taking so long."

"It was no problem to wait," Cassian said reassuringly.

"Admiral Hawksford is here to see you," he added, introducing me with a flourish of his hand as he backed away from the door.

"Good evening, Admiral," Mattheia said, trying to downplay how happy he was to see me, though it glistened in his eyes. "You can come in," he added.

I turned to Officer Cassian and tipped my head. "Thank you. You may take your leave now."

"Please let the guards at the end of the hall know if you need anything," Cassian said. Unlike me, my crew did not have specific, personal escorts. There were only a few soldiers stationed at the very entrance of the residential hall. "Have a good evening." He bowed his head slightly and turned to leave.

"Goodnight, Officer," I replied.

"Where have you been?" Mattheia asked, just after his door slid closed behind us. He took one of my hands into his and brushed the palm of his other across my cheek. "I was a little worried about you."

His grey t-shirt felt extremely soft as I wrinkled it with my fingers; he'd left his jacket draped over a nearby chair.

I gazed into his sky blue eyes and he gazed back longingly. A million thoughts bounced through my mind, like bullets ricocheting from wall to wall, but when his warm touch graced my skin, my worries came to a halt, like shots frozen in time.

My pulse quickened.

I'm scared.

I saw something horrible and...

I don't know how to explain this, but...

My fingers twisted the fabric of his shirt and then I pulled him into a kiss.

Maybe a kiss couldn't make things right or settle my racing mind.

Or, *maybe*, it could.

I just wanted a moment of privacy and quiet—a moment to shut out the day's events and truly feel at ease.

He embraced me tightly, as if he could taste the fear and anxiety on my lips. And as the kiss deepened, his hands came up to clasp my face, and my back pressed against the wall beside the doorframe. My anxieties evaporated.

A single, fleeting moment of passion made me feel better.

For a moment...

His fingers traced the side of my neck and his lips separated from mine. Instead of saying a word, he took both my hands into his and walked me toward a long blue velvet chaise nearby. He patted the chair and I sat first, then he sat beside me and wrapped an arm around my waist.

"Tell me what's wrong," he said, gazing thoughtfully into my eyes. He lifted his other hand and swept it over my ear, letting it slowly drift down my jaw line and neck.

"I told him we were married," I said quietly.

"Told who?"

"Officer Cassian."

"The one who trained me this afternoon?"

"Yes."

He smirked. "Well, I suppose we will be, soon enough. Any particular reason why you told him that?"

"It was getting dark by the time I'd returned, so I couldn't leave my room due to castle rules. I explained our situation to Officer Cassian and he was compelled to let me come see you."

Mattheia cocked an eyebrow. "You sure do have a way of nicely convincing men to break rules for you."

"Would you like me to go?"

"No." He squeezed me in closer. "Of course not."

I scooted over and nuzzled his shoulder with my face. Then I rested my head against him as he lifted both arms to embrace me.

His heat and warm scent soothed my body, but nothing could calm my mind.

Nothing could erase the violent memory of the bloodmane smashing into the cage bars over and over again. Vivid imagery of bright red blood oozing down its face breached my thoughts.

"Valhara?" Mattheia's grasp on me tightened. "You're shaking."

My eyes welled with tears and shallow breaths made my lungs quiver.

"Valhara?" Mattheia shifted and grasped onto my shoulders. "What is it? What happened?"

The bright white bolts of electricity coiling between the metal bars and shooting through the bloodmane's system blinded my thoughts and evoked horrendous memories of the creature crumbling to its death inside the enclosure.

I pushed tears from my cheeks with both hands and glanced up at Mattheia.

He studied my face intently. "What did you see today? What did they call you away for?" he asked.

I sniffled and swiped my fingers across my face again. "I'm sorry I'm falling apart."

"You can tell me anything," he whispered, pressing his index finger below my chin and looking me in the eye.

"They captured a bloodmane."

"Th-they did?" He drew back slightly. "How?"

"I don't know, exactly, but after they called me over to take a look at it..." I sucked in a labored breath and tried to compose myself; my throat tightened. "They killed it right there in front of me."

A look of disgust twisted on his face.

I cleared my congested throat. "They pumped millions of volts of electricity through its body. It was in a cage. A strong cage suspended above a deep cavern pit. It couldn't actually get to me, but it tried, and then the cage started to swing and..." I lost my breath and buried my face against his chest.

"It's okay, Valhara," he whispered, cupping the back of my head with one hand.

"It was larger than I could have imagined," I muttered against his shirt. "And so angry. Roaring. Hissing. Thrashing at the bars until it drew its own blood." I pushed away from his chest and looked him in the eye. "And then... then it spoke to me."

Mattheia gazed in disbelief.

"It spoke words I could hardly hear, but Firagia heard them, too. It called me a traitor and then it said, 'False king.' Why would it say that?"

He squinted. "I-I don't know." He looked to the side, his hands still holding me firmly.

"Who's the false king?" he asked. "What does that even mean? Why would some creature show up out of nowhere and make such an accusation? Did you tell the king?"

"I'm afraid to," I replied with a shake of my head. "He's been pushing me around since I arrived, and he won't listen to anything I have to say. I need to find a way to help Jacksiun, but I don't know how. I'm not a sorceress who can snap her fingers and make all the bloodmanes go away. They're here for a reason, Mattheia, and I don't know what that reason is. We found human blood in the old ruins, and the king claims they have been killing innocent people since they appeared. But they haven't tried to attack since we arrived. What if King Vincent is lying to us? What if there's more to this than he's telling me? Mattheia, I—"

"We'll find out soon enough," he interrupted, tipping my face up toward his. "We'll learn the truth. Together. I'm sorry you had to witness such a terrible thing, and if I could take away the bad memories, I would. But I can't." He leaned over and kissed my forehead. "I love you, and I'm here for you."

"Thank you." I smiled weakly, but with sincerity. "I'm frightened, Mattheia. Frightened of what I may have gotten myself into."

"What *we* may have gotten ourselves into," he corrected. "You're not in this alone, Valhara." He lay back on the soft, velvety cushion of the chaise and motioned for me to join him. "We'll deal with this tomorrow," he said, as I pulled my feet up onto the chaise so I could lie against him, and he embraced me from behind, pulling my body in close to his. "Tomorrow is a new day," he added.

He was so warm and his voice so reassuring. Even in a time like this.

I had to let go, if only for a few minutes... or hours. I had to rest my thoughts so I could think clearly in the morning.

He kissed the side of my neck and I sighed with contentment, entwining my arms around his.

Yes. Tomorrow would be a new day.

Shuffling noises disturbed my slumber and my eyes eased open just as Mattheia walked out of the shower room, shirtless. A darkened ridge of scar tissue extended diagonally across his chest, and the sight of it made me cringe. Not because of the way it looked—scars didn't bother me—but because of the memories that surfaced, prompting me to vividly recall how he'd gotten the wound.

"Doze off?" he asked, heading over to the dresser on the other side of the room to pull open a drawer and rummage around. He'd left me alone not too long ago, so he could clean up, as he hadn't the chance after his fencing bout with Cassian earlier in the day. I must have fallen asleep on the chaise; it was rather comfortable.

"Yes," I replied. "I was resting my eyes and..." He turned his back to me and I trailed off.

I couldn't stop thinking about the scar.

I tried to hold my tongue, but...

"I'm sorry," came out of my mouth before I could stop it.

"What?" He turned toward me, a balled-up, clean shirt in one hand.

"I'm sorry I let that happen to you." I nodded toward him, my gaze grazing over the line across his chest.

He narrowed his eyes and took a step closer. "Let *what* happen?"

Did he really not know what I meant?

"Um..." I lifted my fingertips toward my collar bone and looked away.

"Oh. This?" He glanced down briefly and then back at me. "This happened months ago." He shrugged. "It's over and forgotten. I don't even think about it."

I swung my legs off the chaise and set my feet onto the hardwood. "Really?" I leaned over and rested my elbows on my knees.

"Yes. We're enlisted. Things happen." He approached me. "This isn't the first, and it won't be the last scar I get before I die."

I didn't know how to respond, so I just sat there silently until my line of sight dropped to the floor.

"But if it makes you uncomfortable..." He unclenched his hand and looked down at the wrinkled shirt. "I'll be sure to—"

"No." I jolted up from the seat and grasped on to the shirt, tugging it from his hand. "It *doesn't* make me uncomfortable. Nothing about you does." I moved closer to him, pressing a flattened hand against his chest. The freshly bathed skin was smooth and hot to touch, and felt nice beneath my fingertips. "I only regret the circumstances of it. I shouldn't have put you in danger like that."

His chest rose and fell with a slow, patient sigh. "Valhara, it's done with," he replied, cupping his hand over mine to press my fingers against his skin. "We survived. We're together." Then he brought my hand to his lips and kissed my knuckles. "It doesn't bother me, so it shouldn't bother you, either."

I nodded and smiled sheepishly. "You're right. I'm sorry."

"Stop. There's nothing to feel sorry about." He lifted my chin with his fingers and kissed me.

He reached for my hand and I absent-mindedly dropped his shirt so I could intertwine my fingers with his.

How he could make all the wrong in the world feel right with just a kiss baffled me.

I would have been happy to stay there forever in that moment—his warm, taut chest rising and falling under my touch.

But we didn't have forever...

We only had tonight.

"I love you," he whispered, his breath caressing my lips.

"I know." I smiled and inhaled deeply, taking in the fresh, crisp scent of eucalyptus that lingered on him from his shower. Strong and refreshing, it suited him.

"Ah." His gaze swept down to the floor where he spotted the t-shirt, and then he bent to pick it up. He slipped it on over his head and pushed his arms through, unrolling the fabric down his torso. "There. Good as new." He grinned, swiping flattened hands down his chest.

I took one of his hands into mine and looked him in the eye. "Don't ever feel that you need to hide anything from me, Mattheia."

"Never." He squeezed my fingers gently. "The same goes for you. My wife shouldn't feel the need to hide anything from me." A coy smile stretched across his face. He hooked an arm around me to press his fingers against the small of my back, draw me in, and then kiss me again.

Sunlight poured through the shutters onto the bed, coaxing me awake with refreshing brightness and warmth. I rolled from my side onto my back; Mattheia's arm was draped over my waist and he was sound asleep. I sat up slowly, so as to not disturb him, and let my gaze rest upon his peaceful expression, watching as dawn shimmered across his pale golden hair.

My fingers swept his brow, and my gaze lingered on the soft glow of morning accentuating his beautiful face. He'd be my husband soon enough, and the thought of it filled my heart with anticipation and joy. I glanced at the ring he'd given me, the polished silver details catching the sun's rays. Mattheia made me happy, and I was lucky to have him in my life.

But a new day had begun, and I couldn't stay there watching him forever. I stretched an arm out to the end table and clicked off his alarm clock.

For now, I would let him sleep in; it wasn't something he could do at Silver Diamond, and I'd kept him up late last night with my concerns, so it was only fair.

I set my feet onto the floor, pushed up from the bed, and walked over to the nearby chair where I'd left the rest of my uniform. My undershirt was wrinkled, but no one would notice.

I shook out my white, button-up over-shirt first and tossed it on over my shoulders, buttoning it down the center and tucking it in. Then I slipped on my dark green jacket over that and did-up the buttons.

I liked how my new uniform was a similar cut and style compared to my Celestial Galaxy one, but that it had brassy, gold trim on all the accents and sleeves, and a diamond-shaped insignia on the outer biceps. The uniform helped me fit in at Silver Diamond since it represented my new department, but it also differentiated me from other personnel.

I tugged my cuffs straight and turned to look into the mirror. A twinkle of silver caught my eye—the Pegasus Sword lay across a wooden chest at the foot of the bed, glittering in the sunlight. Thankfully, Jacksiun had been able to get our weapons back for us. I felt out of place without the Azure Phoenix in my custody.

I washed my face, adjusted my cherry-blossom hairclip, and then took a glimpse over my shoulder at Mattheia, who was still asleep. Hopefully he wouldn't be upset that I'd turned off his alarm. It was my call, as this was technically *my* assignment, after all.

I left his room and made my way to the end of the hall.

Near the guard post, Officer Cassian stood waiting.

How long had he been waiting for me?

"Good morning, Officer Cassian," I said with a tip of my head, as I approached.

"Good morning, Admiral. Is Commander Draven available?"

"Not yet," I replied. "What is it?"

"I have news that may interest you." Cassian smiled. "Colonel Hammonds declared that you no longer require an escort within the castle, so I decided to come ask if Commander Draven would like to train again with me today, in lieu of my former duties."

"I'm sure he'd enjoy that," I replied confidently. "Thank you, Officer, for volunteering your time to teach him."

"You are welcome, Admiral. I enjoy helping others. He shows a lot of promise, and I would hate to see a great commander miss an opportunity to expand his skill set." He cocked his head and rested a hand on the pommel of his saber. "Where did you learn, if I may ask?"

"Most of what I know is self-taught, but after I began training extensively with Prince Jacksiun in my free time, our captain decided to establish an official course with an emphasis on sword fighting techniques."

"Prince Jacksiun was good with a blade even when we were children. I imagine, with the excess training he has garnered over the years, he is unmatched by now."

"If you don't count *me* as an adversary." I smirked.

His eyes widened and his smile went straight. "Y-you have bested Prince Jacksiun?"

"More than once, but who's counting?"

Cassian shook his head in disbelief.

"We've learned from each other," I clarified, "but he plays by the book quite predictably, and I've memorized his favored moves and patterns."

"Astounding."

"Keep it between us, though," I said in a quiet voice. "You're his friend, too, so I think you understand."

"Of course, Admiral. I hold the crown prince in high regard." A small smile curled the corner of his lip, but then he forced it away. "I believe many would agree that being bested by the Elemental Guardian is not necessarily a thing to be ashamed of. It illustrates your grand expertise, making you the appropriate choice for such an illustrious fate."

I nodded and tried to hide my own grin. I needed to show respect for the king and prince of Alyssia. Assuming King Vincent was the *true* king.

The bloodmane's words resonated in my mind.

"What is it, Admiral?" Cassian asked. "Are you well?"

I regained my focus and our gazes met. "Yes. I lost myself in thought. Tell me, how long has your mother been friends with the queen?"

"My mother?" He appeared caught off-guard and hesitant to answer.

"Yes. You said they were friends, which is how you and Prince Jacksiun became acquainted as children."

"My mother and the queen have known each other since before my father came into the king's service. It was the queen who recommended him for a role in the Royal Allegiance after she married King Vincent. Had it not been for her, I would not be here speaking with you right now, as a member of the royal officers."

"The Royal Allegiance? What is that?"

"The king's finest and most trusted warriors—his knights."

"You're the son of a knight?"

"Yes. Though…" He looked away and sighed. "My father was injured several years ago and had to be released from his post here. He still acts as a dignitary when younger recruits need guidance, but he rarely leaves home anymore and prefers to work on the small farm he earned for his service. We keep horses, even though the animals are obsolete nowadays. He loves the beasts very much. The queen once extended an invitation for my family to live within the castle when my father had been discharged, but my parents declined. They did not want to leave the comforts of their farm behind."

With the advent of machines and vehicles to get people around quickly and efficiently, horsemanship had become a dying art. I had thought no one kept horses anymore, but I had thought wrong.

"But the queen," Cassian continued, "is very fond of horses, too. She has visited several times just to sit and watch them graze. I believe she would have one of her own, had the palace stables not been put out of commission many years ago."

"I had hoped to speak with the queen, but I've not been given an opportunity," I said.

"She is kindhearted above all others and her good nature is quite contagious. Between the two of us, I believe she has rescued the king from more than a few unnecessary political scuffles."

"Behind every great man is an even greater woman," I added with a laugh.

Cassian took a deep breath and cleared his throat. "What are your plans today, Admiral?"

"I was going to ask you if I could possibly speak with your mother."

"My mother? Whatever for?"

"If she is friends with the queen, then perhaps she may have answers to questions which no one here will address."

He narrowed his eyes a little. "You would not be going against anything the king has said, would you? Surely, there are officials here who could answer any query you may have."

"Not this one," I stated firmly. "The king, his general, and the chamberlain have refused to give me the information I require. I have no choice but to ask his people for help. I promise not to go against anything your king has said, Officer, and I would never do anything to put you or your position here in jeopardy. I need you to trust me, as the Elemental Guardian, and as someone who has your country's best interests in mind."

He glared at me suspiciously, at first, taking several moments to study my face, as if he were searching for any indication that I was lying.

He wouldn't find one.

"Very well," he said with a quiet puff of defeat. "I will contact her and see if she is available to speak with you to-day. Today is her Teaday, and she typically keeps to herself in our library, as it is the same day my father checks the fence lines and grooms the horses."

"Teaday?"

"Yes. Do you not have such a day on the Mainlands?"

"No." I shook my head.

Cassian cracked a smile. "Then it will be a pleasant experience. Although not all Alyssians celebrate it on the same day of the week, Teaday is the one day we allow ourselves to sit and enjoy simple pleasures, should it be reading, art, or study of any kind."

"What about you and father?"

"My father is firmly set in his old ways, and I am afraid he has instilled them in me, as well. Duty before pleasure. Always."

"You work very hard, Officer, and I'm sure it will pay off in the end."

"It has paid off already," he corrected me. "I am happy where I am, and my family is content and well off."

"I see," I replied. "That's wonderful."

"Please give me a moment to call home and see if my mother is available for company."

"I don't want to be trouble."

"I am sure she will not mind at all. Excuse me."

I waited patiently in the hall, gazing up at the spectacular stained glass windows lining the top of the cathedral ceiling, spanning from one end of the hall to the other. The castle was aglow with elegant, colored light beaming in from overhead, but also with pure sunlight filtering in through smaller, clear windows far below those, which were within reach from the floor and could be accessed without ladders. The shutters had been left ajar intermittently, and brief gusts of breeze flittered through, lifting tassels and making tapestries perform ghostly dances along both sides of the walls.

I wondered if Mattheia had woken up yet, and if so, had he wondered where I'd gone off to? I could check on him while Cassian spoke with his mother, but...

As I lifted my face to look over at the officer, I noticed he was already walking back toward me.

"My mother said she would be honored to have you over today. Would you like for me to arrange transportation?"

"Is it far?"

"Well, *far* is not the appropriate term for it, but they do live in the country. It is a short ride from here by Royal Trolley, but it would take quite awhile on foot since our roads are not made to accommodate pedestrians."

"I understand. Then please, go ahead and arrange for a trolley. Also, when you see him, would you let Commander Draven know where I've gone?"

"Certainly, Admiral," he replied with a small bow. "If he desires to continue training, I will work with him this afternoon."

"I'm sure he will. Also, please consider allowing him to practice with his own sword, since it has a very different weight and feel to it."

"Yes, Admiral. I will make sure he gets accustomed to the rapier he brought, as soon as he is ready."

I gazed out the window behind my seat on the trolley and watched as the castle disappeared, giving way to miles of flat grasslands stretching to the horizon. Sterile city air mingled with hints of pollen and greenery. Scents of flowers and wilderness filled the car, thrusting me into a new, wild environment.

The car zipped past a few country homes along the way, most of them set so far from the main roadway that I couldn't see them very well, but I did see some animals dashing through the fields. Jade brush-deer with green stripes scattered across their golden coats, making it nearly impossible to focus on them as they blended into tall, swaying grass. I was sure I saw a flairfox, too—with the brightly colored blue and purple tufts perked up along its backside—weaving through the meadow, but it disappeared too quickly for me to know for certain.

The trolley ride to Officer Cassian's family's home was smooth and remarkably brief. Moments after I'd gotten inside the polished, royal blue, bullet-shaped car and sat on the comfortably plush, velvet bench inside, it was announced that I was nearly to my destination.

It came to a halt and the door slid open. I stepped down, my feet sinking slightly into soft dirt, and looked up ahead. A wooden sign with "Cassian" carved in elegant, deep-set lettering, hung out front of a dirt road leading up to a large, scarlet and brown cottage. I was in the right place, so I confirmed with the trolley, and then it took off zooming back toward the castle.

The Mainlands had an intricate network of magnetic hyper trains which we used to get around, but the Alyssian Trolley network seemed more convenient; it was unmanned and controlled by a supercomputer which could navigate the narrow threads of metallic inserts inlaid underground throughout the city. I was quite surprised it could travel to such a rural area, and it did so without so much as a single bump.

I set out down the dirt road leading toward the cottage and looked at the vast pastures flanking both sides of the pathway with cascading yellow and white wildflowers for as far as I could see. Officer Cassian had said they'd been granted a "small farm," but there was too much farmland here to be considered "small." Perhaps, in Alyssia, the land is plentiful and the king is very generous with it.

I walked up the steps toward the front door, which was accented with stained glass and silver metalwork reminiscent of the castle interior. Before I could lift a hand to knock, the door opened and a middle-aged woman in a lilac satin dress greeted me.

"Good afternoon!" she said, smiling warmly. "You must be the admiral my dear Alistair told me about. Come. Come in, please." She flourished her hand and stepped away from the door, tugging the skirt of her long dress to the side to get it out of the way. A ruffled white petticoat peeked out from beneath the shimmering purple fabric. She closed the door and then came up beside me, resting a hand on my back as she guided me past the foyer into what appeared to be a drawing room. A grand crystal chandelier hung over-head, twinkling with prismatic light as the sun's rays illuminated the facets.

"Come sit." She motioned toward a large, elegantly carved wooden chair with curled armrests, and seat and back cushions featuring detailed, vintage tapestry-like im-agery of birds and trees. I lowered myself onto the chair and sunk into the pleasantly soft seat.

"You are just in time for low tea. Would you care to join me?" she asked, her long, delicate fingers curling together eagerly. I nodded and replied "yes," because anything less might be considered rude, even though I had no idea what she'd meant.

"Brilliant. Please give me a few moments to prepare everything and I will be right back." She shuffled off into the kitchen and I suddenly felt like I'd burdened her unnec-essarily.

I hadn't even had the chance to properly introduce my-self, but apparently, in Alyssia, seating a guest and getting them tea was more important than formal introductions.

"*It is,*" Firagia commented. "*In the days of the Old-World, it was customary to make a guest feel at home upon entering a residence. If Lady Cassian is following the old ways, she will likely bring small cakes and other delights for you to savor while you are here. This is what she meant when she said low tea. It has been a custom for centuries here.*"

"I see..."

I glanced down at my uniform; there were small, but visible, wrinkles in my slacks that made me feel unkempt and underdressed.

"*Do not fret, Valhara,*" Firagia continued. "*It is nothing to worry about. It is only a friendly gesture. You need not be concerned with your appearance.*"

My eyes skimmed the rest of the room, taking in the muted grey and blue color scheme flowing across the walls and furniture. The small round table within arm's reach of my chair and the chair beside me had a pale blue doily draped on top with woven lace on the edges that came very close to touching the hardwood flooring. A short ottoman with upholstery matching the chairs stood at the foot of each seat. I didn't feel comfortable putting my dirty boots up on the beautiful piece of furniture, and I also couldn't tell if it was practical or simply for looks.

The room had a very classy and vintage feel to it, like I'd stepped into another century. In a way, Alyssia was another world, and it was becoming quite clear to me where Jacksiun had acquired many of his peculiarities. It was a very formal country steeped in tradition. Citizens of the Mainlands retained few customs from our ancestors, and although we had our manners, I couldn't think of a single tradition as simple as Alyssian low tea.

Lady Cassian came back into the room, her fingers gripping the handles of a long wooden tray with a silver teapot, two porcelain cups with saucers, and a two-tiered cake stand covered in tiny sandwiches and pastries.

She set the tray onto the table in front of me and lifted the shiny silver teapot by the handle, bracing the other side by pressing a small towel against it with her hand so she wouldn't get scalded.

"Normally we serve black tea in the afternoon, but I thought a fine white tea would suit the occasion. It is made from young leaf buds and is more palatable for those not accustomed to the astringency of black tea." She tipped the pot over one of the pretty blue and white teacups and pale amber liquid poured out. "Have you had tea before?" she asked, looking me in the eye and not even watching as she poured.

"Only once—yesterday morning during breakfast at the castle."

"Oh?" she said with a smile, tipping the pot back and then moving to pour herself a cup. "Did they tell you our tea is grown right here in the mountains behind Rayvenstar Castle? Some is imported from the Kodama islands, but since the middle era of the Rayvenstar reign—about..." She paused and wrinkled her lip as she thought. "About four-hundred-and-fifty years ago, if I remember correctly—Alyssia began cultivating its own species of the tea bush. It is actually a tree. Did you know that?"

I shook my head as she passed one of the cups and saucers to me.

"Oh, yes, it is a tree," she continued. "The only reason they call them bushes is because they are kept short so the leaves are easier to harvest. It is one of the few plants we still grow and pick by hand. With everything being so automated nowadays, and so many farms run by machines, I am delighted the one indulgence we can all still count on being pure is our tea."

She picked up the other cup and saucer and sat in the seat across from me.

I looked down at my cup and watched as steam rose from it. It appeared to be too hot to drink, but she already had her cup raised to her lips and was taking a sip.

I rested the saucer in my lap and smiled. "Thank you, Lady Cassian," I said with a small bow of my head. I didn't really know how to speak to, or address, the wife of a knight.

"Please call me Victoria, my dear girl. Or Lady Victoria, if you must adhere to formalities. Either will do." She sipped her tea again and I garnered the courage to try mine.

It wasn't quite as hot as I had thought it would be. The taste was subtle and reminded me of the aroma of freshly cut grass, but lighter and almost fruity.

"What a stunning necklace you have!" Lady Victoria said, leaning forward in her seat and setting her cup down onto the table. She interlaced her fingers through a strand of pearls draping across her collar bone. "Where did you get it?"

"It's a family heirloom, but I don't know where it came from originally. My mother left it to my elder sister who gave it to me as a gift."

"It is absolutely divine! Your mother must have cherished

it. Wait... did you say your mother left it to your sister?"

I nodded, taking another sip of tea. I reached for a tiny white-frosted cake with a rose piped on top and bit into it. It was delightfully sweet and smelled of vanilla. A second bite made it disappear.

"Oh, my poor dear girl. I am so sorry for your loss. No young lady should ever have to... oh, wait." She leaned closer and glanced down at my hand. "Are you married already?"

I lifted my left hand briefly from the side of my teacup and turned it over to hide the ring in my lap. "Engaged, actually," I replied.

"I see. Well, at least you have found someone, though I am sorry your mother will not be able to attend your wedding. It would simply break my heart if I could not attend dear Alistair's wedding."

"Is he engaged, as well?"

"No. No. Unfortunately not, but someday. Perhaps." She glanced toward the window and shook her head. "I hope..." She sighed heavily, as if she were very disappointed at the fact.

"He's still young," I said optimistically. "Younger than my fiancé, even."

"You cannot blame a mother for wanting her son to be happy and loved, now, can you?"

"No. I suppose not. But finding that happiness can take time."

She heaved another sigh and looked back over at me.

"That necklace of yours... May I take a closer look at it, please?" She reached an open hand toward me.

"Of course." I set down my tea. Then I unclasped the

chain from around my neck and laid the heavy piece onto her palm, careful not to prick her fingers with any of the sharp metal edges of the setting.

"Is it a sunstone?" she asked, leaning down to peer into the gem.

"Yes."

"They are extraordinary and rare. I have not seen one since I was a child. There is something strange about this piece, though." She squinted and lifted it toward the window so it caught the sunlight. "Hmm." Her head cocked to the side and then her eyes grew wide and she jerked back, sucking in a sharp gasp as she dropped my necklace. "Enchanted!" she yelped.

It clinked against the floor and tumbled, gemstone-down, onto its face.

I scrambled to grab up my amulet and carefully checked it for damage, turning it over within my hands and looking through the sunstone for any fractures or chips.

"*It is undamaged*," Firagia said.

"Good," I replied out loud. My heart started racing at the thought of my heirloom having been broken.

"I am terribly sorry," Lady Victoria said, clutching her hands together near her mouth. "Enchanted things run rampant in Alyssia. My mother taught me how to spot the signs and to be very wary of them. That piece of jewelry contains great magic. Cursed or blessed? I do not know."

"Neither," I said, looking up at her fiercely. It had ruffled me a bit that she would drop such a precious item as if it had been poisoned. I suppose she hadn't known any better, and if what she said was true, then she might have a justified fear of such things.

I softened my expression toward her and polished the stone on my pant leg before putting the necklace back on around my neck. "It's not cursed, but it *is* enchanted, in a way."

"Oh?"

"What are your opinions on dragons?"

"Dragons?" Lady Victoria tilted her head as her brow crinkled. "I have no opinion of them at all because I do not know enough about them to have formed one. They have been dead for centuries, killed off by the Pendragon reign and the violent scourge of hunters born of that era."

"What if I told you a dragon exists today?"

Lady Victoria studied me a moment, as if she were trying to decide if I were joking or not. "Then I would inquire as to how you came about this knowledge," she replied with a smirk.

"He is a very special friend—a friend who saved my life and the life of my future husband."

Her brow twitched. "Really? Where on earth did you meet this dragon?" Her hands tangled together in her lap as she leaned forward with curiosity twinkling in her eyes.

Although I had been hiding Firagia from the king, my gut convinced me I was in good company with Lady Victoria; I felt like I could trust her.

"I am an Elemental Guardian," I replied. She nodded as if she'd already been made aware of this. "Part of my gift is to have a Spirit Guardian to guide and assist me throughout my journeys. My Spirit also happens to reside inside this amulet." I brought a hand up and cupped it around the necklace. "He doesn't have to stay there, but his soul is tied to the piece, so he inhabits the stone whenever he wishes to stay out of sight, but still close by. His life force stirs within this stone."

Her mouth gaped open.

"He is no danger to you," I added, in case such a fear was blooming in her mind. "He means everything to me. I don't know what kind of experience you have with magic here in Alyssia, but please don't be afraid of mine."

She shook her head. "I have no aversion toward protective amulets. In fact, my husband has one of his own, given to him by King Vincent, himself." She pushed up off the chair. "Let me get it for you." She hiked up her dress and scuttled off into the next room.

I heard rustling and clinking and then the house fell silent again. She returned with a folded piece of blue velvet between her hands.

"This was a gift to my husband on the day he was knighted." She sat in her chair and carefully unfolded the fabric from around the item. As she peeled back the last fold, a shimmer of iridescent, beetle green came to light.

I gasped when I recognized the color.

I'd seen it only yesterday, but it had been emblazoned on my memory.

"What is it?" Lady Victoria asked, bringing the piece close to her chest.

"What is that?" I asked.

"It is a charm of protection worn by the knights of the Royal Allegiance. It is said to have been blessed with the ability to give the wearer strength, wisdom, and protection from harmful magic."

"May I see it?" I stretched out an open hand and braced myself to stop it from shaking.

"Yes." She passed it to me slowly with both hands cupped beneath it. "As you had just said to me, you need not fear its enchantment."

The piece was heavy, forged of precious metals, and the bottom center accented with what had to be a bloodmane scale cabochon. The color-shifting green piece was set below two exquisitely detailed silver curved wings, and in the center were the initials RA in gold. Three delicate chains dangled from the bottom, each ending in a small eight-point star.

"This is magical, too?" I looked at it carefully but could not see anything particularly outstanding, aside from the scale fragment.

"Yes. These medallions have been passed down through the king's allegiance for centuries. All knights, active or retired, are granted permission to retain one for the duration of their lifetime, after which the piece must be forfeited to the crown to be passed on to a new member of the Royal Allegiance."

"How are you able to tell if an item is enchanted?" I asked.

"Bring it here," she said, motioning for me to come over to her chair. I stood and walked the medallion over to her. "Look closely," she said, pointing at the scale fragment. "If you gaze into the stone, you will see a fleeting sparkle. It will appear as dust to the untrained eye, but if you know what you seek, you will recognize the difference immediately.

Look carefully at the iridescence as the light dances across the surface. Then, when it rounds the very edge and fades into shadow, you will see a glimmer of white."

I knelt by her chair and squinted, staring at the piece as she rotated it so sunlight bounced across the color-changing scale fragment. She turned it the opposite direction and a minute glitter of white-hot fire caught my eye, and then faded just as quickly.

"That was it!" Firagia said excitedly. *"That was vagrant energy."*

"I saw it!" I said to Lady Victoria. "It was brief, but I saw it; brilliant white refracting off the surface after the light passed over it."

"Precisely! Though… it took me more than a decade to learn how to spot it. You must have a keen eye for magic!"

"You could say that," I replied with a little chuckle. I'd been searching for enchanted weapons most of my life. Perhaps the ability had been engrained in me for some time. Now it made sense why I'd seen such a light in the crystal embedded in Excalibur. I was more attuned to magic than I'd even realized.

I came to my feet and returned to my chair.

"Your son told me you are very good friends with the queen. Are you aware of what's happening in the kingdom?"

Lady Victoria twisted her lips to the side and looked away as if she were uncomfortable thinking about it. "Yes." She shifted in her seat. "I am not at liberty to discuss details, but the queen has told me about the monsters that now threaten the royal family. Curses and some foul things are at work here, I am sure of it."

"Curses? What makes you think that?"

She clammed up and pressed her lips thin as her eyes darted to the side.

"Lady Victoria, I don't mean to infringe on your privacy or the privacy of the royal family, but King Vincent brought me here to help him fight these creatures, and yet, he won't tell me anything about them. I don't know what I'm up against and I can't wage war against ghosts."

"Ghosts of the past, more like it," she muttered, crossing her arms.

"What?"

She shook her head and went silent again.

"Please tell me anything you can. As little or much as you are comfortable with. The fates of your king, the crown prince, and even your dear Alistair, lie in our hands."

The disconcerted look on her face began to fade and her gaze met mine.

"Please, Lady Victoria." I coaxed her once more.

"Alright," she whispered. "I will tell you all that I know, but you must not repeat it. The queen has confided in me for decades, and I simply cannot misplace her trust."

"I promise to keep the information in confidence."

She clutched the bloodmane medallion tightly. "The first Rayvenstar king was King Westin. He and his army overthrew the Pendragon Empire. Upon the fall of Camelot, King Westin's queen gifted him an enchanted cape adorned with a bloodmane scale, hoping it would grant him long life and impenetrable strength and stamina in battle. But the bloodmane scale was a thing of evil, and it cursed the Rayvenstar family with a dark shadow that would become the Sword of

Damocles to every male heir born since."

Damocles was an ancient tale about a sword hung by a thread of horse hair over a king to illustrate the sense of constant peril and doom that accompanies those in a position of power.

"How so?"

"The crown prince has come of age. If anything were to happen to King Vincent, Prince Jacksiun would immediately assume the role of king, without a regent. His coming of age is what I believe has sparked the rise of the beasts, for it did not occur until his return home."

"But why would the old king's curse affect the new crown prince? Isn't he deserving of the throne, like the princes before him?"

"Well..." She looked me square in the eye. "You will repeat none of this."

I shook my head.

"The Rayvenstar kings must choose their wives carefully. Although the queen has always been a loyal subject to the Rayvenstar crown, followers of the Pendragon reign still exist in our country. It is my belief that the curse has risen to destroy the crown prince because his mother... is a descendant of the Pendragon clan. It is my belief that they have risen to stop the prince from gaining the throne and reversing King Westin's doings by reviving the old ways of the corrupted King Arthur."

"You don't believe Prince Jacksiun to be corrupted, do you?"

"No. I do not. But it is not about *my* beliefs... it is about those of the old queen—King Westin's wife—and her accursed gift."

"So because Prince Jacksiun *might* have a trace of Pendragon blood in his veins, these monsters want him dead? Who will carry on the Rayvenstar bloodline if he dies? King Vincent doesn't have another heir."

Lady Victoria looked down at her hands, which she'd nervously tangled together in her lap. "The queen has been unable to bear another child, and so Prince Jacksiun is the one and only future king. This is why he must live."

"Yes. I know. I can't believe the creatures couldn't understand the circumstances here and let him be. Their logic makes no sense! So if the bloodmanes are here only to kill him, how do I stop them?"

"I do not know, but I would start by finding the cursed cape gifted by the old queen. King Vincent may have it, or it may have been buried in the Tomb of the Old Kings."

"Someone had closed off the tomb. In spite of the warnings posted, I went inside and found remains of human blood, along with fur from the creatures. I think they're using it as a feeding ground. If there is a cape hidden there, I'm not sure if I can risk returning to try to find it."

"It may be the only option," she uttered with a solemn shrug. "I do not know what else to suggest."

Considering how the king's gift had brought such a terrible curse with it over the years, I began to wonder if the knight's medallions might be linked—or cursed—as well. But now was not the time to question a woman already in distress who was telling me more than she had likely intended to.

Had this happened before? Had they been able to stop

the curse and possibly kill the beasts? How else would they have acquired the scales to facet into the medals for the Royal Allegiance? I wanted to ask Lady Victoria so many more questions, but...

"*No, Valhara,*" Firagia said softly in my mind. "*We mustn't overstay our welcome.*"

He was right.

"Thank you for your time, Lady Victoria," I said, standing.

"Y-you wish to depart already?" She stood and took a step closer to me. "You only just arrived. Please, have another cup of tea. I would be happy to pour it." She bent down to lift the teapot.

"No, thank you," I replied, pressing my hand gently against hers. "You've been wonderfully hospitable. Thank you so much for everything. But I really must go. I need to return to the castle and help Prince Jacksiun."

"Say a word of this to no one," she said, her raised voice trembling as she set down the teapot.

I bowed my head to her. "I want the Rayvenstar lineage to live on and I want that to happen by Prince Jacksiun becoming king someday. He has been my dearest friend since childhood and I want nothing more than to see him happy and to know that he and his family are safe."

"Thank you, dear," she replied with a grateful smile. "You have been lovely company and I do hope to see you again. Please feel free to come by. You need not be announced. Oh, and you should bring your dragon friend. They are welcomed, too." She paused and shrugged. "If they fit inside my home, that is." She smiled awkwardly. "I have no idea how big dragons are."

"My friend would love to visit, I'm sure," I said. "He doesn't take up much space, but he does have a big heart."

I felt Firagia's spirit smiling, even though I couldn't see his face.

Lady Victoria grinned, too, as if my words had charmed her.

"I will call for the trolley to pick you up," she said, tucking her husband's medallion into a pocket in her dress. "Allow me to do that now. You may come along as the reception panel is in the foyer." She crossed the room and I followed her into the entrance hall. Beside the doorframe was a small computer screen with a black background and Royal Allegiance logo—matching the medallion I'd been shown earlier—rotating in place. "I would like to request a trolley pick up," she said. The screen flashed to white and a dialog popped up asking her to confirm the time and date. "Right away. One passenger. Admiral... No. Delete." She glanced over at me. "What was your full name again? I apologize."

"Valhara Hawksford."

She turned back to the screen. "Admiral Valhara Hawksford."

The screen displayed a confirmation with estimated arrival time, to which Lady Victoria responded, "Correct. Thank you." She opened the stained glass embellished front door and walked me out.

"You may take a look at the horses as you wait, if you wish. They should be in the pasture to your left. Make a little clicking noise with your tongue if you do not see them."

She proceeded to flick her tongue against the roof of her mouth in demonstration. "Like that. Just a little click or two and they should come. Their names are Thimble and Verity. You should recognize which is which when they come."

"I will. Thank you, again."

"It was lovely having you, Admiral."

"You may call me Valhara," I said, smiling.

"What a lovely name, indeed. It suits you perfectly." She reached out for one of my hands and cupped it tightly between hers. "Good luck, Valhara. We all love King Vincent, but I hold a special admiration for Prince Jacksiun. I have loved him since birth, and he and my dear Alistair were such good friends growing up. The prince does not have a fleck of ill will or evil in his entire body, and I wish these beasts could see that, regardless of his bloodline."

"I will do my best to help."

I waved goodbye and she went back inside.

My feet hit the dirt road and I followed along the fence line beside the house, searching the field for movement. The grass was short, clearly grazed on. I reached the end of the street, where the trolley would arrive within minutes, and rested my elbows on the top wooden rail of the pasture fence.

I flicked my tongue against the roof of my mouth, as Lady Victoria had instructed, and waited.

The wind blew, making the grass sway, but no horses came. I tried again, putting a little more force into the clicks so they might travel a farther distance across the immense open field. After several more minutes of quietly listening to the whispering breeze as it weaved through branches and leaves overhead, I slid my arms off the fence and turned toward the edge of the dirt path. Muffled motor sounds drew my attention and the trolley approached.

The large, polished, bullet-like car came to a halt. A camera scanned my face, verifying my identity, and then the door opened. For the second time, I was its only passenger; something I felt strange about, but understood it may have been a private car sent specifically for me by the castle.

I stepped inside and sat on a bench near a window. Just as the car began to move, I heard a loud whinny in the distance. I twisted in my seat and looked out toward the fields of Cassian farmland, where two animals were charging along the fence line, following the car. One was a massive gold and white draft horse galloping through the grass, its mane and tail braided neatly. Trailing far behind the horse that must have been Verity, was a tiny, stubby brown pony, racing head-first against the wind. Thimble, I presumed. The two chased the car to the end of the fence line and then stopped to watch and neigh excitedly as I rode out of sight.

I'd seen terrifying beasts in recent months—mythical and magical creatures from other people's lifetimes—and I'd been away from Earth for so long that I had forgotten what beautiful, majestic beasts still existed in my own.

Upon my return to the castle, I found several messages blinking on the communication tablet in my room. One was from Mattheia, informing me he'd be training in the field with Officer Cassian this afternoon. Another was from Private Quill—an urgent request to speak with me.

I replied to her request with a time, and we agreed to meet in the library. One, for privacy and quiet, and two, so I could take another look at Excalibur. I'd been given exclusive permission by Prince Jacksiun to peruse the royal library whenever I pleased. It seemed like the one and only permission anyone was willing to grant me without argument.

I waited in the back of the library near a row of tables for patrons, though I hadn't seen others there since my arrival, as the place had been closed off to the public. Not a librarian in sight, either.

I sat down at a table and entwined my hands together

on top of the desk, waiting for Amanda to arrive.

She entered later than I'd expected, looking agitated and disheveled.

"Are you alright?" I asked, standing to greet her.

She saluted me and tried to shake the look of discomfort from her face. "Yes, Admiral. I had trouble getting by the guards."

"I told them you'd be coming."

"Well, they didn't believe I was who I said I was." She crossed her arms and huffed. "They said I was 'too young to be a private.'" She rolled her eyes and shrugged. "Why would someone say something like that nowadays? Don't they know military age restrictions were dropped more than twenty years ago? What decade are they living in here?"

I glanced around the library, noting the antique accents and décor. "Judging by the looks of things, I'd say they're behind a few *centuries*."

Amanda cracked a reluctant smile at my joke.

"Try not to worry too much," I said. "You're a great private, and they don't have any idea how useful you are to Silver Diamond."

She grimaced and looked down. "That's kind of what I've come to talk to you about."

"Oh?" I gestured for her to come closer. "Would you like to sit to discuss this?"

"I'll stand, thank you." She straightened her posture, rolled her shoulders back, and cleared her throat. "Admiral, permission to speak freely?" she asked.

It wasn't like her to be so uptight.

"Of course, Private," I said with a nod. "You're always

encouraged to be open with me." I sat on the edge of the desk in an effort to appear slightly less confrontational. We'd spoken about many things while I was temporarily enrolled at Silver Diamond, and I felt like we could trust each other. That's why I had requested she be on my team for this mission.

Amanda chewed her lip and fidgeted with one of the braids on the side of her head. "Admiral, may I request that you keep this confidential, as well? I mean... please don't tell the prince what I'm about to tell you."

"Why would I have to keep it from him?" I leaned over slightly. "Who does this concern, exactly?"

"Me. Only me, I assure you."

"I can't make a promise like that, but you know you can trust me."

"Okay. I'm sorry, I just..." Her voice wavered. She heaved a sigh. "I'd like to request permission to return to the Mainlands."

"Why?" I narrowed my eyes. "You were very excited about being part of the Citrine Exploration Division *and* about coming with us to Alyssia. Why the sudden change of heart in only two days?"

"I feel I've become a burden to the team, and that being here will only make things difficult for the rest of you. Personal reasons and investments influenced my decision to come along, and they shouldn't have. It was unprofessional and juvenile of me to let my private life get in the way of my work. I'd like to return to Silver Diamond and relieve you of my being here."

"No one has said anything negative about you, and I

wanted you to come because I have faith in your skills. I was aware you had *some* personal interests in this endeavor, which is *also* why I asked you to come, but I didn't think they would pose an issue. Is this about you and Prince Jacksiun?"

Amanda pressed her lips thin, flexed her hands, and flinched. "I'm too distracted to work," she muttered.

"Distracted? How?"

Her eyes met mine and she frowned. "You know..."

I did know she was greatly attracted to my friend, but what she didn't know was that he had specifically asked for me to find a way for him to talk to her while she was here. I wasn't sure if that information was appropriate to share with her, but I wasn't going to let her run off simply because she felt "distracted."

"Private, I don't think this is about you," I said firmly, looking her straight in the eye. "This is about what the palace guards, the king, and other officials here have said to you. Isn't it?"

"Well..." She looked off to the side and swallowed hard. "Maybe."

"You asked me to keep this information secret, and I said I couldn't promise anything. But if you listen very carefully to me, and tell me the truth about your feelings, I'll let *you* in on a little secret I know will change the way you're thinking right now."

She cocked her head. "Oh? What is it?"

"Tell me the truth, first. Are you distracted because of your feelings for Prince Jacksiun?"

Her eyes widened and she gasped.

I waited for her to reply.

"I... well, I..."

"Please, Amanda. You know you can trust me. Before I became your admiral, I was your friend, and I'd like to think I still am. Are you upset about how you've been treated by other officials here?"

"Yes," she blurted, looking away as if the truth made her feel ashamed.

"Well, I feel there are many things the king is not telling us. Things that could make the difference between saving their kingdom or... losing a friend."

"No!" Amanda yelped beneath her breath.

I stood and walked over to her, pressing my hand against her forearm and smiling. "You're brave and you're smart, Amanda. Don't let anyone tell you otherwise. We're here because we stood up to this challenge, and I need you to be strong and stay with me, even if I don't have to call upon your help. I want to know you're here for support. Please reconsider your request to leave. You know I'll let you go if your heart isn't in this, but... I think it is. More than you're telling."

She nodded. "I understand, Admiral, and I'd never want you to think I don't support you. I do. I want to be here to help in any way I can, but... I just don't want my feelings for *him* to affect my judgment."

"Reconsider, please," I pleaded again.

"What if Prince Jacksiun wants me to leave?"

I furrowed my brow at her. "Why would you think that?"

"Well, I've asked to speak with him twice already and he's turned me away both times."

"Did *he* turn you away? Or did his guards?"

She thought on it a moment and then her own brow wrinkled. "His guards did." Her eyes met mine. "How did you know that?"

"Because it's been happening to me at every turn." I grinned and patted her gently on the shoulder. "Prince Jacksiun didn't turn you away, his father did. The king has been ordering me around since I arrived, and you and everyone else on my crew have been getting pushed to the wayside because it is his belief that I am the only person here who matters. The prince would never push you away, Amanda. On the contrary, he..." I stopped myself right there.

Her jaw dropped. She knew where I was going.

I slid my hand from her shoulder. "I'll see if there's anything I can do to get you a meeting with the prince, but I'll only do this for you if you reconsider your request to abandon this mission."

"I never said I wanted to abandon anything!" I think she surprised herself when she raised her voice, because she quickly quieted down again. "I would never abandon you or my team," she whispered earnestly. "I'm here because I want to be, and because you believe in me. Yes, I officially withdraw my request to leave. Thank you for trying to help. I'm sorry I had to bring up such a petty complaint."

"You were worried," I said. "I understand."

"I'll await further commands from you then, Admiral," she said with a salute.

"There is one more thing I need to tell you," I added. "If there's one thing I've learned about the important people in my life, it's that distancing yourself from them in a time of great stress will only cause *them* pain. If you care about

Prince Jacksiun, and want to see him thrive, then you must support him and be here for him. He won't ask you for help, and he definitely won't tell you when he's in pain, because he's too proud, but that doesn't mean he wants to be alone. Someday, this will be Jacksiun's kingdom. I want to see his coronation as much as you do. We need to work together to assure he survives to see that day. Because when that day comes, King Vincent won't be making the rules anymore."

"Thank you," Amanda said, a grateful smile twisting her lips. "I appreciate you saying this to me. I'll stay, and we'll save this kingdom together. We'll save Prince Jacksiun's kingdom."

"Yes, we will." I looked across the room at the large glass case housing the miraculous silver and blue broadsword. "And that sword over there is going to help us."

I requested a meeting with Chamberlain Grennings because I felt the general had been withholding information, and that the king was too stubborn to admit to me the truth of what was happening.

They made me sit in a waiting room for over an hour, which *I* believed was to tire me out before letting me see the chamberlain. I'd been trying very hard to keep my cool, but my true feelings had begun leaching through the surface.

"Admiral Hawksford," a woman in an all white pant suit addressed me. She approached and bowed slightly. "Come this way, please. Chamberlain Grennings will see you now."

I walked alongside her through a set of tall double doors,

past a long hallway lined with blue carpeting, into a hexagonal room with an elaborate white marble desk in the center toward the far wall.

Chamberlain Grennings sat behind that desk and gestured for me to sit in one of the chairs before him.

"I hear you have concerns, Admiral," he said lackadaisically.

"Yes. Several, in fact."

"Speak freely," he added.

"How many men and women have the bloodmanes killed?"

"What?" He veered his head toward me.

"How many people have they killed? Total."

"Well, I am not the one with the exact count, but it has been several. A few dozen perhaps."

"Perhaps? Why don't you know the exact number?"

"Because I have other business to attend to in this castle. How dare you question my competence."

"I'm not questioning you. I only want an exact number, please."

"What difference does it make if it is one or a hundred? They must be stopped. That is all that matters. I can say with certainty that two of my best soldiers were brutally slaughtered just the other day while attempting to cage that foul monster you witnessed in the cavern observatory."

"Fatalities are to be anticipated, and often expected, when trying to take prisoners of war. I'm more concerned with the overall impact these creatures have had on the king's army and his people. Can you tell me when the attacks started exactly? And where?"

"Almost two weeks ago," Chamberlain Grennings said

through the side of his mouth, his lips barely parting.

"Two weeks? And how many killed?"

He raised an eyebrow at me and I rephrased my question. "How many, approximately?"

He pressed his lips together and his jaw tightened. "47, I believe. You would have to ask the general for the exact number."

47? Jacksiun had told me "hundreds" back when he'd come to Silver Diamond for my help. Not that those 47 lives didn't matter, but the numbers were horribly skewed from what the prince had said. Someone wasn't telling the truth, and I was sure that someone was *not* Jacksiun.

"You say this began about two weeks ago," I started. "When did Prince Jacksiun arrive back here?" I was under the impression that he'd returned around the same time.

Chamberlain Grennings stiffened in his chair and his nostrils flared with agitation as he met my gaze with a cold glare. "I believe you are asking the wrong questions, Admiral," he said gruffly.

"With all due respect, Sir, I believe *you* are avoiding my questions altogether. If this has something to do with Prince Jacksiun's arrival, then I need to know, and you and your general need to face the truth instead of ordering me around like I'm some kind of magical creature exterminator. Which I am not!"

"You will not speak that way to me," he growled, forcefully pushing up from his seat. "Who do you think you are?"

"I am Voyage Admiral Valhara Hawksford of the Citrine Exploration Division of Silver Diamond Academy, and my presence was requested here in order to assist with a threat to your king and country. Now either someone tells me what is really going on around here, why the general murdered the only live specimen we had to study, and why there hasn't been an attack since my arrival here, or I may begin to suspect that you don't really want my help. You are next in line for the throne, after all, should King Vincent *and* Prince Jacksiun fall."

His face crinkled like he might let out a furious howl of anger when his mouth next opened...

But instead, he took a deep breath, stiffly tugged the hem of his silver-trimmed jacket, flattened a hand down the sides to smooth it, and then sat back down, suddenly taking on a *much* calmer, more approachable demeanor.

"I have sworn loyalty to King Vincent and Prince Jacksiun," he said. "And I would never wish for them to fall. I would give my life for theirs, if need be, but this fight is far more complicated than that." He reached across his desk, uncapped a crystal decanter, and poured bright purple liquid into a stout glass. "I have been told you have spoken with Lady Cassian. What has she shared with you?" The bottle clinked when he dropped the stopper back on top.

I wasn't sure how much information was too much, nor did I want to incriminate Cassian's mother for telling me the things she had.

"All I know is that these beasts may have risen from their sleep to put an end to the Rayvenstar lineage as we know it, and that judging by the frequency of their raids, they have very specific targets in mind."

He tipped his head in subtle agreement. "What do you need from me, Admiral? Tell me what you need to know, and I will see to it that you get the information required to assist us."

"Thank you, Sir," I replied. "Time is slipping away and I'm trying to gather all the resources possible before I attempt any retaliation. Not to completely segue from the conversation, but the sword in the library—the one found during the Great War—may I take it out to study?"

His face wrinkled with discord and he shook his head. "No. It is a sacred relic, and we do not loan out our ancient artifacts for 'study.'" He scoffed.

"It could be a valuable asset in this fight. There's something unique and special about it that could be used to our advantage."

"No. There is no questioning that. It stays where it is."

"What if Prince Jacksiun requested permission to see it?"

"That would not make a difference. He does not have jurisdiction over the property within the library yet. It is governed only by the king."

It was clear I wasn't going to get anywhere with my inquiry, so I dropped it.

"I understand. Back to the matter at hand—my team found remains of human blood in the temple of the old kings, along with bloodmane fur, but that's all I've been able to uncover. What did the king say when you told him the general disposed of a bloodmane the other day?"

Chamberlain Grennings sighed and broke eye contact with me. "There is something else you should know," he said somberly. "King Vincent has an unhealthy fondness for those creatures. He believes they are sacred, and that harming them will only expedite the fall of his kingdom."

"What would make him think such a thing?"

"There is a legend surrounding the first Rayvenstar king—King Westin—which involves a certain magical cape gifted to him by the first Rayvenstar queen. Some believed it to be an omen of strength and longevity, while others believed it to be a curse upon the throne; some say the queen sold her soul to the leader of the beasts in exchange for his protection over her husband, and that in return, the bloodmane king would be allowed to choose the Rayvenstar heir from that day forward, deciding who lives and who dies on the throne."

What he was telling me was a minor elaboration on what Lady Cassian had said, but without any mention of Jacksiun's mother's lineage.

"Do you think this is something evil, then?" I asked.

"I do not know exactly what the arrival of the bloodmane pack means for our kingdom, but I do know that if the king hesitates to fight back, then we may all perish, as he has no other heirs. I ask you to not disclose the death of the beast to the king. He is far too sympathetic to the old legend, and believes they are an omen of good, even as they attempt to destroy his very reign with force. I believe that is also why he asked you to come. He may have thought your very presence could frighten them away without harming them. I am sorry you are in this situation and that I cannot provide any additional information. Until they attempt an attack again, I cannot offer more guidance."

"When did they last attack and how?" I asked.

"Last week, two bloodmanes came up through a tunnel

in the royal garden, scaled the back of the castle, and then confronted a line of guards outside the prince's room. Three guards were fatally injured and one survived with critical injuries. A spear pierced one of the beasts' sides and a trail of blood was left behind, which we followed to the Tomb of the Old Kings. This is why I had the entrance to the ruins barricaded."

"Prince Jacksiun said to me something about the old ruins being excavated, which may have woken the bloodmanes. Is there any truth to that?"

Chamberlain Grennings shook his head. "We did not wish to make the prince feel as though he could be in danger, so the king and I decided to keep the truth from him. Those monsters destroyed the ruins to build their filthy dwelling, and when we sent troops in to run them out... that is how many of our soldiers perished. We know, for a fact, that bloodmanes bleed, and now we know they can die."

"Yes. I..." My throat tightened as I remembered the horrifying image. "I witnessed that firsthand. Regrettably."

I took a deep breath and tried to push the revolting memory from my mind before it could rattle me again.

"I have been told you and Prince Jacksiun are close," the chamberlain said.

"He is a very good friend."

"Then you must force aside your sympathies for the beasts, if you want to keep your friend alive."

The clinking of metal on metal drew my attention and I perked up as I approached the training field. There, I found Mattheia and Officer Cassian in the midst of a fencing bout. My guess was that they had been training for a few hours now, as they were quite in the thick of it, and I'd never seen Mattheia handle the Pegasus Sword with such control before.

They'd been fitted with mesh masks, thick plastrons, and hardened leather pauldrons made to protect the primary shoulder and underarm. As I approached, they ended their round and lifted their masks to greet me.

"Good afternoon, Admiral," Officer Cassian said cheerily, tipping his head toward me. "I was worried I might have to send someone to rescue you from my mother. She can be very persuasive with her tea and desserts. She did not keep you too long, did she?"

"Not at all. Lady Victoria was very considerate."

"Good. Were you able to see the horses while you were there?"

"They saw me off, actually. Both are beautiful."

"Thank you. My father cares greatly for them. He boards horses for some of the local nobles, as well, but they are kept in another pasture. Perhaps some other day you will see them, too."

"Perhaps."

"Well." He turned to gesture toward Mattheia. "Would you like to know how Commander Draven has been faring?"

I nodded.

"You will be thrilled to know we have progressed swiftly today."

"Yes. I'm getting the hang of this." Mattheia lifted an arm to wipe sweat from his forehead and swipe his hair out of his face. "Officer Cassian is giving me a good workout, that's for sure."

"I'm glad to hear he's a good teacher. I had a feeling he would be." I grinned at Mattheia, who smiled back. I looked around and didn't see any other familiar faces. "Where's Private Quill?"

"She requested to sit this one out," Cassian replied.

"That's a shame. I know she was very interested in learning."

"If we run out of time here," Mattheia spoke up, "I'll teach her anything I can once we get back to Silver Diamond. I know it won't be the same as your expertise, Officer Cassian, or yours." He pointed toward me. "But I can try to help."

"Thank you. I'll check on her later today," I added. "What have you learned?" I took a seat on a nearby tree stump, which appeared to have been left there for that very purpose.

"Today, I've been introduced to the balestra and quartara—"

"Quartata," Cassian corrected.

"Yes, that." Mattheia laughed.

A balestra is a sort of jump forward that can be used to expedite an advance or retreat, and a quartata is one way to avoid an opponent's blade and then counterattack.

"Those are advanced moves," I said, looking over at Officer Cassian. "Don't you think?"

"Yes." He nodded. "But I believe the commander can practice and perfect them all with time. I wanted to give him a good grasp of the main tactics and moves used in generalized fencing, aside from the primary three."

He meant first position, en-garde, and lunge. All things he'd taught him yesterday.

"Would you like to practice with him?" Officer Cassian asked, flipping his foil around and offering it out to me.

"No, thank you," I replied with a flattened hand.

Cassian's gaze shifted and he gasped with surprise. "Your Highness!" He bowed deeply, and I swerved around to see Prince Jacksiun heading our way.

"Good afternoon, Your Highness," I said, clambering to stand from the tree stump and then bow, as all the others with us had already done.

He looked around. "Where... is Private Quill? I had been told she was training with you."

"She declined to come today," I answered with a frown. "I'm sorry."

"Hmm..." His jaw tightened.

"If I may speak with you about that..." I lowered my voice as I approached him. He motioned for his personal guards to give us space.

"Yes?" He turned his back to the others and we stepped a few feet away.

"Private Quill came to me personally about her dissatisfaction with how she's been treated within the castle."

"She did?"

"She wanted to be released from my team and return to Silver Diamond."

He appeared to be surprised and appalled. "How has she been mistreated? I thought she would be comfortable here."

"Aside from an incident where she was questioned about her identity and rank by some of the castle guards, she had also attempted to meet with you twice in the last two days and was turned away on both occasions."

"Twice!?" His voice rose and I noticed others peeking over at us. "I had not even been notified of her first attempt."

"She thought it was your own choice to send her away, and so she told me she felt like a burden to the team, now that her personal feelings were getting in the way."

"Nonsense." He shook his head and growled beneath his breath. "I never turned her away. Please, apologize to her on my behalf."

"Could *you*? It would mean more to her. I'll find a way to make it happen if you'd consider speaking to her yourself."

His brow flinched as he studied my face for some clue as to what I had planned, but he brushed it off when he realized he couldn't read me.

"Alright, but please be careful," he said with a nod. "I do not want you or anyone else getting into trouble with my father."

"I understand."

"Thank you," he whispered and turned back toward the others. "Commander Draven," he called out. "Might I challenge you to a bout?"

One of the four guards who had accompanied the prince to the training field was quick to speak up. "You must wear protective gear!" he said adamantly.

"Commander Draven is only a beginner; today is his second day of formal training," Jacksiun replied, glaring at the guard. "Do you doubt the abilities of your crown prince?"

"N-no, Your Highness," the guard said with a deep bow. "M-my apologies."

"A blade, please," he ordered with a flick of his hand.

His posture was rigid and there was an air of confidence and pride in his voice I hadn't heard before; he was acclimating nicely to the whole *prince* thing.

Officer Cassian jumped at the opportunity to assist and quickly retrieved a simple foil from the nearby rack.

"This is all we have, Your Highness," he said, his voice shaking. "Would you like me to return to the castle to retrieve one more fitting of a crown prince?"

"No need. This will do." Jacksiun laughed and glanced at Mattheia. "Now, Commander, will you accept my challenge?"

Mattheia looked at me and then back at the prince.

"Yes. But… shouldn't we be on equal ground?" He lifted the blade of the Pegasus Sword up and to the side. "This seems like an unfair advantage."

"It is skill which counts in a match such as this," the prince declared, smirking. "You are welcome to use that sword."

Mattheia acknowledged his agreement and then shifted into a ready stance.

"Admiral, what was it you used to say before we sparred?" Jacksiun's eyes met mine and his grin stretched. "Oh, yes. I remember. Mind if I take a stab at this?"

I chuckled. "I'd prefer you *not* stab him. I mean, if you're jealous of our relationship, you can just say so."

Jacksiun laughed heartily. "No. I know you two are perfect for each other." He got into first position. "Though, I will expect the husband of the Elemental Guardian to wield a sword properly."

"Why? Do you think I can't defend myself?" I raised an eyebrow.

"Have I challenged the wrong person, Admiral?" Jacksiun looked over his shoulder at me. "Is there something you need to get off your back?"

"Not at all, Your Highness." I snickered, backing away and bowing slightly, flourishing my hand. "Good luck, you two."

Mattheia cocked an eyebrow at me. "Good luck? We're only practicing, right?"

"If that is how you picture it, you will never learn a thing," Jacksiun said. "Now, defend yourself." He put one hand behind his back and saluted Mattheia with his foil.

Mattheia brushed off his uncertainty and straightened

his posture. "I'm still learning. Give me a break."

"There are no breaks in battle," Jacksiun replied, stepping forward with his sword into en-garde position, only to intimidate Mattheia. He'd often used the tactic to intimidate me, too, but I'd become accustomed to his sneaky ways.

"True," Mattheia added. "But most people aren't *battling* their friends."

Mattheia lifted his sword up and bent his elbow, adjusting his feet into the L-position, shoulder width apart. Then he, too, pointed his sword toward the prince and assumed the en-garde stance.

Jacksiun advanced and lunged. Mattheia retreated and parried the attack, following up with a riposte—a counterattack.

With lightning-fast timing, the prince flicked his foil to defend from the oncoming strike and knocked the Pegasus Sword forcefully from Mattheia's hand. The sword flung to the side and fell, blade-first, burrowing into the grass.

"The commander is off to a good start, but he has much to learn," Jacksiun said, handing his foil off to one of his guards. "I will let you get back to your teachings, Officer." He peered at me and smiled warmly. "I am sure you and Admiral Hawksford will instruct him with more mercy in your advances than I. Patience in my studies was never my forte."

He was right. He learned so quickly that he wasn't typically a good mentor. Genius can't be taught, I suppose.

I walked toward Mattheia, who had lost some of his poise, appearing defeated and discouraged.

"You'll learn, in time," I said, shrugging sympathetically.

"You've got the talent and you have a connection with that sword already. You grip it with a lot of care and dedication, like you believe in it. That sword was meant for you." I glanced over at it and gasped.

It was pulsing with white light.

A vivid yellow beam shot toward the sky, followed by a soft humming sound. I froze in place, recognizing those signals. I swerved to warn the others, but before I could open my mouth, a flapping sound boomed overhead and we all looked up.

Sparkling brown wings cut through the sky, and a beautiful buckskin colt dashed high over the field. After reaching the edge of the clearing, he made a wide turn in the air and headed back toward us. He swooped low, his coat glistening with twinkles of gold, and aimed toward the sword, coming in for a swift, abrupt landing. He hit the grass with a thump and tucked his wings against his sides, approaching the glowing sword slowly, but eagerly.

Jacksiun's guards drew their sabers and rushed in to quickly shuttle Jacksiun behind them.

The pegasus panicked, stomping his hooves against the grass, kicking up dirt, and snorting fearfully as he backed away. He fanned both wings out to the sides and flitted them angrily.

"Whoa! Whoa!" Mattheia dashed after the beast, coming between it and the guards.

"What are you doing?" one of them asked. "That creature is a danger to the crown prince. Move aside!"

"He's not a threat," Mattheia said, holding his hands out to the sides, facing the guards but keeping them separated from the animal. The pegasus continued to snort and shake defensively.

"Then where did it come from? That weapon? Is it cursed?" The guard motioned toward the Pegasus Sword, which was still gleaming.

"No," Mattheia replied, his voice shuddering. "It's not cursed. Please, let me handle this. Take the prince away, if you must, but don't harm this animal."

The pegasus huffed and puffed protectively, neighing and stamping the ground again as Mattheia backed toward him.

"Hold steady," Jacksiun ordered. "Let the commander see to the creature. I am in no immediate danger."

"Whoa, boy," Mattheia whispered, reaching toward the horse's muzzle. "I won't hurt you. It's okay." The whites of the horse's eyes shimmered as he pulled his head back. Then Mattheia moved closer to the sword. "Get back, everyone!"

"Do as he says!" Jacksiun commanded.

I, too, moved away, fearing for Mattheia's safety, but trusting his judgment.

Mattheia's trembling hand stretched out and rested on the pommel of the sword. The beam of light shooting from the center vanished.

"I'm a friend," Mattheia continued in a calm voice. "This is *my* sword now. You don't have to be afraid of me." He knelt beside it and broke eye contact with the horse. Then he held up his other hand, palm up, and waited for a response from the animal.

We all watched as the pegasus analyzed the situation,

tilting his head, stamping his hooves, and shuffling back and forth as he tried to decide what to do.

I was just about to intervene when the creature lowered his head and approached Mattheia, nuzzling his open hand with his snout.

Mattheia's gaze lifted, and as they made eye contact, the beast's wings began to pull in closer to his body; he appeared less fearful now.

"There," Mattheia said, turning his hand slightly to brush the colt's face. It startled him and he jumped back, shaking out his wings again defensively.

"Calm down, please." Mattheia came to his feet and plucked the sword from the grass. The action provoked the pegasus to rear and neigh anxiously. "You don't have to leave. You can stay. You'll be safe."

The creature clomped around, looking as though he might leap back into the sky and disappear at any second.

But he didn't.

He eventually tucked both wings against his sides, lifted his head, and inched closer to Mattheia.

Mattheia introduced himself and then gestured toward me. "That's Valhara—the Elemental Guardian. If anyone can protect you, it's her. But... I think..." He tilted his head and squinted. "I think you may have helped us once before. Is that true?"

The pegasus nodded his head vigorously and let out an excited, shrill whinny.

"It *was* you?" Mattheia grinned. "That's... that's amazing! Thank you for what you did for us. You're a very brave pegasus."

The pegasus approached him and lowered his head toward the sword, allowing Mattheia to stroke his short, black mane.

I looked back toward Jacksiun, who appeared to be rather impressed.

"He is quite the animal whisperer," Jacksiun said, stepping out from the protective circle of his guards.

The pegasus made note of his movements and snorted and staggered back a few steps.

"My apologies," Jacksiun added, freezing where he stood. "Commander, will you be keeping the beast? If it is willing to be kept, that is."

Mattheia looked back at him and shrugged. "Maybe." He glanced at the pegasus and then at the prince again. "Is that even possible?"

"Give me a moment." The prince turned toward one of his guards. "Request Lady Alexandria's presence, please," he said.

We waited for several minutes, watching the majestic winged horse trot around in circles around us, keeping a close eye on our each and every move. He stopped to graze for a few moments and seemed to be calming down.

Around that time, Lady Alexandria, the king's personal secretary and schedule planner, arrived.

"The royal stables have not been used in over a century," she said.

"If I may intervene," Officer Cassian spoke up, approaching us. "May I speak on your behalf, Commander? About the pegasus?" He waited for Mattheia to answer.

"Yes. Go ahead."

"Lady Alexandria, we require only one stall and permission to access the old pastures," he said. "Lord Cassian and I may be able to assist with the training or upkeep, if required. Would getting permissions such as those be too much to ask?"

Alexandria didn't seem keen on the idea, but she shrugged it off. "No. I will have the groundskeepers prepare the stable for you." She glared judgmentally at Mattheia. "Be certain to keep the beast under control at *all times*. We do not need any more wild animals causing problems here."

"You can trust Commander Draven," I replied. "I will accept full responsibility if anything should happen."

Lady Alexandria left and Jacksiun dismissed himself.

"If we are going to board that animal, you need to learn to communicate with it, first," Cassian said, laying his saber down onto the grass so it wouldn't make noise as he walked.

Mattheia sheathed the Pegasus Sword in the scabbard at his waist.

"I do not know if a pegasus can be trained the same way a horse can, but we can try," Cassian added. "Approach it." He pointed toward the distance, to where the animal had wandered off. Mattheia walked slowly out to it.

"When you get within seven or eight paces of the beast, and you are certain his eyes are on you, turn your back to him quickly and begin walking back to us."

Mattheia looked over his shoulder at Cassian, shrugging as if he thought the idea was a little silly.

"Trust me, Commander!" Cassian assured.

Mattheia nodded and returned his focus to the grazing pegasus. When he got within the allotted distance, he veered around and began making his way back.

Instantly, the pegasus lifted his head up from the grass and walked after him. As distance between the two grew, the horse picked up pace, trotting to catch up, until he was only about a yard away.

Mattheia's eyes widened and he looked back at me with shock; he could feel and hear the animal following closely.

"There you go!" Cassian said excitedly. "So they are like horses, then!"

After those words came out, the pegasus immediately halted behind Mattheia and snorted loudly, digging at the grass.

Mattheia turned. "Hey, boy." He inched closer and lifted a hand.

"Do not make eye contact with him!" Cassian shouted.

Mattheia's gaze met the ground, but his hand remained in the air.

"It's okay," he whispered to the pegasus. "I don't think he meant that. You're not just a regular horse. You're something special. I know that."

I glanced at Cassian, whose brow was wrinkled with confusion. "Did that creature understand me?" he muttered.

"I think so." I stifled a small laugh. "You may have to watch your tongue around Mattheia's intelligent new friend."

Cassian shrugged. "Perhaps."

By now, Mattheia had convinced the animal to let him touch his muzzle, and then stroked the pegasus along his withers. "It's okay, boy. You're safe here, and we will treat you with respect. Will you be okay with me? Will you let me keep you here? Please?"

His voice was so quiet and gentle toward the animal.

The pegasus pushed against his shoulder with his nose and flapped his lips, tugging playfully at one of Mattheia's epaulets.

"Whoa. Careful!" Mattheia stumbled forward, startling the horse. "Sorry." He straightened up. "Is that a yes, then?"

The beautiful, sandy-gold pegasus lifted his powerful head and nodded. He understood us quite well, it seemed. But then he also responded to Cassian's horse-related training techniques.

"Will he come to *me*?" I asked.

"I don't know." Mattheia patted the pegasus on the side of its neck. "Will you go to Valhara?" he said.

The pegasus hesitated at first and shook his head.

"She won't hurt you, I promise," he added, rubbing his fingers through the animal's glossy mane. "If she does, I-I give you permission to trot right back over here and... kick me."

"Mattheia!" I shouted unintentionally; what he'd said had infuriated me. I did not want my fiancé getting kicked by a thousand-pound beast!

The pegasus whinnied and snorted, tipping his head toward the grass as if he were... laughing?

"Hey! I didn't think it was funny," I said, raising my voice.

Was I really arguing with an animal?

But then the pegasus stepped past Mattheia, put his head down, and came galloping after me, full-speed!

I dodged to the side, tumbling onto the grass, and Cassian veered off several feet, too, just as the silly creature came to a complete standstill inches away from where I'd stood.

There he remained, shaking his head again, as if he were chuckling at my fall.

"I'm so sorry, Valhara!" Mattheia rushed over to me, offered out a hand, and helped pull me up from the grass.

Good thing my uniform was green...

I brushed flakes of dirt and dead leaves off my slacks and glared back at the animal.

"What was that all about!?" I clenched my fists. "Did you not hear what he said about me earlier? I'm an Elemental Guardian. And that means..." I marched after him and, before I could show off, he neighed with fright and trotted off into the distant field.

"I'm sorry," Mattheia said. "I didn't know he was going to do something stupid like that."

"I would not have predicted that would have happened, either," Cassian added. "Horses are prey animals and would rather run than fight. Apparently, we all have a thing or two to learn about the pegasus. Admiral, are you hurt?"

"I'm fine, thank you, Officer." I composed myself. "Thank you for offering to help us train him. I hope your father won't be bothered by it."

"Not at all." He shook his head. "Lord Cassian loves horses and... I am sure he will love that beast, as well. He needs things to keep him busy. Since his injury and discharge, he has been restless. Getting back to the castle will be good for his morale." He looked off toward the large, abandoned stables in the distance. The sun would be setting in a few hours. "Would you like me to go check on the condition of the stable and be sure it is ready for the night?"

"Yes. Thank you," Mattheia said.

"I will leave you two to speak, and when you are ready, please meet me there."

"Thank you, Officer," I said with an earnest smile. "You work too hard, I think. You're an officer in the king's castle guard, but you wear so very many hats."

"I enjoy the work," he said. "And any day I can get out of the stuffy castle and into the fields, I am happy."

Mattheia and I tipped our heads to Cassian and he scooped his saber up off the grass, sheathed it, and then headed off toward the stables.

I watched the pegasus grazing in the distance and smiled. He was incredible. Iridescent sparkles shone as sunlight caressed his unique coat.

"What do you think?" Mattheia asked, approaching me from the side and sliding a hand behind my back, now that no one was around to see.

"About your sword fighting skills? Or him?" I nodded toward the pegasus.

"*Him.* I guess I have a pegasus." Mattheia laughed. "I just hope Captain Lansfora lets me keep him."

"Why wouldn't he?"

"Because he's a wild animal and we run a military academy, not a zoo."

"Sometimes I think it's both," I replied snarkily.

He scowled.

I chuckled; ruffling his feathers was fun, and I couldn't do it easily, because he was so laid back. I had to take the shot.

"In all seriousness, though," I continued, "he is a rare

and unusual creature you don't see everyday. I'm sure there's a nice warm spot for him somewhere in the hangar, where the other pilots won't mind."

Mattheia laughed. "I see what you did there. Pilot. Flying horse. Nice."

"Well, I've got some things to research back at the castle." I slid from Mattheia's grasp and briefly touched his hand. "Be safe out here with your new..." I looked back at the animal, which was now rolling in the grass. "Pet?"

"Thanks. Let me know if I can do anything at all for you," Mattheia said with a small grin. "I wish they'd trust me with more information, but..."

I put my hand onto his shoulder and smiled. "I'll let you know if I need your help." Then I leaned closer, brushing his collar with my fingertips. "I love you," I whispered. "We'll talk again soon."

"I love you, too," he replied.

Remember what I told you," I whispered, releasing the spark of fire into Amanda's palm. I doubted anyone could hear us behind closed doors, but I had to be careful.

"I will," she replied, closing her hand so only a hint of amber light escaped through the gaps between her fingers. "Thank you."

She exited my room, and I watched as she walked down the long stretch of blue carpet, until she turned and disappeared down the next hall.

I'd devised a way to try to get Amanda a meeting with the prince. The guards changed shifts in the middle of the day, and those outside Jacksiun's door at that time had not met me yet. If everything went as planned, she'd be able to fool them into believing she was me, and then they would likely grant her permission to speak to the crown prince.

A sliver of concern brewed in me for her safety, should

she be found out as an imposter, but I'd come clean to protect her—if need be. I'll do whatever it takes to protect those I care about.

I sat on the edge of my bed, wondering if what I'd done would make things better or worse. I didn't want Amanda leaving because she felt isolated and discriminated against here, and—

"Stay calm. Stay calm," I heard Amanda mutter to herself. The words swirled about in my mind as if she were nearby, although...

I looked around.

She wasn't.

I held my breath and listened, closing my eyes. My vision and focus shifted to a shadowy place with tiny slats of light cutting through the darkness. I felt movement, heat, and fear—the pounding of an anxious heart ripping through me like a tremor.

"Remember what she said," Amanda added. "Be confident."

A little more light seeped in, and then everything went dark as I felt Amanda squeezing her fist tightly closed around the flame I'd given her.

Was I seeing through that flame?

I could nearly feel her perspiration building on my own skin and her anxiety quickening my pulse. Her grasp on the fireball softened and I witnessed her fussing with her uniform and straightening the perfect braids on the sides of her head. Her heart raced, and my stomach twisted while I tried to separate my emotions from hers. She was a bundle of nerves and it was making *me* tremble uncontrollably.

"State your name," a royal guard said sternly.

"Pri—" She coughed and took a deep breath. "Admiral Valhara Hawksford. I am here to speak with Prince Jacksiun per his request."

She remembered it just as I had instructed her to say it.

"The prince's request?" The guard sounded skeptical.

"Yes. As you may know, I am the Elemental Guardian." She lifted her hand and unfurled her fingers, revealing the floating swirl of fire in her palm. Her surroundings became clear—the two guards standing watch, Amanda's feigned confidence, and the familiar doorway of Prince Jacksiun's room.

The guard's eyes widened and he nodded. "Please wait here as I announce you."

"Th-thank you," she added, almost choking on her words from her stifled tension.

He disappeared into the room and closed the door.

Amanda fidgeted with the coil of flame in her palm, rolling it back and forth between her fingers.

The other guard gazed curiously at her, but then looked off straight ahead and said nothing.

"He will see you now," the first guard said, returning from the room moments later. "He is expecting you."

"Of course, he is. I already told you that," she retorted.

The guard furrowed his brow and Amanda clenched her fingers, blinding me again with shadow.

"T-thank you," she added.

She entered the room and I heard nothing for several moments, except nervous breaths as she walked.

Then there was a familiar voice.

"Private Quill?" It was Jacksiun.

"G-good evening," she replied.

"I thought Admiral Hawksford was here to see me. Is she waiting outside?"

Amanda's fingers loosened on the fire and her hands began to shake. My guilty conscience nagged me to allow the fire to dissipate, but I was curious and eager to hear their conversation. It was none of my business, perhaps, but... in a way, it was.

So I did a terrible thing—I eavesdropped on my friends.

"It's only me, Your Highness," she said, her voice breaking. "Valhara gave me this." Amanda raised her hand and slowly unclenched her fingers. "I had to lie to the guards, however, so I hope you aren't angry with me."

Scarlet light bounced off his eyes as he gazed at her hand with wonder. "Remarkable," he said. His face close to the flame, it was as if we were nose to nose. He pulled back and she clasped her hand closed, enveloping me in blackness. "It does not burn your skin?"

"Not at all," she replied.

"I am not angry with you for having to bend the truth in order to see me," he spoke softly. "I had been hoping to speak with you. Is everything okay?"

"I told Admiral Hawksford that I wanted to return to the Mainlands because I felt like a burden here and... I was under the impression that you were avoiding me because I'd been turned away on two occasions already."

"No. No." He scoffed. "I would never do that. There are people I like far less than you to whom I *would* speak. Please do not think I would turn *you* or anyone away like that."

"I'm sorry," she said, looking to the side. I couldn't see her face, but my own felt flush now, as if all her sensations were bleeding through to me. "I didn't know. I want to help you, but, like everyone else here, I am being shut out. I feel as though I simply can't contribute, and that is also why I wanted to forfeit this mission and return to Silver Diamond."

"Please don't," he said, reaching for her hand. She released the fire and it drifted down to the floor, flickering in place like a candle without heat. "I would very much like you to stay." He gazed fondly at her.

"You would?"

"Yes."

"Why?" She shrugged, avoiding eye contact. "I'm not smart like Commander Draven or Admiral Hawksford. I haven't even graduated yet. I'm wasting your resources and time by being here."

"If you are afraid," he started, "or uncertain about things to come, then I would never ask you to stay and put yourself in an uncomfortable position. But... there is such a thing as moral support." His voice softened and he leaned down to try to get her to meet his gaze again. "And I would be grateful and honored if you would grant me yours. I do want to get to know you better, and I do not want my father's ways to intimidate you. Please stay, if only to remind me that I have one more reason to stand and fight."

"Of course!" She cupped her other hand over his and stepped closer, looking him in the eye. "You have my support, Lieutenant!" She gasped. "I'm sorry. I-I mean, Your Highness." She released his hand and turned away, grumbling. "I'm so sorry. I really don't belong here. I'm so stupid.

I can't—"

"No." He approached her from behind and took her hand again, gently tugging her so she'd turn to face him. "I spent the last several years of my life on a military academy in space, growing up beside Admiral Hawksford and others not from noble lineages. A slip of the tongue does not make you stupid in any way. On the contrary, you were chosen to assist the admiral because of your intelligence." He rested his other hand on her shoulder and gazed at her imploringly. "Now please, tell me, will you stay?"

She chewed her lip. "Yes," she uttered quietly. "I-I will. Because you want me to, and because I *want* to support you. I don't want those creatures to hurt you."

"Our lives have been thrust into chaos, but I hope things will quiet down soon," Jacksiun said, smiling confidently. "Thank you, Amanda." He lifted her hand toward his lips and kissed her knuckles; she let out a gasp of surprise. "Your support means a lot to me."

"I'm just happy I could speak with you, Your Highness." She smiled at him shyly, and it made my heart ache. There was so much adoration glistening in her eyes, and I noticed a certain something spark to life in his when he'd kissed her hand.

I'd heard enough and decided not to infringe on their privacy further.

I concentrated on the flame she'd left on the floor and willed the energy to dissipate, the sights and sounds of the room, and their conversation, fading from my mind like echoes into the night.

In the evening, a string of message attachments popped up on the communication tablet in my room—all from Prince Jacksiun.

I took a seat and clicked the attachments—a slew of illustrations scanned from books, photographs, or tapestries from the ancient era. All of them featured King Arthur.

"I believe you are right," Jacksiun said simply in a single text, following the attachments.

I investigated them closely, quickly realizing they were all artistic renderings of the Pendragon king with Excalibur. The sword in the images resembled the sword on display in the Rayvenstar library.

"I knew it," I replied. "We will discuss more soon." When we weren't being monitored and recorded by castle staff. "Goodnight."

"Goodnight," he typed in return.

I initiated a video chat with Mattheia, who appeared to be online. It beeped for a few moments and then he came on screen.

"Hey," he said with a grin. "Can't go a few hours without seeing me?"

"Very funny," I replied with a fake scowl. "I wanted to ask if you got the pegasus put up for the night, and if that went okay?"

"Sort of."

"Sort of?"

"Obviously, he wasn't keen on the idea of being locked up for the night. But then Officer Cassian brought some carrots and apple slices to the stable and that made him change his mind."

"That's nice. I didn't know equines liked apples."

"Neither did I."

"Are you going to name him?" I asked.

"I was..."

"You *were*?"

He cleared his throat and looked off to the side as if he didn't want to say anything else on camera while he was being recorded. "Uh... let's just say he already has one."

"He does? How did you discover that?"

"I'd rather show you in person. Maybe not tonight, but—"

A shrill siren penetrated the walls of my room and my tablet screen turned black.

"Mattheia!?" I swiped at the screen, but it was unresponsive. Or off. I couldn't tell which, and the noise was so loud it made me cringe and cover my ears.

I gritted my teeth and stood from my seat, mustering the strength to endure the painful wailing long enough to scramble over to my bed and strap on my scabbard. Next, I reached for my sword. With the Azure Phoenix securely attached to the hyper magnet now stretched across my back, I hurried to leave.

But the door to my room wouldn't open...

Were we in lock-down during the emergency? How was I supposed to help if I couldn't get out!?

"Open!" I screamed, but it didn't budge. Maybe the electrical blip that crashed my tablet did the same to the door systems. "Open!"

Nothing.

Either that, or they *were* locking us in.

On purpose.

"Okay, then we'll do this the hard way." I lifted my hands and pressed them against the door until they grew warm and bright. The door began to change color, from yellow to red to black, as the material caught fire and crumbled away. A swift kick to the area I'd burned sent ashes flying into the hall and left a big enough gap for me to shimmy through and escape.

I rushed toward the guards who were stationed at the end of the hall.

"What's going on!?" I asked.

They looked at me as if they hadn't known what the alert was for yet, either.

"How did you get out of your room?" one of them asked. A loud beep sounded and he looked away from me to check a small monitor strapped to the inside of his wrist—a screen with text scrolling with codes I didn't understand. Then a tiny map flashed and another row of text.

"What is it!?" I leaned over, but he reached an arm out to keep me back.

"Bloodmanes!" the other guard exclaimed. "Inside the castle!?"

"Where? Tell me where they are," I asked, my pulse racing and my voice becoming gruff.

Just as he was about to respond, the other guard jabbed him in the arm and glared.

"No!" he said. "It is not her duty."

"It is!" I flashed an angry look at them both and let the fire spark to life in my hands. "I was brought here to protect the king and his son. Now tell me where the monsters are! If you care about your king at all..." The flames licked up higher and spread toward my shoulders.

"T-the throne room," the more agreeable guard stammered.

"Thank you." I released the energy of my fire to extinguish the flames, then took off running down the hall.

I turned a corner and realized I had no idea where the throne room was, or how to get there.

That's when I spotted Officer Cassian rushing toward me. "Admiral! I am glad you were released!" he said. "Come with me, please. One of the beasts has broken through!"

I jogged alongside him, down several halls, and then through a door he'd told me was a shortcut used primarily by royal guards. We entered into the hidden passageway—a narrow brick hall lit with strips of soft, white-blue light, which guided us through the secret network. We exited through a hidden door that put us at the far end of the throne room. At the other end, Prince Jacksiun and the king stood, behind a row of armed guards, facing the massive wooden double-doors leading to the main entrance.

About a dozen Royal Allegiance soldiers had swords at the ready, watching as something pounded against the doors until the wood fractured and a wide crack split through one side.

"The Elemental Guardian is here!" Officer Cassian shouted.

Jacksiun and the king veered their heads toward me.

"Your Highness! What can I do to help!?" I asked.

"Get back! All of you! Take the prince away, quickly!" the king ordered, and his men surrounded the prince and ushered him toward the back of the room. They pushed past us, toward the hidden hallway from which we'd exited. "Let the Guardian through!" the king added.

Another loud crack tore at the wood, and the king gestured for me to come over to him.

"How many are there?" I asked.

A third thunderous sound rumbled beneath my feet, and then the double-doors came crashing down, answering my question by revealing a giant, growling bloodmane. This one was *much* larger than the one they'd captured.

"Be careful, Valhara!" Jacksiun raised his voice to be heard against the blaring siren as he was spirited away from the throne room.

I had to assume he would be safe, now that they'd taken him away. A hulking, seething beast stood before me, crouched down on all fours, fangs bared, virulent yellow eyes narrowed and focused on me.

"Stay behind me, Your Highness," I said to the king,

ushering him out of the way. It surprised me how his guards didn't try to remove him from the room first, but maybe he had other plans for dealing with the intruder.

The bloodmane was at least three times the size of Firagia, but much smaller than the ice dragon I'd fought. It was muscular, with sharp, sinewy curves clearly visible through fur. A large line of iridescent green and yellow color shifting scales ran down its face and back, and segments of the armor decorated the outer side of each arm and leg. It flicked its head, tousling its scarlet mane, and then roared at us. Large paws covered in reddish-brown fur clawed against the floor, tearing up stretches of blue carpeting with extended black claws, each the length of a human hand.

"Murderer..." the beast hissed through clenched teeth and then clamped its jaws together several times. Elongated fangs extended past its lips—one on each side of its muzzle—and a hooked, beak-like appendage protected its nostrils.

"I'm no murderer!" I reached over my shoulder for my sword and the creature lunged at me. In a flash of golden light, Firagia exploded from my necklace, plowing into the bloodmane to deflect the attack.

King Vincent stumbled back several steps at the sight of my dragon.

Furious screeching and growling noises filled the room, and I panicked, fearing Firagia would get injured by the creature as they thrashed around. Finally, he broke free and flew overhead.

The bloodmane neared the king and I held out my sword, which was now ablaze with vivid violet and amber fire. "Don't come any closer," I shouted, knowing that if the creature could speak, it may very well have been able to understand my words.

The bloodmane tromped nearer, a stream of blood drizzling down its forehead from the scuffle. "You murdered the young one," it said, the words shakily rolling off its beastly tongue.

"She murdered no one!" Firagia roared, landing beside me. "Go back to your ruins!"

"I'm not afraid to fight you," I continued, locking eyes with the monster.

"Lies," it hissed. "More lies..." The thunderous whispers made my skin prickle with goose bumps.

"What is it talking about!?" the king yelled. "And shut off that blasted siren!"

The ear-piercing alarm continued to shriek throughout the castle.

"Your Highness," I turned halfway toward him as I spoke, "the general captured a bloodmane earlier."

"Nonsense! I would have been told!" He sneered at the creature. "This beast lies. I would never harm your kind, but you must leave us be. I have already asked this of you. Why do you refuse to listen? The Elemental Guardian can defeat you, if you prompt her to fight."

It roared and then lunged again, kicking off its powerful hindquarters, coming at me like an arrowhead.

I dodged and rolled out of the way, but it quickly swerved and swiped an enormous paw my way, grazing my shoulder. Firagia came down onto all fours and charged at the creature, jabbing the quills along his head and neck into the bloodmane's ribs, which sent it toppling onto its side.

The castle siren finally silenced.

The bloodmane scrambled to its feet and hissed, then turned its face toward the ceiling and let out a loud, dual-tone howl, as if two different animals were calling out simultaneously. One was sharp and piercing and the other was dull and reverberated through the floor.

The bright yellow gaze met mine once more and the beast pawed at the carpet again, shredding it beneath massive claws. "Protect the false one and die," it growled.

"Who is the false one?" I asked, but then King Vincent shoved me away and stood in my place, stretching his arms out to the sides in front of me.

"No, Your Highness! Get away from it!"

"I do not know whose death you speak of, but it was not of my doing," the king said.

"It was the general!" I repeated, glancing helplessly at Firagia, as all control over the situation slipped through my grasp. I couldn't protect the king if he didn't want to be protected.

I dropped the Azure Phoenix to the floor and slid it across to him. "Take my sword!" I yelled.

King Vincent glanced down at it and shook his head, ignoring my offer.

What is wrong with him!?

"Take me in his place and be done with it!" he howled at the beast. "I have been a loyal subject. Respect my decision to grant my son the throne."

"That is not your decision," the bloodmane snarled.

I didn't know what the king was trying to do, but he was in danger, and I had to do something. Fast!

With few choices left, I forcefully pushed both arms forward and lit a line of fire across the throne room floor, separating the king from the bloodmane with a wall of flame that quickly grew, rising high above them both. I could still see the beast's silhouette as it paced angrily on the other side of the wall, the shimmer of its armor peeking through cascading gold.

Surely the thing couldn't vault over a wall of scorching fire.

King Vincent approached the barrier and I warned him to stay back or risk being burned. I couldn't choose which part of the wall would singe flesh, only that the entirety of it be fueled by violent heat.

The bloodmane neared the towering line of fire and snarled, running along it to check for openings, though it found none. Then it turned, lowered its head, and dashed across the room. It pounced and hoisted itself up the stone wall, catching on paintings and tapestries, tearing them down as it climbed toward the stained glass windows in the ceiling. It clawed and dug long, black, grappling hook-like talons into mortar joints between stones, but slipped every few feet and had to try again.

"Let it go!" I screamed at the guards behind us. "Open the main entrance so it can leave before it destroys everything!"

The king affirmed my commands so the guards would listen. We watched anxiously as the beast continued to scale the walls and destroy nearly every piece of art surrounding us. Portraits of kings and queens crashed to the floor, their faces transformed into tattered canvases and paint. Threads from priceless tapestries dangled between cracks in thousand-year-old stone.

"The gate is open!" a guard shouted from behind us.

I vaguely remembered how we'd entered the castle upon our arrival, so I recalled enough to know how to direct the creature back out into the grounds.

Firagia flew up above us and dive-bombed the bloodmane, sending it tumbling to the floor in a fury. Then I moved closer and pushed the raging wall of flames toward it, bending the line of fire into a half circle so small, it encroached upon the animal and forced it out into the main hall. It scurried off in a panic and then veered off in another direction before it reached the castle entryway.

"Where is it going!?" I scooped up the Azure Phoenix off the floor and snapped it to my back, then ran after the beast. I couldn't keep up, so Firagia took to the air. He followed until he came upon a massive hole in the floor, into which the bloodmane dove like a mole and vanished from sight.

"*Should I go after it?*" Firagia asked.

"*No.*"

"*Very well.*" He returned and followed me back into the throne room where he landed nearby.

We surveyed the mess; so many treasured heirlooms and artifacts torn to shreds and strewn across the floor.

"A dragon!?" King Vincent said, approaching us slowly and looking Firagia up and down. "You did not tell me you had a dragon!" He walked toward him and narrowed his eyes as he studied him closely, grazing over his iridescent scales and following the line of sharp quills trailing from his tail to the tip of his snout.

Firagia's wings extinguished and the king gasped.

"Forgive me, Your Highness," Firagia said.

"It speaks!?" He stepped back.

"He's not to be feared," I said, moving toward my scaly friend to pat his shoulder. "He is my Spirit Guardian. We work together."

"He is magnificent," King Vincent added, gathering the courage to approach us again.

"Thank you for your kind words, My Lord." Firagia bowed deeply. "Firagia of Alyssia, at your service."

"Your dialect." The king cocked his head. "It is odd."

I noticed Firagia's inflections differed slightly from others in the castle, but hadn't thought anything of it.

"I was born in the ancient times of Camelot and the dark king, Arthur," Firagia replied. "As you may have heard, the legends speak the truth about the fall of the dragon race, and I am the last of my kind."

"That would explain your rather ancient lilt. It is dignified, nonetheless." The king tipped his head toward Firagia. "Thank you for your assistance with that beast. You are a brave serpent, indeed."

"I prefer dragon, Your Highness," Firagia spoke up. "Please. I am no reptile."

"Then, you are a brave dragon," the king corrected himself.

"Your Highness," I interrupted. "We must speak immediately about this issue. The bloodmane tried to say something to you and you—"

"We are done here," the king raised a flattened hand and his guards swooped in and came between us.

"No! I need to talk to you!"

Firagia's wings ignited again and he growled at the men marching toward me.

"Stand down, Firagia," I commanded.

"But you must get answers!" he said.

"And I will get them," I replied in a hushed tone. "Return to me."

He reached out to touch my arm, where the bloodmane had struck me, and flinched as he drew my wound away, absorbing it into his own body. A line of torn flesh opened on his shoulder.

"Thank you," I whispered.

He bowed his head, then faded into a haze of scarlet light and drifted back into my necklace.

I was then forced out of the throne room by a handful of guards and dumped back into the other hall that led to my room and also split off toward the south wing.

"Stop!" a voice boomed from the distance—a familiar voice.

"Prince Jacksiun!?" One of the guards approached him. "What are you doing back? You were supposed to stay under the council's protection until it was deemed safe for you to leave."

"I will not be told what to do," he said, sneering. "Release the admiral, at once!"

Everyone distanced themselves as Jacksiun came closer.

"Are you hurt?" he asked.

"No."

He pointed at the tears in my sleeve and grimaced. "Perhaps our definition of injury differs."

"It's nothing. I'll be fine. Firagia healed it." I looked up at him and took a deep breath. "Prince Jacksiun, we must speak to your father about what's happening. There are... things you need to know. He's hiding something from us."

"I know," he whispered. "I know something is amiss here. I have already inquired about the sword, and yet he refuses to allow me to study it. Next, a beast breaks into my castle and—"

"They're after you," I blurted.

He froze up. "Wh-what do you mean?"

"I think the bloodmanes are after you because, well..."

"What, Valhara? What is it?"

"According to Chamberlain Grennings, the bloodmanes are supposed to be some kind of protective army meant to guard Rayvenstar Castle and its kings. He told me that, in exchange for that power and protection in battle, the bloodmanes are allowed to choose who assumes the throne."

"So they have started a war with my kingdom because," he paused and his brow furrowed deeply, "they do not want *me* to become king!? What did I do to bring them to this decision?"

"It's not what you did. It's *who* you are."

"Who I am? I am Prince Jacksiun Rayvenstar of Alyssia. The crown prince of the Rayvenstar throne and I—"

"I know who you are," I cut him off. "I am not the one questioning your birthright. Chamberlain Grennings told me your mother may be a descendant of King Arthur Pendragon, and he believes this is what has upset the balance and brought the wrath of the bloodmanes down upon this castle."

"A Pendragon!? That is not possible. They were eradicated

from Alyssia centuries ago by King Westin."

"Westin is the same king whose queen cursed him with an enchanted cape decorated with the scale of a bloodmane."

"The Cape of the Old King," Jacksiun uttered, his voice fading off.

"You've seen it!?" I perked up. "Where is it? Our only chance at stopping the beasts may be to destroy the origin of the curse."

"Yes, I have seen it, but only a glimpse—when I was very little. It was encased in glass and locked away in a safe place within the castle, but I was never told where. I cannot tell you where to find it if I do not know where it is."

"But you've seen it? You're sure?"

"Only as sure as a brief and wavering childhood memory."

"Then I'll do my best to find it, or at least find where it's been hidden."

"I will ask around and see if I can get a castle pig to squeal. Everyone has been keeping me in the dark for too long. That ends now."

"We'll figure something out, Jacksiun," I said, looking up at him confidently. "I won't let my best friend get hurt."

"And I will not let my people lie to me any longer." He huffed a heavy sigh. "Did you see that creature? How big it was? Did you see how it got inside and how quickly it destroyed the reinforced doors?"

"Yes, I—"

"But you were able to fend it off with your fire, right? Did you kill it?"

"No. I didn't know how to, and the king seems hesitant

to put them to death because he believes the curse protects the castle. And…" The heart-wrenching memory of the small bloodmane's violent execution in the observation cavern made me flinch. "The general already killed one of them. I think that's why they attacked again tonight, to avenge that one's death."

"How do you know all this?" Jacksiun asked, cocking an eyebrow. "How do you know what these *monsters* are thinking?"

"Because they spoke to me."

"Spoke to you!?" His eyes widened.

"They told me that if I supported you, I, too, would become their enemy. I think I'm in danger now, as well, but that's a consequence I'll deal with."

"So they want you? No." He growled and looked away. "I will not let them come for you, too. I asked for your help. Regardless of how deceptively my father may have demanded you here, I *asked* for your help, and you came of your own accord."

"I did, but there's much more going on here than I had originally thought. How do we fight a creature your father doesn't want to kill, even though it *does* want to kill us? How is it possible to cage an entire pack of those dangerous creatures? You read that documentation from the scientist and his lab's experiments on resurrecting the bloodmane years ago. The one they created destroyed everything and killed dozens of people. They can't be stopped easily, and they certainly can't be caged for long."

"Then we will not cage them," Jacksiun hissed, his tone shaping into something dark and vengeful—a little frightening to my ears, in fact, because it was unlike him.

"Then what?"

"If those," he sucked a breath through his clenched teeth, "*things* are going to say I am not the rightful king because of a ridiculous rumor that my mother carries Pendragon blood in her veins, then they will face their demise with the same weapon the king they despise wielded in battle."

"Do you mean—"

"Excalibur."

Words wouldn't come to my lips for several moments. My heart thumped and a lump formed in my throat.

"H-how?" The word barely escaped my quivering lip.

"I am going to retrieve it, whether my father wants me to or not. That sword may very well be the key to putting an end to this war. I would rather die fighting than surrender to those accursed beasts. Somehow, I will claim that sword, and I will stand against them in the sacred ruins of my ancestors, which they have shamefully defiled to make their den. They will pay for their sins, and their blood will stain the ground of the tombs they have desecrated." He looked me in the eye, a spark of determination and fury glistening amidst bright blue. "Will you help me free Excalibur?"

"I will," I replied with a nod. "Anything for the heir of the Rayvenstar throne."

Jacksiun rolled his shoulders back and stood a little taller, a bittersweet smile twisting his lips. "You are a true friend, Valhara," he said. "Thank you for your faith in me."

The castle was in utter disarray after the attack, with staff and military personnel frantic in the halls. I made my way to the south wing, where Mattheia and my team were housed, only to find the commander enraged.

"Where have you been!?" he asked in a low, gruff voice; a group of palace guards congregated nearby. "What happened, and why did they lock us in our rooms? What kind of place locks people in during an emergency!?" His voice trembled with anger and fear. "I'm about 30 seconds away from calling Captain Lansfora and demanding permission to abandon this mission."

"Calm down," I replied. "I'll explain."

"Please, do it quickly." He took a deep breath. "I'm getting a little tired of how they've been treating us."

"I know, and I am, too. Prince Jacksiun understands what's going on, but... there's a lot more here than you realize." I pointed toward his room. "Can we talk privately? I don't think I should be discussing this with you where others might hear."

"Sure, if they don't lock us *both* in this time," he said with a scowl.

"If they do," I said, lifting a hand surrounded by glowing fire, "I have a way of getting out." I smirked. "They're going to have to fix my door now."

He scoffed. "That's what they get for trying to hold back the Elemental Guardian. Wish I could say the same." He shrugged.

We returned to his room and he commanded the door to open. After passing the threshold and waiting for the door to close, I nudged him gently in the arm. "Would getting locked in a room together be the worst thing ever?" I smiled, hoping the joke would calm him down a little.

"No. It wouldn't." He sighed and went over to his desk, where he pulled out a chair for me. He sat on the edge of the bed and gestured for me to take the seat across from him. I sat beside him, instead.

"So... what do I need to know in order to *not* try to get this ridiculous mission called off immediately?" he asked, raising an eyebrow.

"Jacksiun's in trouble."

"Why?" His expression shifted to one of surprise and then to worry. "How?" He leaned forward, listening intently now.

"Because the bloodmanes are targeting him. It's hard to explain everything quickly, but you'll have to take my word on this."

"Can you tell me why you believe he's their target?"

"Well, I just witnessed one with a clear opportunity to attack the king, yet it chose not to. It went after me instead because it thought I was a supporter of the prince—which I am, of course, but..."

"Wait!? It went after you!? When was this?"

"When the alarm went off. It went off because a blood-mane had breached the castle and was trying to get into the throne room. I burned down my door and ran to help, but I was only able to scare the thing away with my fire."

"And while all this was happening, I was trapped in my room... unable to help at all." He growled beneath his breath and lowered his head.

"Mattheia." I rested a hand on his knee. "You wouldn't have been able to do anything in that room. It was a mad-house and that beast was enraged—climbing the walls and destroying everything in sight. I barely got away, myself. Firagia helped me."

"He couldn't help enough to prevent that," he said, raising a hand to point out the tear and bloodied fabric in my sleeve at my shoulder. The brass-colored diamond outline was fraying and metallic threads dangled down my arm.

"And you wouldn't have been able to, either." I gazed over at him sympathetically. "This is more complicated than any of us could have predicted, especially since the king doesn't want us to kill any of the beasts. It's not a matter of swooping in, scaring off a bunch of wild animals, and then swooping back to the Mainlands. These bloodmanes are in-telligent and they have the skills and ability to plot against us. We can't treat them like animals anymore. We have to start treating them like humans—very large and very strong humans."

Then it dawned on me... how very ignorant I was to have judged a threat so lightly and to have put several soldiers in harm's way by doing so.

Why wasn't I thinking more clearly?

What if someone had gotten hurt because of me?

Mattheia was a superb leader. Clearly, I was not.

"Are you okay, Valhara?" Mattheia asked, turning to face me while reaching up to cup my cheek with his hand.

"Yes." My eyes met his.

"You stopped talking."

"Did I make a mistake by bringing you and the others here?" I asked.

"Why would you say that?"

"Because I didn't properly assess the situation, and I'm worried I may be putting my team at risk. That I may be putting you in danger, too."

"I came because Captain Lansfora asked me to, and *you* came because your best friend, Prince Jacksiun, asked you to. So unless you're saying Jacksiun would deliberately put you in harm's way in order to save his own skin, then I don't think you've made a mistake. You've got what it takes to become a great leader, but it takes time and experience to learn how to view situations with your head and not just your heart." He smiled with encouragement. "I'm only angry because of how the king has been treating us—like caged animals. If you believe your friend's life is at stake, then I will do whatever I can to help him. I owe it to him." His hand slipped from my face, and he looked down at his lap and sighed. "I wouldn't have you in my life, if it weren't for him."

"I'd like to send the others away," I said, rolling my shoulders back.

"You would?" His face came back up. "Why?"

"Because I need to handle this on my own."

"Valhara." He shook his head. "The first thing you need to learn about being a leader is that you don't abandon your team. They came because it was their duty. Some of them even *wanted* to come. Private Quill, for example. She's very loyal to you and to Silver Diamond, and she's been working hard to prove that loyalty through example. Don't let her and the others down because things have gotten a little stickier than you'd anticipated. They'll understand."

"Do you think they will?" I cocked an eyebrow. "What if they get hurt or—"

"We are here to support *you*, Admiral." He looked me square in the eye, and I could tell by his determined gaze that he spoke honestly and earnestly for the entire crew.

"Thank you," I replied and stood from the bed. "Now there's something important I need to do."

"Let me help." He stood, too.

"Prince Jacksiun wants to steal Excalibur from the library."

"He wants to steal his own kingdom's sword? Why doesn't he just ask his father for it?"

"Because it's an heirloom from the Great War, and it seems like no one here is willing to allow him to lay a finger on it, no matter how much we inquire."

"They still don't know it's Excalibur, do they?"

215

"No, but they'll find out soon enough."

"How can I help?"

"Everyone is in a frenzy out there because of what happened earlier with the bloodmane, and I'm sure they are scurrying trying to find a way to cover up the hole the creature came from—"

"Hole?"

"It came up through the main hall through a tunnel it dug under the castle."

"Then why hasn't it gone after the prince if it can get inside so easily?"

"I don't know, but I don't think they were quite as desperate until the king's general murdered one of their kind."

Mattheia's face twisted with disgust. "So it's personal now?" He rolled his eyes and grunted with discontent. "Great."

"Yes. In more ways than one. Jacksiun's mother is also rumored to have Pendragon blood in her background, so there is a belief that the bloodmanes want to tear Jacksiun from the kingdom before he can become king and soil the Rayvenstar bloodline."

"That's absurd."

"I know, but all they care about is keeping a pure Rayvenstar on the throne, which was seized from the Pendragon reign almost a thousand years ago. It's complicated, but I hope that's enough information for you to go on. I have to get going." I turned away, but felt his fingers wrap tightly around my wrist.

"Valhara, you never said how I could help."

I turned back toward him and shrugged. "I'm sorry. I don't know right now. I need to go to the library with Jacksiun.

He said he'd meet me there soon. If we all go, it may cause alarm, and we don't need any more suspicion from the guards."

"Alright, but be safe."

"Actually, there is one thing you can do," I added. "Inform the rest of the crew that Jacksiun's safety is our main priority right now, and please ask them not to lose morale over the way things have been going. I understand what the problem is, and I'm doing my absolute best to rectify it and get my team acknowledged and taken care of properly."

"That's what a good leader would say," Mattheia said, smiling proudly. "You're better at this than you think."

I took in a deep breath and exhaled. "Only because you believe in me."

"Let me know when you get back, please."

"I will."

I left his room and made my way down the hall, winding through crowds of disgruntled, alarmed workers and guards, toward the library.

The usual guards who stood outside the main entryway were there, but appeared distressed. They were also focused intently on Prince Jacksiun, who stood nearby, quietly awaiting my arrival.

"Your Highness," I said, bowing.

He tipped his head slightly. "Thank you for coming."

He approached the archway and glared sternly at the guards. "Alert me if anyone comes looking for me, but do not let them into the library. I will not be long. The Elemental Guardian and I have important matters to discuss."

"Yes, Your Highness," they replied in tandem, bowing deeply.

I followed Jacksiun inside the library and noticed how the guards didn't give me a second glance, for once.

"How is the commander?" Jacksiun asked quietly, looking at me from the side.

"He's... angry."

"Rightfully so," he continued with a nod. "My father is not making this easy for any of you, and when the sirens sounded, all the doors were locked in an effort to 'keep guests safe,' but it only made things worse. How did you get out, by the way?" He turned his face toward me as we walked through the aisles of books.

"I burned a hole in the door," I said with a chuckle, wondering what the bill might be to repair the high-tech, royal equipment I'd ruined. "A *really big* hole."

Jacksiun laughed fairly heartily, but then cleared his throat and stopped himself.

"Oops?" I added.

Another brief snicker escaped his lips. "I will make sure it is taken care of. Do not fret." He shook his head with disbelief. "I do wish to see your powers in action someday."

"Your wish may come true soon, I'm afraid." We weaved our way through aisles laden with old books and rare armor and artifacts encased beneath glass and illuminated softly with special lights.

Then we came upon it—the mythical Excalibur. The overhead lighting shimmered off white metal and blue accents, making the crystal in the crossbars glisten hypnotically.

"How do you propose we rescue the sword from its glass prison?" Jacksiun asked, his determined blue eyes piercing mine.

"I'm not sure. I need to look more closely at the seams in the glass." I peered at the edges where the case came together, investigating the corners to see how the glass panels had been assembled.

"How hot can your fire become?" Jacksiun asked, looking at me through the other side of the case.

"I don't know, exactly. Fairly hot, I think."

"Hot enough to burn a hole in a metal composite door," he said matter-of-factly.

"I thought the door to my room was made of wood?" I peeked over at him from the other side of the case.

"No," he continued. "This castle was originally built from stone, but has since been reinforced with composite metal and titanium—aside from a few places, like where that bloodmane dug its way in from."

"Oh." Apparently, what I had destroyed should have posed more of a challenge than it had, meaning my fire could rise to temperatures hot enough to burn through metal.

I looked back at the entryway; the guards weren't paying attention to us. It came across as a little taboo to stare at royalty in Alyssia, and I was alright with that.

I peered up at the ceiling and then followed along the corners of the room. "Are there cameras in here?"

"No."

"Really?" I glanced at several artifacts around the room and then back at him. "But, I'd assume..."

"We don't have much trouble with thievery in Alyssia, especially in the library, since we allow so very few people to enter."

"Good. At least we don't need to worry about cameras."

I felt slightly relieved.

Only slightly.

"Do you think I do not know my own castle?" He raised an eyebrow. "That I would ask you to help me with an impossible task?"

"You haven't been home in eight years."

He looked me sternly in the eye. "And *nothing* has changed."

"Change is good sometimes," I muttered.

"Tell my father that," Jacksiun replied, our eyes meeting a moment before he returned his focus to the sword.

I pressed my flattened hand against the side of the cold, inch-thick glass. I didn't know exactly how hot my fire could get, but if it could burn through metal composite, it could probably melt glass.

"Are you sure about this? Your father won't get angry with us for stealing the sword, will he?"

"I do not steal from my own kingdom," Jacksiun said with a sneer. "These artifacts will be mine someday. I am only seizing it in advance, in an effort to make that future possible. The king refuses to acknowledge my opinions, so I will make him see that I am not a useless figurehead."

"I don't think he thinks that about you."

"Then why has he hidden so much of the truth from me?"

"I think he's trying to protect you."

"Then he is protecting me poorly." Jacksiun's voice became gruff again. "Ignorance solves nothing."

"I know that, but I'm sure things have changed since you left, even if those changes are not obvious." I pressed a hand engulfed in flame against the glass panel to test the strength of the case.

"If this legend about the bloodmanes is true," Jacksiun continued, "the king must have known about it for some time. Yet, he hid it from me, even though it could cost me my life."

My fingers began to sink into the glass. "Look," I said, raising my voice only slightly, so as to not draw attention. I didn't want the case to shatter by heating it too quickly, so I continued pressing against it and allowing the temperature to rise gradually. Then I concentrated on willing all the vagrant energy around us into my hand, focusing on making the circumference of my fingers as hot as I possibly could.

The glass began to soften beneath my touch, morphing into a bright, lava-like orange. Jacksiun's eyes widened and he held his breath. I kept pushing my hand against the glass until it broke through to the other side, the area around it changing from orange to yellow and then to white-hot, molten glass. It welled near the bottom of the pedestal the case sat upon. I then reached through the opening, grasped the sword by the grip, and slid it out, careful to avoid molten glass bubbling around the hole.

I struggled to grasp it with both hands; the old blade was sharp, and extremely heavy compared to the Azure Phoenix. A gorgeous broadsword, but one which would fatigue me quickly in battle. At least, until I grew accustomed to the extra weight.

"Now, how do we get this out of here without anyone noticing?" I asked. "We can't just walk out with it."

Jacksiun looked down at the melted pool of liquid glass

dripping down the side of the case. "I had not exactly thought that far ahead yet. I apologize. I suppose I thought you might have a plan."

"Nice to know, as I stand here holding a heavy sword near a pool of red-hot glass."

"Let me have it," he said, moving closer. I carefully gave it to him, relieved to be free of the hefty thing.

"I'm an Elemental Guardian, not a magician." I scrunched my lips to the side. "I'm beginning to wonder what's going to stop the guards from knowing I am the one who took this sword to begin with."

"I will protect you from their wrath, Valhara," Jacksiun said firmly, looking at me with great confidence in his expression. "I have always done my best to keep you out of harm's way, and I will continue to do so in my home."

"Thank you."

"*If I may...*" Firagia's voice echoed in my mind.

"Go on," I replied. Jacksiun furrowed his brow, but I flattened a hand toward him to stop him from speaking up while I listened.

"*I can get the sword out of the library for you.*"

"How?"

Jacksiun continued to stare at me as if I was on fire and hadn't noticed it.

"*Is there some place inside I may materialize safely?*" Firagia asked.

I looked down the lengthy hall of high-rise shelves and started to walk toward one of the aisles, gesturing for Jacksiun to follow. He came along, carefully holding the sword close to his body while facing away from the entryway to hide it from sight.

I came upon a long corridor of books that led to a dead end.

"This will do."

A flash of light shot from my amulet and the dragon manifested at the far end of the hall.

Jacksiun gasped faintly, and then bowed his head in shame. "I will become better acquainted with his entrances eventually. I promise."

"Do not worry, Prince," Firagia replied with a kind-hearted smile. "Now, may I have the sword?"

Jacksiun hesitated at first, but then passed Excalibur over to the dragon, who took hold of the hilt with a delicate, scaly hand. "Follow me," Firagia said, walking upright on his back legs toward the end of the aisle. As he approached the corner, he poked his head around.

"Wait here," he said and then scurried off into the main hall of the library.

I swallowed hard, worried he'd quickly be spotted by the guards because of his size, but I also knew I needed to trust him or he'd feel my doubt, and that would affect his confidence. Firagia was an ancient dragon who knew much more than I did.

A few moments later, I heard him in the distance. "Come," he said.

Jacksiun and I inched into the main room and looked around.

"Where did he...?" Jacksiun asked.

"I am here," the dragon spoke, this time much nearer.

I jerked my head up toward the direction of his voice

and gasped. A subtle, transparent vapor rippled in the air overhead, distorting the background slightly.

"You're... invisible?" I whispered, gazing at the ghostly haze.

"You have seen my fiery wings come and go," he continued. "The same power allows me to fade entirely into nothing more than a mirage."

"Should we go?" Jacksiun asked.

"Yes." I looked toward the wispy shape again. "Will you be okay?"

"Yes, Valhara. I will return the sword to you shortly, as soon as I believe it is safe to leave."

"Thank you."

"Where might I find you?" Firagia asked.

I looked to Jacksiun for the answer.

He thought on it, and then replied, "The solarium on the third floor balcony of the west wing. Do you think you can make it up there?"

"Yes," Firagia answered. "It should not be a problem at all. I will escape through one of the windows and make my way there."

Jacksiun and I exited the library, and I did my best to play off my guilt and discomfort in front of the guards, although they appeared to be paying no attention to us at all.

I didn't like hiding things... literally or figuratively.

The castle guards were still bustling about the halls in a panic, complaining of the monstrous disruption and discussing how they might find the right people at this hour to quickly repair the gaping hole in the main entrance hall. Jacksiun and I slipped by rather easily, and I was shocked we weren't stopped several times. I was certain the guards had not yet been alerted that Jacksiun was the bloodmanes' primary target.

We headed swiftly to the west wing, where I was directed to a tall, spiraling flight of stairs hidden off in a little corner of the hall. Jacksiun gestured for me to go first and followed behind me closely as we ascended the colossal stone steps.

The air became cooler as we neared the third floor, and each passing step brought me closer to the growing scent of pine—from the forest surrounding the castle.

"Allow me," he said as we neared a stately silver door with an intertwining pattern illuminated in thin lines of pulsating blue light. A round disc was set in the upper center of the door with an imprint of a hand in it, traced with pale purple light.

Jacksiun lifted his hand and pressed it to the panel. The door chimed subtly and the color began to shift to blue. There was a click and then the door slid open.

I'd never seen an identity scanner quite like it before.

He entered before me and we walked down a very short tunnel until we reached a vast, plant-filled solarium. I looked up through the glass and saw the stars beginning to peek through dusk, the moon barely visible in the distance overhead. But the glass was so clear, it was like looking through nothing. The only reason I could tell there were walls at all was because several small plants and pine trees had been pushed up against the corners and their branches folded slightly inwards, contained by near-invisible panels.

"How is it so clear?" I asked, running a finger along one of the cool-to-touch walls. "What kind of glass is this?"

"It is not glass," Jacksiun replied, walking toward the far end of the room to open a large door—presumably for Firagia—leading directly onto the castle roof. "It is crystal."

"Crystal!? How does one make walls out of crystal?"

"Very carefully," he said with a smirk.

I scowled.

"My apologies," he added. "Our craftsman discovered a way to melt down a variety of crystal shards, removing the impurities through a proprietary method that creates the crystal-clear panels you see here."

I recalled the unique, matte-black glass panels that made up the exterior of Silver Diamond Academy and began to wonder if the technology used may have been related in some way. I knew so very little about architecture.

A long beige sofa and round, wooden table were in the center of the solarium, along with a lovely little fountain off to the side. A dainty marble maiden poured water into a small pond via an oversized clamshell in her hands. Two colorful fish darted around the basin as I walked past.

"It's very pretty up here," I said, looking at the plants surrounding us. "Was this built for you?"

"No. My mother," Jacksiun replied, turning away from the door to walk back over to me. He sat down on a Victorian style loveseat and took a deep breath. "She does not use it as much as she used to, but it was built for her before I was born. Castle staff tend to the plants and fountain, but the queen does not come here much anymore." He reached up to gently prod a mauve clematis flower hanging from an overhead trellis.

"Why not?"

"I am afraid she missed me too much while I was away," he said, withdrawing from the flower. "She used to bring me up here each evening and teach me about the constellations. It was the first step of my journey into space—the catalyst, if you will." He glanced over at me as I sat across from him in a woven wicker chair with extremely comfortable cushions. "You were the second step."

I smiled. I had been the one who convinced him to come along to Celestial Galaxy, but now my career hung in the balance because of our friendship.

A twinge rippled through my mind as I felt my dragon approaching, so I twisted toward the open door and pointed to alert Jacksiun.

There was a thump against the floor.

"Hello, again," Firagia said, materializing from transparent distortions. He let his wings fade away and approached us with Excalibur cradled between his hands.

"Your Highness," he started, nearing Jacksiun, who had stood from the loveseat. "I feel great energy emanating from this sword—a life-force of some kind. While I do not sense darkness, there is something very strange here. Please examine Excalibur with great care." He lifted it up to Jacksiun and bowed his head.

The polished white and blue metal glittered when moonlight shone upon it, and the large gemstone in the crossbar sparkled with unbelievable brilliance.

Jacksiun examined the blade carefully, wrapping both hands around the grip and testing its weight with a few smooth strikes at the air. "She is perfect," he said, resting the tip of the blade against the floor and a hand on the pommel.

"But," he bent over to look into the large gemstone, "this stone…" He brushed his fingers over the surface. "What is it, exactly? It is like no other stone I have seen before."

The gem began to glow and pulsate, but Jacksiun held fast to the sword even as the metal hummed softly. Then he stiffened, his eyes growing wider as he stared up at nothing.

"What is it?" I asked, moving nearer and debating if I should try to take the sword away. "What do you see, Jacksiun?"

A wisp of white smoke drifted up from the glowing stone and floated in the air before us, growing larger and rounder. A fleck of white sparkles spun and glistened inside the shape, and then it became opaque, with some golden color coming through the white.

A large round head with intense, dark eyes.

Feathers formed and wings stretched out to the sides.

Then a screech and a whoosh as a large bird swooped over our heads, smashing into the glass and falling at our feet.

Jacksiun dropped Excalibur to the floor.

"Wait!" I shouted, but he'd approached the thing before I could stop him.

He knelt and reached both hands out toward the panicked owl.

"Are you hurt?" he asked the regal gold and white bird.

It tumbled around on the floor as it tried to get its bearings and, with a little help from Jacksiun, came to its feet. It chirped and clicked nervously, flapping about in place and glaring up at Jacksiun with intense focus.

"I am sorry," he said softly to the bird.

I gasped and shot a confused glance at Firagia, who was

standing quietly behind me, observing.

"Yes, yes, I know," he continued, speaking to the frightened barn owl as it fluffed its feathers, twitched its wings, and clicked its beak loudly. "They are made of crystal, not glass. Please, do not be angry. I did not mean for it to harm you."

Was it talking to him?

I watched the two of them for a bit longer. He introduced himself to it next, and then the bird responded with an assortment of strange noises.

The owl quieted down and Jacksiun lifted his forearm up above it. "Go ahead," he said. The owl flapped its wings and leapt off the ground, landing on his arm. He flinched as its talons locked onto him. He stood, but left the sword where it lay.

"Now can I ask what that was all about?" I spoke up.

He turned toward me. The owl looked Firagia and me over for several seconds, rotating its head in strange, almost unnatural ways.

"I take it you cannot hear her?" Jacksiun asked, nodding toward the bird.

"No, but it was entertaining watching you two have a conversation about whatever that was."

He chuckled. "She was complaining about the walls because she could not see them, even though she claims to have the immaculate ability to see all. Not composite crystal, apparently."

The owl let out a short clicking sound and hooted softly.

"My word!" Firagia chimed, pressing a hand onto my shoulder. "Do you know who that is?"

I shook my head.

"I believe that is King Arthur's Spirit," he said, nearing the bird. She shifted in place as if seeing his face close-up had made her uncomfortable, but then she cooed and stood straight, flexing her claws on Jacksiun's arm.

He cringed.

As if she could tell she was hurting him, the owl immediately thrust herself off his arm and landed on the back of the loveseat.

"King Arthur's Spirit?" I repeated. "But how?" I recalled that the evil king had slaughtered his precious Spirit Guardian, or so I had been told.

"I feel great amounts of energy within her," Firagia continued. "She did not die as we had all believed."

The owl turned to Jacksiun and chirped loudly.

"No," Jacksiun spoke up, approaching her and reaching out a hand to stroke the top of her head. She nestled down as if she liked the gesture and whirred softly. "She pretended to die, and then returned to the sword so the king would not know the truth."

She stretched out her wings, revealing rows of white feathers fringed with metallic gold as she bowed toward him.

"Her name is Noctua," Jacksiun said, lifting his hand from her. "And she is an astrologist."

"An astrologist owl?" I asked.

Noctua glared at me and squawked in my direction, making known her disapproval of my comment.

"I do not believe I need to translate that," Jacksiun noted with a grin.

"No." I tipped my head to her in apology. "How did you

summon her? I didn't think normal people could summon someone else's Spirit."

"They cannot," Jacksiun said, glancing at the owl. "She said it was because of my bloodline that she could connect with me and also because she felt the direness of our situation, which led her to choose to become visible again."

"Your *Pendragon* blood?"

Jacksiun nodded.

"The owl resided in the stone by choice," Firagia noted. "Without being bound to a Guardian, she may be free to come and go as she pleases."

"But *you* couldn't, could you?" I asked the dragon. "The amulet you were originally bound to—you couldn't just leave it, right?"

He drew back his head. "No. I suppose I could not. I was asleep inside, until we became one."

"If that is true," Jacksiun inquired toward Noctua, "how are you here now? I am no Elemental Guardian." His eyes darted to mine. "Am I?"

Firagia shook his head, easing my rising concern. "No. We would know that by now, I believe."

Noctua chattered quietly and then suddenly faded from sight, her body becoming completely transparent, aside from the twinkle of dozens of tiny white lights dotting her form as if it were a constellation.

"What happened to her!?" I asked.

"Are you okay?" Jacksiun asked, looking at the bedazzling outline of tiny, sparkling stars. He listened and then nodded, lifting his arm up for her to use as a perch once more.

"Come with me, Valhara," he said. "Bring the sword."

I lifted the heavy Excalibur from the floor and brought it alongside him as we passed the threshold leading to the rest of the rooftop and moved into open air.

Noctua turned opaque again.

"Without moonlight, or a Guardian host, she cannot sustain her physical form and... she fades," Jacksiun said solemnly. "The crystal walls must have blocked pure moonlight from touching her." He looked down at her. "I am very sorry, Noctua."

"What can we do for her?" I asked.

"I—"

Noctua fluttered anxiously as a buzzing resounded from Jacksiun's jacket pocket. He reached his hand in and removed his phone, which displayed several rows of scrolling messages.

"Ugh!" Jacksiun shook his head and clenched his teeth.

"What is it?" I leaned closer but couldn't read any of the texts.

"The king requests your presence." He squinted at his screen and scowled. "And... he is asking where I have gone off to."

He moved his arm to type a reply, but it was difficult with Noctua still perched there. She seemed to understand his predicament and swiftly scurried up his arm to sit on his shoulder, nestling down near his neck to tuck into as little space as possible and flexing her feet to grasp him less firmly. She pulled her wings in close until she appeared like a round ball of white and gold flecks balancing next to his head.

"Thank you," he uttered to her from the side of his mouth,

and went back to typing a reply on his phone.

"I will tell him where I am. Do you wish to see him tonight?"

I tilted my head. "Do I have a choice? He *is* the king."

"Yes," Jacksiun agreed, looking me in the eye. "But he is my father, and I will tell him no, on your behalf, if you do not wish to speak with him tonight."

"It's probably important, considering what happened earlier with the bloodmane breaking in."

"You may be right, but we all need our rest if we are to face more dangers tomorrow."

"Or tonight..."

"Very well." Jacksiun acknowledged my concerns with a nod. "I will tell him to expect you shortly."

"Thanks. Where should I meet him?"

Jacksiun stared at his phone, watching new messages scroll by before responding, "The North Hall."

I didn't know where that was, exactly, but I could assume it was... north, and somewhere near my living quarters. I took a deep breath and sighed, not looking forward to dealing with any of the king's demands at this hour, but knowing that I had to.

"Do you mind?" I said to Firagia, touching my amulet. "It will be safer for you here."

"Not a problem," he said with a sweet, dragon smile. He looked at Jacksiun and the owl and bowed his head. "Goodnight, Prince Jacksiun and Noctua." They both tipped their heads in response.

Firagia disappeared into a burst of fiery light which vanished into my necklace.

"I can go with you, if you like," Jacksiun said, turning to face me as I entered back into the solarium.

"Thank you for the offer, but I'll be fine."

"Good luck." He smiled with encouragement. "Be strong, and remember *you* are the Elemental Guardian, Valhara."

G ood evening, Admiral." Officer Cassian greeted me in the hall, near the entryway to the stairwell leading to the solarium.

"I thought your shift ended a few hours ago," I said.

"Yes, but the king personally requested I escort you to the North Hall."

"I'm sorry to trouble you, then."

"No need to apologize," he replied.

We walked down the hall and I watched as several workers passed carrying supplies and pushing carts filled with wood, stone, and a wet, clay-like material that shimmered with metallic particles.

"They are repairing the damage as quickly as possible," Cassian informed me, noticing how closely I'd been watching the traffic.

"How bad is it?"

Cassian sighed. "The damage is substantial and runs deep; it seems the beasts have been planning the attack for some time."

"Where does the tunnel lead?"

"We do not know yet. A drone has been sent in to determine the length and output area of the breach, and we are still waiting on the results. The tunnel appears to fork in multiple directions, meaning other areas of the castle could be at risk."

Concerns for Mattheia and my team began to grow, and the discomfort must have shown on my face because Cassian was quick to address it.

"Do not worry about your team. They did not find a tunnel branching toward the south wing. The beasts have concerned themselves more with striking the heart of our monarchy—the king and his son." He cleared his throat and bowed his head. "I apologize, but I am not able to say more on the subject."

"I understand," I replied.

Secrecy ran rampant in Rayvenstar Castle...

Upon arriving at the North Hall, Officer Cassian escorted me inside an unfamiliar room and then exited, per King Vincent's orders.

The king sat on a throne much smaller and less elaborate than his usual one. His elbow was propped on an armrest and he was leaning to the side, resting his chin on his fist, while a tired, depressed look tugged on his face.

"You wanted to see me, Your Highness," I said, approaching him slowly. He looked up.

"Those things struck us deeply, and there is no turning back from the imminent danger that lies ahead," he grumbled.

"I understand, but I still don't know how to stop them."

"It feared your fire," he said. "It fled because of what you did."

"Are you sure? It appeared panicked and—"

His expression twisted into a bitter one as he forced himself up from the throne. "Marry the prince!" he barked, glaring at me with piercing determination and seriousness.

I gasped.

"No!" I curled a fist and squeezed my fingers tightly. "Why would I do that, and most importantly, why would you even ask me to do such a thing!?"

"Surely you have known each other long enough to make it a successful union," he added. "Do not worry about the prince. I will make sure he obliges."

"You can't do that!" I sneered and shook my head. "You can't make me marry my friend simply because you are king. Besides, how will that remotely help in this situation?"

The king came closer and looked down his nose at me. His eyes narrowed and his lips wrinkled into a judgmental scowl.

"You are powerful," he growled. "You are the Elemental Guardian and you will be an asset at his side. The beast feared you, so you can keep them at bay and protect Prince Jacksiun by becoming his bride. Any woman would be a fool to turn down a proposal from the future king of Alyssia."

"I am no fool!" I hissed and grit my teeth. "This is ludicrous. You asked me—"

"I *commanded you!*"

I huffed angrily and swallowed hard, trying to calm myself long enough to form a careful reply. "You *asked* me to help save your kingdom. I never would have come had I known you would try to coerce me into doing something so ridiculous."

"Fine," the king said with a villainous grin. "Then I will *order* you to marry him."

"No." I curled both hands into fists and sensed fiery heat welling in my fingertips. "You cannot force me."

"How will you stop me?"

"I am already engaged!" I held up my left hand so he would see the ring.

"To whom, exactly!?" He lifted his chin and gazed at me as if he had assumed I was lying.

"Commander Draven of Silver Diamond."

"The young man in black and silver?" The king chuckled. "Is such an engagement not a conflict of interest in your academy? Or does your captain allow incompetence to thrive beneath his very nose?"

"Do not speak that way about my captain!" I raised my voice.

"You will watch your tone in my presence," he retorted. "Call off the engagement, then. You will marry my son, or else..."

Livid, I could no longer hold back the bright red and gold light emanating from my skin.

"Do you threaten me?" King Vincent asked.

"No. Never."

"Then stop that at once. This is your only warning."

I swallowed hard and tried to force the fire to dissipate. "I will not marry Prince Jacksiun. I will marry Commander Draven, as I have promised him and because I have free will to choose. I will *also* do my best to protect you and your son from those beasts."

"What if they leave and then return at a later date? What then?" the king asked, glaring.

My jaw tightened. I didn't know how to respond to that.

"General Cain explained to me how you murdered the beast they had captured," King Vincent continued.

"No! I didn't do anything to it, *they*—"

"It turned to ash!" the king roared. "How else would that have happened!?"

"I. Didn't. Kill it," I spoke through gritted teeth.

"And did you think I would not find out that you stole from me? That treasured artifact from our library has gone missing and you are the only person with access who has the ability to conjure fire and *melt glass*. How stupid do you think I am?"

"I didn't steal it. I helped Prince Jacksiun retrieve it because *you* wouldn't allow him to have it. He believes it might help in this fight and—"

"Lastly, you threaten me with your fire."

"No! You provoked it in me. I had no control over—"

"You have forgone your only means of absolution by refusing a marriage proposal to the prince. Elemental Guardian or not, you will not do as you please in my kingdom. If you break the law in Rayvenstar Castle, you will be punished."

He stretched out an arm toward me.

"Guards!"

The doors flung open and several members of the Royal Allegiance marched in.

"What are you going to do to me!?" I had the urge to reach for my sword but resisted.

"Seize her and take her to the cells."

Cells!?

"When she is ready to speak reasonably," the king added, crossing his arms, "I will see her again."

"*May I stop them!?*" Firagia asked in a panic.

"*No,*" I replied to him in my mind. "*I will handle it.*"

"*Very well, but be careful.*"

I lowered my hands to my sides and allowed two well-decorated soldiers to grasp my forearms firmly. Another tore the sword from my back and tossed it away, out of my reach. A fourth went up ahead and pulled a long tapestry to the side, revealing a rickety metal gate hidden behind.

It opened with an ear-splitting creak, and I flinched as the soldiers squeezed my arms and forced me to walk toward the door. It was dark beyond the entrance and I couldn't see much aside from a steep spiral of stone steps.

We passed several torches that ignited as we neared and I shivered as a gust of frigid air whooshed past, sending goose bumps up my arms. What lied at the very bottom of the lengthy flight of stairs answered the question I'd posed earlier: Alyssia *did* have a dungeon.

A dark, damp, primordial dungeon.

Were they really going to throw me into a cell beneath the castle!? How archaic was King Vincent!?

At the foot of the steps were an archway and a path forking in three directions. I was escorted down the center path, toward a large, rusty jail cell lined with sand and rocks. The bars were warped and slanted, leading me to wonder if the ceiling might collapse at any moment.

The door was unlocked and forced opened with some difficultly, and then I was shoved into the small, musty place and the door slammed behind me. One guard weaved a thick steel chain between the bars and locked it with a robust padlock that also probably wasn't from this century.

"You're making a mistake," I shouted at the guards as they turned to leave. "I stole nothing. That sword will be the prince's someday!"

"Silence!" one of the men snapped. "You will stay imprisoned here until you have had enough time to think about your actions. When you are ready to negotiate, tell him." He pointed at a guard standing outside my cell. "He will bring you to the king. Until then..." Three of them turned their backs in sequence and disappeared down the tunnel leading back toward the steps.

I huffed loudly and looked away from the gate, ignoring the one guard who had been left behind to observe me.

Melting the bars might have been possible, but what good would it do me to escape without having a plan?

Mattheia would be enraged, as soon he found out they'd put me in here. Jacksiun, too. Locking me away unjustly could start a war. What was King Vincent thinking? Had he completely lost his mind?

I crossed my arms, crouched down onto the floor, and sat cross-legged on the sand.

How dare he ask me to nullify my engagement to Mattheia!

What a terrible... terrible...

I took a deep breath and bit down.

There had to be some way out of this.

This was Jacksiun's kingdom and, even if his father had (apparently) gone crazy, I didn't want any of his people to be harmed.

"Are you certain you do not wish for me to get you out of here?" Firagia asked.

I shook my head. *"No. I'll find a way, or the others will come for me."*

I pressed my back against the bars and inhaled deeply.

They would come for me... Right?

Fatigue settled in as the night wore on, and I quickly tired of counting spiders and watching dancing shadows cast by the torchlight near the cell gate.

Several hours must have passed.

No one had come for me.

"How long am I to be down here?" I asked the guard.

He remained silent.

"Excuse me? I asked you how long I am supposed to be stuck down here in this dusty cage?"

No reply.

I flicked my fingertips and hurled a bolt of fire his way, singeing some hairs on the back of his neck. He yelped and patted his collar frantically.

Then he veered around and shot an angry glare my way. "What was that!?"

"Oh, so you *can* speak!"

He squinted.

"How long—"

"Until the king commands us to release you," he cut me off and turned away.

"You do know who I am, don't you?"

"You are the Elemental Guardian. There is no need to reiterate that with childish behavior." He rubbed the back of his neck and shook his head, grunting angrily.

"I'm sorry. Next time, please don't ignore me."

"*I could give him quite a scare,*" Firagia remarked snarkily.

I chuckled to myself and the guard looked over his shoulder at me.

"What are you laughing about?" he asked.

"Nothing." I quieted and rested my head back against the stone wall.

Spending a night... or two... or three... in a craggy old dungeon that smelled of dust and dead bugs was never on my bucket list.

My throat was dry and my eyes itched severely. I rolled onto my back and rubbed my face with my sandy hands, releasing grains unintentionally into my eyes. I sat up with a start, grimaced, and hunched over in pain. I'd forgotten where I was momentarily, and after several minutes of my watery eyes trying to expel foreign bodies of sand, I could focus again on my surroundings—the crooked metal bars of the ancient cell in the crazy king's dungeon.

My scalp itched. I pulled the tie from my pony tail and shook my head vigorously, forking my fingers through strands to loosen the sand. Then I pulled my hair back tightly and tied it up again.

The guard out front was a different man than I recalled seeing earlier. Not that I noted many details about the first one through the dim light and bustling it took to get me down here.

I came to my feet and brushed more sand from my slacks. "Any word on when I'll be released?" I asked.

He said nothing.

"Oh, great. The silent treatment again. Did the last guard tell you—"

"You will be notified of updates as they are made available to us," he replied flatly, not even turning to look at me.

"Thanks."

I stretched my arms up high over my head and scowled at the enormous, furry black spider dangling there to greet me. I stepped to the side to avoid being directly under it.

I wondered how Jacksiun had been faring with Excalibur and Noctua. Had his father already confiscated the sword from him?

What was Mattheia doing? He had to know something was wrong by now.

Maybe I should have just burned the bars down and stormed my way back up to the main floor to confront the king.

But that was dangerous.

My team did not have a menageric of dragons to protect them, and I doubted one free-spirited pegasus stood a chance.

"Can I get something to eat?"

The guard didn't turn. "Soon."

My stomach grumbled.

"What time is it?" I asked. It could have been the middle of the night, for all I knew.

"Is it morning? Can't you tell me that, at least?"

"It is morning."

I rolled my eyes and heaved a sigh.

How much longer would I be trapped?

I pressed my back to the bars and slid down to the floor, bringing my knees up to my chest and resting my head on my crossed arms. What else could I do?

The earth shook beneath me and I staggered to my feet, clasping onto the rusty cell bars until my knuckles went white.

"What's going on!?" I yelled.

The guard stood wide-eyed in front of my cell and his gaze darted from wall to wall. "I-I do not know!"

A crack split open in the floor and sand began sifting through, disappearing into black. I backed myself as far as I could go and flattened my body against the wall.

"Let me out! PLEASE!"

The guard reached into a pocket and fumbled to find the key to unlock the chains. Every passing second allowed the jagged line in the floor to grow wider and the hole deeper. If it gave way, I'd fall to my death!

Finally, a silver key came into the light. The guard struggled to remove the lock, and just as the key clicked and the shank lifted, the ground opened up and a massive, hairy arm reached out and grasped onto my leg. Long, glossy black claws tore into my flesh and I cried out in pain, losing my footing as the thing yanked me forward. I fell and hit my head. My vision spun.

Everything went completely black, and all manner of things came flying at my face. Things I couldn't see.

Things that *hurt*.

I squinted, trying to protect my face with my hands to avoid rocks and dirt that flew at me as I was furiously dragged straight down into the earth. Then my back hit the ground again and I was pulled through a long, dark passageway.

"Stop!" I tried to call out, but the word wouldn't escape my scratched lips.

A thunderous growl resonated from the beast, but I couldn't tell what it was. It held fast to my ankle, and the scuffs and scratches of being dragged so forcefully through the tunnel had begun to sting my entire body.

"Let me go!" I yelled, but dirt got in my mouth, threatening my airways and garbling the phrase. I summoned my fire as quickly as I could and sparks of golden light flickered at my fingertips. A whirlwind of yellow and orange shot out in front of me and hit the beast.

Suddenly, the thing dropped me and swerved around, snarling angrily. Firelight sparkled off iridescent green as the monster loomed over me now, its hooked face armor reflecting the flames. Bright yellow eyes glared and a huge mouth lined with long, sharp fangs gaped open. My body and heart pulsed so fervently that I could no longer control the fire and it fizzled into the atmosphere. A sickness plummeted into my stomach.

A shrill two-toned howl echoed from somewhere deep

within the cavern.

The creature snorted, howled back, and then reached for my leg once more, and began dragging me off again. My surroundings went completely black, and a swirl of dizziness overcame me.

Mold. Damp wood. Detritus.

I was lying on my stomach on the ground, barely able to flex my arms as I opened my eyes and attempted to turn over. It hurt to move my fingers. My entire body ached. Blackness surrounded me.

I wiped a tender spot on my face and felt something wet. Blood?

"W-where...?" I could hardly speak; trying made me cough hard on all the dirt and dust still in my throat.

Through excruciating pain, I lifted an open palm and willed a small flame to come so I could survey my surroundings. A giant room with a manmade floor. I lowered my hand. Carved stone? I squinted but couldn't see well; my head pounded and my vision had become distorted.

Pulsating pain throbbed through my ankle and up my calf. I bent over to touch the area and then pulled up a pant leg to look closer, still cupping the fire in my other hand. An inflamed circle of flesh with several swollen puncture marks. The skin felt raw and hot to touch.

I staggered to my feet with some degree of difficulty, grunting as intense pain made bearing weight on the wounded leg arduous. My gaze swept over my surroundings and I made every attempt to quiet anxious breaths.

Then my amulet began to glow.

"No," I said. "Firagia, wait. Please."

Until I knew exactly where I was, I didn't want him to join me.

"*Valhara... I must help.*"

"*No. Not yet,*" I replied silently, shaking my head in the darkness.

My labored breaths echoed from all sides.

I stumbled forward, narrowly avoiding walls with what I could see from my flame. The serrations in my leg stung, and sweat dripped from my forehead into my eyes. I shook it off and wiped my face with the back of my sleeve.

A fever? Did I have a fever? Were bloodmane claws venomous? Why did everything on my planet have to be venomous!?

Firelight wavered in my hands and my body became unbearably heavy, weighing on me until I fell to my knees again, the stone floor scratching my skin through my slacks.

Without permission, Firagia burst free of the amulet and flickered to life in front of me. My fire fading and my mind hazier, I could only hear him growling fiercely at something I could not see.

"Firagia!? What is it!?" I asked hoarsely, my throat dry and sore.

A shuffle shook the floor, and a violent clamor of beastly noises erupted. Then the room went dark again, my own energy too weak to sustain the light.

My surroundings lit and I found myself and Firagia in another round room illuminated by torches set in sconces around the perimeter. The architecture looked vaguely familiar, but I couldn't remember from where I'd recognized it. The squares of stone beneath my feet had each been carved with depictions of knights in full armor, surrounded by various swirls and spirals reminiscent of those in Rayvenstar Castle and the Goliath.

"Guuuarddddiannnn..." a deep, fierce voice spoke. I lifted my head and widened my eyes, though they stung immensely. Firagia arched his back like a cat and hissed toward the thing that spoke. I pushed up off the ground and stood, wobbling until Firagia helped to steady me.

"Who are you?" I asked, narrowing my eyes and blinking rapidly. There were still remnants of dust or sand in them, but I pushed the discomfort aside.

"This is *my* castle," it said. The voice—although powerful and with great presence—had a strange clumsiness to it, as if it were coming from a mouth not quite intended for speech. "Rayvenstar..."

"This is King Vincent's castle," I replied weakly and choked again on grit in my throat. "And it will soon be his son's."

"Silence!" A glimmer of virulent blue eyeshine shot by in the distance.

The ground vibrated.

I lifted a hand fearfully. Amber light emanated from my fingertips.

"That is not a wise decision," the voice continued. "Fire will not singe my armor."

Armor?

I wiped the corners of my eyes to sweep away tears I'd shed from all the debris, and then struggled to focus toward where the voice had manifested from. Firagia stood by my side, took me by the arm, and helped stabilize my approach.

A towering stone throne stood in the center of the room. Upon it, sat a bloodmane—substantially larger than the previous few I'd encountered—reclined in a very human-like pose. His front paws grasped onto the arm rests, each long black claw digging marks into the stone as if it were soft as clay.

I lifted my head to gaze upon the massive creature—its scales sparkled with blues, oranges, and greens, and a thin rim of jewel-encrusted silver circled its broad forehead—a crown.

"I am the first king," he said, leaning forward in his throne, his paws flexing. "All the bloodmanes who lie here are my blood: my son, grandson, and all the heirs born after. But you... you murdered my son. You took him from our order in cold blood, and for this, you will repent."

"I didn't have anything to do with that creature's death. General Cain and his staff set that cage alive with electricity. I was forced to watch that poor animal suf—"

"Edward was no animal!" the bloodmane roared, rising from his throne a few inches, looking as though he was debating charging after me for that comment.

He settled back down and took in a long breath. He

exhaled slowly and looked down his muzzle at me, the hooked, beak-like armor on his snout shifting color from blue to green in the firelight.

"The Queen's Order has protected this land for hundreds of years," he said.

"Protected it from what?"

"Not what." He lifted a paw and pointed a long, glossy-black talon my way. "Who."

"Then who?"

"False kings."

I'd heard that before. The bloodmane that had been captured by General Cain had said it to me.

"Who is this false king your kind speak of, and how does he encroach upon your reign?"

"The one who seeks the throne but who does not deserve it," he hissed. "The one with hair as dark as night and eyes as blue as the sky. The one whose features do not mirror the true king's. *He* will not seize our kingdom."

King Vincent didn't have blue eyes...

"Prince Jacksiun isn't trying to steal anything. His father is—"

"The prince deceives you," the bloodmane muttered through clenched fangs.

"How?" My legs weakened and I swayed uncontrollably where I stood. Firagia grasped my arm again to steady me. "And... ugh... What did you do to me?"

"We will destroy the false one and take back our throne. We will protect what is ours—what belongs here."

"I won't let you hurt him or his people anymore."

"You have no choice. You are poisoned and only we may

choose to relieve your suffering. The venom will quiet you, unless you agree to do our bidding and repent for the sin of murder you cast upon my son."

"I won't do anything for you!"

"Fight with us or die!" the monster roared, baring his teeth. The light reflected off his bright blue eyes and his bloody mane shook angrily.

I squeezed my hands into fists. Firagia pressed a hand onto my shoulder.

"*Wait, Valhara,*" he whispered.

"We stand with the prince," he said, knowing full well how I felt.

The bloodmane tilted his head. "The dragon speaks, does it? Who are you?" he asked.

"I am Firagia of Alyssia—a dragon born and raised on this great land. I fight for truth, and I fight by my Elemental Guardian's side to protect her beliefs and her life."

"Dragons are rare," the beast continued.

"I-I am aware of no others at this time," Firagia stammered. A sense of fear brewed inside him. I could feel it in my blood, and it did little to calm my own nerves.

"Then save your scales," the creature said. "Raise your talons against the false king."

"If you're referring to Crown Prince Jacksiun, then I must disagree," I retorted, clenching my fists, though my body was growing weaker by the minute. "He deserves to be king, regardless of who he is. He is my friend; I believe in him and his love for this country. Don't you want a compassionate king on the throne? Or will you continue to support King Vincent, whose suggestions as of late have been nothing but conceited and cruel?"

"The prince will come for you," the bloodmane snarled, grinning like a proud cat. The iridescent gleam of the scales down his forehead and face glittered as he nodded. "Then, we will dispose of him."

"You won't harm the prince. I'll stop you!"

"You cannot. We are strong."

"But not invincible. *Nothing* is invincible." I brought my hands together and conjured a red-hot fireball between them. They parted and the flame grew larger and larger until I could barely see over it as it swirled rapidly in front of me. "I will not fight you if you renounce your mission to kill the prince."

"Then... we... fight." The king slid off his throne and onto all fours, and skulked toward me with malice in his eyes. He picked up speed and started to charge.

I released the fire in his direction and then shielded my eyes as he ignited, his entire body quickly consumed by flames.

But instead of crying out in agony, the beast said nothing, and the cavern fell quiet. Watching the glowing bloodmane approach made a sickening feeling spiral through my stomach.

Firagia and I backed away as the monster, still ablaze, continued to draw nearer, slower than before, and his body raging with vivid, dancing waves of heated light. With each step, the fire shrank away and sloughed off the sides of the bloodmane like liquid ash, falling to the floor and shriveling into dying embers against the cold stone below his feet.

He appeared unaffected.

They were fireproof!? But the one in the throne room had—

"Our blessed armor protects us from trivial things," the king snarled.

If I couldn't use my fire against them, and I didn't have the Azure Phoenix, what could I do? Mattheia and the others might take hours... or even *days* to find me in the labyrinth of underground tunnels.

"Are you going to kill me?" I was shaking now, even though I tried to contain my fear. Firagia attempted to brace me, but worry made him tremble, too.

"In time..." the bloodmane replied. "If you refuse to side with the rightful king, you side with the enemy."

He lifted his jaws toward the ceiling and let out a whistle-like howl that echoed through the cavern. The same two-toned, disconcerting noise the previous ones had sounded.

Two smaller bloodmanes came up beside him and bowed deeply. He made a sound, resembling a hawk's call, and then they hurried over to me, snarling fiercely and creeping closer in hunched down positions low to the ground. Firagia pushed in front of me, came down onto all fours, and arched his back high again, igniting his wings until they burned so intensely, they grazed the ceiling of the cave and caught stray roots on fire along the walls.

"Leave her alone!" he roared.

"Stand down, dragon," the bloodmane king bellowed, "or you will, indeed, be the last of your kind."

"Why are you keeping her alive if your only desire is to kill her? What game are you playing?" he asked.

"The crown prince will come for her." The beast sneered.

"He will come, and then we will take his life."

There had to be some way to warn the others before they fell into this trap, but... how? Firagia was attached to his skin now, and teleporting through walls was not possible. They'd surely see him vanish and then they'd retaliate.

Then it came to me.

"Firagia!" I put out a hand to calm him. "I'll wait here. I won't resist them."

I looked into his confused, anxious eyes and communicated with him my true intentions.

"Pretend to go back into my amulet. Vanish into camouflage as you did in the library, but make it appear as though you are returning to me. When they stop watching us, you can escape to the surface and alert the others."

He tilted his head. Doubt brewed in his heart, but he did as I asked.

"Return to my amulet, Spirit," I said, loudly enough for the creatures to hear.

Firagia burst into a stream of light and appeared to go back into my necklace. In reality, he faded into the shadows and I could not see him anymore.

I felt the soft sensation of a hand on my back.

Now I had to find a way to vanquish these powerful creatures before they could murder my best friend. Electrocution wasn't an option at the moment, though it had proved fatal in the past.

Where were we? Under the castle? Somewhere else?

"I've sent my dragon away," I said. "I won't cause trouble for you. Please, don't hurt me."

I tried my best to be convincing and that wasn't difficult,

considering my voice continued to tremble. The ache in my calf grew vehement and I had to bite down to stop from cowering in pain in front of them.

"Follow them," the bloodmane king said, pointing a burly, furry arm out toward the two subordinate beasts that had lumbered closer to me and were staring me down with looming yellow-gold gazes.

The two lackeys turned somewhat grouchily and one of them flicked its long tail forward, indicating I should follow. Even the beast's tail had a row of shimmering scales trailing down toward the tuft of fur at the end. Their bodies were covered in a mostly short, bristly brown coat, but large grey tufts ran down the back of each leg, matching the roots of their ruddy manes. The smaller bloodmane's scales were greenish yellow, instead of the broader spectrum of greens, blues, and oranges of the king beast.

I picked up walking after the two creatures.

"I don't feel very well," I muttered; the venom—or whatever coursed through me—made it feel like I was walking on air, even though stones were below my boots. I was afraid I'd fall and hit my head.

Then Firagia's hand clasped onto my forearm firmly, and I felt him walking alongside me carefully. We followed the creatures out of the round throne room until the two beasts stopped abruptly, sat, and then pointed forward.

"Go..." one of them uttered, with a heavy sigh of discontent and a click of its tongue.

I stepped between them and inched forward until I came to a ledge overhanging a deep chasm with a pool of water at the bottom. The pool was aglow with eerie blue light.

"Go," the beast growled, more loudly this time.

"Okay! I don't want to fall and die!" But as I looked over the edge, it appeared the pool was quite deep. I had no choice but to jump, so I held my breath and leapt off the edge.

I hit down with a splash and sunk several feet below the water.

It was *much* deeper than I'd predicted.

I pushed up to the surface and gasped for breath. The place smelled like the ocean, but Rayvenstar Castle was nowhere near the shoreline. Saltwater must have been siphoned in through the ground from some other source.

I swam toward an alcove in the distance and climbed up onto slippery rocks. Sharp, crystalline edges dug into my skin and I flinched as I hoisted myself up, nicking my hands in the process.

I swiped water from my face and shook my head.

Great. Now my clothes were drenched. I unbuckled my leather scabbard and laid it on the rocks beside me so it could dry; I didn't want the hyper magnet to rust. Then I squeezed water from my pony tail and flung the wet hair back over my shoulder. I pulled off both boots, dumped out water, and set them nearby.

Specks of white and blue glittered off the wall of the cave. They must have been lined with a variety of crystals, just like the floor. Salt deposits, perhaps. The water shimmered with a strange glow I'd never seen before—some kind of bioluminescent algae or organisms. I brushed off my arms, trying to get rid of the residue illuminating my skin, but it wouldn't come off. Particles of light stuck to tiny hairs on my body and refused to budge.

"Agh!" I yelped from a tingling sensation shooting through me. My leg began to feel ice cold. I rolled up my pant leg and gasped. The wound was infested with glowing, moving specks. A creepy feeling came over me and I felt itchy and anxious, with the urge to violently wash my leg to remove the lights. But the only water around... was the pool.

The cold feeling subsided and I watched as swollen skin began to calm, the darkened patches of dried blood and torn tissue disappearing as the organisms appeared to heal my leg.

Once I realized what was happening, I dragged myself to the water's edge and dunked my leg in. The light began to separate from me and drift off, returning to the water, while leaving behind freshly regenerated skin.

I lifted a hand to stroke my fingers across my cut cheek. Nothing but smooth skin there, too.

"*Are you alright, Valhara?*" Firagia spoke to me from overhead. I looked up but couldn't see him from where I was.

"*Yes,*" I replied in my mind so as to not alert the blood-manes.

"*I am sorry I did not jump in after you, but I did not want to make a splash.*"

I chuckled a little.

"*Oh, I see. That is an expression,*" Firagia said with a quiet laugh.

"*I understood what you meant,*" I added. "*Do you know what's in the water?*"

"*No,*" he replied. "*I have never seen such an intriguing*

life form before. Do be careful. There is something very peculiar about the air here."

"It healed me."

"Oh? I would have done the same for you before you jumped down, but those beastly brutes did not leave me enough time. How did the water do it?"

"The microorganisms swarmed over me after I fell in, mended the wound, and then dispersed back into the water."

"I am not familiar with such creatures. Hmm... We may have to research them when we are back at the Mainlands," he suggested.

"If I make it out of here alive," I said in jest, but—

"Do not say such awful things, Valhara!" Firagia said. A plume of unsettling fear roiled in him against my comment. I felt foolish for making the tasteless joke.

"I'm sorry." I pulled my leg out of the water and returned to where I'd left my things.

"I will go get help," he said.

"Thank you."

It then became very quiet, aside from the soft trickle of water feeding the pond. All I could do was wait for help to come. It was possible I could get back up the ledge with Firagia's assistance, but the bloodmanes were surely nearby and I had no defense against them. Maybe Mattheia and the others wouldn't be able to do anything, either, but they would at least try. At least until I could come up with a better plan.

Out of one prison and into another.

I was trapped in a new place—one more beautiful than

the dusty, itchy sand pile of King Vincent's ancient dungeon—but it was getting cold in the cavern, and my body had started shaking from the water cooling on my skin.

I was technically joking when I'd said it to Firagia, but the thought really was beginning to creep into my mind. I didn't want to die here. Here, in this dark, damp cave full of mystical, microscopic organisms that could magically heal broken skin and... apparently cure bloodmane venom; I didn't feel dizzy or weak anymore.

Had the bloodmanes known this would happen? Is that why they threw me down here? To grant me an antidote since I agreed to come quietly?

There was nothing in the place but water and stone—no wood or scraps by which to make a fire. But I didn't need kindling.

I pressed my hands together and willed a spark of light to come to them. A small golden fleck appeared and grew slightly larger, more slowly than usual. It shifted color from yellow to red and then to a softer violet hue. Then the small flame crackled and burst into shards of light that spit outward, away from me, and fizzled against wet stone.

Why can't I conjure fire here? Is there no vagrant energy in this place?

"Ugh..." I grunted and shuddered again, the cold surging across my skin becoming unbearable.

Maybe I should have climbed back into the pool; perhaps the creatures had a cure for hypothermia.

Fear grew in me for the fates of my fiancé, best friend, and the rest of my crew. I *was* scared for their lives.

But now I was also scared for my own...

I wanted to explore the cavern, but I felt too cold and too tired to wander off, especially since help could arrive at any moment. I closed my eyes and sat cross-legged in silence in an attempt to conserve energy. Resting may have been an option, but in the condition I was in—shuddering, shaking, and soaked to the core—I didn't want to take a chance of putting myself at risk by letting down my guard.

Firagia shared with me glimpses of his journey back up to the surface. He struggled to find his way in the pitch darkness and had to stop and take long whiffs of air to catch wind of the direction he needed to go. There were moments when fear sprouted in his heart—which I felt—because he worried he might let me down.

For his sake and mine, I mustered the strength to remain focuscd and keep my morale up. Someone would come. Right?

According to King Vincent, *I* was supposed to be the

hero, but... who was going to save *me*? Mattheia didn't have magical powers. He had a pegasus now, but what good is a flying horse *underground*?

Jacksiun had claimed Excalibur (in a way), but what assistance could a fading magical owl offer me?

When I had come to the king's aid earlier when that other bloodmane had burst into the throne room, I cast a wall of fire and sent it away. When I tried it again, the bloodmane king simply walked straight through, claiming—and demonstrating—that fire could not singe his armor. Why did the first beast flee if it were not afraid?

"King Vincent," Firagia's thoughts eased into my head.

"Maybe, but—"

"No," he corrected. *"The king—I've found him."*

I assumed Firagia's sight and could now see through his eyes.

He'd made it out of the underground tunnels and stood before the king.

"You made it! Good. Have you told anyone? Have you found Mattheia?"

"I have not yet located the commander. I did not want your betrothed to feel the need to rush into an attempt to rescue you. Please do not be angry with me for hesitating to alert him first."

I knew exactly why he hadn't told Mattheia. It was Jacksiun the bloodmanes wanted, and Mattheia was powerless to change that.

"They will not harm me," the king said. "I will go and negotiate with them for my son's life."

"Certainly not!" Firagia snapped, lifting a flattened

hand toward the king. "As a loyal servant to the crown, I will not allow my king to put himself in danger. We must devise a plan first." He bowed deeply. "Your Highness."

"What other way is there, then? The bloodmanes will not stop until they can guarantee an heir of their choosing will sit on the throne after my passing. And I cannot sacrifice the lives of any more beasts or men. I have no other heirs."

"Then I will put an end to this," a frigid voice interrupted.

Firagia turned sharply toward the intruder; Jacksiun entered the room, Excalibur secured at his side in a chainmail scabbard I'd never seen him with before. He wore an elegant, fitted leather and chainmail jacket with stunning silver rivets along the center and decorative coils across the epaulets in vine-like patterns. A strip of bright platinum metal shimmered through the top of his high collar, likely a practical accent put there to prevent a fatal blow to the neck.

His thick leather gloves with fine mesh threading would stop sharp objects from piercing his hands, and on his forearm was a black leather bracer—possibly to accommodate Noctua's talons or for deflecting a strike. The circlet crown he wore was more prominent than the previous, making his stature obvious from a distance. The ensemble appeared to be sturdy and clearly tailored for battle.

"You cannot stop them," King Vincent said, approaching Jacksiun. Through Firagia's eyes, I saw anger and sadness in the king's expression. Hopelessness, even.

"*Tell him the truth,*" I said to Firagia, who then repeated my words to the king.

"Your Highness," he said quietly, "perhaps you should

tell the prince the truth about who he really is."

"*All of it*," I added firmly; Firagia relayed my words.

"I have heard enough secrets," Jacksiun muttered, turning away from his father and toward the dragon. "Take me to Valhara."

"Very well, Your Highness," Firagia replied with a bow.

"No!" The king grabbed Jacksiun by the arm.

Jacksiun veered toward him, a furious look in his eyes. "What now, Father?"

"I-I must tell you the truth. If you are to face the bloodmane king, you must know the truth," the king said, frowning.

"Bloodmane king?" Jacksiun scowled. "King of *what*, exactly?"

"Alyssia," his father added somberly. "King of Rayvenstar Castle. Ancestor of all Rayvenstar heirs... except you."

Those words made a chill rush up my spine.

Jacksiun swallowed hard and furrowed his brow. "What do you mean *except me*?"

"The admiral told me one of the bloodmanes used the words 'false king' to describe you. You are not a false king, but you are also not a blood heir of the Rayvenstar throne."

Jacksiun's breaths hastened. "But I am not the king, at all. *You* are."

"Not yet," the king added, looking away. "But you are eighteen and able to legally assume the throne, should something happen to me."

"You are in good health, Father. Why would—"

"Allow me to explain everything, please."

Jacksiun's jaw tightened and he pressed his lips thin. Then he gestured for his father to continue.

"King Westin Rayvenstar," King Vincent began, "the king who overthrew the Pendragon rule many decades ago, married a sorceress whose love for him was so great, it cursed the Rayvenstar bloodline. In an effort to protect her husband, their heir, and all future Rayvenstar kings, the sorceress gifted to King Westin a bloodmane-skin cape decorated with blood-soaked fur at the collar. It had been made from the last bloodmane in existence, upon its natural death. They called it the Queen's Blessing, and on the back—resting between the shoulder blades—she had sewn a scale with magical runes etched into it, representing protection and strength. The iridescent green scale was as hard as steel. King Westin wore the cloak always, and upon his death, he left it to his son, Prince Edward. The prince accepted the gift with great honor and joy in his heart, for he wished nothing more than to carry on his father's legacy, and to rule his kingdom with strength and knowledge." King Vincent paused and took a breath before continuing. Firagia's gaze remained locked on him.

"But the cape carried a great burden," he continued. "King Edward took a queen, and upon the birth of their first child, they found a curious mark upon the babe's back—a bright green scale—fastened firmly to the infant's supple skin, right between his shoulder blades."

Jacksiun lifted his chin slightly. "Like the one on the cape?"

"Yes. Only his grandmother's magic did more than bless the bloodmane cape, she cursed the Rayvenstar bloodline with her desire to protect us all. About a century ago, an army from the south attacked our kingdom, but they were destroyed before a solider in the king's army had a chance to raise a sword or arrow. Our ancestors, the Rayvenstar kings, were resurrected from their sleeping deaths, changed and revitalized with new forms and new hungers for battle. They had all been transformed into beasts that awaken only when Rayvenstar Castle is in need of protection."

"But why would they rise against us?" Jacksiun asked.

"They rise against *you*, Jacksiun." King Vincent's frown deepened as he lifted a hand to his son's shoulder. "You are the successor of my throne and I, in good faith, had all intentions of leaving this kingdom in your capable hands. But until I could find a way to destroy the Queen's Blessing, I made the difficult choice to drive you away for your own good. I knew you would keep your distance if I continued to be overtly strict. I did not expect you to return home so soon from the academy. You were supposed to go to Aquarius—where you would continue to be under my protection—but, instead—"

"I had to see Mother again," Jacksiun cut in. "I missed her dearly."

"And so you should have, as she is your blood mother." He shook his head and let his fingers slip from his son's shoulder. "While I am *not* your blood father."

Jacksiun's eyes widened.

Firagia and I gasped.

"Your biological father was a knight in the Royal Allegiance—a battalion leader and trusted friend. Upon my command, I unintentionally sent him to his death—a trap set by a group of savages bent on stealing cargo from a supply ship coming in from the northwest. I did not know they had plotted a way to ambush my soldiers, and against your father's judgment, advice, and concerns, I ordered them to progress, straight through the Red Canyons—straight into a valley from which he had no chance of escaping. I later came to know that his widow was with child—*you*. I harbored so much guilt and anger over what I had done to my friend that I offered to marry her and make her my queen, and to accept and raise her child as my own—the next heir to the Rayvenstar throne."

"But Mother has told me numerous times how much she loves you. If she were already married—" Jacksiun's reddened eyes glistened.

"She learned to, because of you. Because of how much you meant to me, regardless of the fact that you were not my descendant."

"Then, why no brothers or sisters if you were concerned about my lineage and the curse?"

"It would seem heirs of my own flesh and blood were not in the cards for me. Even so, it only would have made things difficult because of how much I would have prized you above any other children. Jacksiun, you became a part of me, and your mother and I grew close because of our shared affections for you."

"That explains why I look so much like her and... less like you," Jacksiun said, staring off at nothing as the revelation struck him.

"You should thank her for your handsome features, as they suit you well," the king added, patting him on the arm and smiling. "Your father was a strong, kind-hearted man, and I see much of him in you. I do not have the patience you have, but I do know you will make a good king."

"That is also why you were hesitant to kill the creatures," Jacksiun said softly. "They are not beasts; they are your ancestors, and that is why they rose from the old tombs."

It was then that I realized the blood Lieutenant Claire had found on the stones there was probably not blood of someone they'd killed or eaten, but likely their own—human blood pouring from the wounds of a bloodmane. It would also explain why there were not nearly as many fatalities as I'd been told there were originally. King Vincent was desperate for help but didn't know how to get it without killing the old kings...

So he drove me to my wit's end, and then told me to marry his son in hopes I could protect him somehow.

But it wasn't up to me anymore.

It was up to King Westin—the bloodmane king.

"Where is the cape?" Jacksiun asked. "I will destroy it!"

"Impossible," the king replied with a firm shake of his head.

"Why not!? It is the source of this nightmare."

"It was lost centuries ago."

"No!" Jacksiun hissed. "The one I saw when I was a child, it—"

"Is a replica created to deceive and frighten our enemies—a reminder of the Queen's Blessing." King Vincent clasped his hands together and turned to Firagia. "Please, help him. Help my son. You and the Guardian are strong. If you must destroy the old kings in order to save my son, then—"

"Valhara is in danger," Firagia said, looking the king square in the eye. "She is trapped in the underground labyrinth made by the creatures, taken from safety because of your ill decision to throw her into the castle dungeon."

"You threw Valhara into the dungeon!?" Jacksiun growled. "I-I did not even know we still used it. I-I do not even know where it is!"

"The entrance is in the main room of the North Hall," Firagia said, trying to be helpful.

"What century are we living in, Father!?" Jacksiun continued. "How could you?"

"I had no intention of harming her," he replied sheepishly, avoiding eye contact with his son and the dragon. "It was only in an attempt to coerce her into..." He froze up and his eyes darted around the room.

"Into *what,* Father?" Jacksiun's eyes narrowed.

The king's lips wrinkled with embarrassment. "Into marrying you."

"She is engaged!" Jacksiun scoffed and swerved away, clenching his hands into fists and driving them down to his sides. "Why would you demand she do such a thing? Why, Father?" He turned back and tilted his head down to glare at the king.

"Because she is strong and she may be able to keep the beasts at bay."

"No," Firagia interrupted.

"No?" The king turned to him. "B-but I saw that beast turn and flee after the Guardian cast the fire spell."

"It is my belief that the creature fled only because it did not want to harm you," Firagia informed him. "Valhara attempted to use her fire again after she had been taken prisoner by the bloodmanes, but... to no avail. The bloodmanes are immune to her magic."

Jacksiun huffed impatiently, rested a hand on the pommel of Excalibur, and said, "I am going to find her." He looked at Firagia. "You said the North Hall main room?"

The dragon nodded, and the prince began to walk off.

"I will send an army with you!" his father yelped, chasing after the prince, who was now marching off toward the dungeon entrance.

"No!" Jacksiun shouted over his shoulder. "I will go alone, and I will put an end to this mess... somehow." He shook his head angrily.

The king rushed after his son, and Firagia followed alongside him.

"You should trust the prince," he said. "If he is to be king someday, you must respect his decision to face the bloodmanes on his own."

King Vincent came to a halt and dropped his head down. "I understand," he uttered, defeated. "But I love him, and cannot imagine a world devoid of his presence."

"Then tell him that. It will give him strength and morale," Firagia suggested.

"Wait!" King Vincent shouted after Jacksiun, who was nearly at the end of the room now.

"What, Father?" He stopped and turned on his heel to face him.

"Be careful, my son. I love you and I believe in you, and I am sorry for all the times I made you think otherwise."

The frustration creasing Jacksiun's face softened and his mouth eased open in surprise.

"I..." He swallowed hard and rolled his shoulders back. "I appreciate the sentiment, Father. Now I must go rescue my friend."

"Should I inform Commander Draven of your—" Firagia began asking me.

"No. Please, don't. You know what happened last time. He will stop at nothing, and he will risk everything for me. I'm afraid the sorry reality is that he doesn't have the ability to fight this battle. If he comes down here and faces off against the bloodmanes, they might—"

"Very well," he replied, without letting me finish. He sensed the pain welling in my chest.

I wouldn't risk losing Mattheia again.

"I will go with him," Firagia said to King Vincent, bowing low. "I will do my best to protect the crown prince."

"Thank you," King Vincent said, smiling with appreciation for what seemed like the first time since my arrival.

Firagia trotted off after Jacksiun, and the two of them headed toward the dungeon steps.

I heaved a sigh and then stopped sharing Firagia's sight, returning my gaze to the dark, watery cave that imprisoned me. The cold continued to rattle my bones, and I rubbed my arms with my hands in a futile attempt to warm myself.

The cave walls must have been blocking out all vagrant energy, unlike the rest of Alyssia, which seemed saturated with it, considering how I'd demolished the barricades at the entrance of the old ruins without even trying.

My chest ached and my stomach felt sick. There was little I could do now but wait for the prince to find me.

A prince... having to rescue a damsel in distress—a situation I never thought I'd find myself entangled in.

How can you not recall where they have imprisoned her?" Jacksiun asked. The irritated tone of his voice caught my attention and Firagia invited me to share his sight once more.

"As you can see, Your Highness," Firagia replied, pushing a large patch of scraggly tree roots out of Jacksiun's path, "it is dark and there are many tunnels down here."

"How did you find your way back up?" the prince inquired.

"I could taste the air and feel the shift in scents and temperature wafting from some paths but not from others. Now, I cannot tell, as everything seems the same. Darkness. Dampness. Roots and stone. I cannot tell if we are going further down or further across. I am sorry. I am trying my best."

"What do we do? What if we cannot find her and those things decide to—"

A soft glow radiated from the crystal on Excalibur's crossbars; Jacksiun lowered his hand to it and paused.

"What is it?" Firagia asked, bending over to peek at the gemstone. "Is it Noctua? What is she saying?"

Jacksiun drew Excalibur from his scabbard and held it up in front of him, the sharp tip of the blade sparkling with reflections of firelight from Firagia's wings.

They started walking again down one of the dirt tunnels, and when they came to a split where two paths opened up ahead, he raised Excalibur out toward one of the tunnels, then turned and pointed it toward the other. A halo of white light engulfed the sword and it pulsed.

"Noctua will guide me," Jacksiun said, looking over his shoulder at Firagia while smiling with a new bud of confidence. "She is not only master of the stars, but she can also sense the direction and location of great magic."

The comment confused me. Did *I* possess "great magic?" Not in this old, wet cave, I didn't...

Noctua would prove indispensable at the Citrine Exploration Division, and she would be useful for assisting us in finding other ancient artifacts and weapons. But she was with Jacksiun now, and he deserved the prized artifact and Spirit—if his father would allow him to keep them.

Thinking on it now, my gun—the Platinum Galaxy— might have come in handy for fighting the bloodmanes, since it had electrified bullets, but I didn't want to be responsible for hurting or *killing* an old king.

My focus returned to them and I watched as they navigated the tunnels, each turn making Excalibur glisten or dim, depending upon the direction faced.

I stopped paying attention after a few moments, my soaked, bitterly cold clothes making me tremble. It was difficult to focus with all my muscles starting to ache and burn.

I hope Mattheia understands why I didn't want him to come...

He's going to be furious.

I hope I survive to apologize for it...

It wasn't that I didn't believe in his abilities to be a leader and make the right decisions. He didn't need to risk his life in a war that started because of my best friend's existence. The bloodmanes didn't care about me or anyone other than the prince, and while it seemed like they had been avoiding taking the lives of those uninvolved, they didn't hesitate to if those people got in the way.

My skin prickled with goose bumps and I gasped as an eerie feeling washed over me. Then I heard muffled voices and an echo of footsteps.

"Down there," I heard Firagia whisper. I stood and walked to the water's edge.

"Jacksiun? Firagia?" I called back to them.

"Where are you?" Jacksiun asked.

I couldn't see either of them from where I stood.

"I'm a few feet back—beneath the overhang. You won't be able to see me unless I jump into the water again and—"

"Absolutely not!" Firagia snapped, in a very paternal sort of way. "You are already soaked. Why have you not yet used your fire to warm yourself?"

"I tried, but I couldn't conjure anything in here. It's as if there's no vagrant energy inside this cave."

"Then what are the lights that healed you made of?" Firagia asked.

"I don't know, but please get me out of here before I get hypothermia. I'm so cold right now, I—"

"How?" I heard Jacksiun ask. "Should we look for some tree roots or..."

"No. I can help her," Firagia replied. "Stand back, Valhara."

With a whispery whooshing sound, Firagia sprung from the ledge above, pivoted in the air, and then glided down toward me. He landed on the damp rocks and smiled as he approached. "I am glad you are safe. Now, let me warm you before we go back up."

He forced more light into his wings until they grew larger and hotter, then he brought them in close around my body, nearly embracing me with fire. The water evaporated from my clothes and heat made my body ache less and feel stronger. I briskly brushed my arms with my hands until I felt completely dry—which happened quickly with Firagia's powerful wings wicking the moisture from me.

"Thank you." I scooped up my scabbard and strapped it over my shoulder and across my back.

"Valhara, I must now return to the amulet in order to get you safely back up to where the prince waits."

I nodded in understanding and he slowly began to fade into light. The light drifted through the air and entered the sunstone on my necklace, making it radiate vivid orange fire.

"Step away from the ledge, Jacksiun," I called out.

"I have," he shouted back, as softly as he could shout,

but the words still echoed all around.

"Okay, Firagia, do your thing."

A warm feeling coursed through my ribcage and then a shot of heat rippled up my spine. Wings of brilliant yellow and white fire burst from my back and I was catapulted off the ledge and out over the water so quickly, I lost my breath.

And in that one moment, I glanced down at the pool and at the majestic swirls of living blue and white light drifting through the water like fireflies in the night sky. My gaze lifted and I watched as a rocky cave wall covered in patches of otherworldly color and life passed by. Then the ledge of the overhang came into view, and I made eye contact with Jacksiun, who stared at me with eyes so wide, you'd have thought he'd seen a ghost.

Firelight from my wings reflected off the shimmering blue of his irises, and his mouth gaped open as I drifted back down until my feet were firmly on the ground. The wings dispersed.

"How..." he began, but then shook his head and chuckled. "Why am I even asking? You are an Elemental Guardian. You can probably do anything, right?"

"Not quite. You can thank Firagia for that." I pointed to my necklace.

"Well, thank you, Firagia," he said, leaning a little closer so he could gently tap a finger against the sunstone.

"Nice armor, by the way," I said, gesturing to his finely tailored, hardened leather and chainmail jacket and bracer. "I wouldn't mind having something like that. It looks easy to move in but also sturdy."

"It is. And... if we survive this—"

"Which we will."

"I could commission something like it for you."

The thought brought fleeting happiness with it. Then I remembered where we were and why we were down in a cold, dark cave in the depths of Alyssia.

I took a deep breath and exhaled. "Well, Your Highness, where to? How do we get out of here and what's your plan to deal with the bloodmanes?"

"We can get out with Noctua's help, but I need to do something about *them* first. They will not stop terrorizing my kingdom as long as I am alive, but I am going to do my best to negotiate another solution. Why not go up to the surface with Firagia and—"

"No."

His brow flinched. "No? Valhara, Mattheia is up there probably being driven out of his mind with worry for you. You have an opportunity to get out and return to him— *safely*. I did not come down here to save you, only to put you in danger again."

"You're my friend, Jacksiun." I looked him sternly in the eye. "I won't let you face them alone. We've been through a lot together and, right now, our friendship is being tested."

A frown pulled on his lips and he stared at me with sadness in his eyes. "I know, Valhara, but..."

"All those years in academy training, I managed to keep up with you. Even though you made exams look so easy, they were really difficult for me. But in the end, we both excelled because we studied together and worked hard." I smiled confidently. "I'm not going to leave you behind on this one, and I won't let this be the one test you fail."

Jacksiun's eyebrows flinched and he tried to stifle the look of discomfort creasing his face. He glanced down, took a breath, and then came back up to meet my gaze.

"Okay, but I will not disappoint the commander. I helped him save your life once; I certainly will not be responsible for tearing you away from him."

"Deal," I said jokingly.

"Do you know how you got here?" he asked, looking back through the pitch-black cave behind us.

"No. It was dark. They dragged me down from somewhere much higher. Some large room made of carved stone. A throne room of some kind. Manmade, I'm certain."

"Throne room?" Jacksiun deliberated on the thought for several moments and I waited silently. "If I recall correctly, the Tomb of the Old Kings was once used as a coronation chamber, but they stopped that ceremony centuries ago— back when they had decided to make the location of the temple a secret. There may be an old throne room in there, if that is where they are."

"Well, if the bloodmanes *are* the old kings, then it makes perfect sense," I said with a shrug.

"Noctua." He looked down at Excalibur—which had been sheathed earlier—and pressed his palm against the pommel. "Can you take us to the Tomb of the Old Kings?"

The crystal illuminated.

"She will," he said with a nod.

He slid the sword out and held it toward the tunnel up ahead.

I followed close behind him, and we used Excalibur's light to see where we were headed. Along the way, I tried numerous times to ignite flames in my palm, but they continued to fizzle out.

I gasped.

A gust of fresh air whipped through the tunnel, causing some dirt to crumble from the ceiling onto my head.

I took a breath and asked, "Do you smell that!?"

"Yes. We are getting closer to the surface."

I lifted my hands out in front of me and tried again to will the energy in the air to come.

A spark of red light formed in my hands, shifting from orange to purple and then to white—more vivid and colorful than my usual flame.

"Your fire has returned?" Jacksiun said, looking over his shoulder at me.

"Yes. Magic energy in Alyssia seems very strong, but down there, I could do nothing."

We came upon a new tunnel made of brick and stone. The glow of Excalibur faded and then Jacksiun sheathed the sword. He looked at me and said, "Noctua has informed me that we can find our way from here."

Judging by the manmade tunnel we now found ourselves in, I agreed.

A sloping path opened up that looked like a sandy trail leading into a darkened room. I lifted a hand and projected a few sparks of fire up ahead to light the way. We entered the large room and Jacksiun gasped. His eyes met the bloodmane's before mine did.

He reached for Excalibur, but the beast lunged at us. I pushed Jacksiun behind me even as he fought me off, and then I faced the bloodmane head-on.

"Move!" it roared at me, its vile, hot breath sweeping over my cheeks, making me grimace.

"No. The crown prince demands an audience with King Westin. You put me down there in order to draw the prince in, and here he is. I will not abandon him to your whims."

"Valhara, what are you—" Jacksiun reached for my wrist, but I forced him back by igniting my arm. The blaze startled the beast and it raised its head fearfully.

Perhaps only the king was immune?

"Very well..." The bloodmane seethed and growled, baring its long, sinister fangs in contempt. "Come." It turned and lumbered away, flicking its tail forward irritably.

"What are you doing, Valhara?" Jacksiun asked. "Do you have a plan?"

"My plan is to get you out of here—*alive*. That's my plan."

He muttered something to himself, but then spoke up. "How?"

"I don't know, but I'll think of something."

Our bloodmane escort twisted around to face us and hissed loudly, wrinkling his black lips up high. We'd neared another stone archway. It sat below it and stared angrily at us.

"What is it?" I asked.

"The king... You will bow," it slurred, flexing its massive talons threateningly.

As the beast shifted away from the threshold and off to the side, we came upon the room.

King Westin sat in his oversized throne, his back hunched

over and his bristly face resting on a clenched paw. There were almost a dozen smaller bloodmanes sitting around the room in various places, surrounding us with flickers of yellow eyeshine.

I bowed toward him. Jacksiun did not, and instead huffed angrily.

"I will not bow," he spoke through gritted teeth.

"Be respectful," I whispered.

"He does not respect *me*."

"Please, do as they say," I replied, my voice shaking from combined worry and frustration.

He narrowed his eyes and bowed briefly, but shallowly at the bloodmane king.

"Did you think you could escape?" King Westin growled.

"I had no intention of leaving here without dealing with you first," Jacksiun retorted.

"Dealing with me?" the bloodmane repeated scornfully. "And... with the sword of the corrupt king at your side, no less." He laughed. "How very appropriate. You are making this too easy."

Jacksiun lowered his hand to rest it on the pommel of Excalibur as he glared at the king.

"That sword belonged to a king, nonetheless," I cut in, before my friend could make a foolish move. "Perhaps Prince Jacksiun is not a Rayvenstar by blood, but he will be a good king. A *new* king. Regardless of the little Pendragon blood that flows through his veins, he is loyal to the Rayvenstar crown and always has been."

"How dare you speak to a king this way!?" The bloodmane looked off to the side, annoyed by my comments.

"The sword changes nothing. He will be executed, regardless. Take the Guardian!" He pointed a glossy black claw toward me. Two smaller bloodmanes came hulking closer, and Jacksiun began drawing his sword.

"No!" I screamed and fell to my knees before them. "Hear me out, Your Highness!"

"*What on earth, Valhara!?*" Firagia stirred violently in my mind.

"As the Elemental Guardian of fire," I began, trying to stabilize my voice, "chosen by Earth for whatever reasons she may have had, I can assure you that Crown Prince Jacksiun Rayvenstar—compassionate and wise beyond his years— will give this beautiful nation new life and new hope. It is my belief that his heirs will leave you no room for doubt or hatred, and no more thirst for war." I was trembling as I lifted a hand to swipe a tear from my eye and clear my throat. "Because a righteous and good man will be on the throne. I believe this with all my heart, and as the Elemental Guardian, you *must* at least consider my words. The prince did not ask for this unfairness. He has done nothing but uphold the honor and love of his family and the Rayvenstar name, and he knows no other way of life. Listen, please, Your Highness." I lowered my gaze to the ground.

"Get up," Jacksiun snarled, bending over to reach for my arm and grasp it firmly. "Please. You are better than this, Valhara. I will not stand idly by and watch you grovel."

I sniffled and swallowed hard. My gaze met King Westin's piercing blue eyes and then moved to meet Jacksiun's, whose brow quivered with sadness.

"I don't want my best friend to die," I said shakily,

returning my focus to the king. "It would be a grave injustice to me. And—if you truly care about this country—to the Rayvenstar crown."

King Westin combed his talons through the long furry beard on his square chin. "You speak with audacity, Guardian," he said, and then turned his head toward Jacksiun. "And what say you to that, Prince? Speak for yourself. You seem eager to stand and fight, but your death will be the inevitable result of such foolishness. You must know this by now, seeing how the Guardian, herself, could not inflict harm upon me."

"But you do bleed," Jacksiun said firmly. "And you *can* die, just as your son, Edward, did."

King Westin thrust up from his throne and roared at the prince.

A breath caught in my throat and I staggered back in fear, while Jacksiun's feet were firmly planted on the ground and he did not even flinch.

King Westin tromped nearer on all fours, raising his head higher as he approached.

"You are as imprudent as the Guardian," he said with a low growl. "I could kill you instantly, if I wanted to."

"Yes, you could." Jacksiun lifted his chin defiantly. "But not without the possibility of a casualty or two," he added, glancing at the smaller bloodmanes that surrounded us. "As a king, you must protect your loyal servants any way you can; you are no king without them."

King Westin hissed and flared his nostrils, the sides of his lips crinkling upward in a snarl.

"True," he said gruffly. "But what will you sacrifice to protect your kingdom?" The monstrous beast loomed over

Jacksiun, squinting his electric blue eyes judgmentally.

Jacksiun took a step closer. "My life," he replied flatly.

I gasped.

"Really?" King Westin pulled his head back and scowled.

Jacksiun tugged one leather glove off, and then the other, and dropped them near his feet. "It is a simple solution," he continued, unfastening the scabbard from his waist and allowing Excalibur to tumble to the floor. "If you will not accept me as the future king of Alyssia, then I am of no use to this kingdom, and my existence will only endanger my people." He unclasped a row of small buckles along his leather bracer and slid it off his arm.

"My father has no other heir," he continued, "but if you find me so despicable, then let us end this now, so that my father and his people can go on living in peace." He knelt and loosened the ties on his jacket. He slid a thin strip of protective metal from the high collar, leaving his neck vulnerable, and set it on the ground beside his knees. "A blade cannot pass easily through this." He finished untying the laces which kept his armor taut and closed, slipped the chainmail and leather jacket down off his shoulders, and laid it out flat beside the other pieces. Underneath, he wore a white button-up shirt with the Rayvenstar crest embroidered on his back.

As the bloodmanes watched in confusion, he unbuttoned the shirt, removed it, and folded it into a tidy square, facing the illustration toward the ceiling. "I will not tarnish the royal seal," he whispered, sweeping a flattened hand across the fabric to smooth the wrinkles.

Still kneeling, he lifted both empty hands up, reached

slowly off to the side, and drew Excalibur from the scabbard. The bloodmanes began to growl, but King Westin raised a paw to silence them as he watched intently.

Jacksiun lifted the sword up with both hands, and offered it toward the king. "Take my life with the sword of my ancestors. Then sleep, knowing you will no longer be burdened by the eternal curse that forces you to protect this kingdom."

A burst of white light exploded from the gemstone on Excalibur, sending King Westin back a step. Noctua soared out of the light and landed at Jacksiun's side, hooting frantically and flapping her wings. A flurry of small, gold-laced feathers fluttered around her.

"Thank you, Noctua," Jacksiun said with a bittersweet smile of gratitude. "But there is nothing you can do. It is my life, and this is my choice to make. I will make sure you are cared for." He glanced at King Westin, who was staring at them, bewildered. "The Guardian will be allowed to live, in return for my life. Correct?"

King Westin nodded.

"Return to the sword if you wish not to watch," Jacksiun said to the owl. "I will think no less of you for it. I only wish we had more time to get to know each other."

Noctua cooed softly and butted her head against his thigh affectionately. My heart ached to see her painfully reaching out to him, though there was nothing she could do to change his mind.

"Jacksiun!" I called.

I'd try to stop him, too, even if in vain.

He turned his head and his dark, solemn gaze shook

me to the core.

"It is my decision," he reaffirmed.

He was serious, and there would be no changing his mind; his fierce gaze convinced me his intentions were sure as steel.

I held my breath and nodded in acknowledgement of his wishes. "I will take care of her for you," I said, though my quaking heartbeat made it difficult to speak.

He was right—it was his choice to make. The blood-manes would terrorize his kingdom forever; his sacrifice was for the mercy of his people.

King Westin reached out for Excalibur, grasped the grip tightly in his paw, and examined the blade.

"It is a fine sword," he whispered, turning it so torch-light bounced off its polished surface.

Noctua let out a shrill chirp.

I turned my face away and sucked in a sharp breath. My eyes welled with tears and I shuddered uncontrollably. I didn't want my best friend to die, and I couldn't stand there and watch them murder him in cold blood.

"The Guardian is not from Alyssia. How can you claim to be true to your own country and kingdom, when you have allegiances with those from others?" King Westin asked.

I turned my head back toward them and wiped my damp cheeks.

"My allegiances to my friends will not affect my royal duties," Jacksiun replied. "Friendships such as Valhara's have granted me strength and knowledge. They have helped me to understand the needs of my people and my father.

Without her, and others I have grown to know, I would not be who I am today. I would not have the wisdom to rule this great land. Allegiance to another does not make me weak; it gives me the will to carry on—to wisely rule my own lands with determination and pride, because the rest of the world is watching Alyssia and expects only greatness from our fair country."

"So these *associations* make you stronger?"

"Yes. I choose my alliances and my friends. Just as I have chosen not to fight you. Having Pendragon blood does not make me your enemy."

With his mouth partially ajar, and his bright fangs glistening, the king approached Jacksiun, lowered his head down, and looked him in the eye.

Jacksiun stiffened and straightened his posture, gazing back at the bloodmane king with unwavering courage.

With a thunderous thump, King Westin sat back on his hind legs and jerked his head toward some of the nearby bloodmanes. "Bring the cape," he snarled. He gently rested Excalibur down by his side.

Two bloodmanes trotted off out of the room and we waited in excruciating silence for them to return.

Shortly after they'd left, I turned my head to see them reenter the chamber. There was a long wooden dowel carried between them, their jaws clamped, one on each end. Draped over the rod was a sleek, brown cloak fringed with tufts of crimson fur around the collar. On the back, below the collar and between the shoulder blades, was a large metallic green scale etched with a runic symbol.

As they moved closer, the scale shimmered with green

and yellow, like that of an iridescent beetle.

More accurately, like that of a bloodmane.

"Bring it here," King Westin growled impatiently, curling his claws inward.

The two bloodmanes walked the cloak closer and then stood at attention, awaiting further instruction.

"Prince Jacksiun, you were embraced by King Vincent Rayvenstar as if you were his own flesh and blood," King Westin started, "and yet you are not of the Rayvenstar lineage. You do not carry the Queen's Blessing—the mark given to princes who came before you; unlike us, when you die, you will sleep forever. Upon the death of your father, the kings who serve the Rayvenstar bloodline will fade away, and those to come after you will be left unguarded. We are here only to serve the rightful king."

King Westin gestured for the others to bring the cloak one step closer. He reached for it and lifted it gingerly between his enormous hands. As gingerly as a three-thousand pound beast could with dexterous, human-like paws.

"This cape is what started it all. My queen made it for me, and it has protected our legacy for decades." He leaned closer. "Come to one knee, Prince." Jacksiun did as he was told and shifted his position to rest his arm on one knee. "If you wish to be the king of Rayvenstar Castle, will you accept the burden of eternal guardianship once your time as a mortal human passes?"

My eyes widened, and I struggled to remain as quiet as I could, covering my mouth to smother my anxious breaths.

"I will," Jacksiun replied with a confident nod. "I am willing to give my life for my people and my ancestors." He lowered his head.

The bloodmane cracked a sharp, toothy grin, and then he shook out the old cape and rested it on the prince's shoulders, tugging it forward so it laid flat down his back, falling just to his waist.

"Then so be it," King Westin said, releasing the cape onto Jacksiun's back.

Jacksiun let out a gruff, painful groan and crumpled over, clutching the ground as he flinched and grimaced.

I watched, fighting to keep myself where I stood, battling the urge to run to his side as he appeared to be in great agony.

But a few moments later, he took in a shuddering breath and wiped his forehead with the back of his bare arm, composing himself as quickly as he could. He grasped the cape as it began to slip down his back. There, between his shoulder blades and below the base of his neck, was a bright, iridescent green scale, the size of a fist, set flush against his skin, as if... it was part of him.

He pulled the cape back up over his shoulders and adjusted its fit, covering the scale before I could get a better look.

"Now, you are marked, and the Queen's Blessing will carry on in your bloodline," King Westin continued. "Stand, Crown Prince."

Jacksiun brushed his hands together to sweep off the dirt and took in a deep breath as he rose to his feet.

The surrounding bloodmanes, including King Westin, closed their eyes and bowed their heads low.

"We are at your service," King Westin said. "We will

rise to defend Rayvenstar Castle in times of need, and we look forward to fighting by your side, Prince Jacksiun. We await the company of your father when that time comes, and we know he will instill in you the courage, strength, and wisdom to become a great ruler." He paused and sniffed the air, his brow furrowing and his bright eyes narrowing.

King Westin turned and began walking off; all the bloodmanes followed him into an adjoining room. Jacksiun hurried after the pack. Noctua leapt into the air and swooped after him, landing on his shoulder. I followed behind them.

A subtle halo of moonlight peeked in from overhead— a skylight made from a shattered stone ceiling. The carved floor, featuring images of warriors in action, was very familiar, and as a row of large torches ignited around the perimeter of the room, I found myself inside the damaged mausoleum. Something cold and wet dripped onto my neck; I wrinkled my nose and cut a glance at the ceiling. A flurry of soft white particles tumbled down—snow.

But... it wasn't nearly cold enough.

King Westin looked up at the fluffy, white flakes and grinned. "It is time for us to sleep, Prince Jacksiun," he said, his gaze turning forlorn. "May you be blessed with a peaceful reign and wise heirs. If you should need us, we will rise to defend your castle. May that day never come."

King Westin sat beside Jacksiun and I stood nearby, watching as the various bloodmanes strode toward their designated tomb entrances. As they neared the entryways, the creatures turned transparent and ghostlike, fading away into the crypts, one by one, until all but King Westin had returned to their places of rest.

"Thank you," Jacksiun said, standing tall and adjusting the cape around his shoulders, knocking Noctua off balance. She clicked and repositioned her feet. "Sleep well, my kings." He bowed deeply.

King Westin approached his open crypt and peered inside, then he turned and sat promptly by the pile of rubble nearby, lifting his head high. "I will remain here as a reminder to those who come after you," he said with a surprisingly charming, beastly smirk.

The falling snow swept up around him—a mysterious breeze coming from nowhere—and covered his brown fur and red mane with solid white. The bloodmane's brilliant blue eyes glazed over with grey, and his entire body turned to stone.

I shivered and rubbed my arms. "It's so cold," I said, bringing a small plume of flame to life between my hands.

Jacksiun looked over at me and raised an eyebrow. "At least you have on a shirt."

"True." I laughed. "I guess that's not the Cape of Warming, is it?"

Noctua flapped her wings and hooted cheerfully.

"Yes. We are safe now," he said to her. "Thank you for trying to help."

She tucked her head down into her feathers and cooed happily as he scratched the side of her head with his fingertips.

I turned and took a step; a hard object clinked against the ground, pressing into the sole of my boot. I lifted my leg and spotted a metallic fragment on the ground.

"What's this?" The scale shard had iridescent hints of

blue, green, and orange—like King Westin's armor. My face lifted toward the statue of him; his smirk had been immortalized in stone.

"A gift from the king," Jacksiun answered, glancing down at the scale.

J acksiun gathered his things. With Firagia's help and some of the prince's ingenuity, we were able to safely ascend from the Tomb of the Old Kings and return to the castle.

Immediately upon our arrival, we were taken to a secure meeting room and made to wait for the king and others who had been alerted of our return.

King Vincent, several members of the Royal Allegiance, and Mattheia filtered into the room shortly after the notices had gone out.

"Why did you two go off on your own like that?" Mattheia asked with an unexpectedly bitter glare. "Why didn't Firagia come get me, or at least tell me what was happening? Why did I have to hear it from King Vincent after it was too late to help, and the prince had already left?"

"I'm sorry," I said, approaching him. "I didn't want you to get hurt."

"The safety of any situation is to be judged by the captain of the team, not—"

"This is *my* team," I corrected. "I made the decision to keep you out of this because I knew it wasn't safe for you, or *anyone* without magic. It was my evaluation, and if my poor judgment had gotten me killed, then…"

"You're alive," he said. The hardness of his expression softened. "I understand where you're coming from with your decision, but please don't keep secrets because you're afraid of the choices I'll make in a situation. That isn't being fair or considerate. I couldn't do anything, and thinking you didn't believe in me enough to come to me for help hurt."

"I hadn't *planned* on getting myself thrown into the dungeon, either," I replied with a scoff.

"Y-you were thrown in the dungeon!?" He shook his head. "That's not what they told me. They actually have a dungeon here?"

"Mattheia." I took one of his hands and gently squeezed his fingers. "I apologize for leaving you out of this. I will *try* not to be so stubborn in the future. Okay?"

He seemed relieved as he nodded.

"I may not be an Elemental Guardian," he replied, "or a prince with an enchanted sword previously owned by another Guardian, but I *will* be your husband someday." He reoriented his hand and brushed his thumb over my ring. "I will always try to make the best decisions when it comes to our safety. You don't need to make choices alone in order to protect me. I *know* my limitations. That doesn't mean I should be ignored or belittled for them."

"I'd never—"

"I know," he continued, smiling with compassion. "I'm just telling you how I feel. Don't feel bad anymore." He glanced over at Jacksiun, who was conversing with the king. "We should talk to them."

I agreed, and we made our way over to them.

"It suits you," King Vincent said to his son, looking over the bloodmane cloak draped across his shoulders. "I am overjoyed that the old kings have seen your potential and acknowledge you as the true crown prince. I do not know how I would have gone on, had you—"

"Thank you, Father," Jacksiun cut in. "I have wanted nothing more than to make you proud and to serve our country to the best of my abilities."

"And so you shall." He beamed. "But first, you should go onward with your life, pursue knowledge, love, and whatever else your heart desires. I will not hold you back from the life you wish to live." He turned toward me. "I only wish I had not burdened so many others with my fears. I apologize for my actions towards you and your team, Admiral Hawksford. I will see to it that your sword is returned to you promptly."

I bowed my head slightly. "I understand why you acted the way you did, and I made some poor choices myself, as well." I glanced at Mattheia and then back at King Vincent. "Let us move forward in life with open minds and a greater sense of the bonds that we have made here."

"I believe that is something we can *all* agree on," Jacksiun said. "Father, I have no idea where the future will take me, but I am happy you will allow me to walk some of the journey on my own."

"I will be here if you stumble," King Vincent replied. "For as long as I can be." He stretched out his arms and hugged Jacksiun.

Mattheia grasped my hand again. "You did the right thing by helping Prince Jacksiun," he said. "Things didn't go the way we had planned, but does it ever?" He smirked and shrugged.

I grinned.

"I am going to take my leave," said King Vincent, "and arrange to have the Tomb of the Old Kings restored at once." He turned toward me and Mattheia. "Please do not be in a hurry to depart. I understand Silver Diamond Academy wishes to have you back as soon as possible, but please know that you and your team are welcome to stay in the castle for as long as you wish. Good night." He made a shallow bow toward me and then exited the meeting room, leaving the rest of us to speak.

"I'm happy you and your father have reconciled, and that your kingdom will continue to be safe for years to come," I said to Jacksiun.

"Me, too," he replied. "I am relieved to know that his callousness toward me as a child was merely a side effect of his fears for my safety, and that the bloodmane threat is no longer a concern." He paused and furrowed his brow, looking past me as if he had suddenly thought of something. "Before I forget, may I borrow the scale shard that you found in the temple? I will return it before you leave. I promise."

"Sure." I reached into a pocket in my pants and rummaged for the metallic fragment. It was cold to touch and smooth as ice. "Here." I offered it out to him and he took it delicately between his fingers.

Amanda entered the room, her once perfect braids now frizzy and unkempt, and fatigue appearing as dark circles under her eyes. She spotted us and walked quickly to where we had congregated.

"Security is insane out there," she said grumpily, sweeping her hands down her uniform. "But, I understand why." She smiled at Jacksiun and threw open her arms. "Dragons! You're safe!" She plowed into him, ensnaring him with a hug. He stumbled back a step and then had to quickly adjust his crown so it wouldn't tumble off his head.

"Yes," Jacksiun replied, his arms coming in to embrace her. "We are *all* safe now." His voice trembled slightly, as if he'd been caught off-guard—which he had.

She nuzzled her face against his cloak and refused to release him for an awkwardly long moment. It made me laugh, though.

"Oh, my goodness, that is amazingly soft," she said as she reached up to fork her fingers through the fur around the collar of his cape. She'd finally released him. "What is that? Grumble puff?"

"Bloodmane," he replied with a proud smile.

She sucked in a sharp breath. "But they're so big and mean and... Oh, my. You must be so strong." Her cheeks turned bright red.

I was tempted to point out that he hadn't actually slain *anything* to acquire the cape, but thought it better to let him do the talking.

"It was a gift from a past king to a future one," he clarified.

"Oh." Amanda hung on his every word. "I was so worried about you. I'm happy you're safe," she said quietly, clutching him by the arm and gazing up into his eyes.

"Me, too." He smiled sweetly at her. "I did not want to let down any of the people I care about." Then he leaned over slightly and said to her in a hushed voice, "Although I am not bothered by it, it may be considered rude by others here to hug members of the royal family without permission."

There was a hint of sarcasm to his words, but I don't think she could tell.

"I'm so sorry!" Amanda pulled away and covered her face with her hands. "Please don't throw me in the dungeon for that. Or behead me." She looked up at him again. "You wouldn't do that, would you?" She grimaced. "Do you have a dungeon? Do they behead people here? I'm sorry, I—"

He pressed a hand to her shoulder and she froze.

"You will not be put in the dungeon," he said in a calming tone. "And, no, we do not behead people."

She smiled, relieved.

"Often," he added.

Amanda's smile went straight and then he quickly assured her he was only kidding.

She heaved a loud sigh of relief.

"Admiral Hawksford." Officer Cassian approached Mattheia and me after we exited the conference room.

"Hello, Officer." I acknowledged him and we stopped in

the hallway.

"I am relieved to know you and the prince are well," he said. "I have been told that everything has been settled and no more bloodmane attacks will occur. Is that correct?"

"Yes."

"Did you defeat them with your fire?" he asked, the tone of his voice rising with enthusiasm.

"No."

A look of disappointment washed across his face. "Oh?"

"The prince triumphed," I informed him, grinning proudly. "My powers were rather useless against them, but Prince Jacksiun is wise and brave, and he discovered a solution that will cease the bloodshed and bring long-term peace to Rayvenstar Castle."

"Brilliant! I always knew the prince was meant for greatness," Cassian said. "His wit is, most definitely, as sharp as his sword." He glanced at Mattheia and then back at me. "You must be exhausted after everything that has happened. I came to inform you that the door of your room has not yet been repaired. We are having a new insert for the frame cast as we speak, but composite metal takes about a day to cool before it can be installed. Would you like us to prepare another suite for you?"

My gaze met Mattheia's and he tipped his head.

"Do you need a moment to discuss this?" Cassian asked.

"No. I think... I'll stay with the commander tonight. If you could, please have my suitcase brought over."

"Very well. I will have someone deliver your things. If you need anything, please let me know and I will make sure you are taken care of."

"Thank you, Officer."

"Commander Draven?" His gaze shifted to meet Mattheia's. "Would you be interested in training tomorrow morning before you and the admiral return to the Mainlands? I would like to work with you and the buckskin." He looked over at me. "I believe the admiral is more than capable of continuing your fencing instruction, but I am unsure if Silver Diamond has an on-site horse trainer."

"Not yet," Mattheia said, brushing a hand through the back of his hair. "I suppose I'll have to look into that if this is going to be an on-going thing. 'Hey, Captain Lansfora, do you think it is within our budget to build a stable?'" He chuckled and Officer Cassian cracked a smile. "Anyway, yes. I would be interested in training tomorrow."

"I will see you after breakfast," Cassian said with a quick bow. "Thank you, again, for all you have done for Prince Jacksiun and his kingdom. Goodnight, Admiral. Goodnight, Commander."

He walked away.

Things were quieter on this side of the castle than on the other; the construction workers who were repairing damages caused by the bloodmane break-in were nowhere to be seen.

"So what exactly happened to you down there?" Mattheia asked, tracing a finger across my brow and down my hairline. "You look like you've been through a lot. Not to mention all the blood on your leg there, which you keep telling everyone is 'nothing to worry about.' I didn't want to embarrass you about it back there in the conference room, but I'd like to know what happened."

I vividly remembered all the blood that had oozed from the deep claw marks in my calf, and then I lifted a hand toward my cheek as I recalled the painful scratch mark I'd had there, too, before the mysterious water had healed me. It was all there, just hours before. Wasn't it? It was hazy now, and I could scarcely remember anything more about the miraculous, luminous pool of swirling blues and whites—like tiny star clusters dancing across faint ripples in the water.

"Can we walk?" I asked, gesturing in the direction of Mattheia's room.

"We can talk about it in the morning, if you'd prefer," he said softly, walking alongside me.

"I couldn't use my powers," I whispered.

"Why not?" He looked over at me and wrinkled his brow.

"I don't know, but I couldn't. I fell into a pool of water with some form of life in it—bioluminescent algae or microorganisms. They healed my wound, but I couldn't use my fire to warm myself when it became very cold underground in that strange cavern. Jacksiun showed up in time to get me out, and then Firagia used his wings to dry and warm me."

"Judging by the amount of blood on your pants, I'd say it was a fairly severe wound."

I pressed my lips thin, hesitating to reply; I didn't want him to get upset again.

"Hmm." Mattheia's expression twisted with intrigue. "Could we get a sample of those organisms to bring back to the academy for research? Those types of healing abilities would be invaluable."

"I don't want to go back down there," I said firmly.

"Why?"

"Ever since I learned how to use my fire, I've never been to a place where I couldn't conjure it. When we arrived here and investigated the entrance to the old ruins, the vagrant energy in the air was so abundant that I created something much more destructive than I'd anticipated. But down there in that cave with the healing lights, I couldn't even start a small fire to warm myself. I tried, and it fizzled out. So, either the entire cavern was devoid of vagrant energy, or those organisms were feeding off it, leaving none to spare." I looked over at him again. "What if cultivating such a thing could disrupt the energy of the world? What if that hole in the earth is the only thing stopping those organisms from draining everything?"

"Well, that's a morbid thought," Mattheia replied with a shrug. "I suppose we can nix that idea. I wouldn't want to be responsible for wiping out the world's supply of magical energy, and I also wouldn't want to put your powers at risk."

"It's a noble wish, though—to be able to provide near-instant healing to mortal wounds." I looked down at my boots and my gaze traced up the faded bloodstain in my slacks. "But that power might also be dangerous in the wrong hands. What kind of Elemental Guardian would I be without my fire?"

"You have a dragon," Mattheia said, pointing at my amulet.

"I do, but I think we can both agree we don't ever want to put him in harm's way on purpose again."

"Yes, we can definitely agree on that," he said, nodding. "Thank you, again, Firagia."

The sunstone shimmered and an aura of red light flashed

around it.

"He says he would do it again." I translated Firagia's thoughts into spoken words.

"And Prince Jacksiun?" Mattheia continued. We were nearly at his room. "Was he injured?"

"No, thankfully. But I am sure it took a great deal of his pride to do what he did, in order to appease the bloodmanes."

Mattheia's brow lifted. "What... did he do?"

The sight of my best friend, kneeling on the ground, weaponless and without armor to protect him, offering up his head to the bloodmane king, flashed into my mind and made my chest tighten.

"He offered his life, in return for peace."

Mattheia gasped sharply. "He was going to sacrifice himself!?"

"Shh."

He lowered his voice immediately. "Why?"

"Because the bloodmanes were not simply wild beasts, they were the souls of the old Rayvenstar kings, brought to life only to protect the lineage of this castle from being overthrown. Jacksiun's selflessness demonstrated how much he loved this country, and they decided to honor him as one of their own, instead of taking his life."

We turned to the door of Mattheia's room and he requested the door open.

It slid up, we walked inside, and then it closed behind us.

"I'm not sure I would have thought to do such a thing when confronted with danger of that magnitude," he said, frowning with uncertainty. "But declaring war against ghosts seems like a futile endeavor."

"Like Jacksiun, I know you, too, would have made the choice that was right for you," I assured him.

"For us," he said, taking my hand as he stepped closer. "I'd have made the right choice for *us*."

Mattheia left at the crack of dawn to meet Officer Cassian at the stables. I joined them, after a late start and early brunch; yesterday's events had left me drained. It didn't help that Mattheia had closed the shutters before he'd left in the morning, which prevented the sun from waking me.

By the time I'd reached the outdoor pasture, Mattheia and the pegasus appeared to be alone.

I waved to him as I approached and he came jogging over to me.

"Where's Officer Cassian?" I asked.

"He was called back to assist with more important things this morning, but not before we had a few hours to work with that guy." He pointed at the pegasus, who was galloping along the fence line as fast as his legs could carry him. Just as he neared a corner and appeared he might smash right into it, he pushed out his wings like rudders, veered off to the side, and continued running.

"He sure has a lot of energy," I commented, watching the animal race around, seemingly aimlessly.

"He thinks, well, he *knows* he's the fastest animal here, so he's flaunting it for you."

"For me? How sweet." I laughed.

"Do you want to pet him?"

"Can I?" I cocked an eyebrow. "Or will he try to charge me again?"

"I think he'll behave." He shrugged.

"You... think?"

A sharp whistle cut through the air and the pegasus came to an abrupt halt, jerking his head toward us. He snorted and trotted over.

"Whoa!" Mattheia raised his hands before the animal could get any closer to me. "Be good, okay? Calm down." He patted the pegasus on his neck and rubbed his mane briskly. The animal seemed to enjoy it and lowered his head.

"That means he's comfortable right now," Mattheia informed me. "When horses put their head down, it's a submissive gesture. Either that, or they're thinking about bucking at you." He patted him again. "But we've talked about that, haven't we?"

Had he already tried to kick him?

"You can come closer," Mattheia said in a low voice. "Slowly, though."

The pegasus pulled his head back up, flicking his mane and snorting at me.

"Are you sure?" I was becoming skeptical.

"Yes."

As the animal twitched nervously, Mattheia brushed a hand down his withers. "Calm down. Stop acting like you're scared."

Why was he talking to him like that? You can't *talk* a horse out of being scared, can you?

"Hi there, boy," I uttered. "How are you?" I held out a hand, but the pegasus stepped back.

"Okay. Change of plans," Mattheia said. "Stay where you are, but turn around."

"T-turn around? Why? What if he decides to ram into me or—"

"He won't. Just do it. You'll be fine."

"Okay." I paused and slowly turned my back to them. I didn't hear anything for a few moments and I was beginning to wonder if it was some kind of joke. "How long do I have to stand here?"

Before Mattheia could answer me, bristly hairs prickled the back of my neck and a steamy hot breath swept over my skin. I froze up; the pegasus was just behind me, sniffing my shoulder. I tried very hard not to flinch from the sensation of the massive creature pressing the bridge of his nose against my back.

"He's not going to bite, is he?"

"No." Mattheia came up beside me. "There you go, boy. She's okay. She's a friend."

"Can I turn around yet?"

"Do it slowly."

I did.

"Hi, again," I said, meeting gazes with the blue-eyed colt. He snorted lightly and then reached out to try to nibble the chain of my amulet. "Hey! Hey!" I backed away and it spooked him. "Sorry. You can't chew on that, though."

The pegasus took in a deep breath and sighed loudly, as if he were making a point to show me how disappointed he was.

I reached down and plucked a clump of lush grass from the ground. "So what's his name? And how did you find out what it was?" I asked, offering the grass out in an effort to entice the animal back over to me. He huffed and shook his head in defiance. "Tough crowd." I dropped the grass and brushed my hands together.

"I'll let *him* tell you." Mattheia walked off toward the fence line, ducked down, and reached through the wood slats for his sword.

"How?" I couldn't take my eyes off the horse out of fear he'd charge at me or do something else crazy. He had a strange look on his face. Like he was scheming.

"This sword," Mattheia began, sliding it from its scabbard as he returned, "allows me to hear things. I was working with Officer Cassian and inadvertently placed my hand at my side, touching the stone set in the crossbars." He gestured to the large yellow topaz.

I pressed against the stone with one finger; it was ice-cold.

"Tell her your name," Mattheia said.

A faint voice resonated in the back of my mind—not unlike Firagia's, but clumsier and very juvenile.

"Zandergale?" I repeated the name I'd just heard. The

pegasus whinnied excitedly and clomped his hooves against the grass.

"That's it!" Mattheia affirmed. "That's what he told me, too. Although I asked if I could shorten it and he seemed to be okay with that." He rubbed the bright golden fur on the pegasus' neck. "Right, Zander?"

"*Yes. Yes!*" the voice echoed through my mind. Zander nodded vigorously. "*Watch! I go fast!*" he said, and then stretched out his wings, pulled them in tightly to his sides, and shot off running across the field.

My fingers slipped off the gemstone.

"He's very talkative," Mattheia said, scratching the back of his neck and smiling awkwardly. "It might take some getting used to."

"Yes. He is. And he has a peculiar accent, too. I can't place it, though." I looked out across the vast pasture at the beautiful creature galloping off. Sunlight sparkled off his wings and he glittered like a gemstone being tossed into the sky. "He's beautiful. What are your plans with him?"

"Not a clue." Mattheia shrugged. "But I'd like to work with him more and see where we get. He's brave, and Silver Diamond is always looking for brave soldiers."

"Will he be okay there? Won't he miss his home?"

"I think, with the help of this sword, I can make him feel at home back at the academy," he continued. "From what I could tell when I spoke to him earlier, he doesn't really have a permanent place to stay. Pegasi are drifters, but he feels it's his responsibility to protect this sword, for some reason."

"Well, I don't want to keep him against his will." I brushed the stone again with the tip of my finger.

"*Run. Run. Run. I go fast. Like wind.*"

I tried to stifle a giggle but couldn't hold it in.

"He's going fast again, isn't he?" Mattheia asked.

I nodded.

"We're going to have to get used to that. It's his favorite." He started laughing. "And don't worry about us keeping him against his will. I told him he's free to leave if he really wants to, but he didn't want to go."

We both looked off at Zander, who had finally come to a standstill, and who was now munching happily on grass.

In the evening, after dinner, just as our plates were being cleared away, Jacksiun entered the banquet hall. Everyone stood at attention as he approached and we all bowed.

"Admiral," he started, walking down my side of the table. "My father and I would like your assistance with a matter of great significance."

"How may I help?"

"It pertains to the Tomb of the Old Kings and King Edward—Westin's son. We wish to give his remains a proper burial and to reseal his tomb. I believe it is the least we can do to honor his sacrifice. Would you join me for the ceremony?"

I wasn't particularly eager to reenter that dark, foreboding place.

"If you are concerned," Jacksiun added, "the entryway to the tombs has been stabilized and it is safe to enter. A temporary staircase has been built for easy access to the inside of the main burial chamber, and we have crews on-site with proper lighting and equipment to assure a safe transition in and out of the temple."

"I think you should go," Mattheia spoke up from beside me. "If you want to, that is."

"I do," I replied.

"Thank you. May we leave now?" Jacksiun asked.

"I believe so." I looked at Mattheia, who shrugged in agreement. We had finished our meals several minutes before the prince had entered.

"Would you like to join us?" Jacksiun asked him.

"I'd be honored," Mattheia replied.

We departed, following Prince Jacksiun and an envoy of Royal Allegiance members toward the castle entrance. It shocked me how quickly the maintenance crew I'd seen last night had reconstructed the hallway leading up to the throne room. Even the carved wooden door had been replaced with a similar new one.

As we followed the group—some guards behind and some ahead of us—I noted a woman in all white carrying a glossy wooden chest in her arms.

"What do you think that is?" Mattheia whispered, leaning toward me.

"I don't know. Remains, perhaps."

After leaving the castle, we were met by a small group of soldiers carrying brightly lit torches perched on poles stretching up high over our heads. The sun had just begun to set, and the colors of the fading horizon bloomed in shades of purple, pink, and blue. A bright line of orange fringed the clouds, making the skyline burn with effervescent light.

The entrance to the Tomb of the Old Kings had been cleared of debris and the wood paneling previously used as a blockade. Metal support beams had been propped up inside the main archway for stability.

We entered and worked our way down the sturdy, spiraling wooden staircase assembled near the edge of the ledge where the floor had collapsed. The place smelled of fresh air and a hint of earth.

Battery-operated lamps had been affixed all around the perimeter of the room, illuminating everything as if it were daylight inside. I glanced down at the stone flooring and could now clearly see and appreciate the detailed relief carvings on each square tile. Each one appeared to document a different Rayvenstar king.

The blood-stained floor had been cleaned, name plates restored to each burial chamber, and broken tomb entryways reassembled with fresh stone and mortar. All but King Edward's, whose nameplate had been carefully placed off to the side on a piece of black velvet, and whose tomb had been left open.

Jacksiun approached me and called over the woman in white who carried the wooden box. She opened it and revealed a pile of translucent grey scales.

"What are those?" Mattheia asked, peering over my shoulder.

"These are King Edward's bloodmane scales—all that is left of him," I answered.

"Help me gather them," Jacksiun said, looking me in the eye.

I reached into the chest and carefully lifted several scales of varying sizes. They were amazingly lightweight, like thin acrylic. I reserved the largest, keystone scale for the prince and waited for him to take the massive piece into both hands as if it were a small shield. It had barely fit into the box.

When King Edward was alive in the cage back at the castle observation lab, his scales glimmered with fiery greens and yellows and refracted light like gemstone facets. Now they had lost all color and were dull and hazy.

"They were exquisite creatures," Jacksiun said quietly, admiring the large scale. "Would you like to touch it?" He turned and presented it to Mattheia, who seemed hesitant, so I nudged him. He'd never have the opportunity again.

"Deadly but exquisite," I added.

Mattheia's expression shifted to one of astonishment. "It's like glass," he said, withdrawing his hand. "That's incredible."

"I understand why King Westin was angry with us," Jacksiun said softly. "Already, they had chosen to bar me from the throne, and then our general murdered his son. I will make sure King Edward, and the rest of the Rayvenstar kings, are not forgotten." He looked over at the preserved stone body of King Westin in bloodmane form. "I will honor his sacrifice."

Four of Jacksiun's guards entered the open crypt and proceeded to painstakingly push the heavy lid of a carved stone sarcophagus to one side of the coffin. Once the lid had been pushed open, the guards retreated and Jacksiun stepped up, gesturing for me to follow him.

The woman carrying the chest remained at the threshold of the crypt, the box propped open in her arms, as a few smaller scales remained inside.

Jacksiun handed the larger scale off to a guard. "Handle this with the utmost care." Then he gathered the remaining scales from the box and entered the hollowed-out cavern where the coffin lay open and empty.

"What now?" I asked, cupping the scales firmly in my hands.

"We lay King Edward to rest." He carefully arranged several of the grey scales in a column inside the casket, each of them clinking against stone like shards of crystal. I took his lead and matched his actions, ordering the pieces by way of size—larger toward the head and the smaller toward the feet.

"Thank you for your service, loyalty, and protection all these years," Jacksiun said. "I will do everything in my power to protect your legacy." After we had dispersed all the smaller scales, he retrieved the largest scale back from his guard.

He took it with both hands clasped around the edges and rotated it so the long curve of the top faced the head of the casket, and the sharp, shield-like point at the bottom faced the foot end.

"Sleep well, King Edward," he said, lowering the piece into the coffin, right about where one's heart may have been.

He closed his eyes and bowed deeply.

I did the same.

The prince gestured for his men to return to close the casket, but I raised a hand.

"What is it, Admiral?" Jacksiun asked.

"I'd like to try something," I responded.

I thought about what King Westin had said to me—how fire would not singe their armor, but then I also thought about how gemstones are formed (with intense heat and pressure).

I didn't know what to expect, but I wanted to at least try the idea sifting through my mind as I looked down at the cloudy grey scales.

I reached into the coffin and rested my hand on the large keystone scale. A ripple of yellow-red light illuminated my skin and the scale reflected the fiery glow. I flattened my palm against the piece and it grew brighter, consumed by the flame. Then I removed my hand and waited for the heat to cool.

Jacksiun peered over the side of the casket and his eyes narrowed with uncertainty.

As sparks of fire dissolved from the scale, hints of metallic color shone through. Greens and yellows glimmered from inside the casket, casting rays of color around the tomb walls. My focused energy had infused the piece with new magic, restoring its original sheen.

Jacksiun gazed back at me, his eyes welling with the glisten of joy and thankfulness.

ight you stay for one more day?" Jacksiun asked us; we'd returned to the castle and gathered in the main foyer.

"Captain Lansfora would like us back as soon as possible," Mattheia replied. "But, since there are no pertinent situations taking place currently, I believe we can talk him into extending our stay. Why? If I may ask?"

"My father and I would like to publicly thank you for your help. And..." He looked over at me thoughtfully. "I have something for you." He glanced at Mattheia. "For *both* of you."

Mattheia's eyebrow rose. "I'm intrigued."

"So you *will* stay?" Jacksiun reiterated.

"We should be able to squeeze in one more day, without an issue."

"Good. We will send an officer to gather you when we are ready. Goodnight." He tipped his head and then walked away, his guards following closely at his sides.

I took in a deep breath and sighed. "Are you certain Captain Lansfora will not be upset with us staying longer than necessary?"

"Define *necessary*," Mattheia replied, smirking.

"You haven't told him we've solved this ordeal yet, have you?"

He looked up at the ceiling and pressed his lips thin.

"Hmm. I'm not sure I feel right using academy time for an unscheduled vacation. Who's going to be in charge if Commander Lansfora falls ill?"

"We do have a Third Commanding Officer, actually," he said with a guilty, toothy grin.

"You do?" I propped a hand on my hip and scoffed. "How did I not know about them?"

"We make a point not to disclose that information unless we have to, for security reasons."

"So you secretly have a third in command and never told me? Is that how you've managed to sneak away from Silver Diamond *without* getting reprimanded?"

He smiled awkwardly. "Maybe..."

"Then let me guess, it's not Sergeant Vlain, either. Right?"

"Nope."

"So you beat her for the position of Second Commanding Officer, and she was overlooked for third? No wonder she hates you."

"Hate is a strong word," he replied.

"She hates you."

"Yes, she does," Mattheia admitted with a shrug. He looked down the hall and then up at the darkened stained glass windows along the sides of the ceiling. "We should get some rest if we're going to be ready for whatever it is the prince and king have planned."

"I hope it's not too big of an event. I didn't bring any formal clothes."

"We have our uniforms. They're formal," he reminded me.

"True."

"I am *very* curious what Prince Jacksiun has in store for '*us*.'"

"Me, too."

The following morning, Officer Cassian met us outside at the stables and announced—as expected—that the king and prince had requested an audience with us. Mattheia told Zander to behave and the rambunctious beast took off running and bucking rebelliously across the pasture.

"He is taking well to your training, I see," Cassian said with a sliver of sarcasm.

"Oh, he is," Mattheia retorted. "You should see him when he's *not* behaving."

Cassian laughed and then escorted us back to the castle.

We entered the throne room through majestic wooden doors, held open for us by a guard on each side, and walked down the long stretch of carpet to reach the steps leading to the platform upon which the king, queen, and prince sat.

All members of our team, Officer Cassian, and several members of the Royal Allegiance were seated in chairs on both sides of the carpeted aisle. It was intimidating, at first, but when I looked into the small crowd and saw Private Quill beaming back at me with encouragement, I felt some relief.

Prince Jacksiun—still donning the bloodmane cape, but with his finer, more elegant circlet crown atop his head—stood and approached the first step, gesturing for us to come closer. He held a small wooden box.

I wanted to speak up and tell them they didn't need to reward us for our help, but I knew it was impolite to speak to royalty without being addressed first. That, and it would have made us all look ungrateful.

"Admiral Hawksford, on behalf of King Vincent and myself, we would like to present you with a gift. Please step up."

I moved up one stair and turned to face the prince. He pried open the box and held it out toward me, revealing a bright silver medallion with two wings curved into a circle shape, the letters R and A in gold between them, and a metallic cabochon fixed at the bottom of the two wings. Three short chains dangled from the base, each one ending in a gold, eight-point star. I recognized the color of the stone at once. Color-shifting blues and greens flitted over the piece as he tilted it gently in the box. They'd fashioned for me a Royal Allegiance seal with King Westin's scale!

The piece was so beautiful, it took my breath away.

Only the most elite members of the royal guard had received such medallions and none of them were as many shades of color as mine.

King Vincent stood and walked over to me. He lifted the hefty badge from the box and Jacksiun backed away a few steps.

"It is my honor to bestow upon you, Admiral Hawksford of Silver Diamond Academy and Elemental Guardian of fire, a sigil of the Royal Allegiance of Rayvenstar Castle. This rare piece, crafted by the highest-ranking metalsmith in all the land, features a shard of bloodmane scale, which offers protection and strength to the ordained member."

He turned the piece and unclasped the pin back.

"Will you accept this token and the most honorable rank that comes with it, in thanks for your service to my country?"

I bowed my head. "Yes, Your Highness."

King Vincent carefully pinned the brooch onto my left pocket. "From this day forward, you shall be regarded as Admiral Hawksford of the Royal Allegiance, and welcomed internationally as an official dignitary of the crown. Please raise your head and be applauded for your achievements."

The crowd clapped loudly and a sharp whistle cut the air. I jerked my head toward the left side of the audience—where Amanda was sitting—and she ducked down, embarrassed that I'd heard her. I smiled, though. I smiled so hard, it hurt my face.

I hadn't thought I'd really done much to deserve such an honor... had I?

I looked over at Jacksiun, who was grinning proudly from ear to ear, and then at Mattheia, who was smiling, too, one step down from where I stood.

The king lifted his hands and the crowd silenced.

"Commander Draven," King Vincent said to Mattheia. "Please come join Admiral Hawksford." He walked back over to his throne and sat. "Prince Jacksiun would like to speak upon a separate issue."

The prince approached us, smiling as if he might burst from enthusiasm and pride.

"Commander Draven, Admiral Hawksford," Jacksiun addressed us, "there is something we would like to offer you. You may choose to decline the offer and we would not be offended in the least; however, it would be an honor for us to prepare and host your wedding here at Rayvenstar Castle. It would be a wedding for which we would spare no expense, and you would be granted complete control over the details."

It was like my heart stopped right there.

Get married in a castle?

Get married in a castle still used by an actual king!?

Talk about a fairytale wedding...

Wait. Wouldn't that be too fancy?

It wouldn't be right to use my friend's royal status to...

Mattheia took my hand and I gasped, jolting to attention.

"Please do not feel any pressure to decide today," Prince Jacksiun continued.

"Thank you, Your Highness," I replied, my voice breaking. My mouth was so dry, I could barely speak. "I think we would need to discuss this, though," I said to Mattheia.

"What's there to discuss?" he replied, a grin curling his lips. "Really? We could get married in your best friend's castle! That's amazing, don't you think?"

"Of course, it is, but... what about your mother and my sister and..."

"You may invite *anyone* you wish," Jacksiun cut in, "and we will see to it that all transportation and lodging are taken care of."

The hair on the back of my neck stood and tears crept into my eyes as I debated how to respond.

"It's up to you, Valhara," Mattheia said, squeezing my hand gently. "I think it would be an incredible honor to have the king and crown prince of Alyssia at our wedding, but this doesn't mean we have to rush into it, either."

"So you'd be okay with it?" I asked Mattheia. My cheeks were killing me now.

"Yes."

"Okay!" I turned back toward Jacksiun and bowed. "We would be honored for you to host our wedding. Thank you, Your Highness." I bowed toward the king, too. "Thank you so much."

The contented look on Jacksiun's face made me realize that he had wanted this as much as I had, and that he truly wanted to make us happy.

After the decoration ceremony, we were released back into the crowd to mingle with our team and other members of the Royal Allegiance.

Officer Cassian congratulated me but couldn't stay to chat. He hadn't said a word about my lying to him about my marital status—which I appreciated. Maybe he understood the circumstances.

"Colonel Hammonds?" I greeted him as he approached.

"It is *General* Hammonds now," he said with a reserved smile shaping one corner of his lips. "General Cain's practice of keeping secrets from the king did not bode well for his career."

"I see." I had liked Hammonds better from the beginning anyway.

"I must congratulate you and welcome you into the Allegiance, Admiral. What you did to assist the prince and our kingdom has assured a better future for us all."

"The prince did much of the work. He will make a fine king someday."

"I whole-heartedly agree." He glanced over my shoulder at something. "I apologize, but I must be off. Congratulations."

"Thank you."

He walked away to speak to another member of the royal guard.

Amanda came over with a star-struck look in her eyes. "Oh! That is so pretty!" She poked at my RA badge. That's when I saw a silver sparkle on her pocket I hadn't noticed before.

"What's that?" I asked, nodding toward it. It didn't look like mine, but it was similar—a pair of wings with a star dangling from the bottom center.

"This?" She prodded it with her index finger. "I think it's a constellation prize. I mean, *consolation* prize. Sorry. Prince Jacksiun introduced me to that sparkly new owl of his." She pointed toward him. "And I can't stop thinking about her and the stars and what not. Oh! She gave me a feather, too. Do you believe that?" She slid a hand into her jacket. "Let me show you." Out came a white pinfeather with glittery gold lacing on the edge. "Pretty, huh?" She twirled the feather so light danced up and down the metallic accents.

"That is beautiful," I replied.

Amanda tucked it away and buttoned the pocket. Then she gasped. "Oh, here he comes."

Mattheia and I veered around to see Jacksiun walking toward us. Noctua was perched on his shoulder now, her talons safely nestled into the fur around the collar of the bloodmane cape.

"How is she doing?" I asked, gazing at Noctua.

"Better. It seems the skylights and stained glass windows around the castle allow enough light in to sustain her physical form for extended periods of time. The sword has to stay close, though," he added, pointing to Excalibur, which hung in the scabbard at his side. "I chose not to have her out during the main part of the ceremony to avoid distractions. But there were some things about her I had hoped to discuss with you."

"Sure," I replied.

I glanced over at Amanda, who was listening intently to his every word, starry-eyed.

Noctua let out a sharp chirp and hooted.

"What is she asking?" I said, looking up at her.

"I am sorry," he said softly, tickling her forehead. "The truth is, while she claims to be content that I survived the Queen's Blessing, or Rayvenstar Curse—whichever you prefer to call it—my friendship with you has continued to remind her of her solidarity. She would like to know if there are others like her or, more specifically, *you*."

"Elemental Guardians?" I asked.

He nodded in confirmation.

"I'm not quite sure, little one," I said to Noctua, who bobbed her head in acknowledgement. "But I do know someone who may be able to help. Perhaps, he might even be able to offer some advice on your inability to stay in physical form without natural light, too."

Jacksiun craned his neck to the side and brushed the tip of his finger over Noctua's beak. "How do you like that idea?"

She rubbed against him, screeching and clicking happily.

"Kinasetsu," Mattheia said. "If anyone would know, he would."

Amanda blinked at us, confused. "Who?"

"The cleric who saved Valhara's life," Jacksiun informed her.

"C-cleric?" Amanda's eyes widened. She clasped onto Jacksiun's sleeve and scooted closer to him. "No one said anything about a cleric." She glanced up into his eyes.

"There's more to this world than we know," I said with a little laugh. "You're in my department now, Private, and you'll learn a lot more, soon enough." I reached to take Mattheia's hand and entwine fingers with his. "Now we only need to decide if all this is happening *before* or *after* we get married."

Amanda released Jacksiun's arm and latched on to mine, literally tearing me away from Mattheia. "About that!" she started, excitedly. "Can I help? Please! Please! Pleasssse!" She yanked me off to the side and chewed her lip anxiously as she awaited my response.

"Y-you want to help with our wedding?" I asked. Her

grasp on my arm was so tight, I had to struggle to not grimace.

"Yes! Oh, it would be so much fun." She was beaming.

"I didn't know you were interested in that kind of stuff." Though, why wouldn't I have thought that? She'd been boy crazy since we'd first met. One could suppose marriage would be an eventual side effect of being in love with someone.

"Um, YES!" she replied, shaking with excitement. "I mean. HEY! I've already planned out *my* whoooole royal wedding, so I might as well put all that research to good use for a friend, too." Her fingers squeezed harder and I flinched for real. "Oh. You should see my scrapbook of ideas! Turns out lots of things go with blue and silver. How about that!? Who knew!?" She giggled. I looked over my shoulder at Mattheia, Jacksiun, and Noctua, whose heads were all cocked to the side with curiosity, as Amanda proceeded to drag me farther and farther away.

Wedding scrapbook?

Was Amanda planning her wedding already?

To whom?

Then it hit me.

Why did I ask myself a question I could already answer?

BONUS STORY

I'm getting married in a week.

Mattheia had talked things over with Captain Lansfora, and we'd been granted permission to stay in Alyssia for ten more days. Now, I had to pick out everything so the castle could make preparations.

Most people had months, or even years, to think about their wedding.

I had seven days.

SEVEN.

And I'd be okay with that... as soon as day one ended.

Amanda and I sat in the solarium on the third floor of the castle, flipping through a digital scrapbook of wedding-related images she'd collected on her laptop. Most of them were too flamboyant for my taste, but I didn't want to hurt her feelings for sharing with me.

"You could do this with the floor runners! It's so chic."

She pointed to a photograph of someone's customized rug, featuring the bride's and groom's initials with a coat-of-arms behind them. That seemed pretentious to me. I just wanted a nice, *small*, castle wedding. Judging by Amanda's standards, and by what she was showing me in regards to my wishes, I apparently wanted a *tiny* wedding.

I sat with her for a few more hours and she made notes of all the things I liked and didn't like (the list of likes being much shorter), and then started sorting through a pack of color swatches she'd gathered from the royal event planner, Lady Stafford.

The royal event planner had assured me I did not have to pay any attention to the castle's current color scheme, and that everything from the drapes to the carpet could be changed to fulfill my desires.

The problem was I didn't have a lot of desires, and, on top of that, Mattheia told me he'd be content with whatever decisions I made. I was a high-ranking lieutenant turned admiral, at one of the top military academies on the planet, but I knew nothing about wedding planning. Amanda was great help, but I hadn't thought of any of these things before today.

Guest list? I didn't know that many people I wanted to invite.

Flowers? Yes. I liked certain ones.

Cake flavor and style? I wasn't a fan of most sweets.

Picking out dinner wouldn't be too difficult.

Then there was all this talk of having to have live music and a dance.

I didn't know how to dance and I wasn't excited about

having to learn.

The color of rugs we stepped on during the ceremony didn't matter to me.

"You have to at least pick out some colors, Valhara," Amanda said, fanning out another pack of swatches—all shades of purple. Amanda *really* liked purple.

I tilted my head to the side and squinted. I, on the contrary, did not like purple.

"Okay." She sighed and put down the stack of cards. "Let's try another way. What is your favorite color?"

"Um..."

"Don't think about it. Just tell me the first color that comes to mind."

I looked down at my sleeves.

"Green?" I said.

"Are you asking me if your favorite color is green, or telling me that it is?" Amanda replied, skeptical of my answer.

"I *do* like green," I clarified.

"Military green?" She scrunched her lips to one side. "You wear that almost every day. Any other choices?"

"I like the color of Mattheia's eyes." I shrugged, feeling embarrassed about my vague and insufficient answers. "Green really is a favorite color of mine."

"There are different shades of green, too, you know? Dark green. Light green. Neon green." Amanda sifted through the enormous pack of swatches and pulled out a bunch ranging from light blue to an almost black green. She fanned them out in front of me. My eyes were immediately drawn to a pretty light greenish-blue in the middle.

"What's that?" I asked, pointing to the shade. "That's nice."

"That's called 'Mermaid Sky,'" she said. "Do you like that? It's sort of a mix of sea foam green and ocean blue."

"Yes. I do like that." The more I looked at it, the faster I grew attached. "It's perfect. Let's start with Mermaid Sky."

Amanda shuffled through the color cards again and started laying several out on the table. "Kind of a shame we won't be birds of a feather anymore after this," she said, still sorting through cards.

"How so?"

"Well, Draven and Quill don't exactly have the same ring to them." She shrugged and set a card with an unattractive orange gradient down.

I stuck my tongue out and scowled at the sight of it, and then she quickly shuffled it back into the stack.

"Who said I was changing my name to Draven, anyway?" I said. "I'm not. I'll still be Valhara Hawksford to you. Better yet, *Admiral* Hawksford, Private." I cocked an eyebrow.

"Oh, I didn't know if you were taking his name or keeping yours. Guess I'm old fashioned."

"Old fashioned? You're one to talk. Seeing as you've got your heart set on becoming Amanda Rayven..."

Her lips stretched into a huge (almost creepy) toothy grin. "Say it slow...ly. And enunciate."

"Rayven... star..." I dropped my face into my palm. It *was* still a bird, technically.

"Pre-ordained, I tell you." She giggled. "But enough about me." She gestured to the array of new swatches she'd laid out on the table. "There are the colors that will go best with that," she said, running a finger down one of them. "Taupe, for example, is nice."

"Taupe?" It sounded more like slang than a color.

How are you feeling today? Taupe! How about you?

I chuckled, but Amanda was not amused by my undisclosed joke.

"Then there is coral, rose, sand, black, other shades of blue." She scanned my face for a response. "Anything clicking?"

"Gold?" I asked.

"Gold what?" Amanda asked, looking down at the color cards.

"Metallic gold. Gold, gold. Would that go with Mermaid Sky?"

Amanda nibbled her lip and sifted through the swatches. She pressed her finger to one of them. "Gold." Then she clicked her tongue and nodded. "Yup. Checks out. Good choice."

I smiled. Maybe this whole wedding planning thing wouldn't be so difficult after all.

The guest list was next.

I had a few friends at Celestial Galaxy who couldn't make it with such short notice, but I understood their obligations, so it didn't bother me. Amanda was already with me, and so was Jacksiun.

My sister and her fiancé, Captain Ventresca, were the only two left on my side of the invite list. Mattheia's mother had already made arrangements to come. She was also bringing Daisy because all the boarding facilities in her area were booked. Captain Lansfora wanted to attend, but gave us his condolences for being unable to travel—partially because of the short notice. Also, there were rules in place to prevent the Captain and Second Commanding Officer from being away simultaneously.

"How is it that my little sister is getting married before I am?" Atira asked, shaking her head. We'd started a video chat on our computers after Amanda went off to inform Lady Stafford of my color choices.

"Sorry, Sis." I grinned toothily. "When your best friend turns out to be a prince, and then his father—the king—offers to subsidize your wedding and allow you to have it in his castle, you make decisions not everyone is happy with."

"Now I didn't say I wasn't happy for you. I think it's wonderful! I might even be a little jealous, but... that would be wrong of me."

"You two should get married while you're here. It could be a double wedding." I smirked.

"Uh... no thanks. We need a little more time to prepare and plan. But thanks anyway. Besides, they offered to front *your* tab, not ours. You know we can't agree on anything anyway."

I laughed, harder than I should have, because she was so right.

"Speaking of which," she continued. "Have you chosen a color scheme?"

"Yes. Gold and Mermaid Sky. It's sort of a mint, seafoam green."

Atira cocked an eyebrow. "What was I just saying about not agreeing on anything? I'm just kidding. Those sound like very nice colors. I think you'd look beautiful surrounded by them. Mint green would look nice with your hair and skin tone, too."

"I haven't had a chance to think about what we're wearing yet."

"You'd better get going. A week is going to pass in the blink of an eye."

"I know." I fidgeted with my RA badge, making the hanging star dangles chime into each other.

"So, are we invited or not?" Atira asked.

"Oh." I looked back at the screen. "Of course. That's why I called. Do you think you and Captain Ventresca can come?"

"His term with C.G. ends in two weeks. I'll go with him and see if we can request either early termination without consequence, or see if we can extend our terms another week or two to make up for the leave. I am fairly certain *I* can come, but it may not be in the cards for him to join me."

"Oh," I groaned. "I would hate for you to have to travel alone."

"I'll do whatever I have to, Valhara," she said, grinning. "The captain is currently working with the replacement to show her the ropes before he goes."

"I see. I'm really sorry to spring this on you at such short notice. You don't think we should wait, do you?"

"To get married?"

"Yes."

"Why do you need to wait if you feel ready now? The

king is granting you the opportunity of a lifetime. Weddings are expensive, and this will be unforgettable for you two. Unless... you're having second thoughts." She narrowed her eyes.

"No! No!" I shook my head violently. "I want to marry Mattheia; I just wish you both could be here for the wedding."

"We'll try, Sis." Atira took a deep breath. "We really will try."

"Thanks."

"So, what are you going to wear?"

"I don't know yet. I've been thinking about the styles I like, but... I really don't know where to start."

"You'd better figure it out soon. I know you're at a castle and all, but I don't think many people can make a wedding dress in a day."

"Why does it have to be a dress?"

Her expression went straight and she glared at me through the monitor. "It doesn't have to be a dress. But if you try to wear your academy uniform to your wedding," she leaned in closer to the camera, "I will find a way to stop everything until you are dressed properly."

"I'm just kidding." I grinned awkwardly.

There was a knock at my door. I ordered it to open because I had been expecting someone.

"How are things going?" Mattheia asked as he entered.

"I see they fixed your door." He stood there, admiring the shiny new composite metal sliding door they'd installed overnight.

"Yes," I replied without looking up from my laptop; I was browsing dress designs.

"Do you need help with anything?" He came up behind me and looked over my shoulder at my screen. "Oh, that's nice," he said, pointing to a sleeveless, draped chiton style with full-length, pleated skirt. "They still make dresses like that?" The chiton dress had been based on a very old, extinct culture that existed around the time of Julius Caesar. They typically came in white, but looked pretty in other colors, too. I'd already partially settled on something like it, but Mattheia's approval pushed me to fully settle.

"Yes, and I like it, too," I replied, craning my neck back to look up at him. He put a hand onto the back of my chair and leaned down closer until his face was parallel to mine.

"Apparently, we need to discuss a cake of some sort," he said. "Although." He pressed a kiss to my cheek and hugged me by the shoulders from behind. "I have just the right amount of sweetness in my life already."

I laughed.

"But, really," he continued, "the baker said he could make anything we wanted, or he could give us samples from several of their most popular flavors. What do you want to do? I know you're not a big fan of cakes, but maybe we can choose something our guests will like."

"You can take care of it, if you want," I said, leaning my head back against him.

"I can? But I thought girls always wanted to be in control

of everything at their weddings."

"I just want to be married. I really didn't want something big like this, did you?"

He embraced me a bit more tightly. "No. Not really." His tone softened. "I kind of imagined we'd sneak off somewhere on a weekend, come back on a weekday, and already be done with it."

I furrowed my brow. "Really?"

"Yes, but then you'd end up widowed because my mom would probably kill me for not making a bigger deal out of it all."

That was a morbid thought, but also a semi accurate one. Mattheia's mom was overjoyed to hear we'd gotten engaged, and even more excited about us having our wedding in Rayvenstar Castle.

"If you want me to make some of the decisions, I will," Mattheia continued. "I just want to make sure it's okay with you, and I don't want to risk messing anything up or going against what you may have envisioned."

"I have nothing in mind for a cake," I added. "You are more than welcome to do whatever you wish with that. Don't get upset if I end up not eating much of it."

"Understood. Maybe I'll make it a pizza-flavored cake, then." He smirked and raised his eye brows.

"I see where you're going with this, but..."

"I'm joking. In case you couldn't tell."

We both liked pizza. In fact, our relationship was built on that, in an abstract sense. Pizza and at least a dozen other things we both loved.

"I'll take care of the cake and it will *not* be pizza flavored," he assured me. "I promise. Is there anything else I can assist you with?" He rested his hands on my shoulders and caressed my neck with his thumbs.

"I'll let you know if I think of anything."

"Alright. I'm going to head to the stables to take Zander out for a run. Cassian's father offered to work with me if I had time, so I'll give him a call if you don't think you'll need me for anything else today."

"Go ahead. Have fun and don't let him talk back to you."

"Lord Cassian?"

"No. Zander."

"Ah." He smiled. "I should have figured that was who you'd meant."

I rested back in my chair and gazed up at Mattheia. He leaned down to kiss me.

"Don't stress out about all this," he said. "Call me if you need anything at all."

"I'll try not to get too worked up. I'll probably be in the library later today. Come there if you can't find me anywhere else."

"Will do."

The Rayvenstar library was one of the few places I could go, besides my room, where I wouldn't be hounded by castle citizens. Now that the prince was safe and the kingdom no longer under siege, everyone wanted to talk to the Elemental Guardian, but I needed a quiet place to gather my thoughts that felt like home. Books and ancient relics had a way of doing that for me.

I found a cozy, narrow aisle of old tomes, flopped onto the floor, and then propped my back against a shelf, letting out a heavy sigh.

Did we really need all this? I would be completely happy with the king's blessing, some paperwork, and a nice dinner, but it wasn't turning out that way at all. I hadn't expected to have to pick out colors, foods, fabrics, and...

Some people like big soirées so they can invite hundreds of friends and family members and get lots of gifts, but we didn't have that many people in our lives we were close to. I could count on two hands the number of people I wanted to invite. Maybe Atira couldn't, but I could.

I pulled my knees up to my chest, rested my arms on them, and then laid my face on top.

Why was I getting so upset? We were having everything handed to us. There were probably thousands of brides-to-be in the world who would kill for a shot at a pre-paid royal wedding, but not me.

Then Mattheia had to go tell me he hadn't wanted anything big either and that weighed heavily on my mind. Was I going to end up making decisions he wouldn't be happy with?

I sat there on the floor for some time, thinking, until I heard soft footsteps nearing the aisle.

"Ah. There you are," Jacksiun said. "I knew I would find you here."

I lifted my face just as he turned the corner.

He approached me slowly. "May I sit with you?"

I nodded, embarrassed at how pitiful I must have looked

sitting there on the floor, hunched over like a brooding child.

He brushed the hem of his jacket down his backside and lowered himself to the floor to sit beside me with his back pressed to the shelf. Our shoulders touched.

"If all this is too much for you," he started, "please let me know. I never meant for it to cause you any strife. We only wanted to do what we could to make you happy. This was *my* suggestion. The king agreed to go along with it."

"It's not that I'm not happy," I replied, wiping the corner of my eye.

A hand clasping a handkerchief inched into view. "Here."

I took it from his fingers and used it to pat my cheeks.

"Then what is it?" he asked.

"I wanted to have a nice, *small* wedding, with only a few guests, and a nice little dinner after. I didn't want to have to worry about all the frills, dances, and music. Maybe it's every other girl's dream to have a fairytale wedding with all the royal trimmings and fanfare, but…"

"I'm sorry, Valhara," he whispered, looking down at his lap and sighing. "I should have been more considerate about your wishes. I know you well enough to know you're not one for elaborate parties. You just want something intimate and special. Right?"

"Exactly," I muttered. "Mattheia told me he didn't care what size wedding party we had, as long as it made *me* happy."

"Is *this* going to make you happy, Valhara?" He tipped his head down to look me in the eye.

I didn't want to respond.

"May I offer a suggestion, then?" He nudged my elbow gently. "Between friends?"

"Sure."

"Do what makes *you* happy, Valhara. This is going to be an important day in your life. Don't you want to remember it as one you loved and enjoyed? You don't want to look back and think about how stressed out and uncomfortable you were, or how out of place you felt. Just because my father offered to host your wedding does not mean it can't be exactly what *you* want it to be. As big... or *small*... as you desire."

I allowed his words to sink in before responding.

"But won't he be disappointed?" I sniffled.

"No." Jacksiun shook his head adamantly. "Why would he be disappointed about *your* wedding? The only thing he's disappointed about is that you're marrying the commander... and not *me*."

"Is he still upset about that?"

"No. I had a long..." he sighed and groaned, "*difficult* talk with him, and he now realizes that you are with exactly who you were meant to be with."

"Do you really think so?"

"Well, you always did have a thing for blondes."

"Excuse me?" I jabbed him in the arm and he laughed hard.

We both laughed.

"No wonder your sister is marrying the captain. There is not a high-ranking, enlisted, blonde-haired man out there who is safe from a Hawksford woman, apparently."

"Stop!" I chuckled so much I ended up snorting, and

then started giggling again.

He was right, though. I mean, it wasn't *only* Mattheia's blonde hair I was attracted to. In my defense, the color was *very* rare nowadays.

The communication band on Jacksiun's wrist buzzed and he flipped his hand over to read the message. "I am sorry, but I have to go. Will you be alright for now?"

"Yes. I think so." I squeezed the handkerchief with my fingers. "Wait. Do you need this back?"

"No." Jacksiun shook his head.

I patted the corners of my eyes one more time, and then tucked the cloth into my shirt pocket.

He stood and offered his hands out to help pull me up. I clasped them and came to my feet. "Think about what I said, Valhara." Our eyes met and his grasp on me tightened. "Please."

"I will. Thank you, Jacksiun." I tipped my head toward him and then he left the library.

Atira was right; seven days had flashed by like lightning.

"Today, you're going to be the prettiest girl in the entire kingdom," Atira said, combing through a lock of my hair several times and then pinning it above my ear. The king had offered to hire a private team of makeup artists and designers for me, but I politely declined. I took Jacksiun's words to heart and requested only my sister's help to get ready.

Thanks to a few strings pulled by King Vincent, Atira

and Captain Ventresca had attained permission to come.

Sometimes it's nice to have friends in high places.

"Turn toward me," Atira said. I did, and she pinned my cherry blossom barrette into place. She cupped my face in her hands and raised my head slightly to look at me. A quiver of sadness wrinkled her lips and she swallowed hard and tried to push the expression away with a forced smile.

"What is it?" I asked.

She turned away and I heard her sniffle and clear her throat.

"Atira?"

"I'm happy for you, Sis," she replied, turning to face me again. "I am. But when I look at you like this, I see so much of Mom in you. She was young back when she and Dad got married, and you look so much alike, now that your hair is down and you're dressed in this beautiful gown." She sighed. "I'm so sorry. I don't mean to bring you down. You're supposed to be happy today, and I need to make sure everything goes exactly as you imagine it will."

Thinking about Mom made me sad, too. I vaguely remember a wedding photo she'd had on her bedroom dresser. She wore a lilac-colored dress and had her hair down and curled so it caught the sunlight just right in the photo and glistened like copper.

Maybe that's why I didn't want anything purple—it reminded me of her.

Tears welled in my eyes.

"Valhara, don't cry! Please!" Atira scooted a stool over toward my chair and sat beside me, reaching out to grab me by my shoulders and pull me in to a tight embrace.

And there we sat, crying.

Most girls cry on their wedding day because they are overjoyed...

Atira reached across the table for a tissue and used it to pat my cheeks.

"I'm going to have to touch-up your makeup," she whispered.

"I know," I said, sniffling. "I'm sorry."

"Don't be. We have each other." She smiled and hugged me briefly. Her fingers twirled through the long, sheer cascades of lighter green chiffon draping down the fronts and backs of my bare shoulders toward the floor. "Your decision to go with the chiton, wrapped dress was brilliant. It looks like it was meant for you."

"Because they literally made it for me yesterday," I said with a laugh.

"You know what I mean."

"Yes."

I'd decided to go with a sea-foam, light mint-green colored, pleated dress which swept the floor, came up to cross my chest, and wrapped around my waist, with the remaining swag affixed and left to hang across one side. I declined a long train because I wanted something comfortable and easy to walk in.

It was wonderfully soft and roomy but also hugged my silhouette perfectly. The extra lengths of fairer green fabric framing the front and back of my bare shoulders reminded me of resting butterfly wings, the way they drifted along at my sides as I walked, the sheer fabric catching every wisp of air like a blade of grass in the wind.

Cool metal chilled my skin as Atira lowered my amulet down over my neck and clasped the chain. It hung just above the brim of my dress and had been polished to an unbelievable shine by one of the castle's jewelers.

"Here." Atira handed me the pair of custom-made, tie-on gladiator sandals that matched my dress. The soles were not as comfortable as I would have liked, but they did look gorgeous, and the flowy ribbon ties—although hidden under my long skirt—made them enchanting.

I bent over to twist the satiny ties around my ankle and up my calf, and then tied them in to a secure bow. I did the same with the other foot and then pushed up off my chair.

I grasped the sides of my skirt gently and swished the fabric back and forth, rotating my hips so the dress rustled around. "Well, how do I look?" I was tempted to brush my hair back over my shoulder, but resisted the urge and left the gently crimped locks where Atira had painstakingly positioned them.

Our eyes met and I waited for a response.

She just stared.

Right when I thought my heart might plummet into despair, Atira's lips parted and a big toothy grin spread across her face.

"You look perfect," she said.

"Do you think Mattheia will think so, too?"

She chuckled. "Valhara, if his gaze manages to break away from your beautiful face today, he will surely be awestruck by the incredible dress you've chosen. He is very much in love with you, Sis, and I'm sure he thinks you're beautiful in everything you wear."

My hands tangled together. "Thank you, Atira," I muttered, looking down at my feet. I could tell my cheeks and ears had become blazing red.

"Let's go. Your royal audience awaits," Atira said, beaming.

We left the dressing room and entered into the hall, where I was greeted by Officer Cassian and several members of the Royal Allegiance. Atira passed me off to them and went up ahead to join the rest of the attendees.

He offered me his arm, I looped mine around his, and then he walked with me until we reached a decorated double-door adorned with my wedding colors. Two of the guards stepped ahead of us and opened the doors wide for us to enter. I flexed my arm and squeezed Cassian's unintentionally. His gaze shifted toward me.

"Are you alright?" he spoke quietly. I had halted at the threshold of the ballroom.

"Y-yes," I uttered. My heart thumped against my ribcage.

"There is nothing to fear, Admiral," he added, pressing his free hand against my forearm. "You have faced greater adversaries than your own wedding, I am certain." A little smile curled his lips and it relieved some of my anxiety.

"Yes. I know I have, but... this is life-changing."

"And the other events were not?" He looked at me with integrity and curiosity in his eyes.

I thought about that.

Everything I'd feared in life served some purpose. I had hated how Captain Ventresca had chosen me to go to Silver Diamond when he should have sent someone else, but then

I met Mattheia there and my entire life changed—for the better. Together, he and my best friend had saved my life.

Marrying Mattheia would be a big change, but one I really wanted. Maybe I hadn't expected to do it quite so soon, or in a giant castle with a marriage ordained by the king of Alyssia, but that didn't make me want it any less.

I rolled my shoulders back and took a deep breath.

"You're right, Officer Cassian," I said, smiling at him. "Thank you so much for reminding me. You are a good friend."

"F-friend?" He glanced away as if he'd not expected to hear such a thing from me. His face flushed a little, but he attempted to hide it by looking off to the side. "Y-you are welcome, Admiral."

"Shall we go?" I asked.

We entered the surprisingly small, but comfortably sized, ballroom which had only a few rows of chairs set up and a long golden runner stretched out on the floor, leading to a platform up ahead where King Vincent and Mattheia waited.

Atira had already been seated in one of the chairs near the front.

Cassian released me and bowed deeply, backing away as another figure stepped up beside me, to whom he also bowed.

"You look exquisite, Valhara," Jacksiun said, tipping his head. "The dressmakers did incredible work, I see." His eyes narrowed joyfully with his genuine smile. It was odd seeing him in shades of green and gold again, as he'd not been since we'd arrived in Alyssia, but now he wore a color other than blue—one that complimented the hues I'd chosen for the event.

"Yes," I replied. "They did. I'm in love with the gown."

"The color suits you," he added.

"Thank you." I glanced around the room. There were about 20 people seated—and I knew every single one of them. I looked to one side and saw Amanda, beaming at me through the row of my other team members. On the other side was Mattheia's mother clutching Daisy in her arms. She looked as though she'd been crying for quite awhile, and her eyes were glassy and red; she also had a huge smile on her face and a clump of tissues in her grasp, bundled up alongside Daisy's golden fur. Tears of joy, I presumed.

"Is everything okay?" Jacksiun asked. "I hope this is not too small for you. After we had spoken, I—"

"It's perfect," I interrupted. "I'm surprised, because I didn't expect this."

"Did you not trust me with your wishes?" The prince cocked an eyebrow at me.

"I should have," I replied softly. "Thank you, my dear friend. I can't tell you how much this means to me."

"I think I know," he said, smiling. "Your groom is waiting." He lifted his arm up and bowed. "Shall we proceed?"

I nodded and hooked my arm through his.

An enchanting violin solo filled the air, as the musician we'd commissioned began to play a delicate tune; the audience silenced. My heart started racing again as I took my first step down the aisle on the golden carpet.

My arm flexed anxiously around Jacksiun's.

I took another step and suddenly felt warmth filling my chest. My amulet began to glow and I flinched as a coil of brilliant gold and orange light twirled around my shoulders toward my back. I tried to keep calm, but I didn't know what was happening. Firagia was working his magic in some strange way, and I had to trust him.

Jacksiun remained close, and astoundingly calm, as the flickering flames collected behind me, forming a radiant pair of fire wings on my back. I couldn't see them very well, but the expressions on everyone's faces convinced me they were grand. A choir of oohs and aahs filled the room.

I turned my head to the side to catch a glimpse of my reflection passing across distant windows.

"A small gift to add to your beauty on this special day," Firagia said in my mind.

"Thank you," I replied.

The wings were beautiful and iridescent, shimmering from gold to red to orange, in a spectrum that accentuated the soft greens of my dress.

We continued toward the platform and I couldn't help but smile as everyone's eyes followed me closely. Firagia's joy filled me and I could no longer resist the excitement bubbling up inside as I made eye contact with Mattheia.

As we neared, I could see that he was nervous, too, but the moment Jacksiun walked me up the first step of the platform, that anxiety melted away. Mattheia heaved a sigh and an inviting smile twisted his lips as the blue of his eyes sparkled with anticipation.

He wore dark slacks and a lovely sage-green suit jacket with pale gold trim and accents on the sleeves that mimicked those of the Royal Allegiance members. Underneath, he wore a darker, complimentary green vest with an intricate pattern stitched into the fabric. Black and silver suited him well, but natural colors complimented his skin tone. I was taken aback by how handsome he looked and how the layered and multi-toned shades of his blonde hair were accented by the neutral greens and golds.

Jacksiun released my arm and backed down from the platform. He smiled at us both before taking a seat in the front row, beside Amanda.

Mattheia and I joined hands. A lump formed in my throat as the excitement and realization of what was really happening to me finally began to sink in. I trembled, but Mattheia only clasped my hands more firmly and mouthed the words, "It's okay."

His calming demeanor helped settle my nerves enough that I could focus on what King Vincent had to say. My fiery wings became less intense.

"We are gathered here today to witness the union of High Commander Mattheia Draven and Voyage Admiral Valhara Hawksford. The responsibilities of marriage are not so unlike those of a military institution. You must defend your honor and the honor of others, respect one another, and be willing to make sacrifices.

"The two of you have made many sacrifices, and it is clear that you truly love and cherish each other. Many of you here today have only joy in your hearts for this union, but if anyone here may show just cause as to why these two shall not be lawfully married, let them speak now or forever hold their peace."

The moment of silence made me nervous again, and my gaze shifted toward the audience. Mattheia's fingers squeezed mine and our eyes met.

I didn't need to worry... did I?

"With no objections from our witnesses, I shall now continue the ceremony." King Vincent looked at me. "Do you, Valhara Hawksford, take Mattheia Draven to be your lawfully wedded husband? To protect, honor, and respect, and to whom you will remain faithful for as long as the fire of your lifeline burns?"

"I do," I replied, glancing at the brilliant silver ring on my finger. We had chosen to leave out the ring exchange portion of the ceremony since we'd already partaken in it in our own way.

The king turned to Mattheia. "And do you, Mattheia Draven, take Valhara Hawksford to be your lawfully wedded wife? To protect, honor, and respect, and to whom you will remain faithful for as long as the fire of your lifeline burns?"

Mattheia's grasp on me tightened as he firmly replied, "I do."

King Vincent placed his hands around ours and smiled.

"With the power vested in me, as king of Alyssia and ruler of Rayvenstar Castle, I hereby declare you lawfully wedded husband and wife."

He released us and took a step back.

Only after I heard clapping from the audience did I realize the king had finished speaking, and before I could process everything, Mattheia tugged me closer and kissed me.

And in that moment, the applause and cheering faded out, as the passion in his kiss distracted me.

Our lips parted, but he held steadfast to my hands, the smile in his eyes also manifesting across his lips.

"You are the most beautiful woman in the world," he said. "Especially in *that*."

His azure eyes sparkled with admiration and I didn't know what to say in return.

"I'm... glad you like my dress," I muttered.

We turned toward our guests and made our way down the platform and back into the aisle.

Officer Cassian escorted us to another room off to the side—a banquet hall with beautiful round tables set with elegant place settings and decorations featuring a calligraphy arrangement of the entwined letters D and H.

"Valhara," Mattheia spoke softly, turning me toward a smaller table featuring a silver tiered tray of frosted cupcakes topped artfully with blackberries, raspberries, strawberries, and blueberries. I gasped at the sight of the incredible display, and at the wonderfully sweet-looking (and familiar) treats.

"You didn't want a cake," he announced, "so I asked my mom if she could help."

It was true, I didn't like many desserts, but when I'd first had dinner with Mattheia and his mother, his mother had baked me home-made berry cupcakes. They quickly became a favorite of mine and she'd made them for me every visit since.

I turned toward Mattheia and threw my arms around his neck, pulling him into an enthusiastic kiss. "Thank you! I love you so much!"

His hands gracefully clasped my waist and he smiled. "I love you, too. I just wanted you to be happy, Valhara."

"I am! I really, really am!" I hugged him so tightly, he grunted. "Sorry."

"I'm joking," he replied. "You can hug me as hard as you want."

I squeezed him one more time for good measure and then turned back to the cupcake display.

"Do you want dinner?" Mattheia asked, brushing a hand over my shoulder to swipe a lock of hair to my back.

My eyes met his and I bit my lip. "Maybe." I glanced at the cupcakes again.

"I see where this is going, and I'm okay with that, too." He walked me closer to the table and, together, we reached over the tiered tray to lift up one of the cupcakes. The blackberries and raspberries on top glistened in the warm lighting of the room. "Ladies first," he said, smirking.

He peeled back the paper liner and shuttled it closer to my mouth. I took a bite; it tasted even better than I had remembered it. Next, I confiscated the remainder of it and peeled back another corner of it to offer it to him.

He bit off part of the cake and laughed, wiping the corner of his mouth with the back of his hand and searching the table for a napkin. A spot of buttercreme remained on the edge of his lips and I grinned mischievously at him, stepping closer, until I was near enough to kiss him once more and rescue him from the stray frosting. I savored the sweet berry flavor.

Then we turned back toward the center of the room, only to discover that everyone had been standing there the entire time watching us make fools out of ourselves.

Mattheia and I burst out laughing and then everyone else did, too.

Shortly after, Jacksiun and Amanda approached us.

"Congrats!" Amanda threw out her arms and hugged me. *Tightly*. I tried to stifle a grunt of discomfort.

"Thank you," I replied, smiling while holding back a grimace.

She curtsied toward Mattheia, her pretty, gold, knee-length dress shimmering as light danced over iridescent chiffon. "Congrats to you, too, Commander," she said. "I look forward to serving the most awesome power-couple in all of Silver Diamond."

"Congratulations, Commander," Jacksiun said, offering out his hand. They shook hands firmly and then he jerked Mattheia in to a brief, manly embrace. After that, the prince looked over at me and took a step closer. "Congratulations, my friend," he said softly, reaching out to hug me. He pressed a kiss to my cheek and I closed my eyes and smiled. "Thank you for allowing me the opportunity to make this day special for you."

I opened my eyes. "No. Thank *you*. It's perfect. I hope I can be as helpful to you someday."

"Actually," Jacksiun started, clearing his throat as he took a step back to stand beside Amanda. He reached for her hand. "As my best friend, you should know that, after my father got it through his head that I was *not* going to marry *you*, I announced to him that I wanted permission to court another young woman."

My eyes widened and Amanda gazed back at me with her grin stretched into a toothy, exaggerated one. She lifted their entwined hands. "That's a fancy way of saying we're dating now," she said, giggling.

"Oh!" I covered my mouth with both hands to muffle the

squeal of joy coming out. "You guys! Ah!" I reached out my arms and hugged them both tightly. "I am so happy for you!"

I knew Amanda had delusions of marrying Jacksiun, but I wasn't quite sure how far it would get. The reserved but enthusiastic smile forming on his face made it clear he *was* looking forward to spending a lot more time with her.

Really, they looked adorable together.

"So do we have your consent, then?" Jacksiun asked me.

"Of course! I love both of you so much. Congratulations! I hope everything works out and that you'll be okay with a long distance relationship."

Amanda and Jacksiun looked at each other and smiled.

"We are willing to try," he said, looking back at me. "I am not afraid of a challenge."

"Neither am I!" Amanda added cheerfully. "You look gorgeous, by the way." She gestured to my dress. "And that fire thing... Dragons!"

"It *was* actually my dragon's idea," I responded.

Her expression went flat and her eyes grew wide. "Oh?" Amanda leaned over and pointed at my necklace. "Well, thank you, good dragon, Sir," she whispered toward my amulet. "Valhara looked amazing."

I sensed Firagia's laughter in my heart.

"Well, we will not hold you hostage from the rest of the party," Jacksiun said. "Enjoy your dinner." He bowed and the two of them walked off to sit together at one of the tables.

Because I didn't want the stress of having to take lessons, we'd also decided not to have a formal dance and, instead, had an area with music set aside for those who wanted to enjoy it. No one seemed bothered that we'd chosen to have an informal wedding.

After dinner, Mattheia's mother came over to us with Daisy tagging alongside her feet. "Oh, I know I said this earlier, but I just can't tell you how happy I am for you two!" she said.

"Thank you," we replied in unison.

"I knew you'd be back for my sweet little Mattheia," she said, reaching out to grab me by the arm and side-hug me.

"Mom..." Mattheia furrowed his brow.

"Oh, don't act offended," she continued. "I'll march over to the kitchen and tell them to take back those cupcakes right now."

"Thank you again for those," I said, trying to take the focus off Mattheia. "They were delicious."

"You're very welcome, dear. I worked with the head baker to make sure they were as beautiful as you two are right now."

My cheeks were getting warm.

"Again, congratulations," she said, standing up on her tip-toes to kiss her son on the cheek and then me next. "You make a precious couple. I promise to love you like my own daughter, Valhara."

"I feel like you already do," I added, smiling gratefully.

"Oh, sweetie, I'm glad you do." She tipped her head and then turned. "I'm not going to keep you. Have a good night!" She bent down toward her dog. "Come along, Daisy." The two of them scurried off.

"So when's your sister getting married?" Mattheia asked, turning to me. I glanced over his shoulder at Atira and Captain Ventresca slow dancing to some serene music playing at the far end of the room.

"I'm not sure. She said she needed more than seven days to plan her wedding."

Mattheia chuckled. "I'm glad we didn't." He lifted a hand and brushed his fingertips across my cheek.

"Me, too. I'm happy with how this turned out. You, Amanda, and Jacksiun did great things and it's absolutely perfect."

"Well." He looked down at the floor and his voice lowered. "I hope there's room for one more surprise."

I narrowed my eyes. "Another surprise?"

He looked back up at me and smiled. "Just a *little* something..."

I took his hand. "Of course there's room."

"Do you mind if we leave?" He grasped my hand firmly.

"I don't mind. No. But... our guests...?"

"I'll handle it."

We started walking and then Mattheia halted near the center of the room and cleared his throat loudly. The music softened. "Thank you everyone for making today magical for us, and for giving me and my lovely wife one of the most unforgettable days of our life together. We'll be retiring for the night but wish you all a fantastic evening."

The way he so naturally called me his "wife" made the hairs on the back of my neck stand on end.

Everyone cheered and waved goodbye to us as we exited the room.

"Where are we going?" I asked as we walked down an unfamiliar hallway of the castle. I'd hiked my dress up a few inches off the floor so it wouldn't tangle around my feet.

Several guards acknowledged and congratulated us as we passed, until we came upon a large door that had been left propped opened, revealing the outside of the castle. We passed the threshold and a charming little Old-World style, open carriage awaited us, trimmed in sparkling gold lights that twinkled in the fading light of dusk. A chauffer held open the side door of the carriage and assisted me up and inside. Mattheia came in next and sat on the plush, velvety seat beside me.

There were no horses attached, but within moments, the motorized carriage started off, taking us down a long, winding road.

The evening breeze was cool and fresh, and I rested my head against Mattheia's shoulder as we rode into the night.

It wasn't long before the vehicle came to a stop. I lifted my face and looked up, my gaze scaling the side of a tall, stone tower that resembled a castle turret.

"What is that?" I asked.

Mattheia propped open the door of the carriage, hopped down, and then turned and offered me his hand.

"You'll see," he replied.

Bright golden flames swayed from torches at both sides of a stone archway. We entered beneath it and made a sharp turn toward a mysterious tunnel just off to the side which had also been lit with sconces.

"Come with me," Mattheia said.

He took me by the hand and led me up a winding stone

staircase with a long, carpet runner padding each step. Candles at both sides of the narrow hallway flickered with soft, yellow light.

With each step we ascended, a cool, earthy breeze filtered in more and more through the arched windows in both sides of the spiraling path. I peeked out them as we passed, observing how the ground began to drift down, disappearing beneath a layer of evening fog.

"How much farther?" I asked, squeezing Mattheia's warm hand.

"Just a few more steps."

I felt like we might touch the sky if we continued up the staircase for much longer. I thought it was the narrowness that made it seem as though we were going higher than we actually were, but then we passed a few more windows and a fluffy green mound of treetops came into view. Moonlight danced off the rustling leaves.

"Stop," Mattheia said quietly, his grasp on my hand tightening. We'd come upon a large wooden door decorated with elegant swirls of golden metalwork. A round panel shimmered dimly in the candlelight; Mattheia lifted his free hand and pressed it flat against the disc. A sparkle of white light ignited the diameter of the panel, and then the door eased open.

A rush of fresh air hit me, and as the door swung open, a bright white halo of light appeared in the distance overhead—the moon.

"Watch your step," he said, walking up ahead of me and turning to help me past the raised threshold.

"Where are we?" I gazed out at the endless dark sky; stars

twinkled and moonlight faintly illuminated the rooftop.

We walked up ahead and he stopped me. "Turn around," he said.

I slowly stepped in a small circle, my shoes clicking softly against stone, until I came face to face with a riveting Rayvenstar Castle skyline. Aglow with torchlight peeking through crenellations, the castle battlements produced an astounding horizon against the darkness of night.

It was just far enough away that we could see everything, but close enough to revel in its grandeur and detail.

"You can breathe now," Mattheia whispered into my ear.

I took in a sharp breath.

"It's so beautiful," I said, staring in awe; I *had* nearly forgotten to breathe.

He came up behind me and wrapped his arms around my waist, pulling me close against his chest. A rush of contentment and joy swelled inside me, and I clasped onto his arms, my eyes remaining locked on the beautiful castle silhouette. A subtle glow of fire illuminated my skin, even as I tried to calm it. I was so content, and I couldn't hide my feelings.

Since I'd become an Elemental Guardian, my emotions had become punctuated with fire. But it was a warm, intense light that consumed my body and flushed a delightful, magical feeling across my skin, casting a soft glow on Mattheia's.

"There's something else I want to show you," he spoke quietly, and coaxed me to turn toward the other side of the rooftop.

My amulet began to pulse.

"Firagia!?"

A beam of color and light shot from the sunstone and Firagia burst from me. The dragon drifted before us, aglow with cascading rays of orange and yellow, his iridescent scales shifting color from red to green.

"Congratulations, Mattheia and Valhara," he said, bowing his head. "I wish you two a bright and wonderful future together."

"Thank you," Mattheia and I replied in tandem.

"I will be around if you need me," he added. "Goodnight." And with a powerful flap of his flaming wings, Firagia swooped up high above us and then dove down, sweeping around the perimeter of the rooftop and setting ablaze hundreds of candles that had, apparently, been hiding there in the darkness.

I looked around; a cozy array of furniture had been placed out for us, making the space into a comfortable little outdoor bedroom illuminated by warm candlelight. My eyes welled with tears.

"You said you wanted something small and quiet," Mattheia said, rubbing my shoulder.

A lovely wooden table presented a tiered tray of different snacks and was surrounded by two padded cast iron chairs. Beside that was an array of flowers, arranged in rows of complementary colors. I took a deep breath of fresh jasmine and honeysuckle. A few sprigs of lavender also resided nearby, but far enough away as to not overpower the perfectly married aromas of the other flowers.

A bit of a ways away from the flowers and snack tray was a thick, cozy stack of pillows and blankets, laid out atop a low mattress.

"This is so beautiful," I mumbled, straining to get the words out, because I was choking on tears of joy. "It's like a sanctuary under the stars." I turned to him. "Did you plan all this?"

"Most of it," he answered with a nod. "I explained to the planner about how we used to sit on the roof of Silver Diamond, and about how important those calm moments were for us." His fingers swept over my cherry blossom barrette and he smiled sweetly. "I fell in love with you before I'd even realized it, but I think *you* fell in love with me on that rooftop." He took my hand and brought it up toward his face to kiss the backs of my knuckles. "We've come so far, Valhara. I'm so lucky to have you in my life."

"I loved you for a while, but I didn't want to admit it," I said, shaking my head in disbelief. "Thank you for being patient with me, and for giving me a second chance to come to terms with my feelings." I wiped the tears from my cheeks and sniffled.

"Be thankful I'm stubborn and loyal to a fault." He smirked. "Oh, and there's one more little surprise I have to show you." He removed his jacket, folded it gently, and draped it over a nearby chair.

"Another one? But, this is—"

"Come with me." He led me over to the inviting bed, which was covered in various layers of furs and downy blankets, and came down onto it. He lay back and gestured for me to crawl up beside him.

I removed my shoes first, as they had been hurting my feet for some time, and set them beside the bed, flexing my feet. I pressed a hand onto the blankets and my jaw dropped, taken aback by how immaculately soft the fabric was. The welcoming sensation drew me in and I melted onto the bed, next to Mattheia, snuggling up close to his side. It was like lying on a cloud.

"I like the texture of this a lot," I said, stroking my fingers down the unique embroidery on his leafy green vest. "This looks wonderful on you. I'm sorry I didn't say anything earlier, but I *was* thinking it."

"You had a lot to take in today," he replied, stretching his arm out to the side; I laid my head on it and looked up at the sky. "Now, apparently, it's only visible from Alyssia a few weeks a year," he started, "but I thought it was an interesting coincidence." He lifted his other arm up and pointed toward the sky. "Right there."

I followed the path of his hand and gasped as a shiver went up my spine.

There, near the tip of his finger, was a bright golden bead of light glistening in the distance—Celestial Galaxy, my previous home and academy.

I smiled so hard that it made my face ache; tears were coming again.

"Hey, don't cry!" Mattheia shifted onto his side and stroked his fingers across my forehead, brushing my hair out of my face. "This is supposed to be a happy day, remember?" He tipped my face toward his. "I worked really hard to make today exactly what you had hoped for."

"I didn't know what I wanted, Mattheia," I said, laughing lightly as I worked hard to gain control of my emotions. "I had no idea what I really wanted out of this, but..." I came up onto my elbows and forked a hand through his hair.

"You did. Thank you." I sniffled again and smiled through the tears. "I love you so much, and I am so grateful our paths crossed, and that you changed the course of my life for the better, even when I didn't know how much of a change I really needed. Thank you."

Candlelight glistened off his eyes, and I could tell he was trying to hold some of his feelings back.

He cleared his throat and released my face briefly to swipe a hand across the corners of his eyes.

"No fair," he said. "Look what you've done to me."

Watching him fight back tears made me chuckle.

His eyes met mine briefly, but then his gaze drifted toward my lips.

He leaned closer and kissed me; my heart thumped in my ribcage.

"I love you, Valhara," he whispered.

The tears had ceased and a gush of contentment swelled in my chest.

"Whatever happens," he spoke softly, our noses almost touching as he gazed into my eyes. "Whether we're facing down an overgrown spider, a dragon the size of a two-story building, or arguing over dishes and laundry duty, we're in this together. Got that?"

I grinned and nodded.

"But right now, it's none of those things." He kissed my forehead. "It's just you, me, and the universe. And I don't think you need to worry about the universe..."

Start the adventure from the beginning!

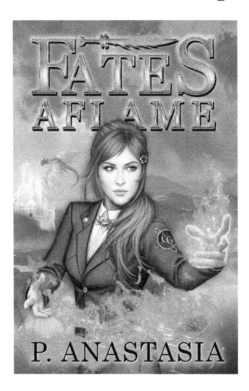

Fa*tes Aflame* is a breathtaking journey through a new world in the tradition of beloved epics

In a society fueled by unbridled magic and turbulent political landscapes, Lieutenant Hawksford is torn between prophecy and duty. With the threads of her fate tugged in all directions, uncertainty shrouds her future.

She has the ability to conjure fire at will, but the birth of her powers awakens a curse and a perilous trial unfolds, putting the lives of those she loves in jeopardy. When extinct beasts brought forth by ancient magic threaten her life, she has no choice but to take a stand, and in the blink of an eye, her carefree life is extinguished.

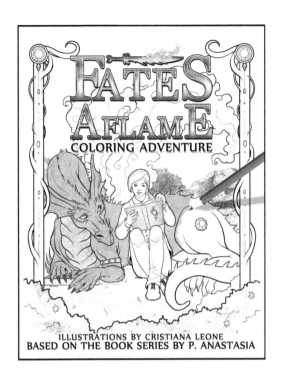

Get the coloring book and see all your favorite characters and scenes come to life!

Available at most online retailers
ISBN 978-0-9974485-2-8

A NOVEL

DARK DIARY

P. ANASTASIA

A young woman with a dark past encounters a young man with an even darker one. More human than vampire, *Dark Diary* is a quaint, sophisticated romance detailing the accounts of two lovers who have paid **the *ultimate price...***

This timeless, standalone, genre-crossing love story with supernatural undertones and a flourish of historical romance, will capture your heart and never let go.

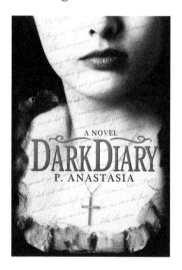

Forbidden romance in the vein of classics like *Wuthering Heights*, frosted with the seductive allure of immortality, *Dark Diary* documents a pair torn apart by time. The story is told by a 400-year-old immortal and a 21-year-old modern-day artist.

He's trapped in a never-ending circle of guilt over the loss of a friend and lover.

She's haunted nightly by visions of her own untimely death.

Together, they find solace by sharing secrets beneath the light of the moon.

WWW.DARKDIARYNOVEL.COM
VISIT THE WEBSITE FOR A FREE PREVIEW!

Fluorescence

 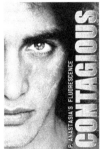  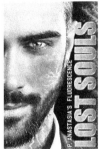

**My name's Alice Green.
I hope, for your sake, you *never* meet me.**

A riveting paranormal romance, *Fluorescence* is engaging and unabashed—a coming-of-age urban science fiction unlike any other.

It lives in her bloodstream. It's unpredictable and could flare up any time, exposing her secret. Alice was a normal teenager, until a dying race of aliens chose her and a handful of others to preserve bio-luminescent DNA known as Fluorescence. Now, she and the others must hide their condition from the rest of the world, while trying to learn the truth behind the living light.

In a unique genre, *Fluorescence* is a striking blend of audacious young love, fantasy, and science fiction.

Each full-length novel in the complete tetralogy is narrated by a different character, driving the story forward in a new and exciting way. It evolves from a quiet beginning into a gripping saga, exploring the real-life limitations encountered while harboring a volatile secret.

HaveYouBeenStarted.com

P. Anastasia's fresh take on storytelling resonates with darkness, charm, and passion—the embodiment of her unique writing style. With origins tracing back to the late nineties, the creative fire that became Fates Aflame was drawn from P.'s love of role-playing games, mythology, and all things magical.

Drawn to the craft in childhood, she began attempting to produce her first book at age 11. While working toward her college degree, she wrote news and editorial columns for two campus newspapers. After graduating with a degree in Communications and spending a year studying abroad in Kofu, Japan, she followed her heart to her publishing aspirations. She currently resides in the beautiful, green state of Kentucky with her husband and her ever-inspiring fur-babies. On the side, she serves as a professional voice talent for radio, television, and audio books.

P. Anastasia is also the author of the *Fluorescence* series and the historical-paranormal romance, *Dark Diary*.

CPSIA information can be obtained
at www.ICGtesting.com
Printed in the USA
LVHW111619050319
609565LV00007B/128/P

9 780997 448566